SPECIAL MESSAGE TO

D0723719

THE ULVERSCROFT FOUNDATION
(registered UK charity number 264873)

was established in 1972 to provide funds for research, diagnosis and treatment of eye diseases. Examples of major projects funded by the Ulverscroft Foundation are:-

- The Children's Eye Unit at Moorfields Eye Hospital, London
- The Ulverscroft Children's Eye Unit at Great Ormond Street Hospital for Sick Children
- Funding research into eye diseases and treatment at the Department of Ophthalmology, University of Leicester
- The Ulverscroft Vision Research Group, Institute of Child Health
- Twin operating theatres at the Western Ophthalmic Hospital, London
- The Chair of Ophthalmology at the Royal Australian College of Ophthalmologists

You can help further the work of the Foundation by making a donation or leaving a legacy. Every contribution is gratefully received. If you would like to help support the Foundation or require further information, please contact:

THE ULVERSCROFT FOUNDATION
**The Green, Bradgate Road, Anstey
Leicester LE7 7FU, England
Tel: (0116) 236 4325**

website: www.foundation.ulverscroft.com

THE MYSTERY OF A HANSOM CAB

Mr. Royston is driving his hansom through the night-time streets of Melbourne when he is hailed by a man supporting a slumped, intoxicated figure, and requesting that the cabman take the unfortunate fellow home — before proceeding to drop his burden and make a rapid exit. Bundling the drunken man onto the seat, the cabman is startled by the reappearance of the good Samaritan, who joins his acquaintance inside — but jumps out before the end of the journey. And when Royston, receiving no response to his inquiries about directions, peers into the cab, he finds that his passenger is now a corpse . . .

FERGUS HUME

THE MYSTERY OF A HANSOM CAB

Complete and Unabridged

ULVERSCROFT
Leicester

First published in Australia in 1886

This Large Print Edition
published 2015

A catalogue record for this book is available
from the British Library.

ISBN 978–1–4448–2435–3

Published by
F. A. Thorpe (Publishing)
Anstey, Leicestershire

Set by Words & Graphics Ltd.
Anstey, Leicestershire
Printed and bound in Great Britain by
T. J. International Ltd., Padstow, Cornwall

This book is printed on acid-free paper

Contents

Preface

In its original form, 'The Mystery of a Hansom Cab' has reached the sale of 375,000 copies in this country, and some few editions in the United States of America. Notwithstanding this, the present publishers have the best of reasons for believing, that there are thousands of persons whom the book has never reached. The causes of this have doubtless been many, but chief among them was the form of the publication itself. It is for this section of the public chiefly that the present edition is issued. In placing it before my new readers, I have been asked by the publishers thoroughly to revise the work, and, at the same time, to set at rest the many conflicting reports concerning it and myself, which have been current since its initial issue. The first of these requests I have complied with, and the many typographic, and other errors, which disfigured the first edition, have, I think I can safely say, now disappeared. The second request I am about to fulfil; but, in order to do so, I must ask my readers to go back with me to the beginning of all things, so far as this special book is

1

concerned. The writing of the book was due more to accident than to design. I was bent on becoming a dramatist, but, being quite unknown, I found it impossible to induce the managers of the Melbourne Theatres to accept, or even to read a play. At length it occurred to me I might further my purpose by writing a novel. I should at all events secure a certain amount of local attention. Up to that time I had written only one or two short stories, and the 'Cab' was not only the first book I ever published, but the first book I ever wrote; so to youth and lack of experience must be ascribed whatever was wanting in the book. I repeat that the story was written only to attract local attention, and no one was more astonished than I when it passed beyond the narrow circle for which it had originally been intended.

My mind made up on this point, I enquired of a leading Melbourne bookseller what style of book he sold most of. He replied that the detective stories of Gaboriau had a large sale; and as, at this time, I had never even heard of this author, I bought all his works — eleven or thereabouts — and read them carefully. The style of these stories attracted me, and I determined to write a book of the same class; containing a mystery, a murder, and a description of low life in

Melbourne. This was the origin of the 'Cab.' The central idea i.e. the murder in a cab — came to me while driving at a late hour to St. Kilda, a suburb of Melbourne; but it took some time and much thought to work it out to a logical conclusion. I was two months sketching out the skeleton of the novel, but even so, when I had written it, the result proved unsatisfactory, for I found I had not sufficiently well concealed the mystery upon which the whole interest of the book depended. In the first draft I made Frettlby the criminal, but on reading over the M.S. I found that his guilt was so obvious that I wrote out the story for a second time, introducing the character of Moreland as a scape-goat. Mother Guttersnipe I unearthed in the slums off Little Bourke Street; and I gave what I am afraid was perhaps too vivid a picture of her language and personality. These I have toned down in the present edition. Calton and the two lodging-house keepers were actual personages whom I knew very well, and I do not think I have exaggerated their idiosyncracies, although many have, I believe, doubted the existence of such oddities. All the scenes in the book, especially the slums, are described from personal observation; and I passed a great many nights in Little Bourke Street, gathering material.

3

Having completed the book, I tried to get it published, but every one to whom I offered it refused even to look at the manuscript on the ground that no Colonial could write anything worth reading. They gave no reason for this extraordinary opinion, but it was sufficient for them, and they laughed to scorn the idea that any good could come out of Nazareth — i.e., the Colonies. The story thus being boycotted on all hands, I determined to publish it myself, and accordingly an edition of, I think, some five thousand copies was brought out at my own cost. Contrary to the expectations of the publishers, and I must add to my own, the whole edition went off in three weeks, and the public demanded a second. This also sold rapidly, and after some months, proposals were made to me that the book should be brought out in London. Later on I parted with the book to several speculators, who formed themselves into what they called 'The Hansom Cab Publishing Company.' Taking the book to London, they published it there with great success, and it had a phenomenal sale, which brought in a large sum of money. The success was, in the first instance, due, in no small degree, to a very kind and generous criticism written by Mr. Clement Scott. I may here state that I had nothing to do with the Company, nor did I receive any money for the English sale of the book beyond what I sold it for; and, as a matter of fact, I did not arrive in England until a year after the novel was published. I have heard it declared that the plot is founded on a real criminal case; but such a statement is utterly without foundation, as the story is pure fiction from beginning to end. Several people before and since my arrival in England, have assumed the authorship of the book to themselves; and one gentleman went so far as to declare that he would shoot me if I claimed to have written it. I am glad to say that up to the present he has not carried out his intention. Another individual had his cards printed, 'Fergus Hume. Author of 'The Mystery of a Hansom Cab,' ' and also added the price for which he was prepared to write a similar book. Many of the papers put this last piece of eccentricity down to my account.

I may state in conclusion, that I belong to New Zealand, and not to Australia, that I am a barrister, and not a retired policeman, that I am yet two decades off fifty years of age, that Fergus Hume is my real name, and not a nom-de-plume; and finally, that far from making a fortune out of the book, all I received for the English and American rights, previous to the issue of this Revised Edition by my present publishers, was the sum of fifty pounds. With this I take my leave, and I trust that the present edition may prove as successful as did the first.

1

What the *Argus* Said.

The following report appeared in the *Argus* newspaper of Saturday, the 28th July, 18 —

'Truth is said to be stranger than fiction, and certainly the extraordinary murder which took place in Melbourne on Thursday night, or rather Friday morning, goes a long way towards verifying this saying. A crime has been committed by an unknown assassin, within a short distance of the principal streets of this great city, and is surrounded by an inpenetrable mystery. Indeed, from the nature of the crime itself, the place where it was committed, and the fact that the assassin has escaped without leaving a trace behind him, it would seem as though the case itself had been taken bodily from one of Gaboreau's novels, and that his famous detective Lecoq alone would be able to unravel it. The facts of the case are simply these: —

'On the twenty-seventh day of July, at the hour of twenty minutes to two o'clock in the morning, a hansom cab drove up to the police station in Grey Street, St. Kilda, and

7

the driver made the startling statement that his cab contained the body of a man who he had reason to believe had been murdered. Being taken into the presence of the inspector, the cabman, who gave his name as Malcolm Royston, related the following strange story: —

'At the hour of one o'clock in the morning, he was driving down Collins Street East, when, as he was passing the Burke and Wills' monument, he was hailed by a gentleman standing at the corner by the Scotch Church. He immediately drove up, and saw that the gentleman who hailed him was supporting the deceased, who appeared to be intoxicated. Both were in evening dress, but the deceased had on no overcoat, while the other wore a short covert coat of a light fawn colour, which was open. As Royston drove up, the gentleman in the light coat said, 'Look here, cabby, here's some fellow awfully tight, you'd better take him home!'

'Royston then asked him if the drunken man was his friend, but this the other denied, saying that he had just picked him up from the footpath, and did not know him from Adam. At this moment the deceased turned his face up to the light of the lamp under which both were standing, and the other seemed to recognise him, for he recoiled a pace, letting the drunken man fall in a heap on the pavement, and gasping out 'You?' he turned on his heel, and walked rapidly away down Russell Street in the direction of Bourke Street.

'Royston was staring after him, and wondering at his strange conduct, when he was recalled to himself by the voice of the deceased, who had struggled to his feet, and was holding on to the lamp-post, swaying to and fro. 'I wan' g'ome,' he said in a thick voice, 'St. Kilda.' He then tried to get into the cab, but was too drunk to do so, and finally sat down again on the pavement. Seeing this, Royston got down, and lifting him up, helped him into the cab with some considerable difficulty. The deceased fell back into the cab, and seemed to drop off to sleep; so, after closing the door, Royston turned to remount his driving-seat, when he found the gentle-man in the light coat whom he had seen holding up the deceased, close to his elbow. Royston said, 'Oh, you've come back,' and the other answered, 'Yes, I've changed my mind, and will see him home.' As he said this he opened the door of the cab, stepped in beside the deceased, and told Royston to drive down to St. Kilda. Royston, who was glad that the friend of the deceased had come to look after him, drove as he had been directed, but near the Church of England Grammar School, on the St. Kilda Road, the gentleman in the light coat called out to him to stop. He did so, and the gentleman got out of the cab, closing the door after him.

''He won't let me take him home,' he said, 'so I'll just walk back to the city, and you can drive him to St. Kilda.'

''What street, sir?' asked Royston.

''Grey Street, I fancy,' said the other, 'but my friend will direct you when you get to the Junction.'

''Ain't he too much on, sir?' said Royston, dubiously.

''Oh, no! I think he'll be able to tell you where he lives — it's Grey Street or Ackland Street, I fancy. I don't know which.'

'He then opened the door of the cab and looked in. 'Good night, old man,' he said — the other apparently did not answer, for the gentleman in the light coat, shrugging his shoulders, and muttering 'sulky brute,' closed the door again. He then gave Royston half-a-sovereign, lit a cigarette, and after making a few remarks about the beauty of the night, walked off quickly in the direction of Melbourne. Royston drove down to the Junction, and having stopped there, according to his instructions he asked his 'fare' several times where he was to drive him to.

Receiving no response and thinking that the deceased was too drunk to answer, he got down from his seat, opened the door of the cab, and found the deceased lying back in the corner with a handkerchief across his mouth. He put out his hand with the intention of rousing him, thinking that he had gone to sleep. But on touching him the deceased fell forward, and on examination, to his horror, he found that he was quite dead. Alarmed at what had taken place, and suspecting the gentleman in the light coat, he drove to the police station at St. Kilda, and there made the above report. The body of the deceased was taken out of the cab and brought into the station, a doctor being sent for at once. On his arrival, however, he found that life was quite extinct, and also discovered that the handkerchief which was tied lightly over the mouth was saturated with chloroform. He had no hesitation in stating that from the way in which the handkerchief was placed, and the presence of chloroform, that a murder had been committed, and from all appearances the deceased died easily, and without a struggle. The deceased is a slender man, of medium height, with a dark complexion, and is dressed in evening dress, which will render identification difficult, as it is a costume

11

which has no distinctive mark to render it noticeable. There were no papers or cards found on the deceased from which his name could be discovered, and the clothing was not marked in any way. The handkerchief, however, which was tied across his mouth, was of white silk, and marked in one of the corners with the letters 'O.W.' in red silk. The assassin, of course, may have used his own handkerchief to commit the crime, so that if the initials are those of his name they may ultimately lead to his detection. There will be an inquest held on the body of the deceased this morning, when, no doubt, some evidence may be elicited which may solve the mystery.'

In Monday morning's issue of the *Argus* the following article appeared with reference to the matter: —

'The following additional evidence which has been obtained may throw some light on the mysterious murder in a hansom cab of which we gave a full description in Saturday's issue: —

'Another hansom cabman called at the police office, and gave a clue which will, no doubt, prove of value to the detectives in their search for the murderer. He states that he was driving up the St. Kilda Road on Friday morning about half-past one o'clock, when he

12

was hailed by a gentleman in a light coat, who stepped into the cab and told him to drive to Powlett Street, in East Melbourne. He did so, and, after paying him, the gentleman got out at the corner of Wellington Parade and Powlett Street and walked slowly up Powlett Street, while the cab drove back to town. Here all clue ends, but there can be no doubt in the minds of our readers as to the identity of the man in the light coat who got out of Royston's cab on the St. Kilda Road, with the one who entered the other cab and alighted therefrom at Powlett Street. There could have been no struggle, as had any taken place the cabman, Royston, surely would have heard the noise. The supposition is, therefore, that the deceased was too drunk to make any resistance, and that the other, watching his opportunity, placed the handkerchief saturated with chloroform over the mouth of his victim. Then after perhaps a few ineffectual struggles the latter would succumb to the effects of his inhalation. The man in the light coat, judging from his conduct before getting into the cab, appears to have known the deceased, though the circumstance of his walking away on recognition, and returning again, shows that his attitude towards the deceased was not altogether a friendly one.

'The difficulty is where to start from in the

13

search after the author of what appears to be a deliberate murder, as the deceased seems to be unknown, and his presumed murderer has escaped. But it is impossible that the body can remain long without being identified by someone, as though Melbourne is a large city, yet it is neither Paris nor London, where a man can disappear in a crowd and never be heard of again. The first thing to be done is to establish the identity of the deceased, and then, no doubt, a clue will be obtained leading to the detection of the man in the light coat who appears to have been the perpetrator of the crime. It is of the utmost importance that the mystery in which the crime is shrouded should be cleared up, not only in the interests of justice, but also in those of the public — taking place as it did in a public conveyance, and in the public street. To think that the author of such a crime is at present at large, walking in our midst, and perhaps preparing for the committal of another, is enough to shake the strongest nerves. In one of Du Boisgobey's stories, entitled 'An Omnibus Mystery,' a murder closely resembling this tragedy takes place in an omnibus, but we question if even that author would have been daring enough to write about a crime being committed in such an unlikely place as a hansom cab. Here is a great chance for some of our detectives to render themselves famous, and we feel sure that they will do their utmost to trace the author of this cowardly and dastardly murder.'

2

The Evidence at the Inquest.

At the inquest held on the body found in the hansom cab the following articles taken from the deceased were placed on the table: —

1. Two pounds ten shillings in gold and silver.

2. The white silk handkerchief which was saturated with chloroform, and was found tied across the mouth of the deceased, marked with the letters O.W. in red silk.

3. A cigarette case of Russian leather, half filled with 'Old Judge' cigarettes.

4. A left-hand white glove of kid — rather soiled — with black seams down the back.

Samuel Gorby, of the detective office, was present in order to see if anything might be said by the witnesses likely to point to the cause or to the author of the crime.

The first witness called was Malcolm Royston, in whose cab the crime had been committed. He told the same story as had already appeared in the *Argus*, and the following facts were elicited by the Coroner: —

Q. Can you give a description of the

gentleman in the light coat, who was holding the deceased when you drove up?

A. I did not observe him very closely, as my attention was taken up by the deceased; and, besides, the gentleman in the light coat was in the shadow.

Q Describe him from what you saw of him.

A. He was fair, I think, because I could see his moustache, rather tall, and in evening dress, with a light coat over it. I could not see his face very plainly, as he wore a soft felt hat, which was pulled down over his eyes.

Q. What kind of hat was it he wore — a wide-awake?

A. Yes. The brim was turned down, and I could see only his mouth and moustache.

Q. What did he say when you asked him if he knew the deceased?

A. He said he didn't; that he had just picked him up.

Q. And afterwards he seemed to recognise him?

A. Yes. When the deceased looked up he said 'You!' and let him fall on to the ground; then he walked away towards Bourke Street.

Q. Did he look back?

A. Not that I saw.

Q. How long were you looking after him?

A. About a minute.

Q. And when did you see him again?

A. After I put deceased into the cab I turned round and found him at my elbow.

Q. And what did he say?

A. I said, 'Oh! you've come back,' and he said, 'Yes, I've changed my mind, and will see him home,' and then he got into the cab, and told me to drive to St. Kilda.

Q. He spoke then as if he knew the deceased?

A. Yes; I thought that he recognised him only when he looked up, and perhaps having had a row with him walked away, but thought he'd come back.

Q. Did you see him coming back?

A. No; the first I saw of him was at my elbow when I turned.

Q. And when did he get out?

A. Just as I was turning down by the Grammar School on the St. Kilda Road.

Q. Did you hear any sounds of fighting or struggling in the cab during the drive?

A. No; the road was rather rough, and the noise of the wheels going over the stones would have prevented my hearing anything.

Q. When the gentleman in the light coat got out did he appear disturbed?

A. No; he was perfectly calm.

Q. How could you tell that?

A. Because the moon had risen, and I could see plainly.

Q. Did you see his face then?

A. No; his hat was pulled down over it. I only saw as much as I did when he entered the cab in Collins Street.

Q. Were his clothes torn or disarranged in any way?

A. No; the only difference I remarked in him was that his coat was buttoned.

Q. And was it open when he got in?

A. No; but it was when he was holding up the deceased.

Q. Then he buttoned it before he came back and got into the cab?

A. Yes. I suppose so.

Q. What did he say when he got out of the cab on the St. Kilda Road?

A. He said that the deceased would not let him take him home, and that he would walk back to Melbourne.

Q. And you asked him where you were to drive the deceased to?

A. Yes; and he said that the deceased lived either in Grey Street or Ackland Street, St. Kilda, but that the deceased would direct me at the Junction.

Q. Did you not think that the deceased was too drunk to direct you?

A. Yes, I did; but his friend said that the sleep and the shaking of the cab would sober him a bit by the time I got to the Junction.

Q. The gentleman in the light coat apparently did not know where the deceased lived?

A. No; he said it was either in Ackland Street or Grey Street.

Q. Did you not think that curious?

A. No; I thought he might be a club friend of the deceased.

Q. For how long did the man in the light coat talk to you?

A. About five minutes.

Q. And during that time you heard no noise in the cab?

A. No; I thought the deceased had gone to sleep.

Q. And after the man in the light coat said 'good-night' to the deceased, what happened?

A. He lit a cigarette, gave me a half-sovereign, and walked off towards Melbourne.

Q. Did you observe if the gentleman in the light coat had his handkerchief with him?

A. Oh, yes; because he dusted his boots with it. The road was very dusty.

Q. Did you notice any striking peculiarity about him?

A. Well, no; except that he wore a diamond ring.

Q. What was there peculiar about that?

A. He wore it on the forefinger of the right

hand, and I never saw it that way before.

Q. When did you notice this?

A. When he was lighting his cigarette.

Q. How often did you call to the deceased when you got to the Junction?

A. Three or four times. I then got down, and found he was quite dead.

Q. How was he lying?

A. He was doubled up in the far corner of the cab, very much in the same position as I left him when I put him in. His head was hanging on one side, and there was a handkerchief across his mouth. When I touched him he fell into the other corner of the cab, and then I found out he was dead. I immediately drove to the St. Kilda police station and told the police.

At the conclusion of Royston's evidence, during which Gorby had been continually taking notes, Robert Chinston was called. He deposed: —

I am a duly qualified medical practitioner, residing in Collins Street East. I made a post-mortem examination of the body of the deceased on Friday.

Q. That was within a few hours of his death?

A. Yes, judging from the position of the handkerchief and the presence of chloroform that the deceased had died from the effects of anaesthesia, and knowing how rapidly the poison evaporates I made the examination at once.

CORONER: Go on, sir.

DR. CHINSTON: Externally, the body was healthy-looking and well nourished. There were no marks of violence. The staining apparent at the back of the legs and trunk was due to post-mortem congestion. Internally, the brain was hyperaemic, and there was a considerable amount of congestion, especially apparent in the superficial vessels. There was no brain disease. The lungs were healthy, but slightly congested. On opening the thorax there was a faint spirituous odour discernible. The stomach contained about a pint of completely digested food. The heart was flaccid. The right-heart contained a considerable quantity of dark, fluid blood. There was a tendency to fatty degeneration of that organ.

I am of opinion that the deceased died from the inhalation of some such vapour as chloroform or methylene.

Q. You say there was a tendency to fatty degeneration of the heart? Would that have anything to do with the death of deceased?

A. Not of itself. But chloroform administered while the heart was in such a state would have a decided tendency to accelerate the fatal result. At the same time, I may mention that the post-mortem signs of poisoning by chloroform are mostly negative.

Dr. Chinston was then permitted to retire, and Clement Rankin, another hansom cabman, was called. He deposed: I am a cabman, living in Collingwood, and usually drive a hansom cab. I remember Thursday last. I had driven a party down to St. Kilda, and was returning about half-past one o'clock. A short distance past the Grammar School I was hailed by a gentleman in a light coat; he was smoking a cigarette, and told me to drive him to Powlett Street, East Melbourne. I did so, and he got out at the corner of Wellington Parade and Powlett Street. He paid me half-a-sovereign for my fare, and then walked up Powlett Street, while I drove back to town.

Q. What time was it when you stopped at Powlett Street?

A. Two o'clock exactly.

Q. How do you know?

A. Because it was a still night, and I heard the Post Office clock strike two o'clock.

Q. Did you notice anything peculiar about the man in the light coat?

A. No! He looked just the same as anyone else. I thought he was some swell of the town out for a lark. His hat was pulled down over his eyes, and I could not see his face.

Q. Did you notice if he wore a ring?

A. Yes! I did. When he was handing me the half-sovereign, I saw he had a diamond ring on the forefinger of his right hand.

Q. He did not say why he was on the St. Kilda Road at such an hour?

A. No! He did not.

Clement Rankin was then ordered to stand down, and the Coroner then summed up in an address of half-an-hour's duration. There was, he pointed out, no doubt that the death of the deceased had resulted not from natural causes, but from the effects of poisoning. Only slight evidence had been obtained up to the present time regarding the circumstances of the case, but the only person who could be accused of committing the crime was the unknown man who entered the cab with the deceased on Friday morning at the corner of the Scotch Church, near the Burke and Wills' monument. It had been proved that the deceased, when he entered the cab, was, to all appearances, in good health, though in a state of intoxication, and the fact that he was found by the cabman, Royston, after the man in the light coat had left the cab, with a handkerchief, saturated with chloroform, tied over his mouth, would seem to show that he had died through the inhalation of chloroform, which had been deliberately administered. All the obtainable evidence in the case was circumstantial, but, nevertheless, showed conclusively that a crime had been committed. Therefore, as the circumstances of the case pointed to one conclusion, the jury could not do otherwise than frame a verdict in accordance with that conclusion.

The jury retired at four o'clock, and, after an absence of a quarter of an hour, returned with the following verdict: —

'That the deceased, whose name there is no evidence to determine, died on the 27th day of July, from the effects of poison, namely, chloroform, feloniously administered by some person unknown; and the jury, on their oaths, say that the said unknown person feloniously, wilfully, and maliciously did murder the said deceased.'

3

One Hundred Pounds Reward.

V.R.
MURDER.
100 POUNDS REWARD.
'Whereas, on Friday, the 27th day of July, the body of a man, name unknown, was found in a hansom cab. AND WHEREAS, at an inquest held at St. Kilda, on the 30th day of July, a verdict of wilful murder, against some person unknown, was brought in by the jury. The deceased is of medium height, with a dark complexion, dark hair, clean shaved, has a mole on the left temple, and was dressed in evening dress. Notice is hereby given that a reward of 100 pounds will be paid by the Government for such information as will lead to the conviction of the murderer, who is presumed to be a man who entered the hansom cab with the deceased at the corner of Collins and Russell Streets, on the morning of the 27th day of July.'

4

Mr. Gorby Makes a Start.

'Well,' said Mr. Gorby, addressing his reflection in the looking-glass, 'I've been finding out things these last twenty years, but this is a puzzler, and no mistake.' Mr. Gorby was shaving, and, as was his usual custom, conversed with his reflection. Being a detective, and of an extremely reticent disposition, he never talked outside about his business, or made a confidant of anyone. When he did want to unbosom himself, he retired to his bedroom and talked to his reflection in the mirror. This method of procedure he found to work capitally, for it relieved his sometimes overburdened mind with absolute security to himself. Did not the barber of Midas when he found out what was under the royal crown of his master, fret and chafe over his secret, until one morning he stole to the reeds by the river, and whispered, 'Midas has ass's ears?' In the like manner Mr. Gorby felt a longing at times to give speech to his innermost secrets; and having no fancy for chattering to the air, he made his mirror his confidant. So far it had never betrayed him, while for the rest it joyed him to see his own jolly red face nodding gravely at him from out the shining surface, like a mandarin. This morning the detective was unusually animated in his confidences to his mirror. At times, too, a puzzled expression would pass over his face. The hansom cab murder had been placed in his hands for solution, and he was trying to think how he should make a beginning.

'Hang it,' he said, thoughtfully stropping his razor, 'a thing with an end must have a start, and if I don't get the start how am I to get the end?'

As the mirror did not answer this question, Mr. Gorby lathered his face, and started shaving in a somewhat mechanical fashion, for his thoughts were with the case, and ran on in this manner: —

'Here's a man — well, say a gentleman — who gets drunk, and, therefore, don't know what he's up to. Another gent who is on the square comes up and sings out for a cab for him — first he says he don't know him, and then he shows plainly he does — he walks away in a temper, changes his mind, comes back and gets into the cab, after telling the cabby to drive down to St. Kilda. Then he polishes the drunk one off with chloroform, gets out of the cab, jumps into another, and after getting out at Powlett Street, vanishes — that's the riddle I've got to find out, and I don't think the Sphinx ever had a harder one. There are three things to be discovered — First, who is the dead man? Second, what was he killed for? And third, who did it?

'Once I get hold of the first the other two won't be very hard to find out, for one can tell pretty well from a man's life whether it's to anyone's interest that he should be got off the books. The man that murdered that chap must have had some strong motive, and I must find out what that motive was. Love? No, it wasn't that — men in love don't go to such lengths in real life — they do in novels and plays, but I've never seen it occurring in my experience. Robbery? No, there was plenty of money in his pocket. Revenge? Now, really it might be that — it's a kind of thing that carries most people further than they want to go. There was no violence used, for his clothes weren't torn, so he must have been taken sudden, and before he knew what the other chap was up to. By the way, I don't think I examined his clothes sufficiently, there might be something about them to give a clue; at any rate it's worth looking after, so I'll start with his clothes.'

So Mr. Gorby, having dressed and

breakfasted, walked quickly to the police station, where he asked for the clothes of the deceased to be shown to him. When he received them he retired into a corner, and commenced an exhaustive examination of them. There was nothing remarkable about the coat. It was merely a well-cut and well-made dress coat; so with a grunt of dissatisfaction Mr. Gorby threw it aside, and picked up the waistcoat. Here he found something to interest him, in the shape of a pocket made on the left-hand side and on the inside of the garment.

'Now, what the deuce is this for?' said Mr. Gorby, scratching his head; 'it ain't usual for a dress waistcoat to have a pocket on its inside as I'm aware of; and,' continued the detective, greatly excited, 'this ain't tailor's work, he did it himself, and jolly badly he did it too. Now he must have taken the trouble to make this pocket himself, so that no one else would know anything about it, and it was made to carry something valuable — so valuable that he had to carry it with him even when he wore evening clothes. Ah! here's a tear on the side nearest the outside of the waistcoat; something has been pulled out roughly. I begin to see now. The dead man possessed something which the other man wanted, and which he knew the dead one carried about with him. He sees him drunk, gets into the cab with him, and tries to get what he wants. The dead man resists, upon which the other kills him by means of the chloroform which he had with him, and being afraid that the cab will stop, and he will be found out, snatches what he wants out of the pocket so quickly that he tears the waistcoat and then makes off. That's clear enough, but the question is, What was it he wanted? A case with jewels? No! It could not have been anything so bulky, or the dead man would never have carried it about inside his waistcoat. It was something flat, which could easily lie in the pocket — a paper — some valuable paper which the assassin wanted, and for which he killed the other.'

'This is all very well,' said Mr. Gorby, throwing down the waistcoat, and rising. 'I have found number two before number one. The first question is: Who is the murdered man? He's a stranger in Melbourne, that's pretty clear, or else some one would have been sure to recognise him before now by the description given in the reward. Now, I wonder if he has any relations here? No, he can't, or else they would have made enquiries, before this. Well, there's one thing certain, he must have had a landlady or landlord, unless he slept in the open air. He can't have lived in an hotel, as the landlord of any hotel in Melbourne would have recognised him from the description, especially when the whole place is ringing with the murder. Private lodgings more like, and a landlady who doesn't read the papers and doesn't gossip, or she'd have known all about it by this time. Now, if he did live, as I think, in private lodgings, and suddenly disappeared, his landlady wouldn't keep quiet. It's a whole week since the murder, and as the lodger has not been seen or heard of, the landlady will naturally make enquiries. If, however, as I surmise, the lodger is a stranger, she will not know where to enquire; therefore, under these circumstances, the most natural thing for her to do would be to advertise for him, so I'll have a look at the newspapers.'

Mr. Gorby got a file of the different newspapers, and looked carefully through those columns in which missing friends and people who will hear 'something to their advantage' are generally advertised for.

'He was murdered,' said Mr. Gorby to himself, 'on a Friday morning, between one and two o'clock, so he might stay away till Monday without exciting any suspicion. On Monday, however, the landlady would begin to feel uneasy, and on Tuesday she would advertise for him. Therefore,' said Mr. Gorby, running his fat finger down the column, 'Wednesday it is.'

It did not appear in Wednesday's paper, neither did it in Thursday's, but in Friday's issue, exactly one week after the murder, Mr. Gorby suddenly came upon the following advertisement: —

'If Mr. Oliver Whyte does not return to Possum Villa, Grey Street, St. Kilda, before the end of the week, his rooms will be let again. — Rubina Hableton.'

'Oliver Whyte,' repeated Mr. Gorby slowly, 'and the initials on the pocket-handkerchief which was proved to have belonged to the deceased were 'O.W.' So his name is Oliver Whyte, is it? Now, I wonder if Rubina Hableton knows anything about this matter. At any rate,' said Mr. Gorby, putting on his hat, 'as I'm fond of sea breezes, I think I'll go down, and call at Possum Villa, Grey Street, St. Kilda.'

5

Mrs. Hableton Unbosoms Herself.

Mrs. Hableton was a lady with a grievance, as anybody who happened to become acquainted with her, soon found out. It is Beaconsfield who says, in one of his novels, that no one is so interesting as when he is talking about himself; and, judging Mrs. Hableton by this statement, she was an extremely fascinating individual, as she never by any chance talked upon any other subject. What was the threat of a Russian invasion to her so long as she had her special grievance — once let that be removed, and she would have time to attend to such minor details as affected the colony. Mrs. Hableton's particular grievance was want of money. Not by any means an uncommon one, you might remind her; but she snappishly would tell you that 'she know'd that, but some people weren't like other people.' In time one came to learn what she meant by this. She had come to the Colonies in the early days — days when the making of money in appreciable quantity was an easier matter than it is now. Owing to a bad husband, she had failed to save any. The late Mr. Hableton — for he had long since departed this life — had been addicted to alcohol, and at those times when he should have been earning, he was usually to be found in a drinking shanty spending his wife's earnings in 'shouting' for himself and his friends. The constant drinking, and the hot Victorian climate, soon carried him off, and when Mrs. Hableton had seen him safely under the ground in the Melbourne Cemetery, she returned home to survey her position, and see how it could be bettered. She gathered together a little money from the wreck of her fortune, and land being cheap, purchased a small 'section' at St. Kilda, and built a house on it. She supported herself by going out charing, taking in sewing, and acting as a sick nurse, So, among this multiplicity of occupations, she managed to exist fairly well.

And in truth it was somewhat hard upon Mrs. Hableton. For at the time when she should have been resting and reaping the fruit of her early industry, she was obliged to toil more assiduously than ever. It was little consolation to her that she was but a type of many women, who, hardworking and thrifty themselves, are married to men who are nothing but an incubus to their wives and to their families. Small wonder, then, that Mrs. Hableton should condense all her knowledge of the male sex into the one bitter aphorism, 'Men is brutes.'

Possum Villa was an unpretentious-looking place, with one bow-window and a narrow verandah in front. It was surrounded by a small garden in which were a few sparse flowers — the especial delight of Mrs. Hableton. It was her way to tie an old handkerchief round her head and to go out into the garden and dig and water her beloved flowers until, from sheer desperation at the overwhelming odds, they gave up all attempt to grow. She was engaged in this favourite occupation about a week after her lodger had gone. She wondered where he was.

'Lyin' drunk in a public-'ouse, I'll be bound,' she said, viciously pulling up a weed, 'a-spendin' 'is, rent and a-spilin' 'is inside with beer — ah, men is brutes, drat 'em!' Just as she said this, a shadow fell across the garden, and on looking up, she saw a man leaning over the fence, staring at her.

'Git out,' she said, sharply, rising from her knees and shaking her trowel at the intruder. 'I don't want no apples to-day, an' I don't care how cheap you sells 'em.' Mrs. Hableton evidently laboured under the delusion that the man was a hawker, but seeing no hand-cart with him, she changed her mind.

'You're takin' a plan of the 'ouse to rob it, are you?' she said. 'Well, you needn't, 'cause there ain't nothin' to rob, the silver spoons as belonged to my father's mother 'avin' gone down my 'usband's throat long ago, an' I ain't 'ad money to buy more. I'm a lone pusson as is put on by brutes like you, an' I'll thank you to leave the fence I bought with my own 'ard earned money alone, and git out.' Mrs. Hableton stopped short for want of breath, and stood shaking her trowel, and gasping like a fish out of water.

'My dear lady,' said the man at the fence, mildly, 'are you — '

'No, I ain't,' retorted Mrs. Hableton, fiercely, 'I ain't neither a member of the 'Ouse, nor a school teacher, to answer your questions. I'm a woman as pays my rates an' taxes, and don't gossip nor read yer rubbishin' newspapers, nor care for the Russings, no how, so git out.'

'Don't read the papers?' repeated the man, in a satisfied tone, 'ah! that accounts for it.'

Mrs. Hableton stared suspiciously at the intruder. He was a burly-looking man, with a jovial red face, clean shaven, and his sharp, shrewd-looking grey eyes twinkled like two stars. He was well-dressed in a suit of light clothes, and wore a stiffly-starched white waistcoat, with a massive gold chain stretched across it. Altogether he gave Mrs. Hableton finally the impression of being a well-to-do tradesman, and she mentally wondered what he wanted.

'What d'y want?' she asked, abruptly.

'Does Mr. Oliver Whyte live here?' asked the stranger.

'He do, an' he don't,' answered Mrs. Hableton, epigrammatically. 'I ain't seen 'im for over a week, so I s'pose 'e's gone on the drink, like the rest of 'em, but I've put sumthin' in the paper as 'ill pull him up pretty sharp, and let 'im know I ain't a carpet to be trod on, an' if you're a friend of 'im, you can tell 'im from me 'e's a brute, an' it's no more but what I expected of 'im, 'e bein' a male.'

The stranger waited placidly during the outburst, and Mrs. Hableton, having stopped for want of breath, he interposed, quietly —

'Can I speak to you for a few moments?'

'An' who's a-stoppin' of you?' said Mrs. Hableton, defiantly. 'Go on with you, not as I expects the truth from a male, but go on.'

'Well, really,' said the other, looking up at the cloudless blue sky, and wiping his face with a gaudy red silk pocket-handkerchief, 'it is rather hot, you know, and — '

38

Mrs. Hableton did not give him time to finish, but walking to the gate, opened it with a jerk.

'Use your legs and walk in,' she said, and the stranger having done so, she led the way into the house, and into a small neat sitting-room, which seemed to overflow with antimacassars, wool mats, and wax flowers. There were also a row of emu eggs on the mantelpiece, a cutlass on the wall, and a grimy line of hard-looking little books, set in a stiff row on a shelf, presumably for ornament, for their appearance in no way tempted one to read them.

The furniture was of horsehair, and everything was hard and shiny, so when the stranger sat down in the slippery-looking arm-chair that Mrs. Hableton pushed towards him; he could not help thinking it had been stuffed with stones, it felt so cold and hard. The lady herself sat opposite to him in another hard chair, and having taken the handkerchief off her head, folded it carefully, laid it on her lap, and then looked straight at her unexpected visitor.

'Now then,' she said, letting her mouth fly open so rapidly that it gave one the impression that it was moved by strings like a marionette, 'Who are you? what are you? and what do you want?'

The stranger put his red silk handkerchief into his hat, placed it on the table, and answered deliberately —

'My name is Gorby. I am a detective. I want Mr. Oliver Whyte.'

'He ain't here,' said Mrs. Hableton, thinking that Whyte had got into trouble, and was in danger of arrest.

'I know that,' answered Mr. Gorby.

'Then where is 'e?'

Mr. Gorby answered abruptly, and watched the effect of his words.

'He is dead.'

Mrs. Hableton grew pale, and pushed back her chair. 'No,' she cried, 'he never killed 'im, did 'e?'

'Who never killed him?' queried Mr. Gorby, sharply.

Mrs. Hableton evidently knew more than she intended to say, for, recovering herself with a violent effort, she answered evasively —

'He never killed himself.'

Mr. Gorby looked at her keenly, and she returned his gaze with a defiant stare.

'Clever,' muttered the detective to himself; 'knows something more than she chooses to tell, but I'll get it out of her.' He paused a moment, and then went on smoothly: 'Oh, no! he did not commit suicide; what makes

40

you think so?' Mrs. Hableton did not answer, but, rising from her seat, went over to a hard and shiny-looking sideboard, from whence she took a bottle of brandy and a small wine-glass. Half filling the glass, she drank it off, and returned to her seat.

'I don't take much of that stuff,' she said, seeing the detective's eyes fixed curiously on her, 'but you 'ave given me such a turn that I must take something to steady my nerves; what do you want me to do?'

'Tell me all you know,' said Mr. Gorby, keeping his eyes fixed on her face.

'Where was Mr. Whyte killed?' she asked.

'He was murdered in a hansom cab on the St. Kilda Road.'

'In the open street?' she asked in a startled tone.

'Yes, in the open street.'

'Ah!' she drew a long breath, and closed her lips, firmly. Mr. Gorby said nothing. He saw that she was deliberating whether or not to speak, and a word from him might seal her lips, so, like a wise man, he kept silent. He obtained his reward sooner than he expected.

'Mr. Gorby,' she said at length, 'I 'ave 'ad a 'ard struggle all my life, which it came along of a bad husband, who was a brute and a drunkard, so, God knows, I ain't got much inducement to think well of the lot of you, but — murder,' she shivered slightly, though the room was quite warm, 'I didn't think of that.'

'In connection with whom?'

'Mr. Whyte, of course,' she answered, hurriedly.

'And who else?'

'I don't know.'

'Then there is nobody else?'

'Well, I don't know — I'm not sure.'

The detective was puzzled.

'What do you mean?' he asked.

'I will tell you all I know,' said Mrs. Hableton, 'an' if 'e's innocent, God will 'elp 'im.'

'If who is innocent?'

'I'll tell you everythin' from the start,' said Mrs. Hableton, 'an' you can judge for yourself.'

Mr. Gorby assented, and she began:

'It's only two months ago since I decided to take in lodgers; but charin's 'ard work, and sewin's tryin' for the eyes, So, bein' a lone woman, 'avin' bin badly treated by a brute, who is now dead, which I was allays a good wife to 'im, I thought lodgers 'ud 'elp me a little, so I put a notice in the paper, an' Mr. Oliver Whyte took the rooms two months ago.'

'What was he like?'

'Not very tall, dark face, no whiskers nor moustache, an' quite the gentleman.'

'Anything peculiar about him?'

Mrs. Hableton thought for a moment.

'Well,' she said at length, 'he 'ad a mole on his left temple, but it was covered with 'is 'air, an' few people 'ud 'ave seen it.'

'The very man,' said Gorby to himself, 'I'm on the right path.'

'Mr. Whyte said 'e 'ad just come from England,' went on the woman.

'Which,' thought Mr. Gorby, 'accounts for the corpse not being recognised by friends.'

'He took the rooms, an' said 'e'd stay with me for six months, an' paid a week's rent in advance, an' 'e allays paid up reg'ler like a respectable man, tho' I don't believe in 'em myself. He said 'e'd lots of friends, an' used to go out every night.'

'Who were his friends?'

'That I can't tell you, for 'e were very close, an' when 'e went out of doors I never know'd where 'e went, which is jest like 'em; for they ses they're goin' to work, an' you finds 'em in the beershop. Mr. Whyte told me 'e was a-goin' to marry a heiress, 'e was.'

'Ah!' interjected Mr. Gorby, sapiently.

'He 'ad only one friend as I ever saw — a Mr. Moreland — who comed 'ere with 'm, an' was allays with 'im — brother-like.'

'What is this Mr. Moreland like?'

'Good-lookin' enough,' said Mrs. Hableton sourly, 'but 'is 'abits weren't as good as 'is face — 'andsom is as 'andsom does, is what I ses.'

'I wonder if he knows anything about this affair,' thought Gorby to himself 'Where is Mr. Moreland to be found?' he asked.

'Not knowin', can't tell,' retorted the landlady, ''e used to be 'ere reg'lar, but I ain't seen 'im for over a week.'

'Strange! very!' said Gorby, shaking his head. 'I should like to see this Mr. Moreland. I suppose it's probable he'll call again?'

''Abit bein' second nature I s'pose he will,' answered the woman, ''e might call at any time, mostly 'avin' called at night.'

'Ah! then I'll come down this evening on chance of seeing him,' replied the detective. 'Coincidences happen in real life as well as in novels, and the gentleman in question may turn up in the nick of time. Now, what else about Mr. Whyte?'

'About two weeks ago, or three, I'm not cert'in which, a gentleman called to see Mr. Whyte; 'e was very tall, and wore a light coat.'

'Ah! a morning coat?'

'No! 'e was in evenin' dress, and wore a light coat over it, an' a soft 'at.'

'The very man,' said the detective below his breath; 'go on.'

'He went into Mr. Whyte's room, an' shut the door. I don't know how long they were talkin' together; but I was sittin' in this very room and heard their voices git angry, and they were a-swearin' at one another, which is the way with men, the brutes. I got up and went into the passage in order to ask 'em not to make such a noise, when Mr. Whyte's door opens, an' the gentleman in the light coat comes out, and bangs along to the door. Mr. Whyte 'e comes to the door of 'is room, an' 'e 'ollers out, 'She is mine; you can't do anything' an' the other turns with 'is 'and on the door an' says, 'I can kill you, an' if you marry 'er I'll do it, even in the open street.' '

'Ah!' said Mr. Gorby, drawing a long breath, 'and then?'

'Then he bangs the door to, which it's never shut easy since, an' I ain't got no money to get it put right, an' Mr. Whyte walks back to his room, laughing.'

'Did he make any remark to you?'

'No; except he'd been worried by a loonatic.'

'And what was the stranger's name?'

'That I can't tell you, as Mr. Whyte never told me. He was very tall, with a fair moustache, an' dressed as I told you.'

Mr. Gorby was satisfied.

'That is the man,' he said to himself, 'who got into the hansom cab, and murdered Whyte; there's no doubt of it! Whyte and he were rivals for the heiress.'

'What d'y think of it?' said Mrs. Hableton curiously.

'I think,' said Mr. Gorby slowly, with his eyes fixed on her, 'I think that there is a woman at the bottom of this crime.'

6

Mr. Gorby Makes Further Discoveries.

When Mr. Gorby left Possum Villa no doubt remained in his mind as to who had committed the murder. The gentleman in the light coat had threatened to murder Whyte, even in the open street — these last words being especially significant — and there was no doubt that he had carried out his threat. The committal of the crime was merely the fulfilment of the words uttered in anger. What the detective had now to do was to find who the gentleman in the light coat was, where he lived, and, that done, to ascertain his doings on the night of the murder. Mrs. Hableton had described him, but was ignorant of his name, and her very vague description might apply to dozens of young men in Melbourne. There was only one person who, in Mr. Gorby's opinion, could tell the name of the gentleman in the light coat, and that was Moreland, the intimate friend of the dead man. They appeared, from the landlady's description, to have been so friendly that it was more than likely Whyte would have told

Moreland all about his angry visitor. Besides, Moreland's knowledge of his dead friend's life and habits might be able to supply information on two points, namely, who was most likely to gain by Whyte's death, and who the heiress was that the deceased boasted he would marry. But the fact that Moreland should be ignorant of his friend's tragic death, notwithstanding that the papers were full of it, and that the reward gave an excellent description of his personal appearance, greatly puzzled Gorby. The only way in which to account for Moreland's extraordinary silence was that he was out of town, and had neither seen the papers nor heard anyone talking about the murder. If this were the case he might either stay away for an indefinite time or return after a few days. At all events it was worth while going down to St. Kilda in the evening on the chance that Moreland might have returned to town, and would call to see his friend. So, after his tea, Mr. Gorby put on his hat, and went down to Possum Villa, on what he could not help acknowledging to himself was a very slender possibility.

Mrs. Hableton opened the door for him, and in silence led the way, not into her own sitting-room, but into a much more luxuriously furnished apartment, which Gorby guessed at once was that of Whyte's. He looked keenly round the room, and his estimate of the dead man's character was formed at once.

'Fast,' he said to himself, 'and a spendthrift. A man who would have his friends, and possibly his enemies, among a very shady lot of people.'

What led Mr. Gorby to this belief was the evidence which surrounded him of Whyte's mode of life. The room was well furnished, the furniture being covered with dark-red velvet, while the curtains on the windows and the carpet were all of the same somewhat sombre hue.

'I did the thing properly,' observed Mrs. Hableton, with a satisfactory smile on her hard face. 'When you wants young men to stop with you, the rooms must be well furnished, an' Mr. Whyte paid well, tho' 'e was rather pertickler about 'is food, which I'm only a plain cook, an' can't make them French things which spile the stomach.' The globes of the gas lamps were of a pale pink colour, and Mrs. Hableton having lit the gas in expectation of Mr. Gorby's arrival, there was a soft roseate hue through the room. Mr. Gorby put his hands in his capacious pockets, and strolled leisurely through the room, examining everything with a curious eye. The walls were covered with pictures of celebrated horses and famous jockeys. Alternating with these were photographs of ladies of the stage, mostly London actresses, Nellie Farren, Kate Vaughan, and other burlesque stars, evidently being the objects of the late Mr. Whyte's adoration. Over the mantelpiece hung a rack of pipes, above which were two crossed foils, and under these a number of plush frames of all colours, with pretty faces smiling out of them; a remarkable fact being, that all the photographs were of ladies, and not a single male face was to be seen, either on the walls or in the plush frames.

'Fond of the ladies, I see,' said Mr. Gorby, nodding his head towards the mantelpiece.

'A set of hussies,' said Mrs. Hableton grimly, closing her lips tightly. 'I feel that ashamed when I dusts 'em as never was — I don't believe in gals gettin' their picters taken with 'ardly any clothes on, as if they just got out of bed, but Mr. Whyte seems to like 'em.'

'Most young men do,' answered Mr. Gorby dryly, going over to the bookcase.

'Brutes,' said the lady of the house. 'I'd drown 'em in the Yarrer, I would, a settin' 'emselves and a callin' 'emselves lords of creation, as if women were made for nothin' but to earn money 'an see 'em drink it, as my 'usband did, which 'is inside never seemed to 'ave enough beer, an' me a poor lone woman

50

with no family, thank God, or they'd 'ave taken arter their father in 'is drinkin' 'abits.'

Mr. Gorby took no notice of this tirade against men, but stood looking at Mr. Whyte's library, which seemed to consist mostly of French novels and sporting newspapers. 'Zola,' said Mr. Gorby, thoughtfully, taking down a flimsy yellow book rather tattered. 'I've heard of him; if his novels are as bad as his reputation I shouldn't care to read them.'

Here a knock came at the front door, loud and decisive. On hearing it Mrs. Hableton sprang hastily to her feet. 'That may be Mr. Moreland,' she said, as the detective quickly replaced 'Zola' in the bookcase. 'I never 'ave visitors in the evenin', bein' a lone widder, and if it is 'im I'll bring 'im in 'ere.'

She went out, and presently Gorby, who was listening intently, heard a man's voice ask if Mr. Whyte was at home.

'No, sir, he ain't,' answered the landlady; 'but there's a gentleman in his room askin' after 'im. Won't you come in, sir?'

'For a rest, yes,' returned the visitor, and immediately afterwards Mrs. Hableton appeared, ushering in the late Oliver Whyte's most intimate friend. He was a tall, slender man, with a pink and white complexion, curly fair hair, and a drooping straw-coloured moustache — altogether a strikingly aristocratic individual. He was well-dressed in a suit of check, and had a cool, nonchalant air about him.

'And where is Mr. Whyte to-night?' he asked, sinking into a chair, and taking no more notice of the detective than if he had been an article of furniture.

'Haven't you seen him lately?' asked the detective quickly. Mr. Moreland stared in an insolent manner at his questioner for a few moments, as if he were debating the advisability of answering or not. At last he apparently decided that he would, for slowly pulling off one glove he leaned back in his chair.

'No, I have not,' he said with a yawn. 'I have been up the country for a few days, and arrived back only this evening, so I have not seen him for over a week. Why do you ask?'

The detective did not answer, but stood looking at the young man before him in a thoughtful manner.

'I hope,' said Mr. Moreland, nonchalantly, 'I hope you will know me again, my friend, but I didn't know Whyte had started a lunatic asylum during my absence. Who are you?'

Mr. Gorby came forward and stood under the gas light.

'My name is Gorby, sir, and I am a detective,' he said quietly.

'Ah! indeed,' said Moreland, coolly looking him up and down. 'What has Whyte been doing; running away with someone's wife, eh? I know he has little weaknesses of that sort.'

Gorby shook his head.

'Do you know where Mr. Whyte is to be found?' he asked, cautiously.

Moreland laughed.

'Not I, my friend,' said he, lightly. 'I presume he is somewhere about here, as these are his head-quarters. What has he been doing? Nothing that can surprise me, I assure you — he was always an erratic individual, and — '

'He paid reg'ler,' interrupted Mrs. Hableton, pursing up her lips.

'A most enviable reputation to possess,' answered the other with a sneer, 'and one I'm afraid I'll never enjoy. But why all this questioning about Whyte? What's the matter with him?'

'He's dead!' said Gorby, abruptly.

All Moreland's nonchalance vanished on hearing this, and he started up from his chair.

'Dead,' he repeated mechanically. 'What do you mean?'

'I mean that Mr. Oliver Whyte was murdered in a hansom cab.' Moreland stared at the detective in a puzzled sort of way, and passed his hand across his forehead.

'Excuse me, my head is in a whirl,' he said, as he sat down again. 'Whyte murdered! He was all right when I left him nearly two weeks ago.'

'Haven't you seen the papers?' asked Gorby.

'Not for the last two weeks,' replied Moreland. 'I have been up country, and it was only on arriving back in town to-night that I heard about the murder at all, as my landlady gave me a garbled account of it, but I never for a moment connected it with Whyte, and I came down here to see him, as I had agreed to do when I left. Poor fellow! poor fellow! poor fellow!' and much overcome, he buried his face in his hands.

Mr. Gorby was touched by his evident distress, and even Mrs. Hableton permitted a small tear to roll down one hard cheek as a tribute of sorrow and sympathy. Presently Moreland raised his head, and spoke to Gorby in a husky tone.

'Tell me all about it,' he said, leaning his cheek on his hand. 'Everything you know.'

He placed his elbows on the table, and buried his face in his hands again, while the detective sat down and related all that he knew about Whyte's murder. When it was done he lifted up his head, and looked sadly at the detective.

'If I had been in town,' he said, 'this would not have happened, for I was always beside Whyte.'

'You knew him very well, sir?' said the detective, in a sympathetic tone.

'We were like brothers,' replied Moreland, mournfully.

'I came out from England in the same steamer with him, and used to visit him constantly here.'

Mr. Hableton nodded her head to imply that such was the case.

'In fact,' said Mr. Moreland, after a moment's thought, 'I believe I was with him on the night he was murdered.'

Mrs. Hableton gave a slight scream, and threw her apron over her face, but the detective sat unmoved, though Moreland's last remark had startled him considerably.

'What's the matter?' said Moreland, turning to Mrs. Hableton.

'Don't be afraid; I didn't kill him — no — but I met him last Thursday week, and I left for the country on Friday morning at half-past six.'

'And what time did you meet Whyte on Thursday night?' asked Gorby.

'Let me see,' said Moreland, crossing his legs and looking thoughtfully up to the ceiling, 'it was about half-past nine o'clock. I was in the Orient Hotel, in Bourke Street. We had a drink together, and then went up the street to an hotel in Russell Street, where we had another. In fact,' said Moreland, coolly, 'we had several other drinks.'

'Brutes!' muttered Mrs. Hableton, below her breath.

'Yes,' said Gorby, placidly. 'Go on.'

'Well of — it's hardly the thing to confess it,' said Moreland, looking from one to the other with a pleasant smile, 'but in a case like this, I feel it my duty to throw all social scruples aside. We both became very drunk.'

'Ah! Whyte was, as we know, drunk when he got into the cab — and you — ?'

'I was not quite so bad as Whyte,' answered the other. 'I had my senses about me. I fancy he left the hotel some minutes before one o'clock on Friday morning.'

'And what did you do?'

'I remained in the hotel. He left his overcoat behind him, and I picked it up and followed him shortly afterwards, to return it. I was too drunk to see in which direction he had gone, and stood leaning against the hotel door in Bourke Street with the coat in my hand. Then some one came up, and, snatching the coat from me, made off with it, and the last thing I remember was shouting out: 'Stop, thief!' Then I must have fallen down, for next morning I was in bed with all my clothes on, and they were very muddy. I got up and left town for the country by the six-thirty train, so I knew nothing about the matter until I came back to Melbourne to-night. That's all I know.'

'And you had no impression that Whyte was watched that night?'

'No, I had not,' answered Moreland, frankly. 'He was in pretty good spirits, though he was put out at first.'

'What was the cause of his being put out?'

Moreland arose, and going to a side table, brought Whyte's album, which he laid on the table and opened in silence. The contents were very much the same as the photographs in the room, burlesque actresses and ladies of the ballet predominating; but Mr. Moreland turned over the pages till nearly the end, when he stopped at a large cabinet photograph, and pushed the album towards Mr. Gorby.

'That was the cause,' he said.

It was the portrait of a charmingly pretty girl, dressed in white, with a sailor hat on her fair hair, and holding a lawn-tennis racquet. She was bending half forward, with a winning smile, and in the background bloomed a mass of tropical plants. Mrs. Hableton uttered a cry of surprise at seeing this.

'Why, it's Miss Frettlby,' she said. 'How did he know her?'

'Knew her father — letter of introduction, and all that sort of thing,' said Mr. Moreland, glibly.

'Ah! indeed,' said Mr. Gorby, slowly. 'So Mr. Whyte knew Mark Frettlby, the millionaire; but how did he obtain a photograph of the daughter?'

'She gave it to him,' said Moreland. 'The fact is, Whyte was very much in love with Miss Frettlby.'

'And she — '

'Was in love with someone else,' finished Moreland. 'Exactly! Yes, she loved a Mr. Brian Fitzgerald, to whom she is now engaged. He was mad on her; and Whyte and he used to quarrel desperately over the young lady.'

'Indeed!' said Mr. Gorby. 'And do you know this Mr. Fitzgerald?'

'Oh, dear, no!' answered the other, coolly. 'Whyte's friends were not mine. He was a rich young man who had good introductions. I am only a poor devil on the outskirts of society, trying to push my way in the world.'

'You are acquainted with his personal appearance, of course?' observed Mr. Gorby. 'Oh, yes, I can describe that,' said Moreland. 'In fact, he's not at all unlike me, which I take to be rather a compliment, as he is said to be good-looking. He is tall, rather fair, talks in a bored sort of manner, and is altogether what one would call a heavy swell; but you must have seen him,' he went on, turning to Mrs. Hableton, 'he was here three or four weeks ago, Whyte told me.'

'Oh, that was Mr. Fitzgerald, was it?' said Mrs. Hableton, in surprise. 'Yes, he is rather like you; the lady they quarrelled over must have been Miss Frettlby.'

'Very likely,' said Moreland, rising. 'Well, I'm off; here's my address,' putting a card in Gorby's, hand. 'I'm glad to be of any use to you in this matter, as Whyte was my dearest friend, and I'll do all in my power to help you to find out the murderer.'

'I don't think that is a very difficult matter,' said Mr. Gorby, slowly.

'Oh, you have your suspicions?' asked Moreland, looking at him.

'I have.'

'Then who do you think murdered Whyte?'

Mr. Gorby paused a moment, and then said deliberately: 'I have an idea — but I am not certain — when I am certain, I'll speak.'

'You think Fitzgerald killed my friend,' said Moreland. 'I see it in your face.'

Mr. Gorby smiled. 'Perhaps,' he said, ambiguously. 'Wait till I'm certain.'

7

The Wool King.

The old Greek legend of Midas turning everything he touched into gold, is truer than most people imagine. Mediaeval superstition changed the human being who possessed such a power into the philosopher's stone — the stone which so many alchemists sought in the dark ages. But we of the nineteenth century have given back into human hands this power of transformation.

But we do not ascribe it either to Greek deity, or to superstition; we call it luck. And he who possesses luck should be happy notwithstanding the proverb which hints the contrary. Luck means more than riches — it means happiness in most of those things, which the fortunate possessor of it may choose to touch. Should he speculate, he is successful; if he marry, his wife will surely prove everything to be desired; should he aspire to a position, social or political, he not only attains it, but does so with comparative ease. Worldly wealth, domestic happiness, high position, and complete success — all these things belong to the man who has luck.

Mark Frettlby was one of these fortunate individuals, and his luck was proverbial throughout Australia. If there was any speculation for which Mark Frettlby went in, other men would surely follow, and in every case the result turned out as well, and in many cases even better than they expected. He had come out in the early days of the colony with comparatively little money, but his great perseverance and never-failing luck had soon changed his hundreds into thousands, and now at the age of fifty-five he did not himself know the extent of his income. He had large stations scattered all over the Colony of Victoria, which brought him in a splendid income; a charming country house, where at certain seasons of the year he dispensed hospitality to his friends; and a magnificent town house down in St. Kilda, which would have been not unworthy of Park Lane.

Nor were his domestic relations less happy — he had a charming wife, who was one of the best known and most popular ladies of Melbourne, and an equally charming daughter, who, being both pretty and an heiress, naturally attracted crowds of suitors. But Madge Frettlby was capricious, and refused innumerable offers. Being an extremely independent young person, with a mind of her own, she decided to remain single, as she had not yet seen anyone she could love, and with her mother continued to dispense the hospitality of the mansion at St. Kilda.

But the fairy prince comes at length to every woman, and in this instance he came at his appointed time, in the person of one Brian Fitzgerald, a tall, handsome, fair-haired young man hailing from Ireland.

He had left behind him in the old country a ruined castle and a few acres of barren land, inhabited by discontented tenants, who refused to pay the rent, and talked darkly about the Land League and other agreeable things. Under these circumstances, with no rent coming in, and no prospect of doing anything in the future, Brian had left the castle of his forefathers to the rats and the family Banshee, and had come out to Australia to make his fortune.

He brought letters of introduction to Mark Frettlby, and that gentleman, taking a fancy to him, assisted him by every means in his power. Under Frettlby's advice Brian bought a station, and, to his astonishment, in a few years he found himself growing rich. The Fitzgeralds had always been more famous for spending than for saving, and it was an agreeable surprise to their latest representative to find the money rolling in instead of out. He began to indulge in castles in the air concerning that other castle in Ireland, with the barren acres and discontented tenants. In his mind's-eye he saw the old place rise up in all its pristine splendour from out its ruins; he saw the barren acres well cultivated, and the tenants happy and content — he was rather doubtful on this latter point, but, with the rash confidence of eight and twenty, determined to do his best to perform even the impossible.

Having built and furnished his castle in the air, Brian naturally thought of giving it a mistress, and this time actual appearance took the place of vision. He fell in love with Madge Frettlby, and having decided in his own mind that she and none other was fitted to grace the visionary halls of his renovated castle, he watched his opportunity, and declared himself. She, woman-like, coquetted with him for some time, but at last, unable to withstand the impetuosity of her Irish lover, confessed in a low voice, with a pretty smile on her face, that she could not live without him. Whereupon — well — lovers being of a conservative turn of mind, and accustomed to observe the traditional forms of wooing, the result can easily be guessed. Brian hunted all over the jewellers' shops in Melbourne with lover-like assiduity, and having obtained a ring wherein were set turquoise stones as blue as his own eyes, he placed it on her slender finger, and at last felt that his engagement was an accomplished fact.

He next proceeded to interview the father, and had just screwed up his courage to the awful ordeal, when something occurred which postponed the interview indefinitely. Mrs. Frettlby was out driving, and the horses took fright and bolted. The coachman and groom both escaped unhurt, but Mrs. Frettlby was thrown out and killed instantly. This was the first really great trouble which had fallen on Mark Frettlby, and he seemed stunned by it. Shutting himself up in his room he refused to see anyone, even his daughter, and appeared at the funeral with a white and haggard face, which shocked everyone. When everything was over, and the body of the late Mrs. Frettlby was consigned to the earth, with all the pomp and ceremony which money could give, the bereaved husband rode home, and resumed his old life. But he was never the same again. His face, which had always been so genial and so bright, became stern and sad. He seldom smiled, and when he did, it was a faint wintry smile, which seemed mechanical. His whole interest in life was centred in his daughter. She became the sole mistress of the St. Kilda mansion, and her father idolised her. She was apparently the one thing left to him which gave him a pleasure in existence. In truth, had it not been for her bright presence, Mark Frettlby would fain have been lying beside his dead wife in the quiet graveyard.

After a time Brian again resolved to ask Mr. Frettlby for the hand of his daughter. But for the second time fate interposed. A rival suitor made his appearance, and Brian's hot Irish temper rose in anger at him.

Mr. Oliver Whyte had come out from England a few months previously, bringing with him a letter of introduction to Mr. Frettlby, who received him hospitably, as was his custom. Taking advantage of this, Whyte lost no time in making himself perfectly at home in the St. Kilda mansion.

From the outset Brian took a dislike to the new-comer. He was a student of Lavater, and prided himself on his perspicuity in reading character. His opinion of Whyte was anything but flattering to that gentleman; while Madge shared his repulsion towards the new-comer.

On his part Mr. Whyte was nothing if not diplomatic. He affected not to notice the coldness of Madge's reception of him. On the contrary he began to pay her the most marked attentions, much to Brian's disgust. At length he asked her to be his wife, and notwithstanding her prompt refusal, spoke to her father on the subject. Much to the astonishment of his daughter, Mr. Frettlby not only consented to Whyte paying his addresses to Madge, but gave that young lady to understand that he wished her to consider his proposals favourably.

In spite of all Madge could say, he refused to alter his decision, and Whyte, feeling himself safe, began to treat Brian with an insolence which was highly galling to Fitzgerald's proud nature. He had called on Whyte at his lodgings, and after a violent quarrel he had left the house vowing to kill him, should he marry Madge Frettlby. The same night Fitzgerald had an interview with Mr. Frettlby. He confessed that he loved Madge, and that his love was returned. So, when Madge added her entreaties to Brian's, Mr. Frettlby found himself unable to withstand the combined forces, and gave his consent to their engagement.

Whyte was absent in the country for the next few days after his stormy interview with Brian, and it was only on his return that he learnt that Madge was engaged to his rival. He saw Mr. Frettlby, and having learnt from his own lips that such was the case, he left the house at once, and swore that he would never enter it again. He little knew how prophetic were his words, for on that same night he met his death in the hansom cab. He had passed out of the life of both the lovers, and they, glad that he troubled them no more, never suspected for a moment that the body of the unknown man found in Royston's cab was that of Oliver Whyte.

About two weeks after Whyte's disappearance Mr. Frettlby gave a dinner party in honour of his daughter's birthday. It was a delightful evening, and the wide French windows which led on to the verandah were open, letting in a gentle breeze from the ocean. Outside there was a kind of screen of tropical plants, and through the tangle of the boughs the guests, seated at the table, could just see the waters of the bay glittering in the pale moonlight. Brian was seated opposite to Madge, and every now and then he caught a glimpse of her bright face from behind the fruit and flowers, which stood in the centre of the table. Mark Frettlby was at the head of the table, and appeared in very good spirits. His stern features were somewhat relaxed, and he drank more wine than usual.

The soup had just been removed when some one, who was late, entered with apologies and took his seat. Some one in this case was Mr. Felix Rolleston, one of the best known young men in Melbourne. He had an income of his own, scribbled a little for the papers, was to be seen at every house of any pretensions in Melbourne, and was always bright, happy, and full of news. For details of any scandal you were safe in applying to Felix Rolleston. He knew all that was going on, both at home and abroad. And his knowledge, if not very accurate, was at least extensive, while his conversation was piquant, and at times witty. Calton, one of the leading lawyers of the city, remarked that 'Rolleston put him in mind of what Beaconsfield said of one of the personages in Lothair, 'He wasn't an intellectual Croesus, but his pockets were always full of sixpences.' ' Be it said in his favour that Felix was free with his sixpences.

The conversation, which had shown signs of languishing before his arrival, now brightened up.

'So awfully sorry, don't you know,' said Felix, as he slipped into a seat by Madge; 'but a fellow like me has got to be careful of his time — so many calls on it.'

'So many calls in it, you mean,' retorted Madge, with a disbelieving smile. 'Confess, now, you have been paying a round of visits.'

'Well, yes,' assented Mr. Rolleston; 'that's the disadvantage of having a large circle of acquaintances. They give you weak tea and thin bread and butter, whereas — '

'You would rather have something else,' finished Brian.

There was a laugh at this, but Mr. Rolleston disdained to notice the interruption.

'The only advantage of five o'clock tea,' he went on, 'is, that it brings people together, and one hears what's going on.'

'Ah, yes, Rolleston,' said Mr. Frettlby, who was looking at him with an amused smile. 'What news have you?'

'Good news, bad news, and such news as you have never heard of,' quoted Rolleston gravely. 'Yes, I have a bit of news — haven't you heard it?'

Rolleston felt he held sensation in his hands. There was nothing he liked better.

'Well, do you know,' he said, gravely fixing in his eye-glass, 'they have found out the name of the fellow who was murdered in the hansom cab.'

'Never!' cried every one eagerly.

'Yes,' went on Rolleston, 'and what's more, you all know him.'

'It's never Whyte?' said Brian, in a horrified tone.

'Hang it, how did you know?' said Rolleston, rather annoyed at being forestalled.

69

'Why, I just heard it at the St. Kilda station.'

'Oh, easily enough,' said Brian, rather confused. 'I used to meet Whyte constantly, and as I have not seen him for the last two weeks, I thought he might be the victim.'

'How did they find out?' asked Mr. Frettlby, idly toying with his wine-glass.

'Oh, one of those detective fellows, you know,' answered Felix. 'They know everything.'

'I'm sorry to hear it,' said Frettlby, referring to the fact that Whyte was murdered.

'He had a letter of introduction to me, and seemed a clever, pushing young fellow.'

'A confounded cad,' muttered Felix, under his breath; and Brian, who overheard him, seemed inclined to assent. For the rest of the meal nothing was talked about but the murder, and the mystery in which it was shrouded. When the ladies retired they chatted about it in the drawing-room, but finally dropped it for more agreeable subjects. The men, however, when the cloth was removed, filled their glasses, and continued the discussion with unabated vigour. Brian alone did not take part in the conversation. He sat moodily staring at his untasted wine, wrapped in a brown study.

'What I can't make out,' observed Rolleston, who was amusing himself with cracking nuts, 'is why they did not find out who he was before.'

'That is not hard to answer,' said Frettlby, filling his glass. 'He was comparatively little known here, as he had been out from England such a short time, and I fancy that this was the only house at which he visited.'

'And look here, Rolleston,' said Calton, who was sitting near him, 'if you were to find a man dead in a hansom cab, dressed in evening clothes — which nine men out of ten are in the habit of wearing in the evening — no cards in his pockets, and no name on his linen, I rather think you would find it hard to discover who he was. I consider it reflects great credit on the police for finding out so quickly.'

'Puts one in mind of 'The Leavenworth Case,' and all that sort of thing,' said Felix, whose reading was of the lightest description. 'Awfully exciting, like putting a Chinese puzzle together. Gad, I wouldn't mind being a detective myself.'

'I'm afraid if that were the case,' said Mr. Frettlby, with an amused smile, 'criminals would be pretty safe.'

'Oh, I don't know so much about that,' answered Felix, shrewdly; 'some fellows are like trifle at a party, froth on top, but something better underneath.'

'What a greedy simile,' said Calton, sipping his wine; 'but I'm afraid the police will have a more difficult task in discovering the man who committed the crime. In my opinion he's a deuced clever fellow.'

'Then you don't think he will be discovered?' asked Brian, rousing himself out of his brown study.

'Well, I don't go as far as that,' rejoined Calton; 'but he has certainly left no trace behind him, and even the Red Indian, in whom instinct for tracking is so highly developed, needs some sort of a trail to enable him to find out his enemies. Depend upon it,' went on Calton, warming to his subject, 'the man who murdered Whyte is no ordinary criminal; the place he chose for the committal of the crime was such a safe one.'

'Do you think so?' said Rolleston. 'Why, I should think that a hansom cab in a public street would be very unsafe.'

'It is that very fact that makes it safer,' replied Mr. Calton, epigrammatically. 'You read De Quincey's account of the Marr murders in London, and you will see that the more public the place the less risk there is of detection. There was nothing about the gentleman in the light coat who murdered Whyte to excite Royston's suspicions. He entered the cab with Whyte; no noise or

72

anything likely to attract attention was heard, and then he alighted. Naturally enough, Royston drove to St. Kilda, and never suspected Whyte was dead till he looked inside and touched him. As to the man in the light coat, he doesn't live in Powlett Street — no — nor in East Melbourne either.'

'Why not?' asked Frettlby.

'Because he wouldn't have been such a fool as to leave a trail to his own door; he did what the fox often does — he doubled. My opinion is that he went either right through East Melbourne to Fitzroy, or he walked back through the Fitzroy Gardens into town. There was no one about at that time of the morning, and he could return to his lodgings, hotel, or wherever he is staying, with impunity. Of course, this is a theory that may be wrong; but from what insight into human nature my profession has given me, I think that my idea is a correct one.'

All present agreed with Mr. Calton's idea, as it really did seem the most natural thing that would be done by a man desirous of escaping detection.

'Tell you what,' said Felix to Brian, as they were on their way to the drawing-room, 'if the fellow that committed the crime, is found out, by gad, he ought to get Calton to defend him.'

8

Brian Takes a Walk and a Drive.

When the gentlemen entered the drawing-room a young lady was engaged in playing one of those detestable pieces of the *Morceau de Salon* order, in which an unoffending air is taken, and variations embroidered on it, till it becomes a perfect agony to distinguish the tune, amid the perpetual rattle of quavers and demi-semi-quavers. The melody in this case was 'Over the Garden Wall,' with variations by Signor Thumpanini, and the young lady who played it was a pupil of that celebrated Italian musician. When the male portion of the guests entered, the air was being played in the bass with a great deal of power (that is, the loud pedal was down), and with a perpetual rattle of treble notes, trying with all their shrill might to drown the tune.

'Gad! it's getting over the garden wall in a hailstorm,' said Felix, as he strolled over to the piano, for he saw that the musician was Dora Featherweight, an heiress to whom he was then paying attention, in the hope that she might be induced to take the name of Rolleston. So, when the fair Dora had paralysed her audience with one final bang and rattle, as if the gentleman going over the garden wall had tumbled into the cucumber-frame, Felix was loud in his expressions of delight.

'Such power, you know, Miss Feather-weight,' he said, sinking into a chair, and mentally wondering if any of the piano strings had given way at that last crash. 'You put your heart into it — and all your muscle, too, by gad,' he added mentally.

'It's nothing but practice,' answered Miss Featherweight, with a modest blush. 'I am at the piano four hours every day.'

'Good heavens!' thought Felix, 'what a time the family must have of it.' But he kept this remark to himself, and, screwing his eye-glass into his left organ of vision, merely ejaculated, 'Lucky piano.'

Miss Featherweight, not being able to think of any answer to this, looked down and blushed, while the ingenuous Felix looked up and sighed.

Madge and Brian were in a corner of the room talking over Whyte's death.

'I never liked him,' she said, 'but it is horrible to think of him dying like that.'

'I don't know,' answered Brian, gloomily;

'from all I can hear dying by chloroform is a very easy death.'

'Death can never be easy,' replied Madge, 'especially to a young man so full of health and spirits as Mr. Whyte was.'

'I believe you are sorry he's dead,' said Brian, jealously.

'Aren't you?' she asked in some surprise.

'*De mortuis nil nisi bonum*,' quoted Fitzgerald. 'But as I detested him when alive, you can't expect me to regret his end.'

Madge did not answer him, but glanced quickly at his face, and for the first time it struck her that he looked ill.

'What is the matter with you, dear?' she asked, placing her hand on his arm. 'You are not looking well.'

'Nothing — nothing,' he answered hurriedly. 'I've been a little worried about business lately — but come,' he said, rising, 'let us go outside, for I see your father has got that girl with the steam-whistle voice to sing.'

The girl with the steam-whistle voice was Julia Featherweight, the sister of Rolleston's inamorata, and Madge stifled a laugh as she went on to the verandah with Fitzgerald.

'What a shame of you,' she said, bursting into a laugh when they were safely outside; 'she's been taught by the best masters.'

'How I pity them,' retorted Brian, grimly,

as Julia wailed out, 'Meet me once again,' with an ear-piercing shrillness.

'I'd much rather listen to our ancestral Banshee, and as to meeting her again, one interview would be more than enough.'

Madge did not answer, but leaning lightly over the high rail of the verandah looked out into the beautiful moonlit night. There were a number of people passing along the Esplanade, some of whom stopped and listened to Julia's shrill notes. One man in particular seemed to have a taste for music, for he persistently stared over the fence at the house. Brian and Madge talked of divers subjects, but every time Madge looked up she saw the man watching the house. 'What does that man want, Brian?' she asked.

'What man?' asked Brian, starting. 'Oh,' he went on indifferently, as the watcher moved away from the gate and crossed the road on to the footpath, 'he's taken up with the music, I suppose; that's all.'

Madge said nothing, but she could not help thinking there was more in it than the music. Presently Julia ceased, and she proposed to go in.

'Why?' asked Brian, who was lying back in a comfortable seat, smoking a cigarette.

'It's nice enough here.'

'I must attend to my guests,' she answered,

rising. 'You stop here and finish your cigarette,' and with a gay laugh she flitted into the house.

Brian sat and smoked, staring out into the moonlight the while. Yes, the man was certainly watching the house, for he sat on one of the seats, and kept his eyes fixed on the brilliantly-lighted windows. Brian threw away his cigarette and shivered slightly.

'Could anyone have seen me?' he muttered, rising uneasily.

'Pshaw! of course not; and the cabman would never recognise me again. Curse Whyte, I wish I'd never set eyes upon him.'

He gave one glance at the dark figure on the seat, and then, with a shiver, passed into the warm, well-lighted room. He did not feel easy in his mind, and he would have felt still less so had he known that the man on the seat was one of the cleverest of the Melbourne detectives.

Mr. Gorby had been watching the Frettlby mansion the whole evening, and was getting rather annoyed. Moreland did not know where Fitzgerald lived, and as that was one of the primary facts the detective wished to ascertain, he determined to watch Brian's movements, and to trace him home.

'If he's the lover of that pretty girl, I'll wait till he leaves the house,' argued Mr. Gorby to himself, as he took his seat on the Esplanade. 'He won't long remain away from her, and once he leaves the house it will be no difficult matter to find out where he lives.'

When Brian made his appearance early in the evening, on his way to Mark Frettlby's mansion, he wore evening dress, a light overcoat, and a soft hat.

'Well, I'm dashed!' ejaculated Mr. Gorby, when he saw Fitzgerald disappear; 'if he isn't a fool I don't know who is, to go about in the very clothes he wore when he polished Whyte off, and think he won't be recognised. Melbourne ain't Paris or London, that he can afford to be so careless, and when I put the darbies on him he will be astonished. Ah, well,' he went on, lighting his pipe and taking a seat on the Esplanade, 'I suppose I'll have to wait here till he comes out.'

Mr. Gorby's patience was pretty severely tried, for hour after hour passed, and no one appeared. He smoked several pipes, and watched the people strolling along in the soft silver moonlight. A bevy of girls passed by with their arms round one another's waists. Then a young man and woman, evidently lovers, came walking along. They sat down by Mr. Gorby and looked hard at him, to hint that he need not stay. But the detective took no heed of them, and kept his eyes steadily upon the great house opposite. Finally, the lovers took themselves off with a very bad grace. Then Mr. Gorby saw Madge and Brian come out on to the verandah, and heard in the stillness of the night, a sound weird and unearthly. It was Miss Featherweight singing. He saw Madge go in, shortly followed by Brian. The latter turned and stared at him for a moment.

'Ah,' said Gorby to himself as he re-lit his pipe; 'your conscience is a-smiting you, is it? Wait a bit, my boy, till I have you in gaol.'

Then the guests came out of the house, and their black figures disappeared one by one from the moonlight as they shook hands and said good-night.

Shortly after Brian came down the path with Frettlby at his side, and Madge hanging on her father's arm. Frettlby opened the gate and held out his hand.

'Good-night, Fitzgerald,' he said, in a hearty voice; 'come soon again.'

'Good-night, Brian, dearest,' said Madge, kissing him, 'and don't forget to-morrow.'

Then father and daughter closed the gate, leaving Brian outside, and walked back to the house.

'Ah!' said Mr. Gorby to himself, 'if you only knew what I know, you wouldn't be so precious kind to him.'

Brian strolled along the Esplanade, and crossing over, passed by Gorby and walked on till he was opposite the Esplanade Hotel. Then he leaned his arms on the fence, and, taking off his hat, enjoyed the calm beauty of the hour.

'What a good-looking fellow,' murmured Mr. Gorby, in a regretful tone. 'I can hardly believe it of him, but the proofs are too clear.'

The night was perfectly still. Not a breath of wind stirred, for what breeze there had been had long since died away. But Brian could see the white wavelets breaking lightly on the sands. The long narrow pier ran out like a black thread into the sheet of gleaming silver, and away in the distance the line of the Williamstown lights sparkled like some fairy illumination.

Over all this placid scene of land and water was a sky such as Dore loved — a great heavy mass of rain-clouds heaped one on top of the other, as the rocks the Titans piled to reach Olympus. Then a break in the woof, and a bit of dark blue sky could be seen glittering with stars, in the midst of which sailed the serene moon, shedding down her light on the cloudland beneath, giving to it all, one silver lining. Somewhat to the annoyance of Mr. Gorby, who had no eye for the picturesque, Brian gazed at the sky for several minutes, admiring the wonderful beauty of its broken masses of light and shade. At length he lit a cigarette and walked down the steps on to the pier.

'Oh, suicide, is it?' muttered Mr. Gorby. 'Not if I can help it.' And he lit his pipe and followed him.

He found Brian leaning over the parapet at the end of the pier, looking at the glittering waters beneath, which kept rising and falling in a dreamy rhythm, that soothed and charmed the ear. 'Poor girl! poor girl!' the detective heard him mutter as he came up. 'If she only knew all! If she — '

At this moment he heard the approaching step, and turned round sharply. The detective saw that his face was ghastly pale in the moonlight, and his brows wrinkled in anger.

'What the devil do you want?' he burst out, as Gorby paused.

'What do you mean by following me all over the place?'

'Saw me, watching the house,' said Gorby to himself. 'I'm not following you, sir,' he said aloud. 'I suppose the pier ain't private property. I only came down here for a breath of fresh air.'

Fitzgerald did not answer, but turned sharply on his heel, and walked quickly up the pier, leaving Gorby staring after him.

'He's getting frightened,' soliloquised the detective to himself, as he strolled easily along, keeping the black figure in front well in view. 'I'll have to keep a sharp eye on him or he'll be clearing out of Victoria.'

Brian walked rapidly up to the St. Kilda station, for on looking at his watch he found that he would just have time to catch the last train. He arrived a few minutes before it started, so, getting into the smoking carriage at the near end of the platform, he lit a cigarette, and, leaning back in his seat, watched the late-comers hurrying into the station. Just as the last bell rang he saw a man rush along, to catch the train. It was the same man who had been watching him the whole evening, and Brian felt confident that he was being followed. He comforted himself, however, with the thought that this pertinacious follower might lose the train, and, being in the last carriage himself, he kept a look out along the platform, expecting to see his friend of the Esplanade standing disappointed on it. There was no appearance of him, so Brian, sinking back into his seat, lamented his ill-luck in not shaking off this man who kept him under such strict surveillance.

'Confound him!' he muttered softly. 'I expect he will follow me to East Melbourne, and find out where I live, but he shan't if I can help it.'

There was no one but himself in the carriage, and he felt relieved at this because he was in no humour to hear chatter.

'Murdered in a cab,' he said, lighting a fresh cigarette, and blowing a cloud of smoke.

'A romance in real life, which beats Miss Braddon hollow. There is one thing certain, he won't come between Madge and me again. Poor Madge!' with an impatient sigh.

'If she only knew all, there would not be much chance of our marriage; but she can never find out, and I don't suppose anyone else will.'

Here a thought suddenly struck him, and rising out of his seat, he walked to the other end of the carriage, and threw himself on the cushions, as if desirous to escape from himself.

'What grounds can that man have for suspecting me?' he said aloud. 'No one knows I was with Whyte on that night, and the police can't possibly bring forward any evidence to show that I was. Pshaw!' he went on, impatiently buttoning up his coat. 'I am like a child, afraid of my shadow — the fellow on the pier is only some one out for a breath of fresh air, as he said himself — I am quite safe.'

At the same time, he felt by no means easy in his mind, and as he stepped out on to the platform at the Melbourne station he looked round apprehensively, as if he half expected to feel the detective's hand upon his shoulder. But he saw no one at all like the man he had met on the St. Kilda pier, and with a sigh of relief he left the station. Mr. Gorby, however, was not far away. He was following at a safe distance. Brian walked slowly along Flinders Street apparently deep in thought. He turned up Russell Street and did not stop until he found himself close to the Burke and Wills' monument — the exact spot where the cab had stopped on the night of Whyte's murder.

'Ah!' said the detective to himself, as he stood in the shadow on the opposite side of the street. 'You're going to have a look at it, are you? — I wouldn't, if I were you — it's dangerous.'

Fitzgerald stood for a few minutes at the corner, and then walked up Collins Street. When he got to the cab-stand, opposite the Melbourne Club, still suspecting he was followed, he hailed a hansom, and drove away in the direction of Spring Street. Gorby was rather perplexed at this sudden move, but without delay, he hailed another cab, and told the driver to follow the first till it stopped.

'Two can play at that game,' he said,

settling himself back in the cab, 'and I'll get the better of you, clever as you are — and you are clever,' he went on in a tone of admiration, as he looked round the luxurious hansom, 'to choose such a convenient place for a murder; no disturbance and plenty of time for escape after you had finished; it's a pleasure going after a chap like you, instead of after men who tumble down like ripe fruit, and ain't got any brains to keep their crime quiet.'

While the detective thus soliloquised, his cab, following on the trail of the other, had turned down Spring Street, and was being driven rapidly along the Wellington Parade, in the direction of East Melbourne. It then turned up Powlett Street, at which Mr. Gorby was glad.

'Ain't so clever as I thought,' he said to himself. 'Shows his nest right off, without any attempt to hide it.'

The detective, however, had reckoned without his host, for the cab in front kept driving on, through an interminable maze of streets, until it seemed as though Brian were determined to drive the whole night.

'Look 'ere, sir!' cried Gorby's cabman, looking through his trap-door in the roof of the hansom, ''ow long's this 'ere game agoin' to larst? My 'oss is knocked up, 'e is, and 'is blessed old legs is agivin' way under 'im!'

'Go on! go on!' answered the detective, impatiently; 'I'll pay you well.'

The cabman's spirits were raised by this, and by dint of coaxing and a liberal use of the whip, he managed to get his jaded horse up to a pretty good pace. They were in Fitzroy by this time, and both cabs turned out of Gertrude Street into Nicholson Street; thence passed on to Evelyn Street and along Spring Street, until Brian's cab stopped at the corner of Collins Street, and Gorby saw him alight and dismiss his cabman. He then walked down the street and disappeared into the Treasury Gardens.

'Confound it,' said the detective, as he got out and paid his fare, which was by no means a light one, but over which he had no time to argue, 'we've come in a circle, and I do believe he lives in Powlett Street after all.'

He went into the gardens, and saw Brian some distance ahead of him, walking rapidly. It was bright moonlight, and he could easily distinguish Fitzgerald by his light coat.

As he went along that noble avenue with its elms in their winter dress, the moon shining through their branches wrought a fantastic tracery on the smooth asphalt. And on either side Gorby could see the dim white forms of the old Greek gods and goddesses — Venus

Victrix, with the apple in her hand (which Mr. Gorby, in his happy ignorance of heathen mythology, took for Eve offering Adam the forbidden fruit); Diana, with the hound at her feet, and Bacchus and Ariadne (which the detective imagined were the Babes in the Wood). He knew that each of the statues had queer names, but thought they were merely allegorical. Passing over the bridge, with the water rippling quietly underneath, Brian went up the smooth yellow path to where the statue of Hebe, holding the cup, seems instinct with life; and turning down the path to the right, he left the gardens by the end gate, near which stands the statue of the Dancing Faun, with the great bush of scarlet geranium burning like an altar before it. Then he went along the Wellington Parade, and turned up Powlett Street, where he stopped at a house near Cairns' Memorial Church, much to Mr. Gorby's relief, who, being like Hamlet, 'fat and scant of breath,' found himself rather exhausted. He kept well in the shadow, however, and saw Fitzgerald give one final look round before he disappeared into the house. Then Mr. Gorby, like the Robber Captain in Ali Baba, took careful stock of the house, and fixed its locality and appearance well in his mind, as he intended to call at it on the morrow.

'What I'm going to do,' he said, as he walked slowly back to Melbourne, 'is to see his landlady when he's out, and find out what time he came in on the night of the murder. If it fits into the time he got out of Rankin's cab, I'll get out a warrant, and arrest him straight off.'

9

Mr. Gorby is Satisfied at Last.

In spite of his long walk, and still longer drive, Brian did not sleep well that night. He kept tossing and turning, or lying on his back, wide awake, looking into the darkness and thinking of Whyte. Towards dawn, when the first faint glimmer of morning came through the venetian blinds, he fell into a sort of uneasy doze, haunted by horrible dreams. He thought he was driving in a hansom, when suddenly he found Whyte by his side, clad in white cerements, grinning and gibbering at him with ghastly merriment. Then the cab went over a precipice, and he fell from a great height, down, down, with the mocking laughter still sounding in his ears, until he woke with a loud cry, and found it was broad daylight, and that drops of perspiration were standing on his brow. It was no use trying to sleep any longer, so, with a weary sigh, he arose and went to his tub, feeling jaded and worn out by worry and want of sleep. His bath did him some good. The cold water brightened him up and pulled him together.

Still he could not help giving a start of surprise when he saw his face reflected in the mirror, old and haggard-looking, with dark circles round the eyes.

'A pleasant life I'll have of it if this sort of thing goes on,' he said, bitterly. 'I wish I had never seen, or heard of Whyte.'

He dressed himself carefully. He was not a man to neglect his toilet, however worried and out of sorts he might happen to feel. Yet, notwithstanding all his efforts the change in his appearance did not escape the eye of his landlady. She was a small, dried-up little woman, with a wrinkled yellowish face. She seemed parched up and brittle. Whenever she moved she crackled, and one went in constant dread of seeing a wizen-looking limb break off short like the branch of some dead tree. When she spoke it was in a voice hard and shrill, not unlike the chirp of a cricket. When — as was frequently the case — she clothed her attenuated form in a faded brown silk gown, her resemblance to that lively insect was remarkable.

And, as on this morning she crackled into Brian's sitting-room with the *Argus* and his coffee, a look of dismay at his altered appearance came over her stony little countenance.

'Dear me, sir,' she chirped out in her shrill

voice, as she placed her burden on the table, 'are you took bad?' Brian shook his head.

'Want of sleep, that's all, Mrs. Sampson,' he answered, unfolding the *Argus*.

'Ah! that's because ye ain't got enough blood in yer 'ead,' said Mrs. Sampson, wisely, for she had her own ideas on the subject of health. 'If you ain't got blood you ain't got sleep.'

Brian looked at her as she said this, for there seemed such an obvious want of blood in her veins that he wondered if she had ever slept in all her life.

'There was my father's brother, which, of course, makes 'im my uncle,' went on the landlady, pouring out a cup of coffee for Brian, 'an' the blood 'e 'ad was somethin' astoundin', which it made 'im sleep that long as they 'ad to draw pints from 'im afore 'e'd wake in the mornin'.'

Brian had the *Argus* before his face, and under its friendly cover he laughed quietly to himself.

'His blood poured out like a river,' went on the landlady, still drawing from the rich stores of her imagination, 'and the doctor was struck dumb with astonishment at seein' the Nigagerer which burst from 'im — but I'm not so full-blooded myself.' Fitzgerald again stifled a laugh, and wondered that Mrs.

Sampson was not afraid of being treated as were Ananias and Sapphira. However, he said nothing, but merely intimated that if she would leave the room he would take his breakfast.

'An' if you wants anythin' else, Mr. Fitzgerald,' she said, going to the door, 'you knows your way to the bell as easily as I do to the kitching,' and, with a final chirrup, she crackled out of the room.

As soon as the door was closed, Brian put down his paper and roared, in spite of his worries. He had that extraordinary vivacious Irish temperament, which enables a man to put all trouble behind his back, and thoroughly enjoy the present. His landlady, with her Arabian Nightlike romances, was a source of great amusement to him, and he felt considerably cheered by the odd turn her humour had taken this morning. After a time, however, his laughter ceased, and his troubles came crowding on him again. He drank his coffee, but pushed away the food which was before him; and looked through the *Argus*, for the latest report about the murder case. What he read made his cheek turn a shade paler than before. He could feel his heart thumping wildly. 'They've found a clue, have they?' he muttered, rising and pacing restlessly up and down. 'I wonder what it can be? I threw that man off the scent last night, but if he suspects me, there will be no difficulty in his finding out where I live. Bah! What nonsense I am talking. I am the victim of my own morbid imagination. There is nothing to connect me with the crime, so I need not be afraid of my shadow. I've a good mind to leave town for a time, but if I am suspected that would excite suspicion. Oh, Madge! my darling,' he cried passionately, 'if you only knew what I suffer, I know that you would pity me — but you must never know the truth — Never! Never!' and sinking into a chair by the window, he covered his face with his hands. After remaining in this position for some minutes, occupied with his own gloomy thoughts, he arose and rang the bell. A faint crackle in the distance announced that Mrs. Sampson had heard it, and she soon came into the room, looking more like a cricket than ever. Brian had gone into his bedroom, and called out to her from there — 'I am going down to St. Kilda, Mrs. Sampson,' he said, 'and probably I shall not be back all day.'

'Which I 'opes it 'ull do you good,' she answered, 'for you've eaten nothin', an' the sea breezes is miraculous for makin' you take to your victuals. My mother's brother, bein' a sailor, an' wonderful for 'is stomach, which, when 'e 'ad done a meal, the table looked as if a low-cuss had gone over it.'

'A what?' asked Fitzgerald, buttoning his gloves.

'A low-cuss!' replied the landlady, in surprise at his ignorance, 'as I've read in 'Oly Writ, as 'ow John the Baptist was partial to 'em, not that I think they'd be very fillin', tho', to be sure, 'e 'ad a sweet tooth, and ate 'oney with 'em.'

'Oh! you mean locusts,' said Brian now enlightened.

'An' what else?' asked Mrs. Sampson, indignantly; 'which, tho' not bein' a scholar'd, I speaks English, I 'opes, my mother's second cousin 'avin' 'ad first prize at a spellin' bee, tho' 'e died early through brain fever, 'avin' crowded 'is 'ead over much with the dictionary.'

'Dear me!' answered Brian, mechanically. 'How unfortunate!' He was not listening to Mrs. Sampson's remarks. He suddenly remembered an arrangement which Madge had made, and which up till now had slipped his memory.

'Mrs. Sampson,' he said, turning round at the door, 'I am going to bring Mr. Frettlby and his daughter to have a cup of afternoon tea here, so you might have some ready.'

'You 'ave only to ask and to 'ave,' answered

Mrs. Sampson, hospitably, with a gratified crackle of all her joints. 'I'll make the tea, sir, an' also some of my own perticler cakes, bein' a special kind I 'ave, which my mother showed me 'ow to make, 'avin' been taught by a lady as she nussed thro' the scarlet fever, tho' bein' of a weak constitootion, she died soon arter, bein' in the 'abit of contractin' any disease she might chance on.'

Brian hurried off lest in her Poe-like appreciation of them, Mrs. Sampson should give vent to more charnel-house horrors.

At one period of her life, the little woman had been a nurse, and it was told of her that she had frightened one of her patients into convulsions during the night by narrating to her the history of all the corpses she had laid out. This ghoul-like tendency in the end proved fatal to her professional advancement.

As soon as Fitzgerald had gone, she went over to the window and watched him as he walked slowly down the street — a tall, handsome man, of whom any woman would be proud.

'What an awful thing it are to think 'e'll be a corpse some day,' she chirped cheerily to herself, 'tho' of course bein' a great swell in 'is own place, 'e'll 'ave a nice airy vault, which 'ud be far more comfortable than a close, stuffy grave, even tho' it 'as a tombstone an' vi'lets over it. Ah, now! Who are you, impertinence?' she broke off, as a stout man in a light suit of clothes crossed the road and rang the bell, 'a-pullin' at the bell as if it were a pump 'andle.'

As the gentleman at the door, who was none other than Mr. Gorby, did not hear her, he of course did not reply, so she hurried down the stairs, crackling with anger at the rough usage her bell had received.

Mr. Gorby had seen Brian go out, and deeming it a good opportunity for enquiry had lost no time in making a start.

'You nearly tored the bell down,' said Mrs. Sampson, as she presented her thin body and wrinkled face to the view of the detective.

'I'm very sorry,' answered Gorby, meekly. 'I'll knock next time.'

'Oh, no you won't,' said the landlady, tossing her head, 'me not 'avin' a knocker, an' your 'and a-scratchin' the paint off the door, which it ain't been done over six months by my sister-in-law's cousin, which 'e is a painter, with a shop in Fitzroy, an' a wonderful heye to colour.'

'Does Mr. Fitzgerald live here?' asked Mr. Gorby, quietly.

'He do,' replied Mrs. Sampson, 'but 'e's gone out, an' won't be back till the arternoon, which any messige 'ull be

97

delivered to 'im punctual on 'is arrival.'

'I'm glad he's not in,' said Mr. Gorby. 'Would you allow me to have a few moments' conversation?'

'What is it?' asked the landlady, her curiosity being roused.

'I'll tell you when we get inside,' answered Mr. Gorby.

She looked at him with her sharp little eyes, and seeing nothing disreputable about him, led the way upstairs, crackling loudly the whole time. This so astonished Mr. Gorby that he cast about in his own mind for an explanation of the phenomenon.

'Wants oiling about the jints,' was his conclusion, 'but I never heard anything like it, and she looks as if she'd snap in two, she's that brittle.'

Mrs. Sampson took Gorby into Brian's sitting-room, and having closed the door, sat down and prepared to hear what he had to say for himself.

'I 'ope it ain't bills,' she said, 'Mr. Fitzgerald 'avin' money in the bank, and everythin' respectable like a gentleman as 'e is, tho', to be sure, your bill might come down on him unbeknown, 'e not 'avin' kept it in mind, which it ain't everybody as 'ave sich a good memory as my aunt on my mother's side, she 'avin' been famous for 'er dates like a 'istory, not to speak of 'er multiplication tables, and the numbers of people's 'ouses.'

'It's not bills,' answered Mr. Gorby, who, having vainly attempted to stem the shrill torrent of words, had given in, and waited mildly until she had finished; 'I only want to know a few things about Mr. Fitzgerald's habits.'

'And what for?' asked Mrs. Sampson, indignantly. 'Are you a noospaper a-putin' in articles about people who don't want to see 'emselves in print, which I knows your 'abits, my late 'usband 'avin' bin a printer on a paper which bust up, not 'avin' the money to pay wages, thro' which, there was doo to him the sum of one pound seven and sixpence halfpenny, which I, bein' 'is widder, ought to 'ave, not that I expects to see it on this side of the grave — oh, dear, no!' and she gave a shrill, elfish laugh. Mr. Gorby, seeing that unless he took the bull by the horns, he would never be able to get what he wanted, grew desperate, and plunged in *medias res.*

'I am an insurance agent,' he said, rapidly, so as to prevent any interruption, 'and Mr. Fitzgerald desires to insure his life in our company. I, therefore, want to find out if he is a good life to insure; does he live temperately? keep early hours? and, in fact, all about him?'

'I shall be 'appy to answer any enquiries

which may be of use to you, sir,' replied Mrs. Sampson; 'knowin' as I do, 'ow good a insurance is to a family, should the 'ead of it be taken off unexpected, leavin' a widder, which, as I know, Mr. Fitzgerald is agoin' to be married soon, an' I 'opes 'e'll be 'appy, tho' thro' it I loses a lodger as 'as allays paid regler, an' be'aved like a gentleman.'

'So he is a temperate man?' said Mr. Gorby, feeling his way cautiously.

'Not bein' a blue ribbing all the same,' answered Mrs. Sampson; 'and I never saw him the wuss for drink, 'e being allays able to use his latch-key, and take 'is boots off afore going to bed, which is no more than a woman ought to expect from a lodger, she 'avin' to do 'er own washin'.'

'And he keeps good hours?'

'Allays in afore the clock strikes twelve,' answered the landlady; 'tho', to be sure, I uses it as a figger of speech, none of the clocks in the 'ouse strikin' but one, which is bein' mended, 'avin' broke through overwindin'.'

'Is he always in before twelve?' asked Mr. Gorby, keenly disappointed at this answer. Mrs. Sampson eyed him waggishly, and a smile crept over her wrinkled little face.

'Young men, not bein' old men,' she replied, cautiously, 'and sinners not bein' saints, it's not nattral as latch-keys should be made for ornament instead of use, and Mr. Fitzgerald bein' one of the 'andsomest men in Melbourne, it ain't to be expected as 'e should let 'is latch-key git rusty, tho' 'avin' a good moral character, 'e uses it with moderation.'

'But I suppose you are seldom awake when he comes in really late,' said the detective.

'Not as a rule,' assented Mrs. Sampson; 'bein' a 'eavy sleeper, and much disposed for bed, but I 'ave 'eard 'im come in arter twelve, the last time bein' Thursday week.'

'Ah!' Mr. Gorby drew a long breath, for Thursday week was the night upon which the murder was committed.

'Bein' troubled with my 'ead,' said Mrs. Sampson, 'thro' 'avin' been out in the sun all day a-washin', I did not feel so partial to my bed that night as in general, so went down to the kitching with the intent of getting a linseed poultice to put at the back of my 'ead, it being calculated to remove pain, as was told to me, when a nuss, by a doctor in the horspital, 'e now bein' in business for hisself, at Geelong, with a large family, 'avin' married early. Just as I was leavin' the kitching I 'eard Mr. Fitzgerald a-comin' in, and, turnin' round, looked at the clock, that 'avin' been my custom when my late 'usband came in, in the early mornin', I bein' a-preparin' 'is meal.'

'And the time was?' asked Mr. Gorby, breathlessly.

'Five minutes to two o'clock,' replied Mrs. Sampson. Mr. Gorby thought for a moment.

'Cab was hailed at one o'clock — started for St. Kilda at about ten minutes past — reached Grammar School, say, at twenty-five minutes past — Fitzgerald talks five minutes to cabman, making it half-past — say, he waited ten minutes for other cab to turn up, makes it twenty minutes to two — it would take another twenty minutes to get to East Melbourne — and five minutes to walk up here — that makes it five minutes past two instead of before — confound it.' 'Was your clock in the kitchen right?' he asked, aloud.

'Well, I think so,' answered Mrs. Sampson. 'It does get a little slow sometimes, not 'avin' been cleaned for some time, which my nevy bein' a watchmaker I allays 'ands it over to 'im.'

'Of course it was slow on that night,' said Gorby, triumphantly.

'He must have come in at five minutes past two — which makes it right.'

'Makes what right?' asked the landlady, sharply. 'And 'ow do you know my clock was ten minutes wrong?'

'Oh, it was, was it?' asked Gorby, eagerly.

'I'm not denyin' of it,' replied Mrs. Sampson; 'clocks ain't allays to be relied on more than men an' women — but it won't be anythin' agin 'is insurance, will it, as in general 'e's in afore twelve?'

'Oh, all that will be quite safe,' answered the detective, delighted with the information he had obtained. 'Is this Mr. Fitzgerald's room?'

'Yes, it is,' replied the landlady; 'but 'e furnished it 'imself, bein' of a luxurus turn of mind, not but what 'is taste is good, tho' far be it from me to deny I 'elped 'im to select; but 'avin' another room of the same to let, any friends as you might 'ave in search of a 'ome 'ud be well looked arter, my references bein' very 'igh, an' my cookin' tasty — an' if — '

Here a ring at the front door bell called Mrs. Sampson away, so with a hurried word to Gorby she crackled downstairs. Left to himself, Mr. Gorby arose and looked round the room. It was excellently furnished, and the pictures were good. At one end of the room, by the window, there was a writing-table covered with papers.

'It's no good looking for the papers he took out of Whyte's pocket, I suppose,' said the detective to himself, as he turned over some letters, 'as I don't know what they are, and I couldn't tell them if I saw them; but I'd like to find that missing glove and the bottle that held the chloroform — unless he's done away with them. There doesn't seem any sign of them here, so I'll have a look in his bedroom.'

There was no time to lose, as Mrs. Sampson might return at any moment, so Mr. Gorby walked quickly into the bedroom, which opened off the sitting-room. The first thing that caught the detective's eye was a large photograph, in a plush frame, of Madge Frettlby. It stood on the dressing-table, and was similar to that one which he had already seen in Whyte's album. He took it up with a laugh.

'You're a pretty girl,' he said, apostrophising the picture, 'but you give your photograph to two young men, both in love with you, and both hot-tempered. The result is that one is dead, and the other won't survive him long. That's what you've done.'

He put it down again, and looking round the room, caught sight of a light covert coat hanging behind the door and also a soft hat.

'Ah,' said the detective, going up to the door, 'here is the very coat you wore when you killed that poor fellow. Wonder what you have in the pockets,' and he plunged his hand into them in turn. There were an old theatre programme and a pair of brown gloves in one, but in the second pocket Mr. Gorby made a discovery — none other than that of the missing glove. There it was — a soiled white glove for the right hand, with black bands down the back; and the detective smiled in a gratified manner as he put it carefully in his pocket.

'My morning has not been wasted,' he said to himself. 'I've found out that he came in at a time which corresponds to all his movements after one o'clock on Thursday night, and this is the missing glove, which clearly belonged to Whyte. If I could only get hold of the chloroform bottle I'd be satisfied.'

But the chloroform bottle was not to be found, though he searched most carefully for it. At last, hearing Mrs. Sampson coming upstairs again, he gave up the search, and came back to the sitting-room.

'Threw it away, I suspect,' he said, as he sat down in his old place; 'but it doesn't matter. I think I can form a chain of evidence, from what I have discovered, which will be sufficient to convict him. Besides, I expect when he is arrested he will confess everything; he seems to feel remorse for what he has done.'

The door opened, and Mrs. Sampson entered the room in a state of indignation.

'One of them Chinese 'awkers,' she explained, ''e's bin a-tryin' to git the better of me over carrots — as if I didn't know what carrots was — and 'im a-talkin' about a shillin' in his gibberish, as if 'e 'adn't been brought up in a place where they don't know what a shillin' is. But I never could abide furreigners ever since a Frenchman, as taught me 'is language, made orf with my mother's silver tea-pot, unbeknown to 'er, it bein' set out on the sideboard for company.'

Mr. Gorby interrupted these domestic reminiscences of Mrs. Sampson's by stating that, now she had given him all necessary information, he would take his departure. 'An' I 'opes,' said Mrs. Sampson, as she opened the door for him, 'as I'll 'ave the pleasure of seein' you again should any business on be'alf of Mr. Fitzgerald require it.'

'Oh, I'll see you again,' said Mr. Gorby, with heavy jocularity, 'and in a way you won't like, as you'll be called as a witness,' he added, mentally. 'Did I understand you to say, Mrs. Sampson,' he went on, 'that Mr. Fitzgerald would be at home this afternoon?'

'Oh, yes, sir, 'e will,' answered Mrs. Sampson, 'a-drinkin' tea with his young lady, who is Miss Frettlby, and 'as got no end of money, not but what I mightn't 'ave 'ad the same 'ad I been born in a 'igher spear.'

'You need not tell Mr. Fitzgerald I have been here,' said Gorby, closing the gate; 'I'll probably call and see him myself this afternoon.'

'What a stout person 'e are,' said Mrs. Sampson to herself, as the detective walked away, 'just like my late father, who was allays fleshy, bein' a great eater, and fond of 'is glass, but I took arter my mother's family, they bein' thin-like, and proud of keeping 'emselves so, as the vinegar they drank could testify, not that I indulge in it myself.'

She shut the door, and went upstairs to take away the breakfast things, while Gorby was being driven along at a good pace to the police office, to obtain a warrant for Brian's arrest, on a charge of wilful murder.

10

In the Queen's Name.

It was a broiling hot day — one of those cloudless days, with the blazing sun beating down on the arid streets, and casting deep, black shadows — a real Australian December day dropped by mistake of the clerk of the weather into the middle of August. The previous week having been really chilly, it was all the more welcome. It was Saturday morning, and fashionable Melbourne was 'doing the Block.' Collins Street is to the Southern city what Bond Street and the Row are to London, and the Boulevards to Paris.

It is on the Block that people show off their new dresses, bow to their friends, cut their enemies, and chatter small talk. The same thing no doubt occurred in the Appian Way, the fashionable street of Imperial Rome, when Catullus talked gay nonsense to Lesbia, and Horace received the congratulations of his friends over his new volume of society verses. History repeats itself, and every city is bound by all the laws of civilisation to have one special street, wherein the votaries of fashion can congregate. Collins Street is not, of course, such a grand thoroughfare as those above mentioned, but the people who stroll up and down the broad pavement are quite as charmingly dressed, and as pleasant as any of the peripatetics of those famous cities. As the sun brings out bright flowers, so the seductive influence of the hot weather had brought out all the ladies in gay dresses of innumerable colours, which made the long street look like a restless rainbow.

Carriages were bowling smoothly along, their occupants smiling and bowing as they recognised their friends on the side walk. Lawyers, their legal quibbles finished for the week, were strolling leisurely with their black bags in their hands; portly merchants, forgetting Flinder's Lane and incoming ships, walked beside their pretty daughters; and the representatives of swelldom were stalking along in their customary apparel of curly brimmed hats, high collars, and immaculate suits. Altogether, it was a pleasant and animated scene, which would have delighted the heart of anyone who was not dyspeptic, or in love — dyspeptic people and lovers (disappointed ones, of course) being wont to survey the world in a cynical vein.

Madge Frettlby was engaged in that occupation so dear to every female heart

— shopping. She was in Moubray, Rowan, and Hicks', turning over ribbons and laces, while the faithful Brian waited for her outside, and amused himself by looking at the human stream which flowed along the pavement.

He disliked shopping quite as much as the majority of his sex, and though as a lover he felt a certain amount of self-abnegation to be becoming in him, it was difficult to drive away the thoughts of his pleasant club, where he could be reading and smoking, with, perchance, something cooling in a glass beside him.

However, after she had purchased a dozen or more articles she did not want, Madge remembered that Brian was waiting for her, and hurried to the door.

'I haven't been many minutes, have I, dear?' she said, touching him lightly on the arm.

'Oh, dear no,' answered Brian, looking at his watch, 'only thirty — a mere nothing, considering a new dress was being discussed.'

'I thought I had been longer,' said Madge, her brow clearing; 'but still I am sure you feel a martyr.'

'Not at all,' replied Fitzgerald, handing her into the carriage; 'I enjoyed myself very much.'

'Nonsense,' she laughed, opening her sunshade, while Brian took his seat beside her; 'that's one of those social stories — which every one considers themselves bound to tell from a sense of duty. I'm afraid I did keep you waiting — though, after all,' she went on, with a true feminine idea as to the flight of time, 'I was only a few minutes.'

'And the rest,' said Brian, quizzically looking at her pretty face, so charmingly flushed under her great white hat.

Madge disdained to notice this interruption.

'James,' she cried to the coachman, 'drive to the Melbourne Club. Papa will be there, you know,' she said to Brian, 'and we'll take him off to have tea with us.'

'But it's only one o'clock,' said Brian, as the Town Hall clock came in sight. 'Mrs. Sampson won't be ready.'

'Oh, anything will do,' replied Madge, 'a cup of tea and some thin bread and butter isn't hard to prepare. I don't feel like lunch, and papa eats so little in the middle of the day, and you — '

'Eat a great deal at all times,' finished Brian with a laugh.

Madge went on chattering in her usual lively manner, and Brian listened to her with delight. Her pleasant talk drove away the evil spirit which had been with him for the last three weeks. Suddenly Madge made an observation as they were passing the Burke and Wills' monument, which startled him.

'Isn't that the place where Mr Whyte got into the cab?' she asked, looking at the corner near the Scotch Church, where a vagrant of musical tendencies was playing 'Just before the Battle, Mother,' on a battered old concertina.

'So the papers say,' answered Brian, listlessly, without turning his head.

'I wonder who the gentleman in the light coat could have been,' said Madge, as she settled herself again.

'No one seems to know,' he replied evasively.

'Ah, but they have a clue,' she said. 'Do you know, Brian,' she went on, 'that he was dressed just like you in a light overcoat and soft hat?'

'How remarkable,' said Fitzgerald, speaking in a slightly sarcastic tone, and as calmly as he was able. 'He was dressed in the same manner as nine out of every ten young fellows in Melbourne.'

Madge looked at him in surprise at the tone in which he spoke, so different from his usual nonchalant way of speaking. She was about to answer when the carriage stopped at the door of the Melbourne Club. Brian, anxious to escape any more remarks about the murder, sprang quickly out, and ran up the steps into the building. He found Mr. Frettlby smoking complacently, and reading the *Age*. As Fitzgerald entered he looked up, and putting down the paper, held out his hand, which the other took.

'Ah! Fitzgerald,' he said, 'have you left the attractions of Collins Street for the still greater ones of Clubland?'

'Not I,' answered Brian. 'I've come to carry you off to afternoon tea with Madge and myself.'

'I don't mind,' answered Mr. Frettlby, rising; 'but, isn't afternoon tea at half-past one rather an anomaly?'

'What's in a name?' said Fitzgerald, absently, as they left the room. 'What have you been doing all morning?'

'I've been in here for the last half-hour reading,' answered the other, carelessly.

'Wool market, I suppose?'

'No, the hansom cab murder.'

'Oh, d — that thing!' said Brian, hastily; then, seeing his companion looking at him in surprise, he apologised. 'But, indeed,' he went on, 'I'm nearly worried to death by people asking about Whyte, as if I knew all about him, whereas I know nothing.'

'Just as well you don't,' answered Mr. Frettlby, as they descended the steps together; 'he was not a very desirable companion.'

It was on the tip of Brian's tongue to say, 'And yet you wanted him to marry your daughter,' but he wisely refrained, and they reached the carriage in silence.

'Now then, papa,' said Madge, when they were all settled in the carriage, and it was rolling along smoothly in the direction of East Melbourne, 'what have you been doing?'

'Enjoying myself,' answered her father, 'until you and Brian came, and dragged me out into this blazing sunshine.'

'Well, Brian has been so good of late,' said Madge, 'that I had to reward him, so I knew that nothing would please him better than to play host.'

'Certainly,' said Brian, rousing himself out of a fit of abstraction, 'especially when one has such charming visitors.'

Madge laughed at this, and made a little grimace.

'If your tea is only equal to your compliments,' she said lightly, 'I'm sure papa will forgive us for dragging him away from his Club.'

'Papa will forgive anything,' murmured Mr. Frettlby, tilting his hat over his eyes, 'so long as he gets somewhere out of the sun. I can't say I care about playing the parts of Shadrach, Meshach, and Abednego in the fiery furnace of a Melbourne hot day.' 'There now, papa is quite a host in himself,' said Madge mischievously, as, the carriage drew up at Mrs. Sampson's door.

'No, you are wrong,' said Brian, as he alighted and helped her out; 'I am the host in myself this time.'

'If there is one thing I hate above another,' observed Miss Frettlby, calmly, 'it's a pun, and especially a bad one.'

Mrs. Sampson was very much astonished at the early arrival of her lodger's guests, and did not hesitate to express her astonishment.

'Bein' taken by surprise,' she said, with an apologetic cackle, 'it ain't to be suppose as miraculs can be performed with regard to cookin', the fire havin' gone out, not bein' kept alight on account of the 'eat of the day, which was that 'ot as never was, tho', to be sure, bein' a child in the early days, I remember it were that 'ot as my sister's aunt was in the 'abit of roastin' her jints in the sun.'

After telling this last romance, and leaving her visitors in doubt whether the joints referred to belonged to an animal or to her sister's aunt or to herself, Mrs. Sampson crackled away downstairs to get things ready.

'What a curious thing that landlady of yours is, Brian,' said Madge, from the depths of a huge arm-chair. 'I believe she's a grasshopper from the Fitzroy Gardens.'

'Oh, no, she's a woman,' said Mr. Frettlby, cynically. 'You can tell that by the length of her tongue.'

'A popular error, papa,' retorted Madge, sharply. 'I know plenty of men who talk far more than any woman.'

'I hope I'll never meet them, then,' said Mr. Frettlby, 'for if I did I should be inclined to agree with De Quincey on murder as a fine art.'

Brian winced at this, and looked apprehensively at Madge, and saw with relief that she was not paying attention to her father, but was listening intently.

'There she is,' as a faint rustle at the door announced the arrival of Mrs. Sampson and the tea-tray. 'I wonder, Brian, you don't think the house is on fire with that queer noise always going on — she wants oil!'

'Yes, St. Jacob's oil,' laughed Brian, as Mrs. Sampson entered, and placed her burden on the table.

'Not 'avin' any cake,' said that lady, 'thro' not being forewarned as to the time of arrival — tho' it's not ofting I'm taken by surprise

— except as to a 'eadache, which, of course, is accidental to every pusson — I ain't got nothin' but bread and butter, the baker and grocer both bein' all that could be desired, except in the way of worryin' for their money, which they thinks as 'ow I keeps the bank in the 'ouse, like Allading's cave, as I've 'eard tell in the Arabian Nights, me 'avin' gained it as a prize for English in my early girl'ood, bein' then considered a scholard an' industrus.'

Mrs. Sampson's shrill apologies for the absence of cake having been received, she hopped out of the room, and Madge made the tea. The service was a quaint Chinese one, which Brian had picked up in his wanderings. He used it only on special occasions. As he watched Madge he could not help thinking how pretty she looked, with her hands moving deftly among the cups and saucers, so bizarre-looking with their sprawling dragons of yellow and green. He half smiled to himself as he thought, 'If they knew all, I wonder if they would sit with me so unconcernedly.'

Mr. Frettlby, too, as he looked at his daughter, thought of his dead wife and sighed. 'Well,' said Madge, as she handed them their tea, and helped herself to some thin bread and butter, 'you two gentlemen are most delightful company — papa is sighing like a furnace, and Brian is staring at me with his eyes like blue china saucers. You ought both to be turned forth to funerals like melancholy.'

'Why like melancholy?' queried Brian, lazily.

'I'm afraid, Mr. Fitzgerald,' said the young lady with a smile in her pretty black eyes, 'that you are not a student of 'A Midsummer Night's Dream.' '

'Very likely not,' answered Brian; 'midsummer out here is so hot that one gets no sleep, and, consequently no dreams. Depend upon it, if the four lovers whom Puck treated so badly had lived in Australia they wouldn't have been able to sleep for the mosquitoes.'

'What nonsense you two young people do talk,' said Mr. Frettlby, with an amused smile, as he stirred his tea.

'*Dulce est desipere in loco*,' observed Brian, gravely, 'a man who can't carry out that observation is sure not to be up to much.'

'I don't like Latin,' said Miss Frettlby, shaking her pretty head. 'I agree with Heine's remark, that if the Romans had been forced to learn it they would not have found time to conquer the world.'

'Which was a much more agreeable task,' said Brian.

'And more profitable,' finished Mr. Frettlby.

They chattered in this desultory fashion for a considerable time, till at last Madge rose and said they must go.

Brian proposed to dine with them at St. Kilda, and then they would all go to Brock's Fireworks. Madge consented to this, and she was just pulling on her gloves when suddenly they heard a ring at the front door, and presently Mrs. Sampson talking in an excited manner at the pitch of her voice.

'You shan't come in, I tell you,' they heard her say shrilly, 'so it's no good trying, which I've allays 'eard as an Englishman's 'ouse is 'is castle, an' you're a-breakin' the law, as well as a-spilin' the carpets, which 'as bin newly put down.'

Some one made a reply; then the door of Brian's room was thrown open, and Gorby walked in, followed by another man. Fitzgerald turned as white as a sheet, for he felt instinctively that they had come for him. However, pulling himself together, he demanded, in a haughty tone, the reason of the intrusion.

Mr. Gorby walked straight over to where Brian was standing, and placed his hand on the young man's shoulder.

'Brian Fitzgerald,' he said, in a clear voice,

'I arrest you in the Queen's name.'

'For what?' asked Brian, steadily.

'The murder of Oliver Whyte.'

At this Madge gave a cry.

'It is not true!' she said, wildly. 'My God, it's not true.'

Brian did not answer, but, ghastly pale, held out his hands. Gorby slipped the handcuffs on to his wrists with a feeling of compunction, despite his joy in running his man down. This done, Fitzgerald turned round to where Madge was standing, pale and still, as though turned into stone.

'Madge,' he said, in a clear, low voice, 'I am going to prison — perhaps to death; but I swear to you, by all that I hold most sacred, that I am innocent of this murder.'

'My darling!' She made a step forward, but her father stepped before her.

'Keep back,' he said, in a hard voice; 'there is nothing between you and that man now.'

She turned round with an ashen face, but with a proud look in her clear eyes.

'You are wrong,' she answered, with a touch of scorn in her voice. 'I love him more now than ever.' Then, before her father could stop her, she placed her arms round her lover's neck, and kissed him wildly.

'My darling,' she said, with the tears streaming down her white cheeks, 'whatever the world may say, you are always dearest of all to me.'

Brian kissed her passionately, and moved away. Madge fell down at her father's feet in a dead faint.

11

Counsel for the Prisoner.

Brian Fitzgerald was arrested at a few minutes past three o'clock, and by five all Melbourne was ringing with the news that the perpetrator of the now famous hansom cab murder had been caught. The evening papers were full of the affair, and the *Herald* went through several editions, the demand being far in the excess of the supply. Such a crime had not been committed in Melbourne since the Greer shooting case in the Opera House, and the mystery by which it was surrounded, made it even more sensational. The committal of the crime in such an extraordinary place as a hansom cab had been startling enough, but the discovery that the assassin was one of the most fashionable young men in Melbourne was still more so. Brian Fitzgerald being well known in society as a wealthy squatter, and the future husband of one of the richest and prettiest girls in Victoria, it was no wonder that his arrest caused some sensation. The *Herald,* which was fortunate enough to obtain the earliest information about the arrest, made the best use of it, and published a flaming article in its most sensational type, somewhat after this fashion: —

HANSOM CAB TRAGEDY. ARREST OF THE SUPPOSED MURDERER. STARTLING REVELATIONS IN HIGH LIFE.

It is needless to say that some of the reporters had painted the lily pretty freely, but the public were ready to believe everything that came out in the papers.

Mr. Frettlby, the day after Brian's arrest, had a long conversation with his daughter, and wanted her to go up to Yabba Yallook Station until the public excitement had somewhat subsided. But this Madge flatly refused to do.

'I'm not going to desert him when he most needs me,' she said, resolutely; 'everybody has turned against him, even before they have heard the facts of the case. He says he is not guilty, and I believe him.'

'Then let him prove his innocence,' said her father, who was pacing slowly up and down the room; 'if he did not get into the cab with Whyte he must have been somewhere else; so he ought to set up the defence of an alibi.'

'He can easily do that,' said Madge, with a ray of hope lighting up her sad face, 'he was here till eleven o'clock on Thursday night.'

'Very probably,' returned her father, dryly; 'but where was he at one o'clock on Friday morning?'

'Besides, Mr. Whyte left the house long before Brian did,' she went on rapidly. 'You must remember — it was when you quarrelled with Mr. Whyte.'

'My dear Madge,' said Frettlby, stopping in front of her with a displeased look, 'you are incorrect — Whyte and myself did not quarrel. He asked me if it were true that Fitzgerald was engaged to you, and I answered 'Yes.' That was all, and then he left the house.'

'Yes, and Brian didn't go until two hours after,' said Madge, triumphantly. 'He never saw Mr. Whyte the whole night.'

'So he says,' replied Mr. Frettlby, significantly.

'I believe Brian before any one else in the world,' said his daughter, hotly, with flushed cheeks and flashing eyes.

'Ah! but will a jury?' queried her father.

'You have turned against him, too,' answered Madge, her eyes filling with tears.

'You believe him guilty.'

'I am not prepared either to deny or confirm his guilt,' said Mr. Frettlby, coldly. 'I have done what I could to help him — I have engaged Calton to defend him, and, if eloquence and skill can save him, you may set your mind at rest.'

'My dear father,' said Madge, throwing her arms round his neck, 'I knew you would not desert him altogether, for my sake.'

'My darling,' replied her father, in a faltering voice, as he kissed her, 'there is nothing in the world I would not do for your sake.'

Meanwhile Brian was sitting in his cell in the Melbourne Jail, thinking sadly enough about his position. He saw no hope of escape except one, and that he did not intend to take advantage of.

'It would kill her; it would kill her,' he said, feverishly, as he paced to and fro over the echoing stones. 'Better that the last of the Fitzgeralds should perish like a common thief than that she should know the bitter truth. If I engage a lawyer to defend me,' he went on, 'the first question he will ask me will be where was I on that night, and if I tell him all will be discovered, and then — no — no — I cannot do it; it would kill her, my darling,' and throwing himself down on the bed, he covered his face with his hands.

He was roused by the opening of the door of his cell, and on looking up saw that it was Calton who entered. He was a great friend of Fitzgerald's, and Brian was deeply touched by his kindness in coming to see him.

Duncan Calton had a kindly heart, and was anxious to help Brian, but there was also a touch of self interest in the matter. He had received a note from Mr. Frettlby, asking him to defend Fitzgerald, which he agreed to do with avidity, as he foresaw in this case an opportunity for his name becoming known throughout the Australian colonies. It is true that he was already a celebrated lawyer, but his reputation was purely a local one, and as he foresaw that Fitzgerald's trial for murder would cause a great sensation throughout Australia and New Zealand, he determined to take advantage of it as another step in the ladder which led to fame, wealth, and position. So this tall, keen-eyed man, with the clean shaven face and expressive mouth, advanced into the cell, and took Brian by the hand.

'It is very kind of you to come and see me,' said Fitzgerald; 'it is at a time like this that one appreciates friendship.'

'Yes, of course,' answered the lawyer, fixing his keen eyes on the other's haggard face, as if he would read his innermost thoughts. 'I came partly on my own account, and partly because Frettlby asked me to see you as to your defence.'

'Mr. Frettlby?' said Brian, in a mechanical way. 'He is very kind; I thought he believed me guilty.'

'No man is considered guilty until he has been proved so,' answered Calton, evasively.

Brian noticed how guarded the answer was, for he heaved an impatient sigh.

'And Miss Frettlby?' he asked, in a hesitating manner. This time he got a decided answer.

'She declines to believe you guilty, and will not hear a word said against you.'

'God bless her,' said Brian, fervently; 'she is a true woman. I suppose I am pretty well canvassed?' he added, bitterly.

'Nothing else talked about,' answered Calton, calmly. 'Your arrest has for the present suspended all interest in theatres, cricket matches, and balls, and you are at the present moment being discussed threadbare in Clubs and drawing-rooms.'

Fitzgerald writhed. He was a singularly proud man, and there was something inexpressibly galling in this unpleasant publicity.

'But this is all idle chatter,' said Calton, taking a seat.

'We must get to business. Of course, you will accept me as your counsel.'

'It's no good my doing so,' replied Brian, gloomily. 'The rope is already round my neck.'

'Nonsense,' replied the lawyer, cheerfully, 'the rope is round no man's neck until he is on the scaffold. Now, you need not say a word,' he went on, holding up his hand as Brian was about to speak; 'I intend to defend you, whether you like it or not. I do not know all the facts, except what the papers have stated, and they exaggerate so much that one can place no reliance on them. At all events, I believe from my heart that you are innocent, and you must walk out of the prisoner's dock a free man, if only for the sake of that noble girl who loves you.'

Brian did not answer, but put out his hand, which the other grasped warmly.

'I will not deny,' went on Calton, 'that there is a little bit of professional curiosity about me. This case is such an extraordinary one, that I feel as if I were unable to let slip an opportunity of doing something with it. I don't care for your humdrum murders with the poker, and all that sort of thing, but this is something clever, and therefore interesting. When you are safe we will look together for the real criminal, and the pleasure of the search will be proportionate to the excitement when we find him out.'

'I agree with everything you say,' said Fitzgerald, calmly, 'but I have no defence to make.'

'No defence? You are not going to confess you killed him?'

'No,' with an angry flush, 'but there are certain circumstances which prevent me from defending myself.'

'What nonsense,' retorted Calton, sharply, 'as if any circumstances should prevent a man from saving his own life. But never mind, I like these objections; they make the nut harder to crack — but the kernel must be worth getting at. Now, I want you to answer certain questions.'

'I won't promise.'

'Well, we shall see,' said the lawyer, cheerfully, taking out his note-book, and resting it on his knee. 'First, where were you on the Thursday night preceding the murder?'

'I can't tell you.'

'Oh, yes, you can, my friend. You left St. Kilda, and came up to town by the eleven o'clock train.'

'Eleven-twenty,' corrected Brian.

Calton smiled in a gratified manner as he noted this down. 'A little diplomacy is all that's required,' he said mentally.

'And where did you go then?' he added, aloud.

'I met Rolleston in the train, and we took a cab from the Flinders Street station up to the Club.'

'What Club?'

'The Melbourne Club.'

'Yes?' interrogatively.

'Rolleston went home, and I went into the Club and played cards for a time.'

'When did you leave the Club?'

'A few minutes to one o'clock in the morning.'

'And then, I suppose, you went home?'

'No; I did not.'

'Then where did you go?'

'Down the street.'

'Rather vague. I presume you mean Collins Street?'

'Yes.'

'You were going to meet some one, I suppose?'

'I never said so.'

'Probably not; but young men don't wander about the streets at night without some object.'

'I was restless and wanted a walk.'

'Indeed! How curious you should prefer going into the heart of the dusty town for a walk to strolling through the Fitzroy Gardens, which were on your way home! It won't do; you had an appointment to meet someone.'

'Well — er — yes.'

'I thought as much. Man or woman?'

'I cannot tell you.'

'Then I must find out for myself.'

'You can't.'

'Indeed! Why not?'

'You don't know where to look for her.'

'Her,' cried Calton, delighted at the success of his craftily-put question. 'I knew it was a woman.'

Brian did not answer, but sat biting his lips with vexation.

'Now, who is this woman?'

No answer.

'Come now, Fitzgerald, I know that young men will be young men, and, of course, you don't like these things talked about; but in this case your character must be sacrificed to save your neck. What is her name?'

'I can't tell you.'

'Oh! you know it, then?'

'Well, yes.'

'And you won't tell me?'

'No!'

Calton, however, had found out two things that pleased him; first, that Fitzgerald had an appointment, and, second that it had been with a woman. He pursued another line.

'When did you last see Whyte?'

Brian answered with great reluctance, 'I saw him drunk by the Scotch Church.'

'What! you were the man who hailed the hansom?'

'Yes,' assented the other, hesitating slightly, 'I was!'

The thought flashed through Calton's brain as to whether the young man before him was guilty or not, and he was obliged to confess that things looked very black against him.

'Then what the newspapers said was correct?'

'Partly.'

'Ah!' Calton drew a long breath — here was a ray of hope.

'You did not know it was Whyte when you found him lying drunk near the Scotch Church?'

'No, I did not. Had I known it was he I would not have picked him up.'

'Of course, you recognised him afterwards?'

'Yes I did. And, as the paper stated, I dropped him and walked away.'

'Why did you leave him so abruptly?'

Brian looked at his questioner in some surprise.

'Because I detested him,' he said, shortly.

'Why did you detest him?'

No answer. 'Was it because he admired Miss Frettlby, and from all appearances, was going to marry her?'

'Well, yes,' sullenly.

'And now,' said Calton, impressively, 'this is the whole point upon which the case turns. Why did you get into the cab with him?'

'I did not get into the cab.'

'The cabman declares that you did.'

'He is wrong. I never came back after I recognised Whyte.'

'Then who was the man who got into the cab with Whyte?'

'I don't know.'

'You have no idea?'

'Not the least.'

'You are certain?'

'Yes, perfectly certain.'

'He seems to have been dressed exactly like you.'

'Very probably. I could name at least a dozen of my acquaintances who wear light coats over their evening dress, and soft hats.'

'Do you know if Whyte had any enemies?'

'No, I don't; I know nothing about him, beyond that he came from England a short time ago with a letter of introduction to Mr. Frettlby, and had the impertinence to ask Madge to marry him.'

'Where did Whyte live?'

'Down in St. Kilda, at the end of Grey Street.'

'How do you know?'

'It was in the papers, and — and — ' hesitatingly, 'I called on him.'

'Why?'

'To see if he would cease his attentions to Madge, and to tell him that she was engaged to me.'

'And what did he say?'

'Laughed at me. Curse him.'

'You had high words, evidently?'

Brian laughed bitterly.

'Yes, we had.'

'Did anyone hear you?'

'The landlady did, I think. I saw her in the passage as I left the house.'

'The prosecution will bring her forward as a witness.'

'Very likely,' indifferently.

'Did you say anything likely to incriminate yourself?' Fitzgerald turned away his head.

'Yes,' he answered in a low voice, 'I spoke very wildly — indeed, I did not know at the time what I said.'

'Did you threaten him?'

'Yes, I did. I told him I would kill him if he persisted in his plan of marrying Madge.'

'Ah! if the landlady can swear that she

134

heard you say so, it will form a strong piece of evidence against you. So far as I can see, there is only one defence, and that is an easy one — you must prove an alibi.'

No answer.

'You say you did not come back and get into the cab?' said Calton, watching the face of the other closely.

'No, it was some one else dressed like me.'

'And you have no idea who it was?'

'No, I have not.'

'Then, after you left Whyte, and walked along Russell Street, where did you go?'

'I can't tell you.'

'Were you intoxicated?'

'No!' indignantly

'Then you remember?'

'Yes.'

'And where were you?'

'I can't tell you.'

'You refuse.'

'Yes, I do.'

'Take time to consider. You may have to pay a heavy price for your refusal.'

'If necessary, I will pay it.'

'And you won't tell me where you were?'

'No, I won't.'

Calton was beginning to feel annoyed.

'You're very foolish,' he said, 'sacrificing your life to some feeling of false modesty.

'You must prove an alibi.'

No answer.

'At what hour did you get home?'

'About two o'clock in the morning.'

'Did you walk home?'

'Yes — through the Fitzroy Gardens.'

'Did you see anyone on your way home?'

'I don't know. I wasn't paying attention.'

'Did anyone see you?'

'Not that I know of.'

'Then you refuse to tell me where you were between one and two o'clock on Friday morning?'

'Absolutely!'

Calton thought for a moment, to consider his next move.

'Did you know that Whyte carried valuable papers about with him?'

Fitzgerald hesitated, and turned pale.

'No! I did not know,' he said, reluctantly.

The lawyer made a master stroke.

'Then why did you take them from him?'

'What! Had he it with him?'

Calton saw his advantage, and seized it at once.

'Yes, he had it with him. Why did you take it?'

'I did not take it. I didn't even know he had it with him.'

'Indeed! Will you kindly tell me what 'it' is.'

Brian saw the trap into which he had fallen.

'No! I will not,' he answered steadily.

'Was it a jewel?'

'No!'

'Was it an important paper?'

'I don't know.'

'Ah! It was a paper. I can see it in your face. And was that paper of importance to you?'

'Why do you ask?'

Calton fixed his keen grey eyes steadily on Brian's face.

'Because,' he answered slowly, 'the man to whom that paper was of such value murdered Whyte.'

Brian started up, ghastly pale.

'My God!' he almost shrieked, stretching out his hands, 'it is true after all,' and he fell down on the stone pavement in a dead faint.

Calton, alarmed, summoned the gaoler, and between them they placed him on the bed, and dashed some cold water over his face. He recovered, and moaned feebly, while Calton, seeing that he was unfit to be spoken to, left the prison. When he got outside he stopped for a moment and looked back on the grim, grey walls.

'Brian Fitzgerald,' he said to himself 'you did not commit the murder yourself, but you know who did.'

12

She Was a True Woman.

Melbourne society was greatly agitated over the hansom cab murder. Before the assassin had been discovered it had been looked upon merely as a common murder, and one of which society need take no cognisance beyond the bare fact of its committal. But now that one of the most fashionable young men in Melbourne had been arrested as the assassin, it bade fair to assume gigantic proportions. Mrs. Grundy was shocked, and openly talked about having nourished in her bosom a viper which had unexpectedly turned and stung her.

Morn, noon, and night, in Toorak drawing-rooms and Melbourne Clubs, the case formed the principal subject of conversation. And Mrs. Grundy was horrified. Here was a young man, well born — 'the Fitzgeralds, my dear, an Irish family, with royal blood in their veins' — well-bred — 'most charming manners, I assure you, and so very good-looking' and engaged to one of the richest girls in Melbourne — 'pretty enough, madam, no doubt, but he wanted her money, sly dog;' and this young man, who had been petted by the ladies, voted a good fellow by the men, and was universally popular, both in drawing-room and club, had committed a vulgar murder — it was truly shocking. What was the world coming to, and what were gaols and lunatic asylums built for if men of young Fitzgerald's calibre were not put in them, and kept from killing people? And then, of course, everybody asked everybody else who Whyte was, and why he had never been heard of before. All people who had met Mr. Whyte were worried to death with questions about him, and underwent a species of social martyrdom as to who he was, what he was like, why he was killed, and all the rest of the insane questions which some people will ask. It was talked about everywhere — in fashionable drawing-rooms at five o'clock tea, over thin bread and butter and souchong; at clubs, over brandies and sodas and cigarettes; by working men over their mid-day pint, and by their wives in the congenial atmosphere of the back yard over the wash-tub. The papers were full of paragraphs about the famous murder, and the society papers gave an interview with the prisoner by their special reporters, which had been composed by those gentlemen out of the floating rumours which they heard around, and their own fertile imaginations.

As to the prisoner's guilt, everyone was certain of it. The cabman Royston had sworn that Fitzgerald had got into the cab with Whyte, and when he got out Whyte was dead. There could be no stronger proof than that, and the general opinion was that the prisoner would put in no defence, but would throw himself on the mercy of the court. Even the church caught the contagion, and ministers — Anglican, Roman Catholic, and Presbyterian, together with the lesser lights of minor denominations — took the hansom cab murder as a text whereon to preach sermons on the profligacy of the age, and to point out that the only ark which could save men from the rising flood of infidelity and immorality was their own particular church. 'Gad,' as Calton remarked, after hearing five or six ministers each claim their own church as the one special vessel of safety, 'there seems to be a whole fleet of arks!'

For Mr. Felix Rolleston, acquainted as he was with all concerned, the time was one of great and exceeding joy. He was ever to the fore in retailing to his friends, plus certain garnishments of his own, any fresh evidence that chanced to come to light. His endeavour was to render it the more piquant, if not dramatic. If you asked him for his definite opinion as to the innocence or guilt of the accused, Mr. Felix shook his head sagaciously, and gave you to understand that neither he, nor his dear friend Calton — he knew Calton to nod to — had yet been able to make up their minds about the matter. 'Fact is, don't you know,' observed Mr. Rolleston, wisely, 'there's more in this than meets the eye, and all that sort of thing — think 'tective fellers wrong myself — don't think Fitz killed Whyte; jolly well sure he didn't.'

This would be followed invariably by a query in chorus of 'who killed him then?'

'Aha,' Felix would retort, putting his head on one side, like a meditative sparrow; ''tective fellers can't find out; that's the difficulty. Good mind to go on the prowl myself, by Jove.'

'But do you know anything of the detective business?' some one would ask.

'Oh, dear yes,' with an airy wave of his hand; 'I've read Gaboreau, you know; awfully jolly life, 'tectives.'

Despite this evasion, Rolleston, in his heart of hearts, believed Fitzgerald guilty. But he was one of those persons, who having either tender hearts or obstinate natures — the latter is perhaps the more general — deem it incumbent upon them to come forward in championship of those in trouble. There are, doubtless, those who think that Nero was a pleasant young man, whose cruelties were but the resultant of an overflow of high spirits; and who regard Henry VIII in the light of a henpecked husband unfortunate in the possession of six wives. These people delight in expressing their sympathy with great scoundrels of the Ned Kelly order. They view them as the embodiment of heroism, unsympathetically and disgracefully treated by the narrow understanding of the law. If one half the world does kick a man when he is down, the other half invariably consoles the prostrate individual with halfpence.

And therefore, even while the weight of public opinion was dead against Fitzgerald he had his share of avowed sympathy. There was a comfort in this for Madge. Not that if the whole countryside had unanimously con-demned her lover she would have believed him guilty. The element of logic does not enter into the championship of woman. Her love for a man is sufficient to exalt him to the rank of a demi-god. She absolutely refuses to see the clay feet of her idol. When all others forsake she clings to him, when all others frown she smiles on him, and when he dies she reveres his memory as that of a saint and a martyr. Young men of the present day are prone to disparage their womenkind; but a poor thing is the man, who in time of trouble has no woman to stand by him with cheering words and loving comfort. And so Madge Frettlby, true woman that she was, had nailed her colours to the mast. She refused surrender to anyone, or before any argument. He was innocent, and his innocence would be proved, for she had an intuitive feeling that he would be saved at the eleventh hour. How, she knew not; but she was certain that it would be so. She would have gone to see Brian in prison, but that her father absolutely forbade her doing so. Therefore she was dependent upon Calton for all the news respecting him, and any message which she wished conveyed.

Brian's persistent refusal to set up the defence of an alibi, annoyed Calton, the more so as he could conceive no reason sufficiently worthy of the risk to which it subjected his client.

'If it's for the sake of a woman,' he said to Brian, 'I don't care who she is, it's absurdly Quixotic. Self-preservation is the first law of nature, and if my neck was in danger I'd spare neither man, woman, nor child to save it.'

'I dare say,' answered Brian; 'but if you had

my reasons you might think differently.' Yet in his own mind the lawyer had a suspicion which he thought might perhaps account for Brian's obstinate concealment of his movements on the fatal night. He had admitted an appointment with a woman. He was a handsome young fellow, and probably his morals were no better than those of his fellows. There was perhaps some intrigue with a married woman. He had perchance been with her on that night, and it was to shield her that he refused to speak.

'Even so,' argued Calton, 'let him lose his character rather than his life; indeed the woman herself should speak. It would be hard upon her I admit; yet when a man's life is in danger, surely nothing should stop her.'

Full of these perplexing thoughts, Calton went down to St. Kilda to have a talk with Madge. He intended to ask her to assist him towards obtaining the information he needed. He had a great respect for Madge, and thought her a really clever woman. It was just possible, he argued, that Brian's great love might cause him to confess everything to her, at her urgent request. He found Madge awaiting his arrival with anxiety.

'Where have you been all this time?' she said as they sat down; 'I have been counting every moment since I saw you last. How is he?'

'Just the same,' answered Calton, taking off his gloves, 'still obstinately refusing to save his own life. Where's your father?' he asked, suddenly.

'Out of town,' she answered, impatiently. 'He will not be back for a week — but what do you mean that he won't save his own life?'

Calton leaned forward, and took her hand.

'Do you want to save his life?' he asked.

'Save his life,' she reiterated, starting up out of her chair with a cry. 'God knows, I would die to save him.'

'Pish,' murmured Calton to himself, as he looked at her glowing face and outstretched hands, 'these women are always in extremes. The fact is,' he said aloud, 'Fitzgerald is able to prove an alibi, and he refuses to do so.'

'But why?'

Calton shrugged his shoulders.

'That is best known to himself — some Quixotic idea of honour, I fancy. Now, he refuses to tell me where he was on that night; perhaps he won't refuse to tell you — so you must come up and see him with me, and perhaps he will recover his senses, and confess.'

'But my father,' she faltered.

'Did you not say he was out of town?' asked Calton.

'Yes,' hesitated Madge. 'But he told me not to go.'

'In that case,' said Calton, rising and taking up his hat and gloves, 'I won't ask you.' She laid her hand on his arm.

'Stop! will it do any good?'

Calton hesitated a moment, for he thought that if the reason of Brian's silence was, as he surmised, an intrigue with a married woman, he might not tell the girl he was engaged to about it — but, on the other hand, there might be some other reason, and Calton trusted to Madge to find it out. With these thoughts in his mind he turned round.

'Yes,' he answered, boldly, 'it may save his life.'

'Then I shall go,' she answered, recklessly. 'He is more to me than my father, and if I can save him, I will. Wait,' and she ran out of the room.

'An uncommonly plucky girl,' murmured the lawyer, as he looked out of the window. 'If Fitzgerald is not a fool he will certainly tell her all — that is, of course, if he is able to — queer things these women are — I quite agree with Balzac's saying that no wonder man couldn't understand woman, seeing that God who created her failed to do so.'

Madge came back dressed to go out, with a heavy veil over her face.

'Shall I order the carriage?' she asked, pulling on her gloves with trembling fingers.

'Hardly,' answered Calton, dryly, 'unless you want to see a paragraph in the society papers to the effect that Miss Madge Frettlby visited Mr. Fitzgerald in gaol — no — no — we'll get a cab. Come, my dear,' and taking her arm he led her away.

They reached the station, and caught a train just as it started, yet notwithstanding this Madge was in a fever of impatience.

'How slowly it goes,' she said, fretfully.

'Hush, my dear,' said Calton, laying his hand on her arm. 'You will betray yourself — we'll arrive soon — and save him.'

'Oh, God grant we may,' she said with a low cry, clasping her hands tightly together, while Calton could see the tears falling from under her thick veil.

'This is not the way to do so,' he said, almost roughly, 'you'll be in hysterics soon — control yourself for his sake.'

'For his sake,' she muttered, and with a powerful effort of will, calmed herself. They soon arrived in Melbourne, and, getting a hansom, drove up quickly to the gaol. After going through the usual formula, they entered the cell where Brian was, and, when the warder who accompanied them opened the door, they found the young man seated on his bed. He looked up, and, on seeing Madge, rose and held out his hands with a cry of delight. She ran forward, and threw herself on his breast with a stifled sob. For a short time no one spoke — Calton being at the other end of the cell, busy with some notes which he had taken from his pocket, and the warder having retired.

'My poor darling,' said Madge, stroking back the soft, fair hair from his flushed forehead, 'how ill you look.'

'Yes!' answered Fitzgerald, with a hard laugh. 'Prison does not improve a man — does it?'

'Don't speak in that tone, Brian,' she said; 'it is not like you — let us sit down and talk calmly over the matter.'

'I don't see what good that will do,' he answered, wearily, as they sat down hand-in-hand. 'I have talked about it to Calton till my head aches, and it is no good.'

'Of course not,' retorted the lawyer, sharply, as he also sat down. 'Nor will it be any good until you come to your senses, and tell us where you were on that night.'

'I tell you I cannot.'

'Brian, dear,' said Madge, softly, taking his hand, 'you must tell all — for my sake.'

Fitzgerald sighed — this was the hardest temptation he had yet been subjected to. He felt half inclined to yield, and chance the result — but one look at Madge's pure face steeled him against doing so. What could his confession bring but sorrow and regret to one whom he loved better than his life?

'Madge!' he answered, gravely, taking her hand again, 'you do not know what you ask.'

'Yes, I do!' she replied, quickly. 'I ask you to save yourself — to prove that you are not guilty of this terrible crime, and not to sacrifice your life for the sake of — of — ' Here she stopped, and looked helplessly at Calton, for she had no idea of the reason of Fitzgerald's refusal to speak.

'For the sake of a woman,' finished Calton, bluntly.

'A woman!' she faltered, still holding her lover's hand.

'Is — is — is that the reason?'

Brian averted his face.

'Yes!' he said, in a low, rough voice.

A sharp expression of anguish crossed her pale face, and, sinking her head on her hands, she wept bitterly. Brian looked at her in a dogged kind of way, and Calton stared grimly at them both.

'Look here,' he said, at length, to Brian, in

an angry voice; 'if you want my opinion of your conduct I think it's infamous — begging your pardon, Miss Frettlby, for the expression. Here is this noble girl, who loves you with her whole heart, and is ready to sacrifice everything for your sake, comes to implore you to save your life, and you coolly turn round and acknowledge another woman.'

Brian lifted his head haughtily, and his face flushed.

'You are wrong,' he said, turning round sharply; 'there is the woman for whose sake I keep silence;' and, rising up from the bed, he pointed to Madge, as she sobbed bitterly on it. She lifted up her haggard face with an air of surprise.

'For my sake!' she cried in a startled voice.

'Oh, he's mad,' said Calton, shrugging his shoulders; 'I shall put in a defence of insanity.'

'No, I am not mad,' cried Fitzgerald, wildly, as he caught Madge in his arms. 'My darling! My darling! It is for your sake that I keep silence, and I shall do so though my life pays the penalty. I could tell you where I was on that night and save myself: but if I did, you would learn a secret which would curse your life, and I dare not speak — I dare not.'

Madge looked up into his face with a pitiful smile as her tears fell fast.

'Dearest!' she said, softly. 'Do not think of me, but only of yourself; better that I should endure misery than that you should die. I do not know what the secret can be, but if the telling of it will save your life, do not hesitate. See,' she cried, falling on her knees, 'I am at your feet — I implore you by all the love you ever had for me, to save yourself, whatever the consequences may be to me.'

'Madge,' said Fitzgerald, as he raised her in his arms, 'at one time I might have done so, but now it is too late. There is another and stronger reason for my silence, which I have only found out since my arrest. I know that I am closing up the one way of escape from this charge of murder, of which I am innocent; but as there is a God in heaven, I swear that I will not speak.'

There was a silence in the cell, broken only by Madge's convulsive sobs, and even Calton, cynical man of the world as he was, felt his eyes grow wet. Brian led Madge over to him, and placed her in his arms.

'Take her away,' he said, in a broken voice, 'or I shall forget that I am a man;' and turning away he threw himself on his bed, and covered his face with his hands. Calton did not answer him, but summoned the warder, and tried to lead Madge away. But just as they reached the door she broke away from him, and, running back, flung herself on her lover's breast.

'My darling! My darling!' she sobbed, kissing him, 'you shall not die. I shall save you in spite of yourself;' and, as if afraid to trust herself longer, she ran out of the cell, followed by the barrister.

13

Madge Makes a Discovery.

Madge stepped into the cab, and Calton paused a moment to tell the cabman to drive to the railway station. Suddenly she stopped him.

'Tell him to drive to Brian's lodgings in Powlett Street,' she said, laying her hand on Calton's arm.

'What for?' asked the lawyer, in astonishment.

'And also to go past the Melbourne Club, as I want to stop there.'

'What the deuce does she mean?' muttered Calton, as he gave the necessary orders, and stepped into the cab.

'And now,' he asked, looking at his companion, who had let down her veil, while the cab rattled quickly down the street, 'what do you intend to do?'

She threw back her veil, and he was astonished to see the sudden change which had come over her. There were no tears now, and her eyes were hard and glittering, while her mouth was firmly closed. She looked like a woman who had determined to do a certain thing, and would carry out her intention at whatever cost.

'I intend to save Brian in spite of himself,' she said, very distinctly.

'But how?'

'Ah, you think that, being a woman, I can do nothing,' she said, bitterly. 'Well, you shall see.'

'I beg your pardon,' retorted Calton, with a grim smile, 'my opinion of your sex has always been an excellent one — every lawyer's is; stands to reason that it should be so, seeing that a woman is at the bottom of nine cases out of ten.'

'The old cry.'

'Nevertheless a true one,' answered Calton. 'Ever since the time of Father Adam it has been acknowledged that women influence the world either for good or evil more than men. But this is not to the point,' he went on, rather impatiently.

'What do you propose to do?'

'Simply this,' she answered. 'In the first place, I may tell you that I do not understand Brian's statement that he keeps silence for my sake, as there are no secrets in my life that can justify his saying so. The facts of the case are simply these: Brian, on the night in question, left our house at St. Kilda, at eleven

154

o'clock. He told me that he would call at the Club to see if there were any letters for him, and then go straight home.'

'But he might have said that merely as a blind.'

Madge shook her head.

'No, I don't think so. I did not ask him where he was going. He told me quite spontaneously. I know Brian's character, and he would not tell a deliberate lie, especially when there was no necessity for it. I am quite certain that he intended to do as he said, and go straight home. When he got to the Club, he found a letter there, which caused him to alter his mind.'

'From whom was the letter?'

'Can't you guess?' she said impatiently. 'From the person, man or woman, who wanted to see him and reveal this secret about me, whatever it is. He got the letter at his Club, and went down Collins Street to meet the writer. At the corner of the Scotch Church he found Mr. Whyte, and on recognising him, left in disgust, and walked down Russell Street to keep his appointment.'

'Then you don't think he came back.'

'I am certain he did not, for, as Brian told you, there are plenty of young men who wear the same kind of coat and hat as he does. Who the second man who got into the cab was I do not know, but I will swear that it was not Brian.'

'And you are going to look for that letter?'

'Yes, in Brian's lodgings.'

'He might have burnt it.'

'He might have done a thousand things, but he did not,' she answered. 'Brian is the most careless man in the world; he would put the letter into his pocket, or throw it into the waste-paper basket, and never think of it again.'

'In this case he did, however.'

'Yes, he thought of the conversation he had with the writer, but not of the letter itself. Depend upon it, we shall find it in his desk, or in one of the pockets of the clothes he wore that night.'

'Then there's another thing,' said Calton, thoughtfully. 'The letter might have been delivered to him between the Elizabeth Street Railway Station and the Club.'

'We can soon find out about that,' answered Madge; 'for Mr. Rolleston was with him at the time.'

'So he was,' answered Calton; 'and here is Rolleston coming down the street. We'll ask him now.'

The cab was just passing the Burke and Wills' monument, and Calton's quick eye had caught a glimpse of Rolleston walking down the left-hand side. What first attracted Calton's attention was the glittering appearance of Felix. His well-brushed top hat glittered, his varnished boots glittered, and his rings and scarf-pin glittered; in fact, so resplendent was his appearance that he looked like an animated diamond coming along in the blazing sunshine.

The cab drove up to the kerb, and Rolleston stopped short, as Calton sprang out directly in front of him. Madge lay back in the cab and pulled down her veil, not wishing to be recognised by Felix, as she knew that if he did it would soon be all over the town.

'Hallo! old chap,' said Rolleston, in considerable astonishment. 'Where did you spring from?'

'From the cab, of course,' answered Calton, with a laugh.

'A kind of *deus ex machina*,' replied Rolleston, attempting a bad pun.

'Exactly,' said Calton. 'Look here, Rolleston, do you remember the night of Whyte's murder — you met Fitzgerald at the Railway Station.'

'In the train,' corrected Felix.

'Well, well, no matter, you came up with him to the Club.'

'Yes, and left him there.'

'Did you notice if he received any message

while he was with you?'

'Any message?' repeated Felix. 'No, he did not; we were talking together the whole time, and he spoke to no one but me.'

'Was he in good spirits?'

'Excellent, made me laugh awfully — but why all this thusness?'

'Oh, nothing,' answered Calton, getting back into the cab. 'I wanted a little information from you; I'll explain next time I see you — Good-bye!'

'But I say,' began Felix, but the cab had already rattled away, so Mr. Rolleston turned angrily away.

'I never saw anything like these lawyers,' he said to himself.

'Calton's a perfect whirlwind, by Jove.'

Meanwhile Calton was talking to Madge.

'You were right,' he said, 'there must have been a message for him at the Club, for he got none from the time he left your place.'

'And what shall we do now?' asked Madge, who, having heard all the conversation, did not trouble to question the lawyer about it.

'Find out at the Club if any letter was waiting for him on that night,' said Calton, as the cab stopped at the door of the Melbourne Club. 'Here we are,' and with a hasty word to Madge, he ran up the steps.

He went to the office of the Club to find

out if any letters had been waiting for Fitzgerald, and found there a waiter with whom he was pretty well acquainted.

'Look here, Brown,' said the lawyer, 'do you remember on that Thursday night when the hansom cab murder took place if any letters were waiting here for Mr. Fitzgerald?'

'Well, really, sir,' hesitated Brown, 'it's so long ago that I almost forget.' Calton gave him a sovereign.

'Oh! it's not that, Mr. Calton,' said the waiter, pocketing the coin, nevertheless. 'But I really do forget.'

'Try and remember,' said Calton, shortly.

Brown made a tremendous effort of memory, and at last gave a satisfactory answer.

'No, sir, there were none!'

'Are you sure?' said Calton, feeling a thrill of disappointment.

'Quite sure, sir,' replied the other, confidently, 'I went to the letter rack several times that night, and I am sure there were none for Mr. Fitzgerald.'

'Ah! I thought as much,' said Calton, heaving a sigh.

'Stop!' said Brown, as though struck with a sudden idea. 'Though there was no letter came by post, sir, there was one brought to him on that night.'

'Ah!' said Calton, turning sharply. 'At what time?'

'Just before twelve o'clock, sir.'

'Who brought it?'

'A young woman, sir,' said Brown, in a tone of disgust. 'A bold thing, beggin' your pardon, sir; and no better than she should be. She bounced in at the door as bold as brass, and sings out, 'Is he in?' 'Get out,' I says, 'or I'll call the perlice.' 'Oh no, you won't,' says she. 'You'll give him that,' and she shoves a letter into my hands. 'Who's him?' I asks. 'I dunno,' she answers. 'It's written there, and I can't read; give it him at once.' And then she clears out before I could stop her.'

'And the letter was for Mr. Fitzgerald?'

'Yes, sir; and a precious dirty letter it was, too.'

'You gave it to him, of course?'

'I did, sir. He was playing cards, and he put it in his pocket, after having looked at the outside of it, and went on with his game.'

'Didn't he open it?'

'Not then, sir; but he did later on, about a quarter to one o'clock. I was in the room, and he opens it and reads it. Then he says to himself, 'What d — d impertinence,' and puts it into his pocket.'

'Was he disturbed?'

'Well, sir, he looked angry like, and put his

coat and hat on, and walked out about five minutes to one.'

'Ah! and he met Whyte at one,' muttered Calton. 'There's no doubt about it. The letter was an appointment, and he was going to keep it. What kind of a letter was it?' he asked.

'Very dirty, sir, in a square envelope; but the paper was good, and so was the writing.'

'That will do,' said Calton; 'I am much obliged to you,' and he hurried down to where Madge awaited him in the cab.

'You were right,' he said to her, when the cab was once more in motion. 'He got a letter on that night, and went to keep his appointment at the time he met Whyte.'

'I knew it,' cried Madge with delight. 'You see, we will find it in his lodgings.'

'I hope so,' answered Calton; 'but we must not be too sanguine; he may have destroyed it.'

'No, he has not,' she replied. 'I am convinced it is there.'

'Well,' answered Calton, looking at her, 'I don't contradict you, for your feminine instincts have done more to discover the truth than my reasonings; but that is often the case with women — they jump in the dark where a man would hesitate, and in nine cases out of ten land safely.'

'Alas for the tenth!' said Miss Frettlby. 'She has to be the one exception to prove the rule.'

She had in a great measure recovered her spirits, and seemed confident that she would save her lover. But Mr. Calton saw that her nerves were strung up to the highest pitch, and that it was only her strong will that kept her from breaking down altogether. 'By Jove,' he muttered, in an admiring tone, as he watched her. 'She's a plucky girl, and Fitzgerald is a lucky man to have the love of such a woman.'

They soon arrived at Brian's lodgings, and the door was opened by Mrs. Sampson, who looked very disconsolate indeed. The poor cricket had been blaming herself severely for the information she had given to the false insurance agent, and the floods of tears which she had wept had apparently had an effect on her physical condition, for she crackled less loudly than usual, though her voice was as shrill as ever. 'That sich a thing should 'ave 'appened to 'im,' she wailed, in her thin, high voice. 'An' me that proud of 'im, not 'avin' any family of my own, except one as died and went up to 'eaving arter 'is father, which I 'opes as they both are now angels, an' friendly, as 'is nature 'ad not developed in this valley of the shadder to determine 'is feelin's towards 'is father when 'e died, bein'

162

carried off by a chill, caused by the change from 'ot to cold, the weather bein' that contrary.'

They had arrived in Brian's sitting-room by this time, and Madge sank into a chair, while Calton, anxious to begin the search, hinted to Mrs. Sampson that she could go. 'I'm departin', sir,' piped the cricket, with a sad shake of her head, as she opened the door; 'knowin', as I do, as 'e's as innocent as an unborn babe, an' to think of me 'avin' told that 'orrid pusson who 'ad no regard for the truth all about 'im as is now in a cold cell, not as what the weather ain't warm, an' 'e won't want a fire as long as they allows 'im blankets.'

'What did you tell him?' asked Calton, sharply.

'Ah! you may well say that,' lamented Mrs. Sampson, rolling her dingy handkerchief into a ball, and dabbing at her red-rimmed eyes, which presented quite a bacchanalian appearance, due, be it said in justice, to grief, not to liquor. ''Avin' bin beguiled by that serping in light clothes as wanted to know if 'e allays come 'ome afore twelve, which I said 'e was in the 'abit of doin', tho', to be sure, 'e did sometimes use 'is latch-key.'

'The night of the murder, for instance.'

'Oh! don't say that, sir,' said Mrs.

Sampson, with a terrified crackle. 'Me bein' weak an' ailin', tho' comin' of a strong family, as allays lived to a good age, thro' bein' in the 'abit of wearin' flannels, which my mother's father thought better nor a-spilin' the inside with chemistry.'

'Clever man, that detective,' murmured Calton to himself. 'He got out of her by strategy what he never would have done by force. It's a strong piece of evidence against Fitzgerald, but it does not matter much if he can prove an alibi. You'll likely be called as a witness for the prosecution,' he said aloud.

'Me, sir!' squeaked Mrs. Sampson, trembling violently, and thereby producing a subdued rustle, as of wind in the trees. 'As I've never bin in the court, 'cept the time as father tooked me for a treat, to 'ear a murder, which there's no denyin' is as good as a play, 'e bein' 'ung, 'avin' 'it 'is wife over the 'ead with the poker when she weren't lookin', and a-berryin' 'er corpse in a back garding, without even a stone to mark the place, let alone a line from the Psalms and a remuneration of 'er virtues.'

'Well, well,' said Calton, rather impatiently, as he opened the door for her, 'leave us for a short time, there's a good soul. Miss Frettlby and I want to rest, and we will ring for you when we are going.'

'Thank you, sir,' said the lachrymose landlady, 'an' I 'opes they won't 'ang 'im, which is sich a choky way of dyin'; but in life we are in death,' she went on, rather incoherently, 'as is well known to them as 'as diseases, an' may be corpsed at any minute, and as — '

Here Calton, unable to restrain his impatience any longer, shut the door, and they heard Mrs. Sampson's shrill voice and subdued cracklings die away in the distance. 'Now then,' he said, 'now that we have got rid of that woman and her tongue, where are we to begin?'

'The desk,' replied Madge, going over to it. 'It's the most likely place.'

'Don't think so,' said Calton, shaking his head. 'If, as you say, Fitzgerald is a careless man, he would not have troubled to put it there. However; perhaps we'd better look.' The desk was very untidy ('Just like Brian,' as Madge remarked) — full of paid and unpaid bills, old letters, play-bills, ball-programmes, and withered flowers.

'Reminiscences of former flirtations,' said Calton, with a laugh, pointing to these.

'I should not wonder,' retorted Miss Frettlby, coolly. 'Brian always was in love with some one or other; but you know what Lytton says, 'There are many counterfeits, but only one Eros,' so I can afford to forget these things.'

The letter, however, was not to be found in the desk, nor was it in the sitting-room. They tried the bedroom, but with no better result. Madge was about to give up the search in despair, when suddenly Calton's eye fell on the waste-paper basket, which, by some unaccountable reason, they had over-looked. The basket was half-full, in fact; more than half, and, on looking at it, a sudden thought struck the lawyer. He rang the bell, and presently Mrs. Sampson made her appearance.

'How long has that waste-paper basket been standing like that?' he asked, pointing to it.

'It bein' the only fault I 'ad to find with 'im,' said Mrs. Sampson, ''e bein' that untidy that 'e a never let me clean it out until 'e told me pussonly. 'E said as 'ow 'e throwed things into it as 'e might 'ave to look up again; an' I 'aven't touched it for more nor six weeks, 'opin' you won't think me a bad 'ousekeeper, it bein' 'is own wish — bein' fond of litter an' sich like.'

'Six weeks,' repeated Calton, with a look at Madge. 'Ah, and he got the letter four weeks ago. Depend upon it, we shall find it there.'

Madge gave a cry, and falling on her knees,

emptied the basket out on the floor, and both she and Calton were soon as busy among the fragments of paper as though they were rag-pickers.

''Opin' they ain't orf their 'eads,' murmured Mrs. Sampson, as she went to the door, 'but it looks like it, they bein' — '

Suddenly a cry broke from Madge, as she drew out of the mass of paper a half-burnt letter, written on thick and creamy-looking paper.

'At last,' she cried, rising off her knees, and smoothing it out; 'I knew he had not destroyed it.'

'Pretty nearly, however,' said Calton, as his eye glanced rapidly over it; 'it's almost useless as it is. There's no name to it.'

He took it over to the window, and spread it out upon the table. It was dirty, and half burnt, but still it was a clue.

OT VILLA
OORAK

July 26th

Mr Fitzgerald is requeste
on a dying woma
who wants to tell
concerns it
bearers who will

'There is not much to be gained from that, I'm afraid,' said Madge, sadly. 'It shows that he had an appointment — but where?'

Calton did not answer, but, leaning his head on his hands, stared hard at the paper. At last he jumped up with a cry —

'I have it,' he said, in an excited tone. 'Look at that paper; see how creamy and white it is, and above all, look at the printing in the corner — 'OT VILLA, OORAK.' '

'Then he went down to Toorak?'

'In an hour, and back again — hardly!'

'Then it was not written from Toorak?'

'No, it was written in one of the Melbourne back slums.'

'How do you know?'

'Look at the girl who brought it,' said Calton, quickly. 'A disreputable woman, one far more likely to come from the back slums than from Toorak. As to the paper, three months ago there was a robbery at Toorak, and this is some of the paper that was stolen by the thieves.'

Madge said nothing, but her sparkling eyes and the nervous trembling of her hands showed her excitement.

'I will see a detective this evening,' said

Calton, exultingly, 'find out where this letter came from, and who wrote it. We'll save him yet,' he said, placing the precious letter carefully in his pocket-book.

'You think that you will be able to find the woman who wrote that?'

'Hum,' said the lawyer, looking thoughtful, 'she may be dead, as the letter says she is in a dying condition. However, if I can find the woman who delivered the letter at the Club, and who waited for Fitzgerald at the corner of Bourke and Russell Streets, that will be sufficient. All I want to prove is that he was not in the hansom cab with Whyte.'

'And do you think you can do that?'

'Depends upon this letter,' said Calton, tapping his pocket-book with his finger. 'I'll tell you to-morrow.'

Shortly afterwards they left the house, and when Calton put Madge safely into the St. Kilda train, her heart felt lighter than it had done since Fitzgerald's arrest.

14

Another Richmond in the Field.

There is an old adage that says 'Like draws to like.' The antithesis of this is probably that 'Unlike repels unlike.' But there are times when individualism does not enter into the matter, and Fate alone, by throwing two persons together, sets up a state, congenial or uncongenial, as the case may be. Fate chose to throw together Mr. Gorby and Mr. Kilsip, and each was something more than uncongenial to the other. Each was equally clever in their common profession; each was a universal favourite, yet each hated the other. They were as fire and water to one another, and when they came together, invariably there was trouble.

Kilsip was tall and slender; Gorby was short and stout. Kilsip looked clever; Gorby wore a smile of self-satisfaction; which alone was sufficient to prevent his doing so. Yet, singularly enough, it was this very smile that proved most useful to Gorby in the pursuit of his calling. It enabled him to come at information where his sharp-looking colleague might try in vain. The hearts of all went forth to Gorby's sweet smile and insinuating manner. But when Kilsip appeared people were wont to shut up, and to retire promptly, like alarmed snails, within their shells. Gorby gave the lie direct to those who hold that the face is ever the index to the mind. Kilsip, on the other hand, with his hawk-like countenance, his brilliant black eyes, hooked nose, and small thin-lipped mouth, endorsed the theory. His complexion was quite colourless, and his hair was jet black. Altogether, he could not be called fair to look upon. His craft and cunning were of the snake-like order. So long as he conducted his enquiries in secret he was generally successful; but once let him appear personally on the scene, and failure was assured to him. Thus, while Kilsip passed as the cleverer, Gorby was invariably the more successful — at all events, ostensibly.

When, therefore, this hansom cab murder case was put into Gorby's hands, the soul of Kilsip was smitten with envy, and when Fitzgerald was arrested, and all the evidence collected by Gorby seemed to point so conclusively to his guilt, Kilsip writhed in secret over the triumph of his enemy. Though he would only have been too glad to say that Gorby had got hold of the wrong man, yet the evidence was so conclusive that such a thought never entered his head until he received a note from Mr. Calton, asking him to call at his office that evening at eight o'clock, with reference to the murder.

Kilsip knew that Calton was counsel for the prisoner. He guessed that he was wanted to follow up a clue. And he determined to devote himself to whatever Calton might require of him, if only to prove Gorby to be wrong. So pleased was he at the mere possibility of triumphing over his rival, that on casually meeting him, he stopped and invited him to drink.

The primary effect of his sudden and unusual hospitality was to arouse all Gorby's suspicions; but on second thoughts, deeming himself quite a match for Kilsip, both mentally and physically, Gorby accepted the invitation.

'Ah!' said Kilsip, in his soft, low voice, rubbing his lean white hands together, as they sat over their drinks, 'you're a lucky man to have laid your hands on that hansom cab murderer so quickly.'

'Yes; I flatter myself I did manage it pretty well,' said Gorby, lighting his pipe. 'I had no idea that it would be so simple — though, mind you, it required a lot of thought before I got a proper start.'

'I suppose you're pretty sure he's the man

you want?' pursued Kilsip, softly, with a brilliant flash of his black eyes.

'Pretty sure, indeed!' retorted Mr. Gorby, scornfully, 'there ain't no pretty sure about it. I'd take my Bible oath he's the man. He and Whyte hated one another. He says to Whyte, 'I'll kill you, if I've got to do it in the open street.' He meets Whyte drunk, a fact which he acknowledges himself; he clears out, and the cabman swears he comes back; then he gets into the cab with a living man, and when he comes out leaves a dead one; he drives to East Melbourne and gets into the house at a time which his landlady can prove — just the time that a cab would take to drive from the Grammar School on the St. Kilda Road. If you ain't a fool, Kilsip, you'll see as there's no doubt about it.'

'It looks all square enough,' said Kilsip, who wondered what evidence Calton could have found to contradict such a plain statement of fact. 'And what's his defence?'

'Mr. Calton's the only man as knows that,' answered Gorby, finishing his drink; 'but, clever and all as he is, he can't put anything in, that can go against my evidence.'

'Don't you be too sure of that,' sneered Kilsip, whose soul was devoured with envy.

'Oh! but I am,' retorted Gorby, getting as red as a turkey-cock at the sneer. 'You're jealous, you are, because you haven't got a finger in the pie.'

'Ah! but I may have yet.'

'Going a-hunting yourself, are you?' said Gorby, with an indignant snort. 'A-hunting for what — for a man as is already caught?'

'I don't believe you've got the right man,' remarked Kilsip, deliberately.

Mr. Gorby looked upon him with a smile of pity.

'No! of course you don't, just because I've caught him; perhaps, when you see him hanged, you'll believe it then?'

'You're a smart man, you are,' retorted Kilsip; 'but you ain't the Pope to be infallible.'

'And what grounds have you for saying he's not the right man?' demanded Gorby. Kilsip smiled, and stole softly across the room like a cat.

'You don't think I'm such a fool as to tell you? But you ain't so safe nor clever as you think,' and, with another irritating smile, he went out.

'He's a regular snake,' said Gorby to himself, as the door closed on his brother detective; 'but he's bragging now. There isn't a link missing in the chain of evidence against Fitzgerald, so I defy him. He can do his worst.'

At eight o'clock on that night the

soft-footed and soft-voiced detective presented himself at Calton's office. He found
the lawyer impatiently waiting for him. Kilsip
closed the door softly, and then taking a
seat opposite to Calton, waited for him to
speak. The lawyer, however, first handed
him a cigar, and then producing a bottle of
whisky and two glasses from some mysterious recess, he filled one and pushed it
towards the detective. Kilsip accepted these
little attentions with the utmost gravity, yet
they were not without their effect on him, as
the keen-eyed lawyer saw. Calton was a great
believer in diplomacy, and never lost an
opportunity of inculcating it into young
men starting in life. 'Diplomacy,' said
Calton, to one young aspirant for legal
honours, 'is the oil we cast on the troubled
waters of social, professional, and political
life; and if you can, by a little tact, manage
mankind, you are pretty certain to get on in
this world.'

Calton was a man who practised what he
preached. He believed Kilsip to have that
feline nature, which likes to be stroked, to be
made much of, and he paid him these little
attentions, knowing full well they would bear
their fruit. He also knew that Kilsip
entertained no friendly feeling for Gorby,
that, in fact, he bore him hatred, and he

determined that this feeling which existed between the two men, should serve him to the end he had in view.

'I suppose,' he said, leaning back in his chair, and watching the wreaths of blue smoke curling from his cigar, 'I suppose you know all the ins and the outs of the hansom cab murder?'

'I should rather think so,' said Kilsip, with a curious light in his queer eyes. 'Why, Gorby does nothing but brag about it, and his smartness in catching the supposed murderer!'

'Aha!' said Calton, leaning forward, and putting his arms on the table. 'Supposed murderer. Eh! Does that mean that he hasn't been convicted by a jury, or that you think that Fitzgerald is innocent?'

Kilsip stared hard at the lawyer, in a vague kind of way, slowly rubbing his hands together.

'Well,' he said at length, in a deliberate manner, 'before I got your note, I was convinced Gorby had got hold of the right man, but when I heard that you wanted to see me, and knowing you are defending the prisoner, I guessed that you must have found something in his favour which you wanted me to look after.'

'Right!' said Calton, laconically.

'As Mr. Fitzgerald said he met Whyte at the corner and hailed the cab — ' went on the detective.

'How do you know that?' interrupted Calton, sharply.

'Gorby told me.'

'How the devil did he find out?' cried the lawyer, with genuine surprise.

'Because he is always poking and prying about,' said Kilsip, forgetting, in his indignation, that such poking and prying formed part of detective business. 'But, at any rate,' he went on quickly, 'if Mr. Fitzgerald did leave Mr. Whyte, the only chance he's got of proving his innocence is that he did not come back, as the cabman alleged.'

'Then, I suppose, you think that Fitzgerald will prove an alibi,' said Calton.

'Well, sir,' answered Kilsip, modestly, 'of course you know more about the case than I do, but that is the only defence I can see he can make.'

'Well, he's not going to put in such a defence.'

'Then he must be guilty,' said Kilsip, promptly.

'Not necessarily,' returned the barrister, drily.

'But if he wants to save his neck, he'll have to prove an alibi,' persisted the other.

'That's just where the point is,' answered Calton. 'He doesn't want to save his neck.'

Kilsip, looking rather bewildered, took a sip of whisky, and waited to hear what Mr. Calton had to say.

'The fact is,' said Calton, lighting a fresh cigar, 'he has some extraordinary idea in his head. He refuses absolutely to say where he was on that night.'

'I understand,' said Kilsip, nodding his head. 'Woman?'

'No, nothing of the kind,' retorted Calton, hastily. 'I thought so at first, but I was wrong. He went to see a dying woman, who wished to tell him something.'

'What about?'

'That's just what I can't tell you,' answered Calton quickly. 'It must have been something important, for she sent for him in great haste — and he was by her bedside between the hours of one and two on Friday morning.'

'Then he did not return to the cab?'

'No, he did not, he went to keep his appointment, but, for some reason or other, he won't tell where this appointment was. I went to his rooms to-day and found this half-burnt letter, asking him to come.'

Calton handed the letter to Kilsip, who placed it on the table and examined it carefully.

'This was written on Thursday,' said the detective.

'Of course — you can see that from the date; and Whyte was murdered on Friday, the 27th.'

'It was written at something Villa, Toorak,' pursued Kilsip, still examining the paper.

'Oh! I understand; he went down there.'

'Hardly,' retorted Calton, in a sarcastic tone. 'He couldn't very well go down there, have an interview, and be back in East Melbourne in one hour — the cabman Royston can prove that he was at Russell Street at one o'clock, and his landlady that he entered his lodging in East Melbourne at two — no, he wasn't at Toorak.'

'When was this letter delivered?'

'Shortly before twelve o'clock, at the Melbourne Club, by a girl, who, from what the waiter saw of her, appears to be a disreputable individual — you will see it says bearer will wait for him at Bourke Street, and as another street is mentioned, and as Fitzgerald, after leaving Whyte, went down Russell Street to keep his appointment, the most logical conclusion is that the bearer of the letter waited for him at the corner of Bourke and Russell Streets. Now,' went on the lawyer, 'I want to find out who the girl that brought the letter is!'

'But how?'

'God bless my soul, Kilsip! How stupid you are,' cried Calton, his irritation getting the better of him. 'Can't you understand — that paper came from one of the back slums — therefore it must have been stolen.'

A sudden light flashed into Kilsip's eyes.

'Talbot Villa, Toorak,' he cried quickly, snatching up the letter again, and examining it with great attention, 'where that burglary took place.'

'Exactly,' said Calton, smiling complacently. 'Now do you understand what I want — you must take me to the crib in the back slums where the articles stolen from the house in Toorak were hidden. This paper' — pointing to the letter — 'is part of the swag left behind, and must have been used by someone there. Brian Fitzgerald obeyed the directions given in the letter, and he was there, at the time of the murder.'

'I understand,' said Kilsip, with a gratified purr. 'There were four men engaged in that burglary, and they hid the swag at Mother Guttersnipe's crib, in a lane off Little Bourke Street — but hang it, a swell like Mr. Fitzgerald, in evening dress, couldn't very well have gone down there unless — '

'He had some one with him well-known in the locality,' finished Calton, rapidly.

'Exactly, that woman who delivered the letter at the Club guided him. Judging from the waiter's description of her appearance, I should think she was pretty well known about the slums.'

'Well,' said Kilsip, rising and looking at his watch, 'it is now nine o'clock, so if you like we will go to the old hag's place at once — dying woman,' he said, as if struck by a sudden thought, 'there was a woman who died there about four weeks ago.'

'Who was she?' asked Calton, who was putting on his overcoat.

'Some relation of Mother Guttersnipe's, I fancy,' answered Kilsip, as they left the office. 'I don't know exactly what she was — she was called the 'Queen,' and a precious handsome woman she must have been — came from Sydney about three months ago, and from what I can make out, was not long from England, died of consumption on the Thursday night before the murder.'

15

A Woman of the People.

Bourke Street is a more crowded thoroughfare than Collins Street, especially at night.
The theatres that it contains are in themselves
sufficient for the gathering of a considerable
crowd. It is a grimy crowd for the most part.
Round the doors of the hotels a number of
ragged and shabby-looking individuals col-
lect, waiting till some kind friend shall invite
them to step inside. Further on a knot of
horsey-looking men are to be seen standing
under the Opera House verandah giving and
taking odds about the Melbourne Cup, or
some other meeting. Here and there are
ragged street Arabs, selling matches and
newspapers; and against the verandah post, in
the full blaze of the electric light, leans a
weary, draggled-looking woman, one arm
clasping a baby to her breast, and the other
holding a pile of newspapers, while she
drones out in a hoarse voice, ''Erald, third
'dition, one penny!' until the ear wearies of
the constant repetition. Cabs rattle incessantly along the street; here, a fast-looking

hansom, with a rakish horse, bearing some gilded youth to his Club — there, a dingy-looking vehicle, drawn by a lank quadruped, which staggers blindly down the street. Alternating with these, carriages dash along with their well-groomed horses, and within, the vision of bright eyes, white dresses, and the sparkle of diamonds. Then, further up, just on the verge of the pavement, three violins and a harp are playing a German waltz to an admiring crowd of attentive spectators. If there is one thing which the Melbourne folk love more than another, it is music. Their fondness for it is only equalled by their admiration for horse-racing. Any street band which plays at all decently, may be sure of a good audience, and a substantial remuneration for their performance. Some writer has described Melbourne, as Glasgow with the sky of Alexandria; and certainly the beautiful climate of Australia, so Italian in its brightness, must have a great effect on the nature of such an adaptable race as the Anglo-Saxon. In spite of the dismal prognostications of Marcus Clarke regarding the future Australian, whom he describes as being 'a tall, coarse, strong-jawed, greedy, pushing, talented man, excelling in swimming and horsemanship,' it is more likely that he will be a cultured, indolent individual, with an intense appreciation of the arts and sciences, and a dislike to hard work and utilitarian principles. Climatic influence should be taken into account with regard to the future Australian, and our posterity will no more resemble us than the luxurious Venetians resembled their hardy forefathers, who first started to build on those lonely sandy islands of the Adriatic.

This was the conclusion at which Mr. Calton arrived as he followed his guide through the crowded streets, and saw with what deep interest the crowd listened to the rhythmic strains of Strauss and the sparkling melodies of Offenbach. The brilliantly-lit street, with the never-ceasing stream of people pouring along; the shrill cries of the street Arabs, the rattle of vehicles, and the fitful strains of music, all made up a scene which fascinated him, and he could have gone on wandering all night, watching the myriad phases of human character constantly passing before his eyes. But his guide, with whom familiarity with the proletarians had, in a great measure, bred indifference, hurried him away to Little Bourke Street, where the narrowness of the thoroughfare, with the high buildings on each side, the dim light of the sparsely scattered gas-lamps, and the few ragged-looking figures slouching along, formed a strong contrast to the brilliant and crowded scene they had just left. Turning off Little Bourke Street, the detective led the way down a dark lane. It was as hot as a furnace from the accumulated heat of the day. To look up at the clear starlit sky was to experience a sensation of delicious coolness.

'Keep close to me,' whispered Kilsip, touching the barrister on the arm; 'we may meet some nasty customers about here.'

It was not quite dark, for the atmosphere had that luminous kind of haze so observable in Australian twilights, and this weird light was just sufficient to make the darkness visible. Kilsip and the barrister kept for safety in the middle of the alley, so that no one could spring upon them unaware, and they could see sometimes on the one side, a man cowering back into the black shadow, or on the other, a woman with disordered hair and bare bosom, leaning out of a window trying to get a breath of fresh air. There were also some children playing in the dried-up gutter, and their shrill young voices came echoing strangely through the gloom, mingling with a bacchanalian sort of song, sung by a man, as he slouched along unsteadily over the rough stones. Now and then a mild-looking string of Chinamen stole along, clad in their dull-hued blue blouses, either chattering shrilly, like a lot of parrots, or moving silently down the alley with a stolid Oriental apathy on their yellow faces. Here and there came a stream of warm light through an open door, and within, the Mongolians were gathered round the gambling-tables, playing fan-tan, or leaving the seductions of their favourite pastime, to glide soft-footed to the many cook-shops, where enticing-looking fowls and turkeys already cooked were awaiting purchasers. Kilsip turning to the left, led the barrister down another and still narrower lane, the darkness and gloom of which made the lawyer shudder, as he wondered how human beings could live in such murky places. At last, to Calton's relief, for he felt somewhat bewildered by the darkness and narrowness of the lanes through which he had been taken, the detective stopped before a door, which he opened, and stepping inside, beckoned to the barrister to follow. Calton did so, and found himself in a low, dark, ill-smelling passage. At the end a faint light glimmered. Kilsip caught his companion by the arm and guided him carefully along the passage. There was much need of this caution, for Calton could feel that the rotten boards were full of holes, into which one or the other of his feet kept slipping from time to time, while he could hear the rats squeaking and scampering away on all sides. Just as they got to the end of this tunnel, for it could be called nothing else, the light suddenly went out, and they were left in complete darkness.

'Light that,' cried the detective in a peremptory tone of voice. 'What do you mean by dowsing the glim?'

Thieves' argot was, evidently, well understood here, for there was a shuffle in the dark, a muttered voice, and someone lit a candle. Calton saw that the light was held by an elfish-looking child. Tangled masses of black hair hung over her scowling white face. As she crouched down on the floor against the damp wall she looked up defiantly yet fearfully at the detective.

'Where's Mother Guttersnipe?' asked Kilsip, touching her with his foot.

She seemed to resent the indignity, and rose quickly to her feet.

'Upstairs,' she replied, jerking her head in the direction of the right wall. Following her direction, Calton — his eyes now somewhat accustomed to the gloom — could discern a gaping black chasm, which he presumed was the stair alluded to. 'Yer won't get much out of 'er to-night; she's a-going to start 'er booze, she is.'

'Never mind what she's doing or about to do,' said Kilsip, sharply, 'take me to her at once.'

The girl looked him sullenly up and down, then she led the way into the black chasm and up the stairs. They were so shaky as to make Calton fear they might give way. As they toiled slowly up the broken steps he held tightly to his companion's arm. At last they stopped at a door through the cracks of which a faint glimmer of light was to be seen. Here the girl gave a shrill whistle, and the door opened. Still preceded by their elfish guide, Calton and the detective stepped through the doorway. A curious scene was before them. A small square room, with a low roof, from which the paper mildewed and torn hung in shreds; on the left hand, at the far end, was a kind of low stretcher, upon which a woman, almost naked, lay, amid a heap of greasy clothes. She appeared to be ill, for she kept tossing her head from side to side restlessly, and every now and then sang snatches of song in a cracked voice. In the centre of the room was a rough deal table, upon which stood a guttering tallow candle, which but faintly illuminated the scene, and a half-empty rectangular bottle of Schnapps, with a broken cup beside it. In front of these signs of festivity sat an old woman with a pack of cards spread out before her, and from which she had evidently been telling the fortune of a villainous-looking young man who had opened the door, and who stood looking at the detective with no very friendly expression of countenance. He wore a greasy brown velvet coat, much patched, and a black wide-awake hat, pulled down over his eyes. From his expression — so scowling and vindictive was it — the barrister judged his ultimate destiny to lie between Pentridge and the gallows.

As they entered, the fortune-teller raised her head, and, shading her eyes with one skinny hand, looked curiously at the new-comers. Calton thought he had never seen such a repulsive-looking old crone; and, in truth, her ugliness was, in its very grotesqueness well worthy the pencil of a Dore. Her face was seamed and lined with innumerable wrinkles, clearly defined by the dirt which was in them; bushy grey eyebrows, drawn frowningly over two piercing black eyes, whose light was undimmed by age; a hook nose, like the beak of a bird of prey, and a thin-lipped mouth devoid of teeth. Her hair was very luxurious and almost white, and was tied up in a great bunch by a greasy bit of black ribbon. As to her chin, Calton, when he saw it wagging to and fro, involuntarily quoted Macbeth's lines —

'Ye should be women,
And yet your beards forbid me to
    interpret
That ye are so.'

She was no bad representative of the weird sisters.

As they entered she eyed them viciously, demanding what the blazes they wanted.

'Want your booze,' cried the child, with an elfish laugh, as she shook back her tangled hair.

'Get out, you whelp,' croaked the old hag, shaking one skinny fist at her, 'or I'll tear yer 'eart out.'

'Yes, she can go,' said Kilsip, nodding to the girl, 'and you can clear, too,' he added, sharply, turning to the young man, who stood still holding the door open.

At first he seemed inclined to dispute the detective's order, but ultimately obeyed him, muttering, as he went out, something about 'the blooming cheek of showin' swells cove's cribs.' The child followed him out, her exit being accelerated by Mother Guttersnipe, who, with a rapidity only attained by long practice, seized the shoe from one of her feet, and flung it at the head of the rapidly retreating girl.

'Wait till I ketches yer, Lizer,' she shrieked,

with a volley of oaths, 'I'll break yer 'ead for ye!'

Lizer responded with a shrill laugh of disdain, and vanished through the shaky door, which she closed after her.

When she had disappeared Mother Guttersnipe took a drink from the broken cup, and, gathering all her greasy cards together in a business-like way, looked insinuatingly at Calton, with a suggestive leer.

'It's the future ye want unveiled, dearie?' she croaked, rapidly shuffling the cards; 'an' old mother 'ull tell — '

'No she won't,' interrupted the detective, sharply. 'I've come on business.'

The old woman started at this, and looked keenly at him from under her bushy eyebrows.

'What 'av the boys been up to now?' she asked, harshly. 'There ain't no swag 'ere this time.'

Just then the sick woman, who had been restlessly tossing on the bed, commenced singing a snatch of the quaint old ballad of 'Barbara Allen' —

'Oh, mither, mither, mak' my bed,
An' mak' it saft an' narrow;
Since my true love died for me to-day
I'll die for him to-morrow.'

'Shut up, cuss you!' yelled Mother Gutter-snipe, viciously, 'or I'll knock yer bloomin' 'ead orf,' and she seized the square bottle as if to carry out her threat; but, altering her mind, she poured some of its contents into the cup, and drank it off with avidity.

'The woman seems ill,' said Calton, casting a shuddering glance at the stretcher.

'So she are,' growled Mother Guttersnipe, angrily. 'She ought to be in Yarrer Bend, she ought, instead of stoppin' 'ere an' singin' them beastly things, which makes my blood run cold. Just 'ear 'er,' she said, viciously, as the sick woman broke out once more —

'Oh, little did my mither think,
When first she cradled me,
I'd die sa far away fra home,
Upon the gallows tree.'

'Yah!' said the old woman, hastily, drinking some more gin out of the cup. 'She's allays a-talkin' of dyin' an' gallers, as if they were nice things to jawr about.'

'Who was that woman who died here three or four weeks ago?' asked Kilsip, sharply.

''Ow should I know?' retorted Mother Guttersnipe, sullenly. 'I didn't kill 'er, did I? It were the brandy she drank; she was allays drinkin', cuss her.'

'Do you remember the night she died?'

'No, I don't,' answered the beldame, frankly. 'I were drunk — blind, bloomin', blazin' drunk — s'elp me.'

'You're always drunk,' said Kilsip.

'What if I am?' snarled the woman, seizing her bottle. 'You don't pay fur it. Yes, I'm drunk. I'm allays drunk. I was drunk last night, an' the night before, an' I'm a-goin' to git drunk to-night' — with an impressive look at the bottle — ''an' to-morrow night, an' I'll keep it up till I'm rottin' in the grave.'

Calton shuddered, so full of hatred and suppressed malignity was her voice, but the detective merely shrugged his shoulders.

'More fool you,' he said, briefly. 'Come now, on the night the 'Queen,' as you call her, died, there was a gentleman came to see her?'

'So she said,' retorted Mother Guttersnipe; 'but, lor, I dunno anythin', I were drunk.'

'Who said — the 'Queen?' '

'No, my gran'darter, Sal. The 'Queen,' sent 'er to fetch the toff to see 'er cut 'er lucky. Wanted 'im to look at 'is work, I s'pose, cuss 'im; and Sal prigged some paper from my box,' she shrieked, indignantly; 'prigged it w'en I were too drunk to stop 'er?'

The detective glanced at Calton, who nodded to him with a gratified expression on

193

his face. They were right as to the paper having been stolen from the Villa at Toorak.

'You did not see the gentleman who came?' said Kilsip, turning again to the old hag.

'Not I, cuss you,' she retorted, politely. ''E came about 'arf-past one in the morning, an' you don't expects we can stop up all night, do ye?'

'Half-past one o'clock,' repeated Calton, quickly. 'The very time. Is this true?'

'Wish I may die if it ain't,' said Mother Guttersnipe, graciously. 'My gran'darter Sal kin tell ye.'

'Where is she?' asked Kilsip, sharply.

At this the old woman threw back her head, and howled dismay.

'She's 'ooked it,' she wailed, drumming on the ground with her feet. 'Gon' an' left 'er pore old gran' an' joined the Army, cuss 'em, a-comin' round an' a-spilin' business.'

Here the woman on the bed broke out again —

'Since the flowers o' the forest are a'
    wed awa — '

''Old yer jawr,' yelled Mother Guttersnipe, rising, and making a dart at the bed. 'I'll choke the life out ye, s'elp me. D'y want me to murder ye, singin' 'em funeral things?'

194

Meanwhile the detective was talking rapidly to Mr. Calton.

'The only person who can prove Mr. Fitzgerald was here between one and two o'clock,' he said, quickly, 'is Sal Rawlins, as everyone else seems to have been drunk or asleep. As she has joined the Salvation Army, I'll go to the barracks the first thing in the morning and look for her.'

'I hope you'll find her,' answered Calton, drawing a long breath. 'A man's life hangs on her evidence.'

They turned to go, Calton having first given Mother Guttersnipe some loose silver, which she seized on with an avaricious clutch.

'You'll drink it, I suppose?' said the barrister, shrinking back from her.

'Werry likely,' retorted the hag, with a repulsive grin, tying the money up in a piece of her dress, which she tore off for the purpose. 'I'm a forting to the public-'ouse, I am, an' it's the on'y pleasure I 'ave in my life, cuss it.'

The sight of money had a genial effect on her nature, for she held the candle at the head of the stairs, as they went down, so that they should not break their heads. As they arrived safely, they saw the light vanish, and heard the sick woman singing, 'The Last Rose of Summer.'

The street door was open, and, after

groping their way along the dark passage, with its pitfalls, they found themselves in the open street.

'Thank heaven,' said Calton, taking off his hat, and drawing a long breath. 'Thank heaven we are safely out of that den!'

'At all events, our journey has not been wasted,' said the detective, as they walked along. 'We've found out where Mr. Fitzgerald was on the night of the murder, so he will be safe.'

'That depends upon Sal Rawlins,' answered Calton, gravely; 'but come, let us have a glass of brandy, for I feel quite ill after my experience of low life.'

16

Missing.

The next day Kilsip called at Calton's office late in the afternoon, and found the lawyer eagerly expecting him. The detective's face, however, looked rather dismal, and Calton was not reassured.

'Well!' he said, impatiently, when Kilsip had closed the door and taken his seat.

'Where is she?'

'That's just what I want to know,' answered the detective, coolly; 'I went to the Salvation Army head-quarters and made enquiries about her. It appears that she had been in the Army as a hallelujah lass, but got tired of it in a week, and went off with a friend of hers to Sydney. She carried on her old life of dissipation, but, ultimately, her friend got sick of her, and the last thing they heard about her was that she had taken up with a Chinaman in one of the Sydney slums. I telegraphed at once to Sydney, and got a reply that there was no person of the name of Sal Rawlins known to the Sydney police, but they said they would make enquiries, and let me know the result.'

'Ah! she has, no doubt, changed her name,' said Calton, thoughtfully, stroking his chin. 'I wonder why?'

'Wanted to get rid of the Army, I expect,' answered Kilsip, drily. 'The straying lamb did not care about being hunted back to the fold.'

'And when did she join the Army?'

'The very day after the murder.'

'Rather sudden conversion?'

'Yes, but she said the death of the woman on Thursday night had so startled her, that she went straight off to the Army to get her religion properly fixed up.'

'The effects of fright, no doubt,' said Calton, dryly. 'I've met a good many examples of these sudden conversions, but they never last long as a rule — it's a case of 'the devil was sick, the devil a monk would be,' more than anything else. Good-looking?'

'So-so, I believe,' replied Kilsip, shrugging his shoulders.

'Very ignorant — could neither read nor write.'

'That accounts for her not asking for Fitzgerald when she called at the Club — she probably did not know whom she had been sent for. It will resolve itself into a question of identification, I expect. However, if the police can't find her, we will put an advertisement in the papers offering a reward, and send out handbills to the same effect. She must be found. Brian Fitzgerald's life hangs on a thread, and that thread is Sal Rawlins.'

'Yes!' assented Kilsip, rubbing his hands together. 'Even if Mr. Fitzgerald acknowledges that he was at Mother Guttersnipe's on the night in question, she will have to prove that he was there, as no one else saw him.'

'Are you sure of that?'

'As sure as anyone can be in such a case. It was a late hour when he came, and everyone seems to have been asleep except the dying woman and Sal; and as one is dead, the other is the only person that can prove that he was there at the time when the murder was being committed in the hansom.'

'And Mother Guttersnipe?'

'Was drunk, as she acknowledged last night. She thought that if a gentleman did call it must have been the other one.'

'The other one?' repeated Calton, in a puzzled voice. 'What other one?'

'Oliver Whyte.'

Calton arose from his seat with a blank air of astonishment.

'Oliver Whyte!' he said, as soon as he could find his voice. 'Was he in the habit of going there?'

Kilsip curled himself up in his seat like a sleek cat, and pushing forward his head till his nose looked like the beak of a bird of prey, looked keenly at Calton.

'Look here, sir,' he said, in his low, purring voice, 'there's a good deal in this case which don't seem plain — in fact, the further we go into it, the more mixed up it seems to get. I went to see Mother Guttersnipe this morning, and she told me that Whyte had visited the 'Queen' several times while she lay ill, and that he seemed to be pretty well acquainted with her.'

'But who the deuce is this woman they call the 'Queen'?' said Calton, irritably. 'She seems to be at the bottom of the whole affair — every path we take leads to her.'

'I know hardly anything about her,' replied Kilsip, 'except that she was a good-looking woman, of about forty-nine — she come out from England to Sydney a few months ago, then on here — how she got to Mother Guttersnipe's I can't find out, though I've tried to pump that old woman, but she's as close as wax, and it's my belief she knows more about this dead woman than she chooses to tell.'

'But what could she have told Fitzgerald to make him act in this silly manner? A stranger who comes from England, and dies in a

Melbourne slum, can't possibly know any-thing about Miss Frettlby.'

'Not unless Miss Frettlby was secretly married to Whyte,' suggested Kilsip, 'and the 'Queen' knew it.'

'Nonsense,' retorted Calton, sharply. 'Why, she hated him and loves Fitzgerald; besides, why on earth should she marry secretly, and make a confidant of a woman in one of the lowest parts of Melbourne? At one time her father wanted her to marry Whyte, but she made such strong opposition, that he eventually gave his consent to her engage-ment with Fitzgerald.'

'And Whyte?'

'Oh, he had a row with Mr. Frettlby, and left the house in a rage. He was murdered the same night, for the sake of some papers he carried.'

'Oh, that's Gorby's idea,' said Kilsip, scornfully, with a vicious snarl.

'And it's mine too,' answered Calton, firmly. 'Whyte had some valuable papers, which he always carried about with him. The woman who died evidently told Fitzgerald that he did so; I gathered as much from an accidental admission he made.' Kilsip looked puzzled.

'I must confess that it is a riddle,' he said at length; 'but if Mr. Fitzgerald would only speak, it would clear everything up.'

'Speak about what — the man who murdered Whyte?'

'Well, if he did not go quite so far as that he might at least supply the motive for the crime.'

'Perhaps so,' answered Calton, as the detective rose to go; 'but it's no use. Fitzgerald for some reason or another, has evidently made up his mind not to speak, so our only hope in saving him lies in finding this girl.'

'If she's anywhere in Australia you may be sure she'll be found,' answered Kilsip, confidently, as he took his departure. 'Australia isn't so over-crowded as all that.' But if Sal Rawlins was in Australia at all she certainly must have been in some very remote part. All efforts to find her proved futile. It was an open question if she was alive or dead; she seemed to have vanished completely. She was last seen in a Sydney den with a Chinaman whom afterwards she appeared to have left. Since then, nothing whatever was known of her. Notices offering large rewards for her discovery were inserted in all the newspapers, Australian and New Zealand; but nothing came of them. As she herself was unable to read there seemed little chance of her knowing of them; and, if, as Calton surmised she had changed her name, no one would be likely to tell her of them. There was only the bare chance that she might hear of them casually, or that she might turn up of her own accord. If she returned to Melbourne she would certainly go to her grandmother's. She had no motive for not doing so. So Kilsip kept a sharp watch on the house, much to Mrs. Rawlins' disgust, for, with true English pride, she objected to this system of espionage.

'Cuss 'im,' she croaked over her evening drink, to an old crone, as withered and evil-looking as herself, 'why can't 'e stop in 'is own bloomin' 'ouse, an' leave mine alone — a-comin' round 'ere a-pokin' and pryin' and a-perwenting people from earnin' their livin' an' a-gittin' drunk when they ain't well.'

'What do 'e want?' asked her friend, rubbing her weak old knees.

'Wants? — 'e wants 'is throat cut,' said Mother Guttersnipe, viciously. 'An' s'elp me I'll do for 'im some night w'en 'e's a watchin' round 'ere as if it were Pentridge — 'e can git what he can out of that whelp as ran away, but I knows suthin' 'e don't know, cuss 'im.'

She ended with a senile laugh, and her companion having taken advantage of the long speech to drink some gin out of the broken cup, Mother Guttersnipe seized the unfortunate old creature by the hair, and in spite of her feeble cries, banged her head against the wall.

'I'll have the perlice in at yer,' whimpered the assaulted one, as she tottered as quickly away as her rheumatics would allow her. 'See if I don't.'

'Get out,' retorted Mother Guttersnipe, indifferently, as she filled herself a fresh cup.

'You come a-falutin' round 'ere agin priggin' my drinks, cuss you, an' I'll cut yer throat an' wring yer wicked old 'ead orf.'

The other gave a howl of dismay at hearing this pleasant proposal, and tottered out as quickly as possible, leaving Mother Guttersnipe in undisputed possession of the field. Meanwhile Calton had seen Brian several times, and used every argument in his power to get him to tell everything, but he either maintained an obstinate silence, or merely answered, 'It would only break her heart.'

He admitted to Calton, after a good deal of questioning, that he had been at Mother Guttersnipe's on the night of the murder. After he had left Whyte by the corner of the Scotch Church, as the cabman — Royston — had stated, he had gone along Russell Street, and met Sal Rawlins near the Unicorn Hotel. She had taken him to Mother Guttersnipe's, where he had seen the dying woman, who had told him something he could not reveal.

'Well,' said Mr. Calton, after hearing the admission, 'you might have saved us all this trouble by admitting this before, and yet kept your secret, whatever it may be. Had you done so, we might have got hold of Sal Rawlins before she left Melbourne; but now it's a mere chance whether she turns up or not.'

Brian did not answer to this; in fact, he seemed hardly to be thinking of what the lawyer was saying; but just as Calton was leaving, he asked —

'How is Madge?'

'How can you expect her to be?' said Calton, turning angrily on him. 'She is very ill, owing to the worry she has had over this affair.'

'My darling! My darling!' cried Brian, in agony, clasping his hands above his head. 'I did it only to save you.'

Calton approached him, and laid his hand lightly on his shoulder.

'My dear fellow,' he said, gravely, 'the confidences between lawyer and client are as sacred as those between priest and penitent. You must tell me this secret which concerns Miss Frettlby so deeply.'

'No,' said Brian, firmly, 'I will never repeat

205

what that wretched woman told me. When I would not tell you before, in order to save my life, it is not likely I am going to do so now, when I have nothing to gain and everything to lose by telling it.'

'I will never ask you again,' said Calton, rather annoyed, as he walked to the door.

'And as to this accusation of murder, if I can find this girl, you are safe.'

When the lawyer left the gaol, he went to the Detective Office to see Kilsip, and ascertain if there was any news of Sal Rawlins; but, as usual, there was none.

'It is fighting against Fate,' he said, sadly, as he went away; 'his life hangs on a mere chance.'

The trial was fixed to come off in September, and, of course, there was great excitement in Melbourne as the time drew near. Great, therefore, was the disappointment when it was discovered that the prisoner's counsel had applied for an adjournment of the trial till October, on the ground that an important witness for the defence could not be found.

17

The Trial.

In spite of the utmost vigilance on the part of the police, and the offer of a large reward, both by Calton, on behalf of the accused, and by Mr. Frettlby, the much-desired Sal Rawlins still remained hidden. The millionaire had maintained a most friendly attitude towards Brian throughout the whole affair. He refused to believe him guilty, and when Calton told him of the defence of proving an alibi by means of Sal Rawlins, he immediately offered a large reward, which was in itself enough to set every person with any time on their hands hunting for the missing witness. All Australia and New Zealand rang with the extremely plebeian name of Sal Rawlins, the papers being full of notices offering rewards; and handbills of staring red letters were posted up in all railway stations, in conjunction with 'Liquid Sunshine' Rum and 'D.W.D.' Whisky. She had become famous without knowing it, unless, indeed, she had kept herself concealed purposely, but this was hardly probable, as there was no apparent motive for her doing so. If she was above ground she must certainly have seen the handbills, if not the papers; and though not able to read, she could hardly help hearing something about the one topic of conversation throughout Australia. Notwithstanding all this, Sal Rawlins was still undiscovered, and Calton, in despair, began to think that she must be dead. But Madge, though at times her courage gave way, was still hopeful.

'God will not permit such a judicial crime as the murder of an innocent man to be committed,' she declared.

Mr. Calton, to whom she said this, shook his head doubtfully.

'God has permitted it to take place before,' he answered softly; 'and we can only judge the future by the past.'

At last, the day of the long-expected trial came, and as Calton sat in his office looking over his brief, a clerk entered and told him Mr. Frettlby and his daughter wished to see him. When they came in, the banister saw that the millionaire looked haggard and ill, and there was a worried expression on his face.

'There is my daughter, Calton,' he said, after hurried greetings had been exchanged. 'She wants to be present in Court during

Fitzgerald's trial, and nothing I can say will dissuade her.'

Calton turned, and looked at the girl in some surprise.

'Yes,' she answered, meeting his look steadily, though her face was very pale; 'I must be there. I shall go mad with anxiety unless I know how the trial goes on.'

'But think of the disagreeable amount of attention you will attract,' urged the lawyer.

'No one will recognise me,' she said calmly, 'I am very plainly dressed, and I will wear this veil;' and, drawing one from her pocket, she went to a small looking-glass which was hanging on the wall, and tied it over her face.

Calton looked in perplexity at Mr. Frettlby.

'I'm afraid you must consent,' he said.

'Very well,' replied the other, almost sternly, while a look of annoyance passed over his face. 'I shall leave her in your charge.'

'And you?'

'I'm not coming,' answered Frettlby, quickly, putting on his hat. 'I don't care about seeing a man whom I have had at my dinner-table, in the prisoner's dock, much as I sympathise with him. Good-day;' and with a curt nod he took his leave. When the door closed on her father, Madge placed her hand on Calton's arm.

'Any hope?' she whispered, looking at him

through the black veil.

'The merest chance,' answered Calton, putting his brief into his bag. 'We have done everything in our power to discover this girl, but without result. If she does not come at the eleventh hour I'm afraid Brian Fitzgerald is a doomed man.' Madge fell on her knees, with a stifled cry.

'Oh, God of Mercy,' she cried, raising her hands as if in prayer, 'save him. Save my darling, and let him not die for the crime of another. God — '

She dropped her face in her hands and wept convulsively, as the lawyer touched her lightly on the shoulder.

'Come!' he said kindly. 'Be the brave girl you were, and we may save him yet. The hour is darkest before the dawn, you know.'

Madge dried her tears, and followed the lawyer to the cab, which was waiting for them at the door. They drove quickly up to the Court, and Calton put her in a quiet place, where she could see the dock, and yet be unobserved by the people in the body of the Court. Just as he was leaving her she touched his arm.

'Tell him,' she whispered, in a trembling voice, 'tell him I am here.'

Calton nodded, and hurried away to put on his wig and gown, while Madge looked hurriedly round the Court from her point of vantage.

It was crowded with fashionable Melbourne of both sexes, and they were all talking together in subdued whispers. The popular character of the prisoner, his good looks, and engagement to Madge Frettlby, together with the extraordinary circumstances of the case, had raised public curiosity to the highest pitch, and, consequently, everybody who could possibly manage to gain admission was there.

Felix Rolleston had secured an excellent seat beside the pretty Miss Featherweight, whom he admired so much, and he was chattering to her with the utmost volubility. 'Puts me in mind of the Coliseum and all that sort of thing, you know,' he said, putting up his eye-glass and starting round. 'Butchered to make a Roman holiday by jove.'

'Don't say such horrid things, you frivolous creature,' simpered Miss Featherweight, using her smelling-bottle. 'We are all here out of sympathy for that poor dear Mr. Fitzgerald.'

The mercurial Felix, who had more cleverness in him than people gave him credit for, smiled outright at this eminently feminine way of covering an overpowering curiosity. 'Ah, yes,' he said lightly; 'exactly. I daresay Eve only ate the apple because she didn't like to see such a lot of good fruit go to waste.'

Miss Featherweight eyed him doubtfully. She was not quite certain whether he was in jest or earnest. Just as she was about to reply to the effect that she thought it wicked to make the Bible a subject for joking, the judge entered and the Court rose.

When the prisoner was brought in, there was a great flutter among the ladies, and some of them even had the bad taste to produce opera-glasses. Brian noticed this, and he flushed up to the roots of his fair hair, for he felt his degradation acutely. He was an intensely proud man, and to be placed in the criminal dock, with a lot of frivolous people, who had called themselves his friends, looking at him as though he were a new actor or a wild animal, was galling in the extreme. He was dressed in black, and looked pale and worn, but all the ladies declared that he was as good-looking as ever, and they were sure he was innocent.

The jury were sworn in, and the Crown prosecutor rose to deliver his opening address. Most of those present knew the facts only through the medium of the newspapers, and such floating rumours as they had been able to gather. They were therefore unaware of the true history of events which had led to

Fitzgerald's arrest, and they prepared to listen to the speech with profound attention.

The ladies ceased to talk, the men to stare round, and nothing could be seen but row after row of eager and attentive faces, hanging on the words that issued from the lips of the Crown prosecutor. He was not a great orator, but he spoke clearly and distinctly, and every word could be heard in the dead silence.

He gave a rapid sketch of the crime — merely a repetition of what had been published in the newspapers — and then proceeded to enumerate the witnesses for the prosecution.

He would call the landlady of the deceased to show that ill-feeling existed between the prisoner and the murdered man, and that the accused had called on the deceased a week prior to the committal of the crime, and threatened his life. (There was great excitement at this, and several ladies decided, on the spur of the moment, that the horrid man was guilty, but the majority of them still refused to believe in the guilt of such a good-looking young fellow.) He would call a witness who could prove that Whyte was drunk on the night of the murder, and went along Russell Street, in the direction of Collins Street; the cabman Royston could swear to the fact that the prisoner had hailed the cab, and after going away for a short time, returned and entered the cab with the deceased. He would also prove that the prisoner left the cab at the Grammar School, in the St. Kilda Road, and on the arrival of the cab at the junction, he discovered the deceased had been murdered. The cabman Rankin would prove that he drove the prisoner from the St. Kilda Road to Powlett Street in East Melbourne, where he got out; and he would call the prisoner's landlady to prove that the prisoner resided in Powlett Street, and that on the night of the murder he had not reached home till shortly after two o'clock. He would also call the detective who had charge of the case, to prove the finding of a glove belonging to the deceased in the pocket of the coat which the prisoner wore on the night of the murder; and the doctor who had examined the body of the deceased would give evidence that the death was caused by inhalation of chloroform. As he had now fully shown the chain of evidence which he proposed to prove, he would call the first witness, MALCOLM ROYSTON. ROYSTON, on being sworn, gave the same evidence as he had given at the inquest, from the time that the cab was hailed up to his arrival at the St. Kilda Police Station with the dead body of Whyte. In the cross-examination, Calton asked him if he was prepared to swear that the man who hailed the cab, and the man who got in with the deceased, were one and the same person.

WITNESS: I am.

CALTON: You are quite certain?

WITNESS: Yes; quite certain.

CALTON: Do you then recognise the prisoner as the man who hailed the cab?

WITNESS (hesitatingly): I cannot swear to that. The gentleman who hailed the cab had his hat pulled down over his eyes, so that I could not see his face; but the height and general appearance of the prisoner are the same.

CALTON: Then it is only because the man who got into the cab was dressed like the prisoner on that night that you thought they were both the same?

WITNESS: It never struck me for a minute that they were not the same. Besides, he spoke as if he had been there before. I said, 'Oh, you've come back,' and he said,

'Yes; I'm going to take him home,' and got into my cab.

CALTON: Did you notice any difference in his voice?

WITNESS: No; except that the first time I saw him he spoke in a loud voice, and the second time he came back, very low.

CALTON: You were sober, I suppose?

WITNESS (indignantly): Yes; quite sober.

CALTON: Ah! You did not have a drink, say at the Oriental Hotel, which, I believe, is near the rank where your cab stands?

WITNESS (hesitating): Well, I might have had a glass.

CALTON: So you might; you might have had several.

WITNESS (sulkily): Well, there's no law against a cove feeling thirsty.

CALTON: Certainly not; and I suppose you took advantage of the absence of such a law.

WITNESS (defiantly): Yes, I did.

CALTON: And you were elevated?

WITNESS: Yes; on my cab. — (Laughter.)

CALTON (severely): You are here to give evidence, sir, not to make jokes, however clever they may be. Were you, or were you not, slightly the worse for drink?

WITNESS: I might have been.

CALTON: So you were in such a condition that you did not observe very closely the man who hailed you?

WITNESS: No, I didn't — there was no reason why I should — I didn't know a murder was going to be committed.

CALTON: And it never struck you it might

216

be a different man?

WITNESS: No; I thought it was the same man the whole time.

This closed Royston's evidence, and Calton sat down very dissatisfied at not being able to elicit anything more definite from him. One thing appeared clear, that someone must have dressed himself to resemble Brian, and have spoken in a low voice for fear of betraying himself.

Clement Rankin, the next witness, deposed to having picked up the prisoner on the St. Kilda Road between one and two on Friday morning, and driven him to Powlett Street, East Melbourne. In the cross-examination, Calton elicited one point in the prisoner's favour.

CALTON: Is the prisoner the same gentleman you drove to Powlett Street?

WITNESS (confidently): Oh, yes.

CALTON: How do you know? Did you see his face?

WITNESS: No, his hat was pulled down over his eyes, and I could only see the ends of his moustache and his chin, but he carried himself the same as the prisoner, and his moustache is the same light colour.

CALTON: When you drove up to him on the St. Kilda Road, where was he, and what was he doing?

WITNESS: He was near the Grammar School, walking quickly in the direction of Melbourne, and was smoking a cigarette.

CALTON: Did he wear gloves?

WITNESS: Yes, one on the left hand, the other was bare.

CALTON: Did he wear any rings on the right hand?

WITNESS: Yes, a large diamond one on the forefinger.

CALTON: Are you sure?

WITNESS: Yes, because I thought it a curious place for a gentleman to wear a ring, and when he was paying me my fare, I saw the diamond glitter on his finger in the moonlight.

CALTON: That will do.

The counsel for the defence was pleased with this bit of evidence, as Fitzgerald detested rings, and never wore any; so he made a note of the matter on his brief. Mrs. Hableton, the landlady of the deceased, was then called, and deposed that Oliver Whyte had lodged with her for nearly two months. He seemed a quiet enough young man, but often came home drunk. The only friend she knew he had was a Mr. Moreland, who was often with him. On the 14th July, the prisoner called to see Mr. Whyte, and they had a quarrel. She heard Whyte say, 'She is mine, you can't do anything with her,' and the prisoner answered, 'I can kill you, and if you marry her I shall do so in the open street.' She had no idea at the time of the name of the lady they were talking about. There was a great sensation in the Court at these words, and half the people present looked upon such evidence as being sufficient in itself to prove the guilt of the prisoner.

In cross-examination, Calton was unable to shake the evidence of the witness, as she merely reiterated the same statements over and over again.

The next witness was Mrs. Sampson, who crackled into the witness-box dissolved in tears, and gave her answers in a piercingly shrill tone of anguish. She stated that the prisoner was in the habit of coming home early, but on the night of the murder, had come in shortly before two o'clock.

CROWN PROSECUTOR (referring to his brief): You mean after two.

WITNESS: 'Avin' made a mistake once, by saying five minutes after two to the policeman as called hisself a insurance agent, which 'e put the words into my mouth, I ain't a goin' to do so again, it bein' five minutes afore two, as I can swear to.

CROWN PROSECUTOR: You are sure your clock was right?

WITNESS: It 'adn't bin, but my nevy bein' a watchmaker, called unbeknown to me, an' made it right on Thursday night, which it was Friday mornin' when Mr. Fitzgerald came 'ome.

Mrs. Sampson bravely stuck to this statement, and ultimately left the witness-box in triumph, the rest of her evidence being comparatively unimportant as compared with this point of time. The witness Rankin, who drove the prisoner to Powlett Street (as sworn to by him) was recalled, and gave evidence that it was two o'clock when the prisoner got down from his cab in Powlett Street.

CROWN PROSECUTOR: How do you know that?

WITNESS: Because I heard the Post Office clock strike.

CROWN PROSECUTOR: Could you hear it at East Melbourne?

WITNESS: It was a very still night, and I heard the chimes and then the hour strike quite plainly.

This conflicting evidence as to time was a strong point in Brian's favour. If, as the landlady stated, on the authority of the kitchen clock, which had been put right on the day previous to the murder, Fitzgerald had come into the house at five minutes to two, he could not possibly be the man who had alighted from Rankin's cab at two o'clock at Powlett Street.

The next witness was Dr. Chinston, who swore to the death of the deceased by means of chloroform administered in a large quantity, and he was followed by Mr. Gorby, who deposed as to the finding of the glove belonging to the deceased in the pocket of the prisoner's coat.

Roger Moreland, an intimate friend of the deceased, was next called. He stated that he had known the deceased in London, and had met him in Melbourne. He was with him a great deal. On the night of the murder he was in the Orient Hotel in Bourke Street. Whyte came in, and was greatly excited. He was in evening dress, and wore a light coat. They had several drinks together, and then went up to an hotel in Russell Street, and had some more drinks there. Both witness and deceased were intoxicated. Whyte took off his light coat, saying he felt warm, and went out shortly afterwards, leaving witness asleep in the bar. He was awakened by the barman, who wanted him to leave the hotel. He saw that Whyte had left his coat behind him, and took it up with the intention of giving it to him. As he stood in the street some one snatched the coat from him and made off with it. He tried to follow the thief, but he could not do so, being too intoxicated. He then went home, and to bed, as he had to leave early for the country in the morning. In cross-examination: —

CALTON: When you went into the street, after leaving the hotel, did you see the deceased?

WITNESS: No, I did not; but I was very drunk, and unless deceased had spoken to me, I would not have noticed him.

CALTON: What was deceased excited about when you met him?

WITNESS: I don't know. He did not say.

CALTON: What were you talking about?

WITNESS: All sorts of things. London principally.

CALTON: Did the deceased mention anything about papers?

WITNESS (surprised): No, he did not.

CALTON: Are you sure?

WITNESS: Quite sure.

CALTON: What time did you get home?

WITNESS: I don't know; I was too drunk to remember.

This closed the case for the Crown, and as it was now late the case was adjourned till the next day.

The Court was soon emptied of the busy, chattering crowd, and Calton, on looking over his notes, found that the result of the first day's trial was two points in favour of Fitzgerald. First: the discrepancy of time in the evidence of Rankin and the landlady, Mrs. Sampson. Second: the evidence of the cabman Royston, as to the wearing of a ring on the forefinger of the right hand by the man who murdered Whyte, whereas the prisoner never wore rings.

These were slender proofs of innocence to put against the overwhelming mass of evidence in favour of the prisoner's guilt. The opinions of all were pretty well divided, some being in favour and others against, when suddenly an event happened which surprised everyone. All over Melbourne extras were posted, and the news passed from lip to lip like wildfire — 'Return of the Missing Witness, Sal Rawlins!'

18

Sal Rawlins Tells All She Knows.

And, indeed, such was the case. Sal Rawlins had made her appearance at the eleventh hour, to the heartfelt thankfulness of Calton, who saw in her an angel from heaven, sent to save the life of an innocent man.

It was at the conclusion of the trial; and, together with Madge, he had gone down to his office, when his clerk entered with a telegram. The lawyer opened it hastily, and, with a silent look of pleasure on his face, handed the telegram to Madge.

She, womanlike, being more impulsive, gave a cry when she read it, and, falling on her knees, thanked God for having heard her prayers, and saved her lover's life.

'Take me to her at once,' she implored the lawyer.

She was anxious to hear from Sal Rawlins' own lips the joyful words which would save Brian from a felon's death.

'No, my dear,' answered Calton, firmly, but kindly. 'I can hardly take a lady to the place where Sal Rawlins lives. You will know all

224

to-morrow, but, meanwhile, you must go home and get some sleep.'

'And you will tell him?' she whispered, clasping her hands on Calton's arm.

'At once,' he answered promptly. 'And I will see Sal Rawlins to-night, and hear what she has to say. Rest content, my dear,' he added, as he placed her in the carriage, 'he is perfectly safe now.'

Brian heard the good news with a deep feeling of gratitude, knowing that his life was safe, and that he could still keep his secret. It was the natural revulsion of feeling after the unnatural life he had been leading since his arrest. When one is young and healthy, and has all the world before one, it is a terrible thing to contemplate a sudden death. And yet, in spite of his joy at being delivered from the hangman's rope, there mingled with his delight the horror of that secret which the dying woman had told him with such malignant joy.

'I had rather she had died in silence than she should have bequeathed me this legacy of sorrow.'

And the gaoler, seeing his haggard face the next morning, muttered to himself, 'He war blest if the swell warn't sorry he war safe.'

So, while Brian was pacing up and down his cell during the weary watches of the night,

Madge, in her own room, was kneeling beside her bed and thanking God for His great mercy; and Calton, the good fairy of the two lovers, was hurrying towards the humble abode of Mrs. Rawlins, familiarly known as Mother Guttersnipe. Kilsip was beside him, and they were talking eagerly about the providential appearance of the invaluable witness.

'What I like,' observed Kilsip, in his soft, purring tone, 'is the sell it will be for that Gorby. He was so certain that Mr. Fitzgerald was the man, and when he gets off tomorrow Gorby will be in a rage.'

'Where was Sal the whole time?' asked Calton, absently, not thinking of what the detective was saying.

'Ill,' answered Kilsip. 'After she left the Chinaman she went into the country, caught cold by falling into some river, and ended up by getting brain fever. Some people found her, took her in, and nursed her. When she got well she came back to her grandmother's.'

'But why didn't the people who nursed her tell her she was wanted? They must have seen the papers.'

'Not they,' retorted the detective. 'They knew nothing.'

'Vegetables!' muttered Calton, contemptuously. 'How can people be so ignorant! Why, all Australia has been ringing with the case. At any rate, it's money out of their pocket. Well?'

'There's nothing more to tell,' said Kilsip, 'except that she turned up to-night at five o'clock, looking more like a corpse than anything else.'

When they entered the squalid, dingy passage that led to Mother Guttersnipe's abode, they saw a faint light streaming down the stair. As they climbed up they could hear the rancorous voice of the old hag pouring forth alternate blessings and curses on her prodigal offspring, and the low tones of a girl's voice in reply. On entering the room Calton saw that the sick woman, who had been lying in the corner on the occasion of his last visit, was gone. Mother Guttersnipe was seated in front of the deal table, with a broken cup and her favourite bottle of spirits before her. She evidently intended to have a night of it, in order to celebrate Sal's return, and had commenced early, so as to lose no time. Sal herself was seated on a broken chair, and leaned wearily against the wall. She stood up as Calton and the detective entered, and they saw that she was a tall, slender woman of about twenty-five, not bad-looking, but with a pallid and haggard appearance from recent illness. She was clothed in a kind of tawdry blue dress, much soiled and torn, and had over her shoulders an old tartan shawl, which she drew tightly across her breast as the strangers entered. Her grand-mother, who looked more weird and grotesquely horrible than ever, saluted Calton and the detective on their entrance with a shrill yell, and a volley of choice language.

'Oh, ye've come again, 'ave ye,' she screeched, raising her skinny arms, 'to take my gal away from 'er pore old gran'mother, as nussed 'er, cuss her, when 'er own mother had gone a-gallivantin' with swells. I'll 'ave the lawr of ye both, s'elp me, I will.' Kilsip paid no attention to this outbreak of the old fury, but turned to the girl.

'This is the gentleman who wants to speak to you,' he said, gently, making the girl sit on the chair again, for indeed she looked too ill to stand. 'Just tell him what you told me.'

''Bout the 'Queen,' sir?' said Sal, in a low, hoarse voice, fixing her wild eyes on Calton. 'If I'd only known as you was a-wantin' me I'd 'ave come afore.'

'Where were you?' asked Calton, in a pitying tone.

'Noo South Wales,' answered the girl with a shiver. 'The cove as I went with t' Sydney left me — yes, left me to die like a dog in the gutter.'

'Cuss 'im!' croaked the old woman in a sympathetic manner, as she took a drink from the broken cup.

'I tooked up with a Chinerman,' went on her granddaughter, wearily, 'an' lived with 'im for a bit — it's orful, ain't it?' she said with a dreary laugh, as she saw the disgust on the lawyer's face. 'But Chinermen ain't bad; they treat a pore girl a dashed sight better nor a white cove does. They don't beat the life out of 'em with their fists, nor drag 'em about the floor by the 'air.'

'Cuss 'em!' croaked Mother Guttersnipe, drowsily, 'I'll tear their 'earts out.'

'I think I must have gone mad, I must,' said Sal, pushing her tangled hair off her forehead, 'for arter I left the Chiner cove, I went on walkin' and walkin' right into the bush, a-tryin' to cool my 'ead, for it felt on fire like. I went into a river an' got wet, an' then I took my 'at an' boots orf an' lay down on the grass, an' then the rain comed on, an' I walked to a 'ouse as was near, where they tooked me in. Oh, sich kind people,' she sobbed, stretching out her hands, 'that didn't badger me 'bout my soul, but gave me good food to eat. I gave 'em a wrong name. I was so 'fraid of that Army a-findin' me. Then I got ill, an' know'd nothin' for weeks. They said I was orf my chump. An' then I came back 'ere to see gran'.'

'Cuss ye,' said the old woman, but in such a tender tone that it sounded like a blessing.

'And did the people who took you in never tell you anything about the murder?' asked Calton.

Sal shook her head.

'No, it were a long way in the country, and they never know'd anythin', they didn't.'

'Ah! that explains it,' muttered Calton to himself.

'Come, now,' he said cheerfully, 'tell me all that happened on the night you brought Mr. Fitzgerald to see the 'Queen.' '

'Who's 'e?' asked Sal, puzzled.

'Mr. Fitzgerald, the gentleman you brought the letter for to the Melbourne Club.'

'Oh, 'im?' said Sal, a sudden light breaking over her wan face. 'I never know'd his name afore.'

Calton nodded complacently.

'I knew you didn't,' he said, 'that's why you didn't ask for him at the Club.'

'She never told me 'is name,' said Sal, jerking her head in the direction of the bed.

'Then whom did she ask you to bring to her?' asked Calton, eagerly.

'No one,' replied the girl. 'This was the way of it. On that night she was orfil ill, an' I sat beside 'er while gran' was asleep.'

'I was drunk,' broke in gran', fiercely, 'none of yer lies; I was blazin' drunk.'

'An' ses she to me, she ses,' went on the girl, indifferent to her grandmother's interruption, ''Get me some paper an' a pencil, an' I'll write a note to 'im, I will.' So I goes an' gits 'er what she arsks fur out of gran's box.'

'Stole it, cuss ye,' shrieked the old hag, shaking her fist.

'Hold your tongue,' said Kilsip, in a peremptory tone.

Mother Guttersnipe burst into a volley of oaths, and having run rapidly through all she knew, subsided into a sulky silence.

'She wrote on it,' went on Sal, 'an' then arsked me to take it to the Melbourne Club an' give it to 'im. Ses I, 'Who's 'im?' Ses she, 'It's on the letter; don't you arsk no questions an' you won't 'ear no lies, but give it to 'im at the Club, an' wait for 'im at the corner of Bourke Street and Russell Street.' So out I goes, and gives it to a cove at the Club, an' then 'e comes along, an' ses 'e, 'Take me to 'er,' and I tooked 'im.'

'And what like was the gentleman?'

'Oh, werry good lookin',' said Sal. 'Werry tall, with yeller 'air an' moustache. He 'ad party clothes on, an' a masher coat, an' a soft 'at.'

'That's Fitzgerald right enough,' muttered Calton. 'And what did he do when he came?'

'He goes right up to 'er, and she ses, 'Are you 'e?' and 'e ses, 'I am.' Then ses she, 'Do you know what I'm a-goin' to tell you?' an' 'e says, 'No.' Then she ses, 'It's about 'er;' and ses 'e, lookin' very white, 'Ow dare you 'ave 'er name on your vile lips?' an' she gits up an' screeches, 'Turn that gal out, an' I'll tell you;' an' 'e takes me by the arm, an' ses 'e, 'Ere git out,' an' I gits out, an' that's all I knows.'

'And how long was he with her?' asked Calton, who had been listening attentively.

''Bout arf-a-hour,' answered Sal. 'I takes 'im back to Russell Street 'bout twenty-five minutes to two, 'cause I looked at the clock on the Post Office, an' 'e gives me a sov., an' then he goes a-tearin' up the street like anything.'

'Take him about twenty minutes to walk to East Melbourne,' said Calton to himself.

'So he must just have got in at the time Mrs. Sampson said. He was in with the 'Queen' the whole time, I suppose?' he asked, looking keenly at Sal.

'I was at that door,' said Sal, pointing to it, 'an' 'e couldn't 'ave got out unless I'd seen 'im.'

'Oh, it's all right,' said Calton, nodding to Kilsip, 'there won't be any difficulty in proving an alibi. But I say,' he added, turning to Sal, 'what were they talking about?'

'I dunno,' answered Sal. 'I was at the door, an' they talks that quiet I couldn't 'ear 'em. Then he sings out, 'My G —, it's too horrible!' an' I 'ear 'er a larfin' like to bust, an' then 'e comes to me, and ses, quite wild like, 'Take me out of this 'ell!' an' I tooked 'im.'

'And when you came back?'

'She was dead.'

'Dead?'

'As a blessed door-nail,' said Sal, cheerfully.

'An' I never know'd I was in the room with a corpse,' wailed Mother Guttersnipe, waking up. 'Cuss 'er, she was allays a-doin' contrary things.'

'How do you know?' said Calton, sharply, as he rose to go.

'I know'd 'er longer nor you,' croaked the old woman, fixing one evil eye on the lawyer; 'an' I know what you'd like to know; but ye shan't, ye shan't.'

Calton turned from her with a shrug of his shoulders.

'You will come to the Court to-morrow with Mr. Kilsip,' he said to Sal, 'and tell what you have just now told me.'

'It's all true, s'elp me,' said Sal, eagerly; ''e was 'ere all the time.'

Calton stepped towards the door, followed by the detective, when Mother Guttersnipe rose.

'Where's the money for finin' her?' she screeched, pointing one skinny finger at Sal.

'Well, considering the girl found herself,' said Calton, dryly, 'the money is in the bank, and will remain there.'

'An' I'm to be done out of my 'ard earned tin, s'elp me?' howled the old fury. 'Cuss ye, I'll 'ave the lawr of ye, and get ye put in quod.'

'You'll go there yourself if you don't take care,' said Kilsip, in his soft, purring tones.

'Yah!' shrieked Mother Guttersnipe, snapping her fingers at him. 'What do I care about yer quod? Ain't I bin in Pentrig', an' it ain't 'urt me, it ain't? I'm as lively as a gal, I am.'

And the old fury, to prove the truth of her words, danced a kind of war dance in front of Mr. Calton, snapping her fingers and yelling out curses, as an accompaniment to her ballet. Her luxurious white hair streamed out during her gyrations, and with her grotesque appearance and the faint light of the candle, she presented a gruesome spectacle.

Calton remembered the tales he had heard of the women of Paris, at the revolution, and the way they danced 'La Carmagnole.' Mother Guttersnipe would have been in her element in that sea of blood and turbulence he thought. But he merely shrugged his shoulders, and walked out of the room, as with a final curse, delivered in a hoarse voice, Mother Guttersnipe sank exhausted on the floor, and yelled for gin.

19

The Verdict of the Jury.

Next morning the Court was crowded, and numbers were unable to gain admission. The news that Sal Rawlins, who alone could prove the innocence of the prisoner, had been found, and would appear in Court that morning, had spread like wildfire, and the acquittal of the prisoner was confidently expected by a large number of sympathising friends, who seemed to have sprung up on all sides, like mushrooms, in a single night. There were, of course, plenty of cautious people left who waited to hear the verdict of the jury before committing themselves, and who still believed him to be guilty. But the unexpected appearance of Sal Rawlins had turned the great tide of public feeling in favour of the prisoner, and many who had been loudest in their denunciations of Fitzgerald, were now more than half convinced of his innocence. Pious clergymen talked in an incoherent way about the finger of God and the innocent not suffering unjustly, which was a case of counting unhatched chickens, as the verdict had yet to be given.

Felix Rolleston awoke, and found himself famous in a small way. Out of good-natured sympathy, and a spice of contrariness, he had declared his belief in Brian's innocence, and now, to his astonishment, he found that his view of the matter was likely to prove correct. He received so much praise on all sides for his presumed perspicuity, that he soon began to think that he had believed in Fitzgerald's innocence by a calm course of reasoning, and not because of a desire to differ from every one else in their opinion of the case. After all, Felix Rolleston is not the only man who has been astonished to find greatness thrust upon him, and come to believe himself worthy of it. He was a wise man, however, and while in the full tide of prosperity he seized the flying moment, and proposed to Miss Feather-weight, who, after some hesitation, agreed to endow him with herself and her thousands. She decided that her future husband was a man of no common intellect, seeing that he had long ago arrived at a conclusion which the rest of Melbourne were only beginning to discover now, so she determined that, as soon as she assumed marital authority, Felix, like Strephon in 'Iolanthe,' should go into Parliament, and with her money and his brains she might some day be the wife of a premier. Mr. Rolleston had no idea of the political honours which his future spouse intended for him, and was seated in his old place in the court, talking about the case.

'Knew he was innocent, don't you know,' he said, with a complacent smile.

'Fitzgerald's too jolly good-looking a fellow, and all that sort of thing, to commit murder.'

Whereupon a clergyman, happening to overhear the lively Felix make this flippant remark, disagreed with it entirely, and preached a sermon to prove that good looks and crime were closely connected, and that both Judas Iscariot and Nero were beauty-men.

'Ah,' said Calton, when he heard the sermon, 'if this unique theory is a true one, what a truly pious man that clergyman must be!' This allusion to the looks of the reverend gentleman was rather unkind, for he was by no means bad-looking. But then Calton was one of those witty men who would rather lose a friend than suppress an epigram. When the prisoner was brought in, a murmur of sympathy ran through the crowded Court, so ill and worn-out he looked; but Calton was puzzled to account for the expression of his face, so different from that of a man whose life had been saved, or, rather, was about to be saved, for in truth it was a foregone conclusion.

'You know who stole those papers,' he thought, as he looked at Fitzgerald, keenly, 'and the man who did so is the murderer of Whyte.'

The judge having entered, and the Court being opened, Calton rose to make his speech, and stated in a few words the line of defence he intended to take. He would first call Albert Dendy, a watchmaker, to prove that on Thursday night, at eight o'clock in the evening, he had called at the prisoner's lodgings while the landlady was out, and while there had put the kitchen clock right, and had regulated the same. He would also call Felix Rolleston, a friend of the prisoner's, to prove that the prisoner was not in the habit of wearing rings, and frequently expressed his detestation of such a custom. Sebastian Brown, a waiter at the Melbourne Club, would be called to prove that on Thursday night a letter was delivered to the prisoner at the Club by one Sarah Rawlins, and that the prisoner left the Club shortly before one o'clock on Friday morning. He would also call Sarah Rawlins, to prove that she had delivered a note to Sebastian Brown for the prisoner, at the Melbourne Club, at a quarter to twelve on Thursday Night, and that at a few minutes past one o'clock on Friday morning she had conducted the prisoner to a slum off Little Bourke Street, and that he was there between one and two on Friday morning, the hour at which the murder was alleged to have taken place. This being his defence to the charge brought against the prisoner, he would call Albert Dendy.

Albert Dendy, duly sworn, stated: —

I am a watchmaker, and carry on business in Fitzroy. I remember Thursday, the 26th of July last. On the evening of that day I called at Powlett Street East Melbourne, to see my aunt, who is the landlady of the prisoner. She was out at the time I called, and I waited in the kitchen till her return. I looked at the kitchen clock to see if it was too late to wait, and then at my watch. I found that the clock was ten minutes fast, upon which I put it right, and regulated it properly.

CALTON: At what time did you put it right?

WITNESS: About eight o'clock.

CALTON: Between that time and two in the morning, was it possible for the clock to gain ten minutes?

WITNESS: No, it was not possible.

CALTON: Would it gain at all?

WITNESS: Not between eight and two

o'clock — the time was not long enough.

CALTON: Did you see your aunt that night?

WITNESS: Yes, I waited till she came in.

CALTON: And did you tell her you had put the clock right?

WITNESS: No, I did not; I forgot all about it.

CALTON: Then she was still under the impression that it was ten minutes fast?

WITNESS: Yes, I suppose so.

After Dendy had been cross-examined, Felix Rolleston was called, and deposed as follows: —

I am an intimate friend of the prisoner. I have known him for five or six years, and I never saw him wearing a ring during that time. He has frequently told me he did not care for rings, and would never wear them.

In cross-examination: —

CROWN PROSECUTOR: You have never seen the prisoner wearing a diamond ring?

WITNESS: No, never.

CROWN PROSECUTOR: Have you ever seen any such ring in his possession?

WITNESS: No, I have seen him buying rings for ladies, but I never saw him with any ring such as a gentleman would wear.

CROWN PROSECUTOR: Not even a seal ring.

WITNESS: No, not even a seal ring.

Sarah Rawlins was then placed in the witness-box, and, after having been sworn, deposed: —

I know the prisoner. I delivered a letter, addressed to him at the Melbourne Club, at a quarter to twelve o'clock on Thursday, 26th July. I did not know what his name was. He met me shortly after one, at the corner of Russell and Bourke Streets, where I had been told to wait for him. I took him to my grandmother's place, in a lane off Little Bourke Street. There was a dying woman there, who had sent for him. He went in and saw her for about twenty minutes, and then I took him back to the corner of Bourke and Russell Streets. I heard the three-quarters strike shortly after I left him.

CROWN PROSECUTOR: You are quite certain that the prisoner was the man you met on that night?

WITNESS: Quite certin', s'elp me G — .

CROWN PROSECUTOR: And he met you a few minutes past one o'clock?

WITNESS: Yes, 'bout five minutes — I 'eard the clock a-strikin' one just afore he came down the street, and when I leaves 'im agin, it were about twenty-five to two, 'cause it took me ten minits to git 'ome, and I 'eard the clock go three-quarters, jest as I gits to the door.

CROWN PROSECUTOR: How do you know it was exactly twenty-five to two when you left him?

WITNESS: 'Cause I sawr the clocks — I left 'im at the corner of Russell Street, and comes down Bourke Street, so I could see the Post Orffice clock as plain as day, an' when I gets into Swanston Street, I looks at the Town 'All premiscus like, and sees the same time there.

CROWN PROSECUTOR: And you never lost sight of the prisoner the whole time?

WITNESS: No, there was only one door by the room, an' I was a-sittin' outside it, an' when he comes out he falls over me.

CROWN PROSECUTOR: Were you asleep?

WITNESS: Not a blessed wink.

Calton then directed Sebastian Brown to be called. He deposed: —

I know the prisoner. He is a member of the Melbourne Club, at which I am a waiter. I remember Thursday, 26th July. On that night the last witness came with a letter to the prisoner. It was about a quarter to twelve. She just gave it to me, and went away. I delivered it to Mr. Fitzgerald. He left the Club at about ten minutes to one.

This closed the evidence for the defence,

and after the Crown prosecutor had made his speech, in which he pointed out the strong evidence against the prisoner, Calton arose to address the jury. He was a fine speaker, and made a splendid defence. Not a single point escaped him, and that brilliant piece of oratory is still remembered and spoken of admiringly in the purlieus of Temple Court and Chancery Lane.

He began by giving a vivid description of the circumstances, of the murder — of the meeting of the murderer and his victim in Collins Street East — the cab driving down to St. Kilda — the getting out of the cab of the murderer after committing the crime — and the way in which he had secured himself against pursuit.

Having thus enchained the attention of the jury by the graphic manner in which he described the crime, he pointed out that the evidence brought forward by the prosecution was purely circumstantial, and that they had utterly failed to identify the prisoner in the dock with the man who entered the cab. The supposition that the prisoner and the man in the light coat were one and the same person, rested solely upon the evidence of the cabman, Royston, who, although not intoxicated, was — judging from his own statements, not in a fit state to distinguish between the man who hailed the cab, and the man who got in. The crime was committed by means of chloroform; therefore, if the prisoner was guilty, he must have purchased the chloroform in some shop, or obtained it from some friends. At all events, the prosecution had not brought forward a single piece of evidence to show how, and where the chloroform had been obtained. With regard to the glove belonging to the murdered man found in the prisoner's pocket, he picked it up off the ground at the time when he first met Whyte, when the deceased was lying drunk near the Scotch Church. Certainly there was no evidence to show that the prisoner had picked it up before the deceased entered the cab; but, on the other hand, there was no evidence to show that it had been picked up in the cab. It was far more likely that the glove, and especially a white glove, would be picked up under the light of the lamp near the Scotch Church, where it was easily noticeable, than in the darkness of a cab, where there was very little room, and where it would be quite dark, as the blinds were drawn down. The cabman, Royston, swore positively that the man who got out of his cab on the St. Kilda Road wore a diamond ring on the forefinger of his right hand, and the cabman, Rankin, swore to the same thing about the man who got out at Powlett Street. Against this could be placed the evidence of one of the prisoner's most intimate friends — one who had seen him almost daily for the last five years, and he had sworn positively that the prisoner was not in the habit of wearing rings.

The cabman Rankin had also sworn that the man who entered his cab on the St. Kilda Road alighted at Powlett Street, East Melbourne, at two o'clock on Friday morning, as he heard that hour strike from the Post Office clock, whereas the evidence of the prisoner's landlady showed plainly that he entered the house five minutes previously, and her evidence was further supported by that of the watchmaker, Dendy. Mrs. Sampson saw the hand of her kitchen clock point to five minutes to two, and, thinking it was ten minutes slow, told the detective that the prisoner did not enter the house till five minutes past two, which would just give the man who alighted from the cab (presuming him to have been the prisoner) sufficient time to walk up to his lodgings. The evidence of the watchmaker, Dendy, however, showed clearly that he had put the clock right at the hour of eight on Thursday night; that it was impossible for it to gain ten minutes before two on Friday morning, and therefore, the time, five minutes to two, seen by the landlady was the correct one, and the prisoner was in the house five minutes before the other man alighted from the cab in Powlett Street.

These points in themselves were sufficient to show that the prisoner was innocent, but the evidence of the woman Rawlins must prove conclusively to the jury that the prisoner was not the man who committed the crime. The witness Brown had proved that the woman Rawlins had delivered a letter to him, which he gave to the prisoner and that the prisoner left the Club, to keep the appointment spoken of in the letter, which letter, or, rather, the remains of it had been put in evidence. The woman Rawlins swore that the prisoner met her at the corner of Russell and Bourke Streets, and had gone with her to one of the back slums, there to see the writer of the letter. She also proved that at the time of the committal of the crime the prisoner was still in the back slum, by the bed of the dying woman, and, there being only one door to the room, he could not possibly have left without the witness seeing him. The woman Rawlins further proved that she left the prisoner at the corner of Bourke and Russell Streets at twenty-five minutes to two o'clock, which was five minutes before

Royston drove his cab up to the St. Kilda Police Station, with the dead body inside. Finally, the woman Rawlins proved her words by stating that she saw both the Post Office and Town Hall clocks; and supposing the prisoner started from the corner of Bourke and Russell Streets, as she says he did, he would reach East Melbourne in twenty minutes, which made it five minutes to two on Friday morning, the time at which, according to the landlady's statement, he entered the house.

All the evidence given by the different witnesses agreed completely, and formed a chain which showed the whole of the prisoner's movements at the time of the committal of the murder. Therefore, it was absolutely impossible that the murder could have been committed by the man in the dock. The strongest piece of evidence brought forward by the prosecution was that of the witness Hableton, who swore that the prisoner used threats against the life of the deceased. But the language used was merely the outcome of a passionate Irish nature, and was not sufficient to prove the crime to have been committed by the prisoner. The defence which the prisoner set up was that of an alibi, and the evidence of the witnesses for the defence proved conclusively that the prisoner could not, and did not, commit the murder. Finally, Calton wound up his elaborate and exhaustive speech, which lasted for over two hours, by a brilliant peroration, calling upon the jury to base their verdict upon the plain facts of the case, and if they did so they could hardly fail in bringing in a verdict of 'Not Guilty.'

When Calton sat down a subdued murmur of applause was heard, which was instantly suppressed, and the judge began to sum up, strongly in favour of Fitzgerald. The jury then retired, and immediately there was a dead silence in the crowded Court — an unnatural silence, such as must have fallen on the blood-loving Roman populace when they saw the Christian martyrs kneeling on the hot yellow sands of the arena, and watched the long, lithe forms of lion and panther creeping steadily towards their prey. The hour being late the gas had been lighted, and there was a sickly glare through the wide hall.

Fitzgerald had been taken out of court on the retiring of the jury, but the spectators stared steadily at the empty dock, which seemed to enchain them by some indescribable fascination. They conversed among themselves only in whispers, until even the whispering ceased, and nothing could be heard but the steady ticking of the clock, and now and then the quick-drawn breath of some timid on-looker. Suddenly, a woman, whose nerves were over-strung, shrieked, and the cry rang weirdly through the crowded hall. She was taken out, and again there was silence, every eye being now fixed on the door through which the jury would re-issue with their verdict of life or death. The hands of the clock moved slowly round — a quarter — a half — three quarters — and then the hour sounded with a silvery ring which startled everyone. Madge, sitting with her hands tightly clasped together, began to fear that her highly-strung nerves would give way.

'My God,' she muttered softly to herself; 'will this suspense never end?'

Just then the door opened, and the jury re-entered. The prisoner was again placed in the dock, and the judge resumed his seat, this time with the black cap in his pocket, as everyone guessed.

The usual formalities were gone through, and when the foreman of the jury stood up every neck was craned forward, and every ear was on the alert to catch the words that fell from his lips. The prisoner flushed a little and then grew pale as death, giving a quick, nervous glance at the quiet figure in black, of which he could just catch a glimpse. Then came the verdict, sharp and decisive, 'NOT

GUILTY.' On hearing this a cheer went up from everyone in the court, so strong was the sympathy with Brian.

In vain the crier of the Court yelled, 'Order!' until he was red in the face. In vain the judge threatened to commit all present for contempt of court — his voice being inaudible, it did not matter much — the enthusiasm could not be restrained, and it was five minutes before order was obtained. The judge, having recovered his composure, delivered his judgment, and discharged the prisoner, in accordance with the verdict. Calton had won many cases, but it is questionable if he had ever heard a verdict which gave him so much satisfaction as that which proclaimed Fitzgerald innocent. And Brian, stepping down from the dock a free man, passed through a crowd of congratulating friends to a small room off the Court, where a woman was waiting for him — a woman who clung round his neck, and sobbed out —

'My darling! My darling! I knew that God would save you.'

20

The *Argus* Gives its Opinion.

The morning after the trial was concluded the following article in reference to the matter appeared in the *Argus*: —

'During the past three months we have frequently in our columns commented on the extraordinary case which is now so widely known as 'The Hansom Cab Tragedy.' We can safely say that it is the most remarkable case which has ever come under the notice of our Criminal Court, and the verdict given by the jury yesterday has enveloped the matter in a still deeper mystery. By a train of strange coincidences, Mr. Brian Fitzgerald, a young squatter, was suspected of having murdered Whyte, and had it not been for the timely appearance of the woman Rawlins who turned up at the eleventh hour, we feel sure that a verdict of guilty would have been given, and an innocent man would have suffered punishment for the crime of another. Fortunately for the prisoner, and for the interests of justice, his counsel, Mr. Calton, by unwearied diligence, was able to discover the last witness, and prove an alibi. Had it not been for this, in spite of the remarks made by the learned counsel in his brilliant speech yesterday, which resulted in the acquittal of the prisoner, we question very much if the rest of the evidence in favour of the accused would have been sufficient to persuade the jury that he was an innocent man. The only points in favour of Mr. Fitzgerald were the inability of the cabman Royston to swear to him as the man who had got into the cab with Whyte, the wearing of a diamond ring on the forefinger of the right hand (whereas Mr. Fitzgerald wears no rings), and the difference in time sworn to by the cabman Rankin and the landlady. Against these points, however, the prosecution placed a mass of evidence, which seemed conclusively to prove the guilt of the prisoner; but the appearance of Sal Rawlins in the witness-box put an end to all doubt. In language which could not be mistaken for anything else than the truth, she positively swore that Mr. Fitzgerald was in one of the slums off Bourke Street, between the hours of one and two on Friday morning, at which time the murder was committed. Under these circumstances, the jury unanimously agreed, and returned a verdict of 'Not guilty,' and the prisoner was forthwith acquitted. We have to congratulate his counsel, Mr. Calton, for the able speech he made for the defence, and also Mr. Fitzgerald, for his providential escape from a dishonourable and undeserved punishment. He leaves the court without a stain on his character, and with the respect and sympathy of all Australians, for the courage and dignity with which he comported himself through-out, while resting under the shadow of such a serious charge.

'But now that it has been conclusively proved that he is innocent, the question arises in every one's mind, 'Who is the murderer of Oliver Whyte?' The man who committed this dastardly crime is still at large, and, for all we know, may be in our midst. Emboldened by the impunity with which he has escaped the hands of justice, he may be walking securely down our streets, and talking of the very crime of which he is the perpetrator. Secure in the thought that all traces of him have been lost for ever, from the time he alighted from Rankin's cab, at Powlett Street, he has ventured probably to remain in Melbourne, and, for all that anyone knows, he may have been in the court during the late trial. Nay, this very article, may meet his eye, and he may rejoice at the futile efforts which have been made to find him. But let him beware, Justice is not blind, but blind-folded, and when he least expects it, she will tear the bandage from her keen eyes, and drag him forth to the light of day to receive the reward of his deed. Owing to the strong evidence against Fitzgerald, that is the only direction in which the detectives have hitherto looked, but baffled on one side, they will look on the other, and this time may be successful.

'That such a man as the murderer of Oliver Whyte should be at large is a matter of danger, not only to individual citizens, but to the community at large; for it is a well-known fact that a tiger who once tastes human blood never overcomes his craving for it; and, without doubt the man who so daringly and coolly murdered a drunken, and therefore defenceless man, will not hesitate to commit a second crime. The present feeling of all classes in Melbourne must be one of terror, that such a man should be at large, and must, in a great measure, resemble the fear which filled everyone's heart in London when the Marr murders were committed, and it was known that the murderer had escaped. Anyone who has read De Quincy's graphic description of the crime perpetrated by Williams must tremble to think that such another devil incarnate is in our midst. It is an imperative necessity that such a feeling should be done away with. But how is this to be managed? It is one thing to speak, and another to act. There seems to be no possible clue discoverable at present which can lead to the discovery of the real murderer. The man in the light coat who got out of Rankin's cab at Powlett Street, East Melbourne (designedly, as it now appears, in order to throw suspicion on Fitzgerald), has vanished as completely as the witches in Macbeth, and left no trace behind. It was two o'clock in the morning when he left the cab, and, in a quiet suburb like East Melbourne, no one would be about, so that he could easily escape unseen. There seems to be only one chance of ever tracing him, and that is to be found in the papers which were stolen from the pocket of the dead man. What they were, only two persons knew, and one knows now. The first two were Whyte and the woman who was called 'The Queen,' and both of them are now dead. The other who knows now is the man who committed the crime. There can be no doubt that these papers were the motive for the crime, as no money was taken from the pockets of the deceased. The fact, also, that the papers were carried in a pocket made inside the waistcoat of the deceased shows that they were of value.

'Now, the reason we think that the dead woman knew of the existence of these papers is simply this. It appears that she came out from England with Whyte as his mistress, and after staying some time in Sydney came on to Melbourne. How she came into such a foul and squalid den as that she died in, we are unable to say, unless, seeing that she was given to drink, she was picked up drunk by some Samaritan of the slums, and carried to Mrs. Rawlins' humble abode. Whyte visited her there frequently, but appears to have made no attempt to remove her to a better place, alleging as his reason that the doctor said she would die if taken into the air. Our reporter learned from one of the detectives that the dead woman was in the habit of talking to Whyte about certain papers, and on one occasion was overheard to say to him, 'They'll make your fortune if you play your cards well.' This was told to the detective by the woman Rawlins, to whose providential appearance Mr. Fitzgerald owes his escape. From this it can be gathered that the papers — whatever they might be — were of value, and sufficient to tempt another to commit a murder in order to obtain them. Whyte, therefore, being dead, and his murderer having escaped, the only way of discovering the secret which lies at the root of this tree of crime, is to find out the history of the woman who died in the slum. Traced back for some years, circumstances may be discovered which will reveal what these papers contained, and once that is found, we can confidently say that the murderer will soon be discovered. This is the only chance of finding out the cause, and the author of this mysterious murder; and if it fails, we fear the hansom cab tragedy will have to be relegated to the list of undiscovered crimes, and the assassin of Whyte will have no other punishment than that of the remorse of his own conscience.'

21

Three Months Afterwards.

A hot December day, with a cloudless blue sky, and a sun blazing down on the earth, clothed in all the beauty of summer garments. Such a description of snowy December sounds perchance a trifle strange to English ears. It may strike them as being somewhat fantastic, as was the play in 'A Midsummer Night's Dream,' to Demetrius when he remarked, 'This is hot ice and wondrous cold fire.'

But here in Australia we are in the realm of contrariety, and many things other than dreams go by contrary. Here black swans are an established fact, and the proverb concerning them, made when they were considered as mythical a bird as the Phoenix, has been rendered null and void by the discoveries of Captain Cook. Here ironwood sinks and pumice stone floats, which must strike the curious spectator as a queer freak on the part of Dame Nature. At home the Edinburgh mail bears the hardy traveller to a cold climate, with snowy mountains and wintry blasts; but here the further north one goes the hotter it gets, till one arrives in Queensland, where the heat is so great that a profane traveller of an epigrammatic turn of mind once fittingly called it, 'An amateur hell.'

But however contrary, as Mrs. Gamp would say, Nature may be in her dealings, the English race out in this great continent are much the same as in the old country — John Bull, Paddy, and Sandy, all being of a conservative turn of mind, and with strong opinions as to the keeping up of old customs. Therefore, on a hot Christmas day, with the sun one hundred odd in the shade, Australian revellers sit down to the roast beef and plum-pudding of Old England, which they eat contentedly as the orthodox thing, and on New Year's Eve the festive Celt repairs to the doors of his 'freends' with a bottle of whisky and a cheering verse of 'Auld Lang Syne'.

Still it is these peculiar customs that give an individuality to a nation, and John Bull abroad loses none of his insular obstinacy; but keeps his Christmas in the old fashion, and wears his clothes in the new fashion, without regard to heat or cold. A nation that never surrenders to the fire of an enemy cannot be expected to give in to the fire of the sun, but if some ingenious mortal would only invent some light and airy costume, after the fashion of the Greek dress, and Australians would consent to adopt the same, life in Melbourne and her sister cities would be much cooler than it is at present.

Madge was thinking somewhat after this fashion as she sat on the wide verandah, in a state of exhaustion from the heat, and stared out at the wide plains lying parched and arid under the blazing sun. There was a dim kind of haze rising from the excessive heat, hanging midway between heaven and earth, and through its tremulous veil the distant hills looked aerial and unreal.

Stretched out before her was the garden with its intensely vivid flowers. To look at them merely was to increase one's caloric condition. Great bushes of oleanders, with their bright pink blossoms, luxurious rose trees, with their yellow, red, and white blooms, and all along the border a rainbow of many-coloured flowers, with such brilliant tints that the eye ached to see them in the hot sunshine, and turned restfully to the cool green of the trees which encircled the lawn. In the centre was a round pool, surrounded by a ring of white marble, and containing a still sheet of water, which flashed like a mirror in the blinding light.

The homestead of Yabba Yallook station was a long low house, with no upper-storey, and with a wide verandah running nearly round it. Cool green blinds were hung between the pillars to keep out the sun, and all along were scattered lounging chairs of basket-work, with rugs, novels, empty soda-water bottles, and all the other evidences that Mr. Frettlby's guests had been wise, and stayed inside during the noonday heat. Madge was seated in one of these comfortable chairs, and she divided her attention between the glowing beauty of the world outside, which she could see through a narrow slit in the blinds. But she did not seem greatly interested in her book, and it was not long before she let it fall unheeded to the ground and took refuge in her own thoughts. The trial through which she had so recently passed had been a great one, and it had not been without its outward result. It had left its impress on her beautiful face, and there was a troubled look in her eyes. After Brian's acquittal of the murder of Oliver Whyte, she had been taken by her father up to the station, in the hope that it would restore her to health. The mental strain which had been on her during the trial had nearly brought on an attack of brain fever; but here, far from the excitement of town life, in the quiet seclusion of the country, she had recovered her health, but not her spirits.

Women are more impressionable than men, and it is, perhaps, for this reason that they age quicker. A trouble which would pass lightly over a man, leaves an indelible mark on a woman, both physically and mentally, and the terrible episode of Whyte's murder had changed Madge from a bright and merry girl into a grave and beautiful woman. Sorrow is a potent enchantress. Once she touches the heart, life can never be quite the same again. We never more surrender ourselves entirely to pleasure; and often we find so many of the things we have longed for are after all but Dead Sea fruit. Sorrow is the veiled Isis of the world, and once we penetrate her mystery and see her deeply-furrowed face and mournful eyes, the magic light of romance dies all away, and we realise the hard bitter fact of life in all its nakedness.

Madge felt something of all this. She saw the world now, not as the fantastic fairyland of her girlish dreams, but as the sorrowful vale of tears through which we must all walk till we reach the 'Promised Land.'

And Brian, he also had undergone a change, for there were a few white hairs now amid his curly, chestnut locks, and his character, from being gay and bright, had become moody and irritable. After the trial he had left town immediately, in order to avoid meeting with his friends, and had gone up to his station, which was next to that of the Frettlbys'. There he worked hard all day, and smoked hard all night, thinking ever the secret which the dead woman had told him, and which threatened to overshadow his life. Every now and then he rode over and saw Madge. But this was generally when he knew her father to be away from Melbourne, for of late he had disliked the millionaire. Madge could not but condemn his attitude, remembering how her father had stood beside him in his recent trouble. Yet there was another reason why Brian kept aloof from Yabba Yallook station. He did not wish to meet any of the gay society which was there, knowing that since his trial he was an object of curiosity and sympathy to everyone — a position galling enough to his proud nature.

At Christmas time Mr. Frettlby had asked several people up from Melbourne, and though Madge would rather have been left alone, yet she could not refuse her father, and had to play hostess with a smiling brow and aching heart.

Felix Rolleston, who a month since had joined the noble army of benedicts, was there with Mrs. Rolleston, *née* Miss Featherweight, who ruled him with a rod of iron. Having bought Felix with her money, she had determined to make good use of him, and, being ambitious to shine in Melbourne society, had insisted upon Felix studying politics, so that when the next general election came round he could enter Parliament. Felix had rebelled at first, but ultimately gave way, as he found that when he had a good novel concealed among his parliamentary papers time passed quite pleasantly, and he got the reputation of a hard worker at little cost. They had brought up Julia with them, and this young person had made up her mind to become the second Mrs. Frettlby. She had not received much encouragement, but, like the English at Waterloo, did not know when she was beaten, and carried on the siege of Mr. Frettlby's heart in an undaunted manner.

Dr. Chinston had come up for a little relaxation, and gave never a thought to his anxious patients or the many sick-rooms he was in the habit of visiting. A young English fellow, called Peterson, who amused himself by travelling; an old colonist, full of reminiscences of the old days, when, 'by gad, sir, we hadn't a gas lamp in the whole of Melbourne,' and several other people, completed the party. They had all gone off to the billiard-room, and left Madge in her comfortable chair, half-asleep. Suddenly she started, as she heard a step behind her, and turning, saw Sal Rawlins, in the neatest of black gowns, with a coquettish white cap and apron, and an open book. Madge had been so delighted with Sal for saving Brian's life that she had taken her into her service as maid. Mr. Frettlby had offered strong opposition at first that a fallen woman like Sal should be near his daughter; but Madge was determined to rescue the unhappy girl from the life of sin she was leading, and so at last he reluctantly consented. Brian, too, had objected, but ultimately yielded, as he saw that Madge had set her heart on it. Mother Guttersnipe objected at first, characterising the whole affair as 'cussed 'umbug,' but she, likewise, gave in, and Sal became maid to Miss Frettlby, who immediately set to work to remedy Sal's defective education by teaching her to read. The book she held in her hand was a spelling-book, and this she handed to Madge.

'I think I knows it now, miss,' she said, respectfully, as Madge looked up with a smile.

'Do you, indeed?' said Madge, gaily. 'You will be able to read in no time, Sal.'

'Read this?' said Sal, touching 'Tristan: A

Romance, by Zoe.'

'Hardly!' said Madge, picking it up, with a look of contempt.

'I want you to learn English, and not a confusion of tongues like this thing. But it's too hot for lessons, Sal,' she went on, leaning back in her seat, 'so get a chair and talk to me.'

Sal complied, and Madge looked out at the brilliant flower-beds, and at the black shadow of the tall witch elm which grew on one side of the lawn. She wanted to ask a certain question of Sal, and did not know how to do it. The moodiness and irritability of Brian had troubled her very much of late, and, with the quick instinct of her sex, she ascribed it indirectly to the woman who had died in the back slum. Anxious to share his troubles and lighten his burden, she determined to ask Sal about this mysterious woman, and find out, if possible, what secret had been told to Brian which affected him so deeply.

'Sal,' she said, after a short pause, turning her clear grey eyes on the woman, 'I want to ask you something.'

The other shivered and turned pale.

'About — about that?'

Madge nodded.

Sal hesitated for a moment, and then flung herself at the feet of her mistress.

'I will tell you,' she cried. 'You have been kind to me, an' have a right to know. I will tell you all I know.'

'Then,' asked Madge, firmly, as she clasped her hands tightly together, 'who was this woman whom Mr. Fitzgerald went to see, and where did she come from?'

'Gran' an' me found her one evenin' in Little Bourke Street,' answered Sal, 'just near the theatre. She was quite drunk, an' we took her home with us.'

'How kind of you,' said Madge.

'Oh, it wasn't that,' replied the other, dryly. 'Gran' wanted her clothes; she was awful swell dressed.'

'And she took the clothes — how wicked!'

'Anyone would have done it down our way,' answered Sal, indifferently; 'but Gran' changed her mind when she got her home. I went out to get some gin for Gran', and when I came back she was huggin' and kissin' the woman.'

'She recognised her.'

'Yes, I s'pose so,' replied Sal, 'an' next mornin', when the lady got square, she made a grab at Gran', an' hollered out, 'I was comin' to see you.' '

'And then?'

'Gran' chucked me out of the room, an' they had a long jaw; and then, when I come back, Gran' tells me the lady is a-goin' to stay with us 'cause she was ill, and sent me for Mr. Whyte.'

'And he came?'

'Oh, yes — often,' said Sal. 'He kicked up a row when he first turned up, but when he found she was ill, he sent a doctor; but it warn't no good. She was two weeks with us, and then died the mornin' she saw Mr. Fitzgerald.'

'I suppose Mr. Whyte was in the habit of talking to this woman?'

'Lots,' returned Sal; 'but he always turned Gran' an' me out of the room afore he started.'

'And' — hesitating — 'did you ever overhear one of these conversations?'

'Yes — one,' answered the other, with a nod. 'I got riled at the way he cleared us out of our own room; and once, when he shut the door and Gran' went off to get some gin, I sat down at the door and listened. He wanted her to give up some papers, an' she wouldn't. She said she'd die first; but at last he got 'em, and took 'em away with him.'

'Did you see them?' asked Madge, as the assertion of Gorby that Whyte had been murdered for certain papers flashed across her mind.

'Rather,' said Sal, 'I was looking through a

269

hole in the door, an' she takes 'em from under her piller, an' 'e takes 'em to the table, where the candle was, an' looks at 'em — they were in a large blue envelop, with writing on it in red ink — then he put 'em in his pocket, and she sings out: 'You'll lose 'em,' an' 'e says: 'No, I'll always 'ave 'em with me, an' if 'e wants 'em 'e'll have to kill me fust afore 'e gits 'em.' '

'And you did not know who the man was to whom the papers were of such importance?'

'No, I didn't; they never said no names.'

'And when was it Whyte got the papers?'

'About a week before he was murdered,' said Sal, after a moment's thought. 'An' after that he never turned up again. She kept watchin' for him night an' day, an' 'cause he didn't come, got mad at him. I hear her sayin', 'You think you've done with me, my gentleman, an' leaves me here to die, but I'll spoil your little game,' an' then she wrote that letter to Mr. Fitzgerald, an' I brought him to her, as you know.'

'Yes, yes,' said Madge, rather impatiently. 'I heard all that at the trial, but what conversation passed between Mr. Fitzgerald and this woman? Did you hear it?'

'Bits of it,' replied the other. 'I didn't split in Court, 'cause I thought the lawyer would be down on me for listening. The first thing I heard Mr. Fitzgerald sayin' was, 'You're mad — it ain't true,' an' she ses, 'S'elp me it is, Whyte's got the proof,' an' then he sings out, 'My poor girl,' and she ses, 'Will you marry her now?' and ses he, 'I will, I love her more than ever;' and then she makes a grab at him, and says, 'Spile his game if you can,' and says he, 'What's yer name?' and she says — '

'What?' asked Madge, breathlessly.

'Rosanna Moore!'

There was a sharp exclamation as Sal said the name, and, turning round quickly, Madge found Brian standing beside her, pale as death, with his eyes fixed on the woman, who had risen to her feet.

'Go on!' he said sharply.

'That's all I know,' she replied, in a sullen tone. Brian gave a sigh of relief.

'You can go,' he said slowly; 'I wish to speak with Miss Frettlby alone.'

Sal looked at him for a moment, and then glanced at her mistress, who nodded to her as a sign that she might withdraw. She picked up her book, and with another sharp enquiring look at Brian, turned and walked slowly into the house.

22

A Daughter of Eve.

After Sal had gone, Brian sank into a chair beside Madge with a weary sigh. He was in riding dress, which became his stalwart figure well, and he looked remarkably handsome but ill and worried.

'What on earth were you questioning that girl about?' he said abruptly, taking his hat off, and tossing it and his gloves on to the floor.

Madge flushed crimson for a moment, and then taking Brian's two strong hands in her own, looked steadily into his frowning face.

'Why don't you trust me?' she asked, in a quiet tone.

'It is not necessary that I should,' he answered moodily. 'The secret that Rosanna Moore told me on her death-bed is nothing that would benefit you to know.'

'Is it about me?' she persisted.

'It is, and it is not,' he answered, epigrammatically.

'I suppose that means that it is about a third person, and concerns me,' she said calmly, releasing his hands.

'Well, yes,' impatiently striking his boot with his riding whip. 'But it is nothing that can harm you so long as you do not know it; but God help you should anyone tell it to you, for it would embitter your life.'

'My life being so very sweet now,' answered Madge, with a slight sneer. 'You are trying to put out a fire by pouring oil on it, and what you say only makes me more determined to learn what it is.'

'Madge, I implore you not to persist in this foolish curiosity,' he said, almost fiercely, 'it will bring you only misery.'

'If it concerns me I have a right to know it,' she answered curtly. 'When I marry you how can we be happy together, with the shadow of a secret between us?'

Brian rose, and leaned against the verandah post with a dark frown on his face.

'Do you remember that verse of Browning's,' he said, coolly —

'Where the apple reddens
Never pry —
Lest we lose our Edens,
Eve and I.

'Singularly applicable to our present conversation, I think.'

'Ah,' she said, her pale face flushing with anger, 'you want me to live in a fool's paradise, which may end at any moment.'

'That depends upon yourself,' he answered coldly. 'I never roused your curiosity by telling you that there was a secret, but betrayed it inadvertently to Calton's cross-questioning. I tell you candidly that I did learn something from Rosanna Moore, and it concerns you, though only indirectly through a third person. But it would do no good to reveal it, and would ruin both our lives.'

She did not answer, but looked straight before her into the glowing sunshine. Brian fell on his knees beside her, and stretched out his hands with an entreating gesture.

'Oh, my darling,' he cried sadly, 'cannot you trust me? The love which has stood such a test as yours cannot fail like this. Let me bear the misery of knowing it alone, without blighting your young life with the knowledge of it. I would tell you if I could, but, God help me, I cannot — I cannot,' and he buried his face in his hands. Madge closed her mouth firmly, and touched his comely head with her cool, white fingers. There was a struggle going on in her breast between her feminine curiosity and her love for the man at her feet — the latter conquered, and she bowed her head over his.

'Brian,' she whispered softly, 'let it be as you wish. I will never again try to learn this secret, since you do not desire it.'

He arose to his feet, and caught her in his strong arms, with a glad smile.

'My dearest,' he said, kissing her passionately, and then for a few moments neither of them spoke. 'We will begin a new life,' he said, at length. 'We will put the sad past away from us, and think of it only as a dream.'

'But this secret will still fret you,' she murmured.

'It will wear away with time and with change of scene,' he answered sadly.

'Change of scene!' she repeated in a startled tone. 'Are you going away?'

'Yes; I have sold my station, and intend leaving Australia for ever during the next three months.'

'And where are you going?' asked the girl, rather bewildered.

'Anywhere,' he said a little bitterly. 'I am going to follow the example of Cain, and be a wanderer on the face of the earth!'

'Alone!'

'That is what I have come to see you about,' said Brian, looking steadily at her. 'I have come to ask you if you will marry me at once, and we will leave Australia together.'

She hesitated.

'I know it is asking a great deal,' he said, hurriedly, 'to leave your friends, your position, and' — with hesitation — 'your father; but think of my life without you — think how lonely I shall be, wandering round the world by myself; but you will not desert me now I have so much need of you — you will come with me and be my good angel in the future as you have been in the past?'

She put her hand on his arm, and looking at him with her clear, grey eyes, said —

'Yes!'

'Thank God for that,' said Brian, reverently, and there was again a silence.

Then they sat down and talked about their plans, and built castles in the air, after the fashion of lovers.

'I wonder what papa will say?' observed Madge, idly twisting her engagement ring round and round.

Brian frowned, and a dark look passed over his face.

'I suppose I must speak to him about it?' he said at length, reluctantly.

'Yes, of course!' she replied, lightly. 'It is merely a formality; still, one that must be observed.'

'And where is Mr. Frettlby?' asked Fitzgerald, rising.

'In the billiard-room,' she answered, as she followed his example. 'No!' she continued, as she saw her father step on to the verandah. 'Here he is.' Brian had not seen Mark Frettlby for some time, and was astonished at the change which had taken place in his appearance. Formerly, he had been as straight as an arrow, with a stem, fresh-coloured face; but now he had a slight stoop, and his face looked old and withered. His thick, black hair was streaked here and there with white. His eyes alone were unchanged. They were as keen and bright as ever. Brian knew full well how he himself had altered. He knew, too, that Madge was not the same, and now he could not but wonder whether the great change that was apparent in her father was attributable to the same source — to the murder of Oliver Whyte. Sad and thoughtful as Mr. Frettlby looked, as he came along, a smile broke over his face as he caught sight of his daughter.

'My dear Fitzgerald,' he said, holding out his hand, 'this is indeed a surprise! When did you come over?'

'About half-an-hour ago,' replied Brian, reluctantly, taking the extended hand of the millionaire. 'I came to see Madge, and have a talk with you.'

'Ah! that's right,' said the other, putting his

arm round his daughter's waist. 'So that's what has brought the roses to your face, young lady?' he went on, pinching her cheek playfully. 'You will stay to dinner, of course, Fitzgerald?'

'Thank you, no!' answered Brian, hastily, 'my dress — '

'Nonsense,' interrupted Frettlby, hospitably; 'we are not in Melbourne, and I am sure Madge will excuse your dress. You must stay.'

'Yes, do,' said Madge, in a beseeching tone, touching his hand lightly. 'I don't see so much of you that I can let you off with half-an-hour's conversation.'

Brian seemed to be making a violent effort.

'Very well,' he said in a low voice; 'I shall stay.'

'And now,' said Frettlby, in a brisk tone, as he sat down; 'the important question of dinner being settled, what is it you want to see me about? — Your station?'

'No,' answered Brian, leaning against the verandah post, while Madge slipped her hand through his arm. 'I have sold it.'

'Sold it!' echoed Frettlby, aghast. 'What for?'

'I felt restless, and wanted a change.'

'Ah! a rolling stone,' said the millionaire, shaking his head, 'gathers no moss, you know.'

'Stones don't roll of their own accord,' replied Brian, in a gloomy tone. 'They are impelled by a force over which they have no control.'

'Oh, indeed!' said the millionaire, in a joking tone. 'And may I ask what is your propelling force?'

Brian looked at the man's face with such a steady gaze that the latter's eyes dropped after an uneasy attempt to return it.

'Well,' he said impatiently, looking at the two tall young people standing before him, 'what do you want to see me about?'

'Madge has agreed to marry me at once, and I want your consent.'

'Impossible!' said Frettlby, curtly.

'There is no such a word as impossible,' retorted Brian, coolly, thinking of the famous remark in *Richelieu*, 'Why should you refuse? I am rich now.'

'Pshaw!' said Frettlby, rising impatiently. 'It's not money I'm thinking about — I've got enough for both of you; but I cannot live without Madge.'

'Then come with us,' said his daughter, kissing him.

Her lover, however, did not second the invitation, but stood moodily twisting his tawny moustache, and staring out into the garden in an absent sort of manner.

'What do you say, Fitzgerald?' said Frettlby, who was eyeing him keenly.

'Oh, delighted, of course,' answered Brian, confusedly.

'In that case,' returned the other, coolly, 'I will tell you what we will do. I have bought a steam yacht, and she will be ready for sea about the end of January. You will marry my daughter at once, and go round New Zealand for your honeymoon. When you return, if I feel inclined, and you two turtle-doves don't object, I will join you, and we will make a tour of the world.'

'Oh, how delightful,' cried Madge, clasping her hands. 'I am so fond of the ocean with a companion, of course,' she added, with a saucy glance at her lover.

Brian's face had brightened considerably, for he was a born sailor, and a pleasant yachting voyage in the blue waters of the Pacific, with Madge as his companion, was, to his mind, as near Paradise as any mortal could get.

'And what is the name of the yacht?' he asked, with deep interest.

'Her name?' repeated Mr. Frettlby, hastily. 'Oh, a very ugly name, and one which I intend to change. At present she is called the *Rosanna*.'

'Rosanna!'

Brian and his betrothed both started at this, and the former stared curiously at the old man, wondering at the coincidence between the name of the yacht and that of the woman who died in the Melbourne slum.

Mr Frettlby flushed a little when he saw Brian's eye fixed on him with such an enquiring gaze, and rose with an embarrassed laugh.

'You are a pair of moon-struck lovers,' he said, gaily, taking an arm of each, and leading them into the house, 'but you forget dinner will soon be ready.'

23

Across the Walnuts and the Wine.

Moore, sweetest of bards, sings —

'Oh, there's nothing half so sweet in life
As love's young dream.'

But he made this assertion in his callow days, before he had learned the value of a good digestion. To a young and fervid youth, love's young dream is, no doubt, very charming, lovers, as a rule, having a small appetite; but to a man who has seen the world, and drunk deeply of the wine of life, there is nothing half so sweet in the whole of his existence as a good dinner. 'A hard heart and a good digestion will make any man happy.' So said Talleyrand, a cynic if you like, but a man who knew the temper of his day and generation. Ovid wrote about the art of love — Brillat Savarin, of the art of dining; yet, I warrant you, the gastronomical treatise of the brilliant Frenchman is more widely read than the passionate songs of the Roman poet. Who does not value as the sweetest in the whole twenty-four the hour when, seated at an artistically-laid table, with delicately-cooked viands, good wines, and pleasant company, all the cares and worries of the day give place to a delightful sense of absolute enjoyment? Dinner with the English people is generally a very dreary affair, and there is a heaviness about the whole thing which communicates itself to the guests, who eat and drink with a solemn persistence, as though they were occupied in fulfilling some sacred rite. But there are men — alas! few and far between — who possess the rare art of giving good dinners — good in the sense of sociality as well as in that of cookery. Mark Frettlby was one of these rare individuals — he had an innate genius for getting pleasant people together — people, who, so to speak, dovetailed into one another. He had an excellent cook, and his wines were irreproachable, so that Brian, in spite of his worries, was glad that he had accepted the invitation. The bright gleam of the silver, the glitter of glass, and the perfume of flowers, all collected under the subdued crimson glow of a pink-shaded lamp, which hung from the ceiling, could not but give him a pleasurable sensation.

On one side of the dining-room were the French windows opening on to the verandah, and beyond appeared the vivid green of the trees, and the dazzling colours of the flowers, somewhat tempered by the soft hazy glow of the twilight.

Brian had made himself as respectable as possible under the odd circumstances of dining in his riding-dress, and sat next to Madge, contentedly sipping his wine, and listening to the pleasant chatter which was going on around him.

Felix Rolleston was in great spirits, the more so as Mrs Rolleston was at the further end of the table, hidden from his view.

Julia Featherweight sat near Mr. Frettlby, and chatted to him so persistently that he wished she would become possessed of a dumb devil.

Dr. Chinston and Peterson were seated on the other side of the table, and the old colonist, whose name was Valpy, had the post of honour, on Mr. Frettlby's right hand. The conversation had turned on to the subject, ever green and fascinating, of politics, and Mr. Rolleston thought it a good opportunity to air his views as to the Government of the Colony, and to show his wife that he really meant to obey her wish, and become a power in the political world.

'By Jove, you know,' he said, with a wave of his hand, as though he were addressing the

House; 'the country is going to the dogs, and all that sort of thing. What we want is a man like Beaconsfield.'

'Ah! but you can't pick up a man like that every day,' said Frettlby, who was listening with an amused smile to Rolleston's disquisitions.

'Rather a good thing, too,' observed Dr. Chinston, dryly.

'Genius would become too common.'

'Well, when I am elected,' said Felix, who had his own views, which modesty forbade him to publish, on the subject of the coming colonial Disraeli, 'I probably shall form a party.'

'To advocate what?' asked Peterson, curiously.

'Oh, well, you see,' hesitated Felix, 'I haven't drawn up a programme yet, so can't say at present.'

'Yes, you can hardly give a performance without a programme,' said the doctor, taking a sip of wine, and then everybody laughed.

'And on what are your political opinions founded?' asked Mr. Frettlby, absently, without looking at Felix.

'Oh, you see, I've read the Parliamentary reports and Constitutional history, and — and Vivian Grey,' said Felix, who began to feel himself somewhat at sea.

'The last of which is what the author called it, a *Lusus Naturae*,' observed Chinston. 'Don't erect your political schemes on such bubble foundations as are in that novel, for you won't find a Marquis Carabas out here.'

'Unfortunately, no!' observed Felix, mournfully; 'but we may find a Vivian Grey.'

Every one smothered a smile, the allusion was so patent.

'Well, he didn't succeed in the end,' cried Peterson.

'Of course he didn't,' retorted Felix, disdainfully; 'he made an enemy of a woman, and a man who is such a fool as to do that deserves to fall.'

'You have an excellent opinion of our sex, Mr. Rolleston,' said Madge, with a wicked glance at the wife of that gentleman, who was listening complacently to her husband's aimless chatter.

'No better than they deserve,' replied Rolleston, gallantly.

'But you have never gone in for politics, Mr. Frettlby?'

'Who? — I — no,' said the host, rousing himself out of the brown study into which he had fallen. 'I'm afraid I'm not sufficiently patriotic, and my business did not permit me.'

'And now?'

'Now,' echoed Mr. Frettlby, glancing at his daughter, 'I intend to travel.'

'The jolliest thing out,' said Peterson, eagerly. 'One never gets tired of seeing the queer things that are in the world.'

'I've seen queer enough things in Melbourne in the early days,' said the old colonist, with a wicked twinkle in his eyes.

'Oh!' cried Julia, putting her hands up to her ears, 'don't tell me them, for I'm sure they're naughty.'

'We weren't saints then,' said old Valpy, with a senile chuckle.

'Ah, then, we haven't changed much in that respect,' retorted Frettlby, drily.

'You talk of your theatres now,' went on Valpy, with the garrulousness of old age; 'why, you haven't got a dancer like Rosanna.'

Brian started on hearing this name again, and he felt Madge's cold hand touch his.

'And who was Rosanna?' asked Felix, curiously, looking up.

'A dancer and burlesque actress,' replied Valpy, vivaciously, nodding his old head. 'Such a beauty; we were all mad about her — such hair and eyes. You remember her, Frettlby?'

'Yes,' answered the host, in a curiously dry voice.

But before Mr. Valpy had the opportunity to wax more eloquent, Madge rose from the table, and the other ladies followed. The ever polite Felix held the door open for them, and received a bright smile from his wife for, what she considered, his brilliant talk at the dinner table.

Brian sat still, and wondered why Frettlby changed colour on hearing the name — he supposed that the millionaire had been mixed up with the actress, and did not care about being reminded of his early indiscretions — and, after all, who does?

'She was as light as a fairy,' continued Valpy, with wicked chuckle.

'What became of her?' asked Brian, abruptly.

Mark Frettlby looked up suddenly, as Fitzgerald asked this question.

'She went to England in 1858,' said the aged one. 'I'm not quite sure if it was July or August, but it was in 1858.'

'You will excuse me, Valpy, but I hardly think that these reminiscences of a ballet-dancer are amusing,' said Frettlby, curtly, pouring himself out a glass of wine. 'Let us change the subject.'

Notwithstanding the plainly-expressed wish of his host Brian felt strongly inclined to pursue the conversation. Politeness, however, forbade such a thing, and he consoled himself with the reflection that, after dinner, he would ask old Valpy about the ballet-dancer whose name caused Mark Frettlby to exhibit such strong emotion. But, to his annoyance, when the gentlemen went into the drawing-room, Frettlby took the old colonist off to his study, where he sat with him the whole evening talking over old times.

Fitzgerald found Madge seated at the piano in the drawing-room playing one of Mendelssohn's Songs without Words.

'What a dismal thing that is you are playing, Madge,' he said lightly, as he sank into a seat beside her. 'It is more like a funeral march than anything else.'

'Gad, so it is,' said Felix, who came up at this moment. 'I don't care myself about 'Op. 84' and all that classical humbug. Give me something light — 'Belle Helene,' with Emelie Melville, and all that sort of thing.'

'Felix!' said his wife, in a stern tone.

'My dear,' he answered recklessly, rendered bold by the champagne he had taken, 'you observed — '

'Nothing particular,' answered Mrs. Rolleston, glancing at him with a stony eye, 'except that I consider Offenbach low.'

'I don't,' said Felix, sitting down to the piano, from which Madge had just risen, 'and to prove he ain't, here goes.'

He ran his fingers lightly over the keys, and dashed into a brilliant Offenbach galop, which had the effect of waking up the people in the drawing-room, who felt sleepy after dinner, and sent the blood tingling through their veins. When they were thoroughly roused, Felix, now that he had an appreciative audience, for he was by no means an individual who believed in wasting his sweetness on the desert air, prepared to amuse them.

'You haven't heard the last new song by Frosti, have you?' he asked, after he had brought his galop to a conclusion.

'Is that the composer of 'Inasmuch' and 'How so?' ' asked Julia, clasping her hands. 'I do love his music, and the words are so sweetly pretty.'

'Infernally stupid, she means,' whispered Peterson to Brian. 'They've no more meaning in them than the titles.'

'Sing us the new song, Felix,' commanded his wife, and her obedient husband obeyed her.

It was entitled, 'Somewhere,' words by Vashti, music by Paola Frosti, and was one of those extraordinary compositions which may mean anything — that is, if the meaning can be discovered. Felix had a pleasant voice, though it was not very strong, and the music was pretty, while the words were mystical. The first verse was as follows: —

'A flying cloud, a breaking wave,
A faint light in a moonless sky:
A voice that from the silent grave
Sounds sad in one long bitter cry.
I know not, sweet, where you may
   stand,
With shining eyes and golden hair,
Yet I know, I will touch your hand
And kiss your lips somewhere —
Somewhere! Somewhere! —
When the summer sun is fair,
Waiting me, on land or sea,
Somewhere, love, somewhere!'

The second verse was very similar to the first, and when Felix finished a murmur of applause broke from every one of the ladies.

'How sweetly pretty,' sighed Julia. 'Such a lot in it.'

'But what is its meaning?' asked Brian, rather bewildered.

'It hasn't got one,' replied Felix, complacently. 'Surely you don't want every song to have a moral, like a book of Aesop's Fables?'

Brian shrugged his shoulders, and turned away with Madge.

'I must say I agree with Fitzgerald,' said the doctor, quickly. 'I like a song with some meaning in it. The poetry of the one you sang is as mystical as Browning, without any of his genius to redeem it.'

'Philistine,' murmured Felix, under his breath, and then vacated his seat at the piano in favour of Julia, who was about to sing a ballad called, 'Going Down the Hill,' which had been the rage in Melbourne musical circles during the last two months. Meanwhile Madge and Brian were walking up and down in the moonlight. It was an exquisite night, with a cloudless blue sky glittering with the stars, and a great yellow moon in the west. Madge seated herself on the side of the marble ledge which girdled the still pool of water in front of the house, and dipped her hand into the cool water. Brian leaned against the trunk of a great magnolia tree, whose glossy green leaves and great creamy blossoms looked fantastic in the moonlight. In front of them was the house, with the ruddy lamplight streaming through the wide windows, and they could see the guests within, excited by the music, waltzing to Rolleston's playing, and their dark figures kept passing and re-passing the windows while the charming music of the waltz mingled with their merry laughter.

'Looks like a haunted house,' said Brian, thinking of Poe's weird poem; 'but such a thing is impossible out here.'

'I don't know so much about that,' said Madge, gravely, lifting up some water in the palm of her hand, and letting it stream back like diamonds in the moonlight. 'I knew a house in St. Kilda which was haunted.'

'By what?' asked Brian, sceptically.

'Noises!' she answered, solemnly.

Brian burst out laughing and startled a bat, which flew round and round in the silver moonlight, and whirred away into the shelter of a witch elm.

'Rats and mice are more common here than ghosts,' he said, lightly. 'I'm afraid the inhabitants of your haunted house were fanciful.'

'So you don't believe in ghosts?'

'There's a Banshee in our family,' said Brian, with a gay smile, 'who is supposed to cheer our death beds with her howlings; but as I've never seen the lady myself, I'm afraid she's a Mrs. Harris.'

'It's aristocratic to have a ghost in a family, I believe,' said Madge; 'that is the reason we colonials have none.'

'Ah, but you will have,' he answered with a careless laugh. 'There are, no doubt, democratic as well as aristocratic ghosts; but, pshaw!' he went on, impatiently, 'what nonsense I talk. There are no ghosts, except of a man's own raising. The ghosts of a dead youth — the ghosts of past follies — the ghosts of what might have been — these are the spectres which are more to be feared than those of the churchyard.' Madge looked at him in silence, for she understood the meaning of that passionate outburst — the secret which the dead woman had told him, and which hung like a shadow over his life. She arose quietly and took his arm. The light touch roused him, and a faint wind sent an eerie rustle through the still leaves of the magnolia, as they walked back in silence to the house.

24

Brian Receives a Letter.

Notwithstanding the hospitable invitation of Mr. Frettlby, Brian refused to stay at Yabba Yallook that night, but after saying good-bye to Madge, mounted his horse and rode slowly away in the moonlight. He felt very happy, and letting the reins lie on his horse's neck, he gave himself up unreservedly to his thoughts. *Atra Cura* certainly did not sit behind the horseman on this night; and Brian, to his surprise, found himself singing 'Kitty of Coleraine,' as he rode along in the silver moonlight. And was he not right to sing when the future seemed so bright and pleasant? Oh, yes! they would live on the ocean, and she would find how much pleasanter it was on the restless waters, with their solemn sense of mystery, than on the crowded land.

'Was not the sea
Made for the free —
Land for courts and slaves alone?'

Moore was perfectly right. She would learn

that when with a fair wind, and all sail set, they were flying over the blue Pacific waters.

And then they would go home to Ireland to the ancestral home of the Fitzgeralds, where he would lead her in under the arch, with 'CEAD MILLE FAILTHE' on it, and everyone would bless the fair young bride. Why should he trouble himself about the crime of another? No! He had made a resolve, and intended to keep it; he would put this secret with which he had been entrusted behind his back, and would wander about the world with Madge and — her father. He felt a sudden chill come over him as he murmured the last words to himself 'her father.'

'I'm a fool,' he said, impatiently, as he gathered up the reins, and spurred his horse into a canter. 'It can make no difference to me so long as Madge remains ignorant; but to sit beside him, to eat with him, to have him always present like a skeleton at a feast — God help me!'

He urged his horse into a gallop, and as he rushed over the turf, with the fresh, cool night wind blowing keenly against his face, he felt a sense of relief, as though he were leaving some dark spectre behind. On he galloped, with the blood throbbing in his young veins, over miles of plain, with the dark-blue, star-studded sky above, and the pale moon shining down on him — past a silent shepherd's hut, which stood near a wide creek; splashing through the cool water, which wound through the dark plain like a thread of silver in the moonlight — then, again, the wide, grassy plain, dotted here and there with tall clumps of shadowy trees, and on either side he could see the sheep skurrying away like fantastic spectres — on — on — ever on, until his own homestead appears, and he sees the star-like light shining brightly in the distance — a long avenue of tall trees, over whose wavering shadows his horse thundered, and then the wide grassy space in front of the house, with the clamorous barking of dogs. A groom, roused by the clatter of hoofs up the avenue, comes round the side of the house, and Brian leaps off his horse, and flinging the reins to the man, walks into his own room. There he finds a lighted lamp, brandy and soda on the table, and a packet of letters and newspapers. He flung his hat on the sofa, and opened the window and door, so as to let in the cool breeze; then mixing for himself a glass of brandy and soda, he turned up the lamp, and prepared to read his letters. The first he took up was from a lady. 'Always a she correspondent for me,' says Isaac Disraeli, 'provided she does not cross.' Brian's correspondence did not cross, but notwithstanding this, after reading half a page of small talk and scandal, he flung the letter on the table with an impatient ejaculation. The other letters were principally business ones, but the last one proved to be from Calton, and Fitzgerald opened it with a sensation of pleasure. Calton was a capital letter-writer, and his epistles had done much to cheer Fitzgerald in the dismal period which succeeded his acquittal of Whyte's murder, when he was in danger of getting into a morbid state of mind. Brian, therefore, sipped his brandy and soda, and, lying back in his chair, prepared to enjoy himself.

'My dear Fitzgerald,' wrote Calton in his peculiarly clear handwriting, which was such an exception to the usual crabbed hieroglyphics of his brethren of the bar, 'while you are enjoying the cool breezes and delightful freshness of the country, here am I, with numerous other poor devils, cooped up in this hot and dusty city. How I wish I were with you in the land of Goschen, by the rolling waters of the Murray, where everything is bright and green, and unsophisticated — the two latter terms are almost identical — instead of which my view is bounded by bricks and mortar, and the muddy waters of the Yarra have to do duty for your noble river.

Ah! I too have lived in Arcadia, but I don't now: and even if some power gave me the choice to go back again, I am not sure that I would accept. Arcadia, after all, is a lotus-eating Paradise of blissful ignorance, and I love the world with its pomps, vanities, and wickedness. While you, therefore, oh Corydon — don't be afraid, I'm not going to quote Virgil — are studying Nature's book, I am deep in the musty leaves of Themis' volume, but I dare say that the great mother teaches you much better things than her artificial daughter does me. However, you remember that pithy proverb, 'When one is in Rome, one must not speak ill of the Pope,' so being in the legal profession, I must respect its muse. I suppose when you saw that this letter came from a law office, you wondered what the deuce a lawyer was writing to you for, and my handwriting, no doubt suggested a writ — pshaw! I am wrong there, you are past the age of writs — not that I hint that you are old; by no means — you are just at that appreciative age when a man enjoys life most, when the fire of youth is tempered by the experience of age, and one knows how to enjoy to the utmost the good things of this world, videlicet — love, wine, and friendship. I am afraid I am growing poetical, which is a bad thing for a lawyer, for the flower of poetry cannot flourish in the arid wastes of the law. On reading what I have written, I find I have been as discursive as Praed's Vicar, and as this letter is supposed to be a business one, I must deny myself the luxury of following out a train of idle ideas, and write sense. I suppose you still hold the secret which Rosanna Moore entrusted you with — ah! you see I know her name, and why? — simply because, with the natural curiosity of the human race, I have been trying to find out who murdered Oliver Whyte, and as the *Argus* very cleverly pointed out Rosanna Moore as likely to be at the bottom of the whole affair, I have been learning her past history. The secret of Whyte's murder, and the reason for it, is known to you, but you refuse, even in the interests of justice, to reveal it — why, I don't know; but we all have our little faults, and from an amiable though mistaken sense of — shall I say — duty? — you refuse to deliver up the man whose cowardly crime so nearly cost you your life. After your departure from Melbourne every one said, 'The hansom cab tragedy is at an end, and the murderer will never be discovered.' I ventured to disagree with the wiseacres who made such a remark, and asked myself, 'Who was this woman who died at Mother Guttersnipe's?' Receiving no satisfactory answer from myself, I determined to find out, and took steps accordingly. In the first place, I learned from Roger Moreland, who, if you remember, was a witness against you at the trial, that Whyte and Rosanna Moore had come out to Sydney in the *John Elder* about a year ago as Mr. and Mrs. Whyte. I need hardly say that they did not think it needful to go through the formality of marriage, as such a tie might have been found inconvenient on some future occasion. Moreland knew nothing about Rosanna Moore, and advised me to give up the search, as, coming from a city like London, it would be difficult to find anyone that knew her there. Notwithstanding this, I telegraphed home to a friend of mine, who is a bit of an amateur detective, 'Find out the name and all about the woman who left England in the *John Elder* on the 21st day of August, 18 — , as wife of Oliver Whyte.' *Mirabile dictu*, he found out all about her, and knowing, as you do, what a maelstrom of humanity London is, you must admit my friend was clever. It appears, however, that the task I set him was easier than he expected, for the so-called Mrs. Whyte was rather a notorious individual in her own way. She was a burlesque actress at the Frivolity Theatre in London, and, being a very handsome woman, had been photographed innumerable times. Consequently, when she very foolishly went with Whyte to choose a berth on board the boat, she was recognised by the clerks in the office as Rosanna Moore, better known as Musette of the Frivolity. Why she ran away with Whyte I cannot tell you. With reference to men understanding women, I refer you to Balzac's remark anent the same. Perhaps Musette got weary of St. John's Wood and champagne suppers, and longed for the purer air of her native land. Ah! you open your eyes at this latter statement — you are surprised — no, on second thoughts you are not, because she told you herself that she was a native of Sydney, and had gone home in 1858, after a triumphant career of acting in Melbourne. And why did she leave the applauding Melbourne public and the flesh-pots of Egypt? You know this also. She ran away with a rich young squatter, with more money than morals, who happened to be in Melbourne at the time. She seems to have had a weakness for running away. But why she chose Whyte to go with this time puzzles me. He was not rich, not particularly good-looking, had no position, and a bad temper. How do I know all these traits of Mr. Whyte's character, morally and socially?

Easily enough; my omniscient friend found them all out. Mr. Oliver Whyte was the son of a London tailor, and his father being well off, retired into a private life, and ultimately went the way of all flesh. His son, finding himself with a capital income, and a pretty taste for amusement, cut the shop of his late lamented parent, found out that his family had come over with the Conqueror — Glanville de Whyte helped to sew the Bayeux tapestry, I suppose — and graduated at the Frivolity Theatre as a masher. In common with the other gilded youth of the day, he worshipped at the gas-lit shrine of Musette, and the goddess, pleased with his incense, left her other admirers in the lurch, and ran off with fortunate Mr. Whyte. So far as this goes there is nothing to show why the murder was committed. Men do not perpetrate crimes for the sake of light o' loves like Musette, unless, indeed, some wretched youth embezzles money to buy jewellery for his divinity. The career of Musette, in London, was simply that of a clever member of the *demi-monde*, and, as far as I can learn, no one was so much in love with her as to commit a crime for her sake. So far so good; the motive of the crime must be found in Australia. Whyte had spent nearly all his money in England, and, consequently, Musette and her lover arrived in Sydney with comparatively very little cash. However, with an Epicurean-like philosophy, they enjoyed themselves on what little they had, and then came to Melbourne, where they stayed at a second-rate hotel. Musette, I may tell you, had one special vice, a common one — drink. She loved champagne, and drank a good deal of it. Consequently, on arriving at Melbourne, and finding that a new generation had arisen, which knew not Joseph — I mean Musette — she drowned her sorrows in the flowing bowl, and went out after a quarrel with Mr. Whyte, to view Melbourne by night — a familiar scene to her, no doubt. What took her to Little Bourke Street I don't know. Perhaps she got lost — perhaps it had been a favourite walk of hers in the old days; at all events she was found dead drunk in that unsavoury locality, by Sal Rawlins. I know this is so, because Sal told me so herself. Sal acted the part of the good Samaritan — took her to the squalid den she called home, and there Rosanna Moore fell dangerously ill. Whyte, who had missed her, found out where she was, and that she was too ill to be removed. I presume he was rather glad to get rid of such an encumbrance, so he went back to his lodgings at St. Kilda, which, judging from the landlady's story, he must have occupied for some time, while Rosanna Moore was drinking herself to death in a quiet hotel. Still he does not break off his connection with the dying woman; but one night is murdered in a hansom cab, and that same night Rosanna Moore dies. So, from all appearance, everything is ended; not so, for before dying Rosanna sends for Brian Fitzgerald at his club, and reveals to him a secret which he locks up in his own heart. The writer of this letter has a theory — a fanciful one, if you will — that the secret told to Brian Fitzgerald contains the mystery of Oliver Whyte's death. Now then, have I not found out a good deal without you, and do you still decline to reveal the rest? I do not say you know who killed Whyte, but I do say you know sufficient to lead to the detection of the murderer. If you tell me, so much the better, both for your own sense of justice and for your peace of mind; if you do not — well, I shall find out without you. I have taken, and still take, a great interest in this strange case, and I have sworn to bring the murderer to justice; so I make this last appeal to you to tell me what you know. If you refuse, I will set to work to find out all about Rosanna Moore prior to her departure from Australia in 1858, and I am certain sooner or later to discover the secret which led to Whyte's murder. If there is any strong reason why it should be kept silent, I perhaps, will come round to your view, and let the matter drop; but if I have to find it out myself, the murderer of Oliver Whyte need expect no mercy at my hands. So think over what I have said; if I do not hear from you within the next week, I shall regard your decision as final, and pursue the search myself. I am sure, my dear Fitzgerald, you will find this letter too long, in spite of the interesting story it contains, so I will have pity on you, and draw to a close. Remember me to Miss Frettlby and to her father. With kind regards to yourself, I remain, yours very truly,

'DUNCAN CALTON.'

When Fitzgerald had finished the last of the closely-written sheets, he let the letter fall from his hands, and, leaning back in his chair, stared blankly into the dawning light outside. He arose after a few moments, and, pouring himself out a glass of brandy, drank it quickly. Then mechanically lighting a cigar, he stepped out of the door into the fresh beauty of the dawn. There was a soft crimson glow in the east, which announced the approach of the sun, and he could hear the chirping of the awakening birds in the trees. But Brian did not see the marvellous breaking of the dawn. He stood staring at the red light flaring in the east, and thinking of Calton's letter. 'I can do no more,' he said bitterly, leaning his head against the wall of the house. 'There is only one way of stopping Calton, and that is by telling him all. My poor Madge! My poor Madge!'

A soft wind arose, and rustled among the trees, and there appeared great shafts of crimson light in the east; then, with a sudden blaze, the sun peered over the brim of the wide plain. The warm yellow rays touched lightly the comely head of the weary man, and, turning round, he held up his arms to the great luminary, as though he were a fire-worshipper.

'I accept the omen of the dawn,' he cried, 'for her life and for mine.'

25

What Dr. Chinston Said.

His resolution taken, Brian did not let the grass grow under his feet, but rode over in the afternoon to tell Madge of his intended departure.

The servant told him she was in the garden, so he went there, and, guided by the sound of merry voices, and the laughter of pretty women, soon found his way to the lawn-tennis ground. Madge and her guests were there, seated under the shade of a great witch elm, and watching, with great interest, a single-handed match being played between Rolleston and Peterson, both of whom were capital players. Mr. Frettlby was not present. He was inside writing letters, and talking with old Mr. Valpy, and Brian gave a sigh of relief as he noted his absence. Madge caught sight of him as he came down the garden path, and flew quickly towards him with outstretched hands, as he took his hat off.

'How good of you to come,' she said, in a delighted tone, as she took his arm, 'and on such a hot day.'

'Yes, it's something fearful in the shade,' said pretty Mrs. Rolleston, with a laugh, putting up her sunshade.

'Pardon me if I think the contrary,' replied Fitzgerald, bowing, with an expressive look at the charming group of ladies under the great tree.

Mrs. Rolleston blushed and shook her head.

'Ah! it's easy seen you come from Ireland, Mr. Fitzgerald,' she observed, as she resumed her seat. 'You are making Madge jealous.'

'So he is,' answered Madge, with a gay laugh. 'I shall certainly inform Mr. Rolleston about you, Brian, if you make these gallant remarks.'

'Here he comes, then,' said her lover, as Rolleston and Peterson, having finished their game, walked off the tennis ground, and joined the group under the tree. Though in tennis flannels, they both looked remarkably warm, and, throwing aside his racket, Mr. Rolleston sat down with a sigh of relief.

'Thank goodness it's over, and that I have won,' he said, wiping his heated brow; 'galley slaves couldn't have worked harder than we have done, while all you idle folks sat *sub tegmine fagi.*'

'Which means?' asked his wife, lazily.

'That onlookers see most of the game,'

answered her husband, impudently.

'I suppose that's what you call a free and easy translation,' said Peterson, laughing.

'Mrs. Rolleston ought to give you something for your new and original adaptation of Virgil.'

'Let it be iced then,' retorted Rolleston, lying full length on the ground, and staring up at the blue of the sky as seen through the network of leaves. 'I always like my 'something' iced.'

'It's a way you've got,' said Madge, with a laugh, as she gave him a glass filled with some sparkling, golden-coloured liquor, with a lump of ice clinking musically against the side of it.

'He's not the only one who's got that way,' said Peterson, gaily, when he had been similarly supplied.

'It's a way we've got in the army,
It's a way we've got in the navy,
It's a way we've got in the 'Varsity.'

'And so say all of us,' finished Rolleston, and holding out his glass to be replenished; 'I'll have another, please. Whew, it is hot.'

'What, the drink?' asked Julia, with a giggle.

'No — the day,' answered Felix, making a

310

face at her. 'It's the kind of day one feels inclined to adopt Sydney Smith's advice, by getting out of one's skin, and letting the wind whistle through one's bones.'

'With such a hot wind blowing,' said Peterson, gravely, 'I'm afraid they'd soon be broiled bones.'

'Go, giddy one,' retorted Felix, throwing his hat at him, 'or I'll drag you into the blazing sun, and make you play another game.'

'Not I,' replied Peterson, coolly. 'Not being a salamander, I'm hardly used to your climate yet, and there is a limit even to lawn tennis;' and turning his back on Rolleston, he began to talk to Julia Featherweight.

Meanwhile, Madge and her lover, leaving all this frivolous chatter behind them, were walking slowly towards the house, and Brian was telling her of his approaching departure, though not of his reasons for it.

'I received a letter last night,' he said, turning his face away from her; 'and, as it's about some important business, I must start at once.'

'I don't think it will be long before we follow,' answered Madge, thoughtfully. 'Papa leaves here at the end of the week.'

'Why?'

'I'm sure I don't know,' said Madge,

petulantly; 'he is so restless, and never seems to settle down to anything. He says for the rest of his life he is going to do nothing; but wander all over the world.'

There suddenly flashed across Fitzgerald's mind a line from Genesis, which seemed singularly applicable to Mr. Frettlby — 'A fugitive and a vagabond thou shalt be in the earth.'

'Everyone gets these restless fits sooner or later,' he said, idly. 'In fact,' with an uneasy laugh, 'I believe I'm in one myself.'

'That puts me in mind of what I heard Dr. Chinston say yesterday,' she said. 'This is the age of unrest, as electricity and steam have turned us all into Bohemians.'

'Ah! Bohemia is a pleasant place,' said Brian, absently, unconsciously quoting Thackeray, 'but we all lose our way to it late in life.'

'At that rate we won't lose our way to it for some time,' she said laughing, as they stepped into the drawing-room, so cool and shady, after the heat and glare outside. As they entered Mr. Frettlby rose from a chair near the window. He appeared to have been reading, for he held a book in his hand.

'What! Fitzgerald,' he exclaimed, in a hearty tone, as he held out his hand; 'I am glad to see you.'

'I let you know I am living, don't I?' replied

Brian, his face flushing as he reluctantly took the proffered hand. 'But the fact is I have come to say good-bye for a few days.'

'Ah! going back to town, I suppose,' said Mr. Frettlby, lying back in his chair, and playing with his watch chain. 'I don't know that you are wise, exchanging the clear air of the country for the dusty atmosphere of Melbourne.'

'Yet Madge tells me you are going back,' said Brian, idly toying with a vase of flowers on the table.

'Depends upon circumstances,' replied the other carelessly. 'I may and I may not. You go on business, I presume?'

'Well, the fact is Calton — ' Here Brian stopped suddenly, and bit his lip with vexation, for he had not intended to mention the lawyer's name.

'Yes?' said Mr. Frettlby, interrogatively, sitting up quickly, and looking keenly at Brian.

'Wants to see me on business,' he finished, awkwardly.

'Connected with the sale of your station, I suppose,' said Frettlby, still keeping his eyes on the young man's face.

'Can't have a better man. Calton's an excellent man of business.'

'A little too excellent,' replied Fitzgerald,

ruefully, 'he's a man who can't leave well alone.'

'A *propos* of what?'

'Oh, nothing,' answered Fitzgerald, hastily, and just then his eyes met those of Frettlby. The two men looked at one another steadily for a moment, but in that short space of time a single name flashed through their brains — the name of Rosanna Moore. Mr. Frettlby was the first to lower his eyes, and break the spell.

'Ah, well,' he said, lightly, as he rose from his chair and held out his hand, 'if you are two weeks in town, call at St. Kilda, and it's more than likely you will find us there.' Brian shook hands in silence, and watched him pick up his hat, and move on to the verandah, and then out into the hot sunshine.

'He knows,' he muttered involuntarily.

'Knows what, sir?' said Madge, who came silently behind him, and slipped her arm through his. 'That you are hungry, and want something to eat before you leave us?'

'I don't feel hungry,' said Brian, as they walked towards the door.

'Nonsense,' answered Madge, merrily, who, like Eve, was on hospitable thoughts intent. 'I'm not going to have you appear in Melbourne a pale, fond lover, as though I were treating you badly. Come, sir — no,' she continued, putting up her hand as he tried to kiss her, 'business first, pleasure afterwards,' and they went into the dining-room laughing.

Mark Frettlby wandered down to the lawn-tennis ground, thinking of the look he had seen in Brian's eyes. He shivered for a moment in the hot sunshine, as though it had grown suddenly chill.

'Someone stepping across my grave,' he murmured to himself, with a cynical smile.

'Bah! how superstitious I am, and yet — he knows, he knows!'

'Come on, sir,' cried Felix, who had just caught sight of him, 'a racket awaits you.' Frettlby awoke with a start, and found himself near the lawn-tennis ground, and Felix at his elbow, smoking a cigarette.

He roused himself with a great effort, and tapped the young man lightly on the shoulder.

'What?' he said with a forced laugh, 'do you really expect me to play lawn tennis on such a day? You are mad.'

'I am hot, you mean,' retorted the imperturbable Rolleston, blowing a wreath of smoke.

'That's a foregone conclusion,' said Dr. Chinston, who came up at that moment.

'Such a charming novel,' cried Julia, who had just caught the last remark.

'What is?' asked Peterson, rather puzzled.

'Howell's book, 'A Foregone Conclusion,'' said Julia, also looking puzzled. 'Weren't you talking about it?'

'I'm afraid this talk is getting slightly incoherent,' said Felix, with a sigh. 'We all seem madder than usual to-day.'

'Speak for yourself,' said Chinston, indignantly, 'I'm as sane as any man in the world.'

'Exactly,' retorted the other coolly, 'that's what I say, and you, being a doctor, ought to know that every man and woman in the world is more or less mad.'

'Where are your facts?' asked Chinston, smiling.

'My facts are all visible ones,' said Felix, gravely pointing to the company. 'They're all crooked on some point or another.'

There was a chorus of indignant denial at this, and then every one burst out laughing at the extraordinary way in which Mr. Rolleston was arguing.

'If you go on like that in the House,' said Frettlby, amused, 'you will, at all events, have an entertaining Parliament.'

'Ah! they'll never have an entertaining Parliament till they admit ladies,' observed Peterson, with a quizzical glance at Julia.

'It will be a Parliament of love then,' retorted the doctor, dryly, 'and not mediaeval either.'

Frettlby took the doctor's arm, and walked away with him. 'I want you to come up to my study, doctor,' he said, as they strolled towards the house, 'and examine me.'

'Why, don't you feel well?' said Chinston, as they entered the house.

'Not lately,' replied Frettlby. 'I'm afraid I've got heart disease.'

The doctor looked sharply at him, and then shook his head.

'Nonsense,' he said, cheerfully, 'it's a common delusion with people that they have heart disease, and in nine cases out of ten it's all imagination; unless, indeed,' he added waggishly, 'the patient happens to be a young man.'

'Ah! I suppose you think I'm safe as far as that goes,' said Frettlby, as they entered the study; 'and what did you think of Rolleston's argument about people being mad?'

'It was amusing,' replied Chinston, taking a seat, Frettlby doing the same. 'That's all I can say about it, though, mind you, I think there are more mad people at large than the world is aware of.'

'Indeed!'

'Yes; do you remember that horrible story of Dickens', in the 'Pickwick Papers,' about the man who was mad, and knew it, yet successfully concealed it for years? Well, I believe there are many people like that in the world, people whose lives are one long struggle against insanity, and yet who eat, drink, talk, and walk with the rest of their fellow-men, apparently as gay and light-hearted as they are.'

'How extraordinary.'

'Half the murders and suicides are done in temporary fits of insanity,' went on Chinston, 'and if a person broods over anything, his incipient madness is sure to break out sooner or later; but, of course, there are cases where a perfectly sane person may commit a murder on the impulse of the moment, but I regard such persons as mad for the time being; but, again, a murder may be planned and executed in the most cold-blooded manner.'

'And in the latter case,' said Frettlby, without looking at the doctor, and playing with a paper knife, 'do you regard the murderer as mad?'

'Yes, I do,' answered the doctor, bluntly. 'He is as mad as a person who kills another because he supposes he has been told by God to do so — only there is method in his madness. For instance, I believe that hansom cab murder, in which you were mixed up — '

'I wasn't mixed up in it,' interrupted Frettlby, pale with anger.

'Beg pardon,' said Chinston, coolly, 'a slip

of the tongue; I was thinking of Fitzgerald. Well, I believe that crime to have been premeditated, and that the man who committed it was mad. He is, no doubt, at large now, walking about and conducting himself as sanely as you or I, yet the germ of insanity is there, and sooner or later he will commit another crime.'

'How do you know it was premeditated?' asked Frettlby, abruptly.

'Any one can see that,' answered the other. 'Whyte was watched on that night, and when Fitzgerald went away the other was ready to take his place, dressed the same.'

'That's nothing,' retorted Frettlby, looking at his companion sharply. 'There are dozens of men in Melbourne who wear evening dress, light coats, and soft hats — in fact, I generally wear them myself.'

'Well, that might have been a coincidence,' said the doctor, rather disconcerted; 'but the use of chloroform puts the question beyond a doubt; people don't usually carry chloroform about with them.'

'I suppose not,' answered the other, and then the matter dropped. Chinston made an examination of Mark Frettlby, and when he had finished, his face was very grave, though he laughed at the millionaire's fears.

'You are all right,' he said, gaily. 'Action of

the heart a little weak, that's all — only,' impressively, 'avoid excitement — avoid excitement.'

Just as Frettlby was putting on his coat, a knock came to the door, and Madge entered.

'Brian is gone,' she began. 'Oh, I beg your pardon, doctor — but is papa ill?' she asked with sudden fear.

'No, child, no,' said Frettlby, hastily, 'I'm all right; I thought my heart was affected, but it isn't.'

'Not a bit of it,' answered Chinston, reassuringly. 'All right — only avoid excitement.'

But when Frettlby turned to go to the door, Madge, who had her eyes fixed on the doctor's face, saw how grave it was.

'There is danger?' she said, touching his arm as they paused for a moment at the door.

'No! No!' he answered, hastily.

'Yes, there is,' she persisted. 'Tell me the worst, it is best for me to know.'

The doctor looked at her in some doubt for a few moments, and then placed his hand on her shoulder.

'My dear young lady,' he said gravely, 'I will tell you what I have not dared to tell your father.'

'What?' she asked in a low voice, her face growing pale.

'His heart is affected.'

'And there is great danger?'

'Yes, great danger. In the event of any sudden shock — ' he hesitated.

'Yes — '

'He would probably drop down dead.'

'My God!'

26

Kilsip Has a Theory of His Own.

Mr. Calton sat in his office reading a letter he had just received from Fitzgerald, and judging from the complacent smile upon his face it seemed to give him the greatest satisfaction.

'I know,' wrote Brian, 'that now you have taken up the affair, you will not stop until you find out everything, so, as I want the matter to rest as at present, I will anticipate you, and reveal all. You were right in your conjecture that I knew something likely to lead to the detection of Whyte's murderer; but when I tell you my reasons for keeping such a thing secret, I am sure you will not blame me. Mind you, I do not say that I know who committed the murder; but I have suspicions — very strong suspicions — and I wish to God Rosanna Moore had died before she told me what she did. However, I will tell you all, and leave you to judge as to whether I was justified in concealing what I was told. I will call at your office some time next week, and then you will learn everything that Rosanna Moore told me; but once that you are possessed of the knowledge you will pity me.'

'Most extraordinary,' mused Calton, leaning back in his chair, as he laid down the letter. 'I wonder if he's about to tell me that he killed Whyte after all, and that Sal Rawlins perjured herself to save him! No, that's nonsense, or she'd have turned up in better time, and wouldn't have risked his neck up to the last moment. Though I make it a rule never to be surprised at anything, I expect what Brian Fitzgerald has to tell me will startle me considerably. I've never met with such an extraordinary case, and from all appearances the end isn't reached yet. After all,' said Mr. Calton, thoughtfully, 'truth is stranger than fiction.'

Here a knock came to the door, and in answer to an invitation to enter, it opened, and Kilsip glided into the room.

'You're not engaged, sir?' he said, in his soft, low voice.

'Oh, dear, no,' answered Calton, carelessly; 'come in — come in!'

Kilsip closed the door softly, and gliding along in his usual velvet-footed manner, sat down in a chair near Calton's, and placing his hat on the ground, looked keenly at the barrister.

'Well, Kilsip,' said Calton, with a yawn, playing with his watch chain, 'any good news to tell me?'

'Well, nothing particularly new,' purred the detective, rubbing his hands together.

'Nothing new, and nothing true, and no matter,' said Calton, quoting Emerson. 'And what have you come to see me about?'

'The Hansom Cab Murder,' replied the other quietly.

'The deuce!' cried Calton, startled out of his professional dignity. 'And have you found out who did it?'

'No!' answered Kilsip, rather dismally; 'but I have an idea.'

'So had Gorby,' retorted Calton, dryly, 'an idea that ended in smoke. Have you any practical proofs?'

'Not yet.'

'That means you are going to get some?'

'If possible.'

'Much virtue in 'if,'' quoted Calton, picking up a pencil, and scribbling idly on his blotting paper. 'And to whom does your suspicion point?'

'Aha!' said Mr. Kilsip, cautiously.

'Don't know him,' answered the other, coolly; 'family name Humbug, I presume. Bosh! Whom do you suspect?'

Kilsip looked round cautiously, as if to

make sure they were alone, and then said, in a stage whisper —

'Roger Moreland!'

'That was the young man that gave evidence as to how Whyte got drunk?'

Kilsip nodded.

'Well, and how do you connect him with the murder?'

'Do you remember in the evidence given by the cabmen, Royston and Rankin, they both swore that the man who was with Whyte on that night wore a diamond ring on the forefinger of the right hand?'

'What of that? Nearly every second man in Melbourne wears a diamond ring.'

'But not on the forefinger of the right hand.'

'Oh! And Moreland wears a ring in that way?'

'Yes!'

'Merely a coincidence. Is that all your proof?'

'All I can obtain at present.'

'It's very weak,' said Calton, scornfully.

'The weakest proofs may form a chain to hang a man,' observed Kilsip, sententiously.

'Moreland gave his evidence clearly enough,' said Calton, rising, and pacing the room. 'He met Whyte; they got drunk together. Whyte went out of the hotel, and

325

shortly afterwards Moreland followed with the coat, which was left behind by Whyte, and then someone snatched it from him.'

'Ah, did they?' interrupted Kilsip, quickly.

'So Moreland says,' said Calton, stopping short. 'I understand; you think Moreland was not so drunk as he would make out, and that after following Whyte outside, he put on his coat, and got into the cab with him.'

'That is my theory.'

'It's ingenious enough,' said the barrister; 'but why should Moreland murder Whyte? What motive had he?'

'Those papers — '

'Pshaw! another idea of Gorby's,' said Calton, angrily. 'How do you know there were any papers?'

The fact is, Calton did not intend Kilsip to know that Whyte really had papers until he heard what Fitzgerald had to tell him.

'And another thing,' said Calton, resuming his walk, 'if your theory is correct, which I don't think it is, what became of Whyte's coat? Has Moreland got it?'

'No, he has not,' answered the detective, decisively.

'You seem very positive about it,' said the lawyer, after a moment's pause. 'Did you ask Moreland about it?'

A reproachful look came into Kilsip's white face.

'Not quite so green,' he said, forcing a smile. 'I thought you'd a better opinion of me than that, Mr. Calton. Ask him? — no.'

'Then how did you find out?'

'The fact is, Moreland is employed as a barman in the Kangaroo Hotel.'

'A barman!' echoed Calton; 'and he came out here as a gentleman of independent fortune. Why, hang it, man, that in itself is sufficient to prove that he had no motive to murder Whyte. Moreland pretty well lived on Whyte, so what could have induced him to kill his golden goose, and become a barman — pshaw! the idea is absurd.'

'Well, you may be right about the matter,' said Kilsip, rather angrily; 'and if Gorby makes mistakes I don't pretend to be infallible. But, at all events, when I saw Moreland in the bar he wore a silver ring on the forefinger of his right hand.'

'Silver isn't a diamond.'

'No; but it shows that was the finger he was accustomed to wear his ring on. When I saw that, I determined to search his room. I managed to do so while he was out, and found — '

'A mare's nest?'

Kilsip nodded.

'And so your castle of cards falls to the ground,' said Calton, jestingly. 'Your idea is absurd. Moreland no more committed the murder than I did. Why, he was too drunk on that night to do anything.'

'Humph — so he says.'

'Well, men don't calumniate themselves for nothing.'

'It was a lesser danger to avert a greater one,' replied Kilsip, coolly. 'I am sure that Moreland was not drunk on that night. He only said so to escape awkward questions as to his movements. Depend upon it he knows more than he lets out.'

'Well, and how do you intend to set about the matter?'

'I shall start looking for the coat first.'

'Ah! you think he has hidden it?'

'I am sure of it. My theory is this. When Moreland got out of the cab at Powlett Street — '

'But he didn't,' interrupted Calton, angrily.

'Let us suppose, for the sake of argument, that he did,' said Kilsip, quietly. 'I say when he left the cab he walked up Powlett Street, turned to the left down George Street, and walked back to town through the Fitzroy Gardens, then, knowing that the coat was noticeable, he threw it away, or rather, hid it, and walked out of the Gardens through the town — '

'In evening dress — more noticeable than the coat.'

'He wasn't in evening dress,' said Kilsip, quietly.

'No, neither was he,' observed Calton, eagerly, recalling the evidence at the trial.

'Another blow to your theory. The murderer was in evening dress — the cabman said so.'

'Yes; because he had seen Mr. Fitzgerald in evening dress a few minutes before, and thought that he was the same man who got into the cab with Whyte.'

'Well, what of that?'

'If you remember, the second man had his coat buttoned up. Moreland wore dark trousers — at least, I suppose so — and, with the coat buttoned up, it was easy for the cabman to make the mistake, believing, as he did, that it was Mr. Fitzgerald.'

'That sounds better,' said Calton, thoughtfully. 'And what are you going to do?'

'Look for the coat in the Fitzroy Gardens.'

'Pshaw! a wild goose chase.'

'Possibly,' said Kilsip, as he arose to go.

'And when shall I see you again?' said Calton.

'Oh, to-night,' said Kilsip, pausing at, the door. 'I had nearly forgotten, Mother

Guttersnipe wants to see you.'

'Why? What's up?'

'She's dying, and wants to tell you some secret.'

'Rosanna Moore, by Jove!' said Calton. 'She'll tell me something about her. I'll get to the bottom of this yet. All right, I'll be here at eight o'clock.'

'Very well, sir!' and the detective glided out.

'I wonder if that old woman knows anything?' said Calton to himself, as he resumed his seat. 'She may have overheard some conversation between Whyte and his mistress, and intends to divulge it. Well, I'm afraid when Fitzgerald does confess, I shall know all about it beforehand.'

27

Mother Guttersnipe Joins the Majority.

Punctual to his appointment, Kilsip called at Calton's office at eight o'clock, in order to guide him through the squalid labyrinths of the slums. He found the barrister waiting impatiently for him. The fact is, Calton had got it into his head that Rosanna Moore was at the bottom of the whole mystery, and every new piece of evidence he discovered went to confirm this belief. When Rosanna Moore was dying, she might have confessed something to Mother Guttersnipe, which would hint at the name of the murderer, and he had a strong suspicion that the old hag had received hush-money in order to keep quiet. Several times before Calton had been on the point of going to her and trying to get the secret out of her — that is, if she knew it; but now fate appeared to be playing into his hands, and a voluntary confession was much more likely to be true than one dragged piecemeal from unwilling lips.

By the time Kilsip made his appearance Calton was in a high state of excitement.

331

'I suppose we'd better go at once,' he said to Kilsip, as he lit a cigar. 'That old hag may go off at any moment.'

'She might,' assented Kilsip, doubtfully; 'but I wouldn't be a bit surprised if she pulled through. Some of these old women have nine lives like a cat.'

'Not improbable,' retorted Calton, as they passed into the brilliantly-lighted street; 'her nature seemed to me to be essentially feline. But tell me,' he went on, 'what's the matter with her — old age?'

'Partly; drink also, I think,' answered Kilsip. 'Besides, her surroundings are not very healthy, and her dissipated habits have pretty well settled her.'

'It isn't anything catching, I hope,' cried the barrister, with a shudder, as they passed into the crowd of Bourke Street.

'Don't know, sir, not being a doctor,' answered the detective, stolidly.

'Oh!' ejaculated Calton, in dismay.

'It will be all right, sir,' said Kilsip, reassuringly; 'I've been there dozens of times, and I'm all right.'

'I dare say,' retorted the barrister; 'but I may go there once and catch it, whatever it is.'

'Take my word, sir, it's nothing worse than old age and drink.'

'Has she a doctor?'

'Won't let one come near her — prescribes for herself.'

'Gin, I suppose? Humph! Much more unpleasant than the usual run of medicines.' In a short time they found themselves in Little Bourke Street, and after traversing a few dark and narrow lanes — by this time they were more or less familiar to Calton — they found themselves before Mother Guttersnipe's den.

They climbed the rickety stairs, which groaned and creaked beneath their weight, and found Mother Guttersnipe lying on the bed in the corner. The elfish black-haired child was playing cards with a slatternly-looking girl at a deal table by the faint light of a tallow candle.

They both sprang to their feet as the strangers entered, and the elfish child pushed a broken chair in a sullen manner towards Mr. Calton, while the other girl shuffled into a far corner of the room, and crouched down there like a dog. The noise of their entry awoke the hag from an uneasy slumber into which she had fallen. Sitting up in bed, she huddled the clothes round her. She presented such a gruesome spectacle that involuntarily Calton recoiled. Her white hair was unbound, and hung in tangled masses over her shoulders in snowy profusion. Her face, parched and wrinkled, with the hooked nose, and beady black eyes, like those of a mouse, was poked forward, and her skinny arms, bare to the shoulder, were waving wildly about as she grasped at the bedclothes with her claw-like hands. The square bottle and the broken cup lay beside her, and filling herself a dram, she lapped it up greedily.

The irritant brought on a paroxysm of coughing which lasted until the elfish child shook her well, and took the cup from her.

'Greedy old beast,' muttered this amiable infant, peering into the cup, 'ye'd drink the Yarrer dry, I b'lieve.'

'Yah!' muttered the old woman feebly. 'Who's they, Lizer?' she said, shading her eyes with one trembling hand, while she looked at Calton and the detective.

'The perlice cove an' the swell,' said Lizer, suddenly. 'Come to see yer turn up your toes.'

'I ain't dead yet, ye whelp,' snarled the hag with sudden energy; 'an' if I gits up I'll turn up yer toes, cuss ye.'

Lizer gave a shrill laugh of disdain, and Kilsip stepped forward.

'None of this,' he said, sharply, taking Lizer by one thin shoulder, and pushing her over to where the other girl was crouching; 'stop there till I tell you to move.'

Lizer tossed back her tangled black hair, and was about to make some impudent reply, when the other girl, who was older and wiser, put out her hand, and pulled her down beside her.

Meanwhile, Calton was addressing himself to the old woman in the corner.

'You wanted to see me?' he said gently, for, notwithstanding his repugnance to her, she was, after all, a woman, and dying.

'Yes, cuss ye,' croaked Mother Guttersnipe, lying down, and pulling the greasy bedclothes up to her neck. 'You ain't a parson?' with sudden suspicion.

'No, I am a lawyer.'

'I ain't a-goin' to have the cussed parsons a-prowlin' round 'ere,' growled the old woman, viciously. 'I ain't a-goin' to die yet, cuss ye; I'm goin' to get well an' strong, an' 'ave a good time of it.'

'I'm afraid you won't recover,' said Calton, gently. 'You had better let me send for a doctor.'

'No, I shan't,' retorted the hag, aiming a blow at him with all her feeble strength. 'I ain't a-goin' to have my inside spil'd with salts and senner. I don't want neither parsons nor doctors, I don't. I wouldn't 'ave a lawyer, only I'm a-thinkin' of makin' my will, I am.'

'Mind I gits the watch,' yelled Lizer, from

the corner. 'If you gives it to Sal I'll tear her eyes out.'

'Silence!' said Kilsip, sharply, and, with a muttered curse, Lizer sat back in her corner.

'Sharper than a serpent's tooth, she are,' whined the old woman, when quiet was once more restored. 'That young devil 'ave fed at my 'ome, an' now she turns, cuss her.'

'Well — well,' said Calton, rather impatiently, 'what is it you wanted to see me about?'

'Don't be in such a 'urry,' said the hag, with a scowl, 'or I'm blamed if I tell you anything, s'elp me.'

She was evidently growing very weak, so Calton turned to Kilsip and told him in a whisper to get a doctor. The detective scribbled a note on some paper, and, giving it to Lizer, ordered her to take it. At this, the other girl arose, and, putting her arm in that of the child's, they left together.

'Them two young 'usseys gone?' said Mother Guttersnipe. 'Right you are, for I don't want what I've got to tell to git into the noospaper, I don't.'

'And what is it?' asked Calton, bending forward.

The old woman took another drink of gin, and it seemed to put life into her, for she sat up in the bed, and commenced to talk rapidly, as though she were afraid of dying before her secret was told.

'You've been 'ere afore?' she said, pointing one skinny finger at Calton, 'and you wanted to find out all about 'er; but you didn't. She wouldn't let me tell, for she was always a proud jade, a-flouncin' round while 'er pore mother was a-starvin'.'

'Her mother! Are you Rosanna Moore's mother?' cried Calton, considerably astonished.

'May I die if I ain't,' croaked the hag. ''Er pore father died of drink, cuss 'im, an' I'm a-follerin' 'im to the same place in the same way. You weren't about town in the old days, or you'd a-bin after her, cuss ye.'

'After Rosanna?'

'The werry girl,' answered Mother Guttersnipe. 'She were on the stage, she were, an' my eye, what a swell she were, with all the coves a-dyin' for 'er, an' she dancin' over their black 'earts, cuss 'em; but she was allays good to me till 'e came.'

'Who came?'

' 'E!' yelled the old woman, raising herself on her arm, her eyes sparkling with vindictive fury. ''E, a-comin' round with di'monds and gold, and a-ruinin' my pore girl; an' how 'e's 'eld 'is bloomin' 'ead up all these years as if he were a saint, cuss 'im — cuss 'im.'

'Whom does she mean?' whispered Calton to Kilsip.

'Mean!' screamed Mother Guttersnipe, whose sharp ears had caught the muttered question. 'Why, Mark Frettlby!'

'Good God!' Calton rose up in his astonishment, and even Kilsip's inscrutable countenance displayed some surprise.

'Aye, 'e were a swell in them days,' pursued Mother Guttersnipe, 'and 'e comes aphilanderin' round my gal, cuss 'im, an' ruins 'er, and leaves 'er an' the child to starve, like a black-'earted villain as 'e were.'

'The child! Her name?'

'Bah,' retorted the hag, with scorn, 'as if you didn't know my gran'daughter Sal.'

'Sal, Mark Frettlby's child?'

'Yes, an' as pretty a girl as the other, tho' she 'appened to be born on the wrong side of the 'edge. Oh, I've seen 'er a-sweepin' along in 'er silks an' satins as tho' we were dirt — an' Sal 'er 'alf sister — cuss 'er.'

Exhausted by the efforts she had made, the old woman sank back in her bed, while Calton sat dazed, thinking over the astounding revelation that had just been made. That Rosanna Moore should turn out to be Mark Frettlby's mistress he hardly wondered at; after all, the millionaire was but a man, and in his young days had been no better and no

worse than the rest of his friends. Rosanna
Moore was pretty, and was evidently one of
those women who — rakes at heart — prefer
the untrammelled freedom of being a
mistress, to the sedate bondage of a wife. In
questions of morality, so many people live in
glass houses, that there are few nowadays who
can afford to throw stones. Calton did not
think any the worse of Frettlby for his
youthful follies. But what did surprise him
was that Frettlby should be so heartless, as to
leave his child to the tender mercies of an old
hag like Mother Guttersnipe. It was so
entirely different from what he knew of the
man, that he was inclined to think that the
old woman was playing him a trick.

'Did Mr. Frettlby know Sal was his child?'
he asked.

'Not 'e,' snarled Mother Guttersnipe, in an
exultant tone. ''E thought she was dead, 'e
did, arter Rosanner gave him the go-by.'

'And why did you not tell him?'

''Cause I wanted to break 'is 'eart, if 'e 'ad
any,' said the old beldame, vindictively.

'Sal was a-goin' wrong as fast as she could
till she was tuk from me. If she had gone and
got into quod I'd 'ave gone to 'im, and said,
'Look at yer darter! 'Ow I've ruined her as
you did mine.' '

'You wicked woman,' said Calton, revolted

at the malignity of the scheme. 'You sacrificed an innocent girl for this.'

'None of yer preachin',' retorted the hag sullenly; 'I ain't bin brought up for a saint, I ain't — an' I wanted to pay 'im out — 'e paid me well to 'old my tongue about my darter, an' I've got it 'ere,' laying her hand on the pillow, 'all gold, good gold — an' mine, cuss me.'

Calton rose, he felt quite sick at this exhibition of human depravity, and longed to be away. As he was putting on his hat, however, the two girls entered with the doctor, who nodded to Kilsip, cast a sharp scrutinising glance at Calton, and then walked over to the bed. The two girls went back to their corner, and waited in silence for the end. Mother Guttersnipe had fallen back in the bed, with one claw-like hand clutching the pillow, as if to protect her beloved gold, and over her face a deadly paleness was spreading, which told the practised eye of the doctor that the end was near. He knelt down beside the bed for a moment, holding the candle to the dying woman's face. She opened her eyes, and muttered drowsily —

'Who's you? get out,' but then she seemed to grasp the situation again, and she started up with a shrill yell, which made the hearers shudder, it was so weird and eerie.

'My money!' she yelled, clasping the pillow in her skinny arms. 'It's all mine, ye shan't have it — cuss ye.'

The doctor arose from his knees, and shrugged his shoulders.

'Not worth while doing anything,' he said coolly, 'she'll be dead soon.'

The old woman, mumbling over her pillow, caught the word, and burst into tears.

'Dead! dead! my poor Rosanna, with 'er golden 'air, always lovin' 'er pore mother till 'e took 'er away, an' she came back to die — die — ooh!'

Her voice died away in a long melancholy wail, that made the two girls in the corner shiver, and put their fingers in their ears.

'My good woman,' said the doctor, bending over the bed, 'would you not like to see a minister?'

She looked at him with her bright, beady eyes, already somewhat dimmed with the mists of death, and said, in a harsh, low whisper — 'Why?'

'Because you have only a short time to live,' said the doctor, gently. 'You are dying.' Mother Guttersnipe sprang up, and seized his arm with a scream of terror.

'Dyin', dyin' — no! no!' she wailed, clawing his sleeve. 'I ain't fit to die — cuss me; save me — save me; I don't know where I'd go to,

341

s'elp me — save me.'

The doctor tried to remove her hands, but she held on with wonderful tenacity.

'It is impossible,' he said briefly.

The hag fell back in her bed.

'I'll give you money to save me,' she shrieked; 'good money — all mine — all mine. See — see — 'ere — suverains,' and tearing her pillow open, she took out a canvas bag, and from it poured a gleaming stream of gold. Gold — gold — it rolled all over the bed, over the floor, away into the dark corners, yet no one touched it, so enchained were they by the horrible spectacle of the dying woman clinging to life. She clutched some of the shining pieces, and held them up to the three men as they stood silently beside the bed, but her hands trembled so that sovereigns kept falling from them on the floor with metallic clinks.

'All mine — all mine,' she shrieked, loudly. 'Give me my life — gold — money — cuss ye — I sold my soul for it — save me — give me my life,' and, with trembling hands, she tried to force the gold on them. They said no word, but stood silently looking at her, while the two girls in the corner clung together, and trembled with fear.

'Don't look at me — don't,' cried the hag, falling down again amid the shining gold.

'Ye want me to die, — I shan't — I shan't — give me my gold,' clawing at the scattered sovereigns. 'I'll take it with me — I shan't die — G — G — ' whimpering. 'I ain't done nothin' — let me live — give me a Bible — save me, G — cuss it — G — , G — .' She fell back on the bed, a corpse.

The faint light of the candle flickered on the shining gold, and on the dead face, framed in tangled white hair; while the three men, sick at heart, turned away in silence to seek assistance, with that wild cry still ringing in their ears — 'G — save me, G — !'

28

Mark Frettlby Has a Visitor.

According to the copy books of our youth, 'Procrastination is the thief of time.' Now, Brian found the truth of this. He had been in town almost a week, but he had not yet been to see Calton. Each morning — or something very near it — he set out, determined to go direct to Chancery Lane, but he never arrived there. He had returned to his lodgings in East Melbourne, and had passed his time either in the house or in the garden. When perhaps business connected with the sale of his station compelled his presence in town, he drove straight there and back. Curiously enough he shrank from meeting any of his friends. He felt keenly his recent position in the prisoner's dock. And even when walking by the Yarra, as he frequently did, he was conscious of an uneasy feeling — a feeling that he was an object of curiosity, and that people turned to look at him out of a morbid desire to see one who had been so nearly hanged for murder.

As soon as his station should be sold and

he married to Madge he determined to leave Australia, and never set foot on it again. But until he could leave the place he would see no one, nor would he mix with his former friends, so great was his dread of being stared at. Mrs. Sampson, who had welcomed him back with shrill exclamations of delight, was loud in her expressions of disapproval as to the way he was shutting himself up.

'Your eyes bein' 'ollow,' said the sympathising cricket, 'it is nat'ral as it's want of air, which my 'usband's uncle, being a druggist, an' well-to-do, in Collingwood, ses as 'ow a want of ox-eye-gent, being a French name, as 'e called the atmispeare, were fearful for pullin' people down, an' makin' 'em go off their food, which you hardly eats anythin', an' not bein' a butterfly it's expected as your appetite would be larger.'

'Oh, I'm all right,' said Brian, absently, lighting a cigarette, and only half listening to his landlady's garrulous chatter, 'but if anyone calls tell them I'm not in. I don't want to be bothered by visitors.'

'Bein' as wise a thing as Solomon ever said,' answered Mrs. Sampson, energetically, 'which, no doubt, 'e was in good 'ealth when seein' the Queen of Sheber, as is necessary when anyone calls, and not feelin' disposed to speak, which I'm often that way myself on occasions, my sperits bein' low, as I've 'eard tell soder water 'ave that effect on 'em, which you takes it with a dash of brandy, tho' to be sure that might be the cause of your want of life, and — drat that bell,' she finished, hurrying out of the room as the front-door bell sounded, 'which my legs is a-givin' way under me thro' bein' overworked.'

Meanwhile, Brian sat and smoked contentedly, much relieved by the departure of Mrs. Sampson, with her constant chatter, but he soon heard her mount the stairs again, and she entered the room with a telegram, which she handed to her lodger. ''Opin' it don't contain bad noose,' she said as she retreated to the door again, 'which I don't like 'em 'avin' had a shock in early life thro' one 'avin' come unexpected, as my uncle's grandfather were dead, avin' perished of consumption, our family all being disposed to the disease — and now, if you'll excuse me, sir, I'll get to my dinner, bein' in the 'abit of takin' my meals reg'lar, and I studies my inside carefully, bein' easily upset, thro' which I never could be a sailor.'

Mrs. Sampson, having at last exhausted herself, went out of the room, and crackled loudly down the stairs, leaving Brian to read his telegram. He tore open the envelope and found the message was from Madge, to say that they had returned, and to ask him to dine with them that evening. Fitzgerald folded up the telegram, then rising from his seat, he walked moodily up and down the room with his hands in his pockets.

'So he is there,' said the young man aloud; 'and I shall have to meet him and shake hands with him, knowing all the time what he is. If it were not for Madge I'd leave this place at once, but after the way she stood by me in my trouble, I should be a coward if I did so.'

It was as Madge had predicted — her father was unable to stay long in one place, and had come back to Melbourne a week after Brian had arrived. The pleasant party at the station was broken up, and, like the graves of a household, the guests were scattered far and wide. Peterson had left for New Zealand en route for the wonders of the Hot Lakes, and the old colonist was about to start for England in order to refresh his boyish memories. Mr. and Mrs. Rolleston had come back to Melbourne, where the wretched Felix was compelled once more to plunge into politics; and Dr. Chinston had resumed his usual routine of fees and patients.

Madge was glad to be back in Melbourne again, as now that her health was restored she craved for the excitement of town life. It was now more than three months since the murder, and the nine days' wonder was a thing of the past. The possibility of a war with Russia was the one absorbing topic of the hour, and the colonists were busy preparing for the attack of a possible enemy. As the Spanish Kings had drawn their treasures from Mexico and Peru, so might the White Czar lay violent hands on the golden stores of Australia; but here there were no uncultured savages to face, but the sons and grandsons of men who had dimmed the glories of the Russian arms at Alma and Balaclava. So in the midst of stormy rumours of wars the tragic fate of Oliver Whyte was quite forgotten. After the trial, everyone, including the detective office, had given up the matter, and mentally relegated it to the list of undiscovered crimes. In spite of the utmost vigilance, nothing new had been discovered, and it seemed likely that the assassin of Oliver Whyte would remain a free man. There were only two people in Melbourne who still held the contrary opinion, and they were Calton and Kilsip. Both these men had sworn to discover this unknown murderer, who struck his cowardly blow in the dark, and though there seemed no possible chance of success, yet they worked on. Kilsip suspected Roger Moreland, the boon companion of the dead man, but his suspicions were vague and uncertain, and there seemed little hope of verifying them. The barrister did not as yet suspect any particular person, though the death-bed confession of Mother Guttersnipe had thrown a new light on the subject, but he thought that when Fitzgerald told him the secret which Rosanna Moore had confided to his keeping, the real murderer would soon be discovered, or, at least, some clue would be found that would lead to his detection. So, as the matter stood at the time of Mark Frettlby's return to Melbourne, Mr. Calton was waiting for Fitzgerald's confession before making a move, while Kilsip worked stealthily in the dark, searching for evidence against Moreland.

On receiving Madge's telegram, Brian determined to go down in the evening, but not to dinner, so he sent a reply to Madge to that effect. He did not want to meet Mark Frettlby, but did not of course tell this to Madge, so she had her dinner by herself, as her father had gone to his club, and the time of his return was uncertain. After dinner, she wrapped a light cloak round her, and repaired to the verandah to wait for her lover. The garden looked charming in the moonlight, with the black, dense cypress trees standing up against the sky, and the great fountain splashing cool and silvery. There was a heavily-foliaged oak by the gate, and she strolled down the path, and stood under it in the shadow, listening to the whisper and rustle of its multitudinous leaves. It is curious the unearthly glamour which moonlight seems to throw over everything, and though Madge knew every flower, tree, and shrub in the garden, yet they all looked weird and fantastical in the cold, white light. She went up to the fountain, and seating herself on the edge, amused herself by dipping her hand into the chilly water, and letting it fall, like silver rain, back into the basin. Then she heard the iron gate open and shut with a clash, and springing to her feet, saw someone coming up the path in a light coat and soft wide-awake hat.

'Oh, it's you at last, Brian?' she cried, as she ran down the path to meet him. 'Why did you not come before?'

'Not being Brian, I can't say,' answered her father's voice. Madge burst out laughing.

'What an absurd mistake,' she cried. 'Why, I thought you were Brian.'

'Indeed!'

'Yes; in that hat and coat I couldn't tell the difference in the moonlight.'

'Oh,' said her father, with a laugh, pushing his hat back, 'moonlight is necessary to complete the spell, I suppose?'

'Of course,' answered his daughter. 'If there were no moonlight, alas, for lovers!'

'Alas, indeed!' echoed her father. 'They would become as extinct as the moa; but where are your eyes, Puss, when you take an old man like me for your gay young Lochinvar?'

'Well, really, papa,' answered Madge, deprecatingly, 'you do look so like him in that coat and hat that I could not tell the difference, till you spoke.'

'Nonsense, child,' said Frettlby, roughly, 'you are fanciful;' and turning on his heel, he walked rapidly towards the house, leaving Madge staring after him in astonishment, as well she might, for her father had never spoken to her so roughly before. Wondering at the cause of his sudden anger, she stood spell-bound, until there came a step behind her, and a soft, low whistle. She turned with a scream, and saw Brian smiling at her.

'Oh, it's you,' she said, with a pout, as he caught her in his arms and kissed her.

'Only me,' said Brian, ungrammatically; 'disappointing, isn't it?'

'Oh, fearfully,' answered the girl, with a gay laugh, as arm-in-arm they walked towards the house. 'But do you know I made such a curious mistake just now; I thought papa was you.'

'How strange,' said Brian, absently, for indeed he was admiring her charming face, which looked so pure and sweet in the moonlight.

'Yes, wasn't it?' she replied. 'He had on a light coat and a soft hat, just like you wear sometimes, and as you are both the same height, I took you for one another.'

Brian did not answer, but there was a cold feeling at his heart as he saw a possibility of his worst suspicions being confirmed, for just at that moment there came into his mind the curious coincidence of the man who got into the hansom cab being dressed similarly to himself. What if — 'Nonsense,' he said, aloud, rousing himself out of the train of thought the resemblance had suggested.

'I'm sure it isn't,' said Madge, who had been talking about something else for the last five minutes. 'You are a very rude young man.'

'I beg your pardon,' said Brian, waking up. 'You were saying — '

'That the horse is the most noble of all animals — Exactly.'

'I don't understand — ' began Brian, rather puzzled.

'Of course you don't,' interrupted Madge, petulantly; 'considering I've been wasting my eloquence on a deaf man for the last ten minutes; and very likely lame as well as deaf.'

And to prove the truth of the remark, she ran up the path with Brian after her. He had a long chase of it, for Madge was nimble and better acquainted with the garden than he was but at last he caught her just as she was running up the steps into the house, and then — history repeats itself.

They went into the drawing-room and found that Mr. Frettlby had gone up to his study, and did not want to be disturbed. Madge sat down to the piano, but before she struck a note, Brian took both her hands prisoners.

'Madge,' he said, gravely, as she turned round, 'what did your father say when you made that mistake?'

'He was very angry,' she answered. 'Quite cross; I'm sure I don't know why.'

Brian sighed as he released her hands, and was about to reply when the visitor's bell sounded, they heard the servant answer it, and then someone was taken upstairs to Mr. Frettlby's study.

When the footman came in to light the gas, Madge asked who it was that had come to the door.

'I don't know, miss,' he answered; 'he said he wanted to see Mr. Frettlby particularly, so I took him up to the study.'

'But I thought that papa said he was not to be disturbed?'

'Yes, miss, but the gentleman had an appointment with him.'

'Poor papa,' sighed Madge, turning again to the piano. 'He has always got such a lot to do.'

Left to themselves, Madge began playing Waldteufel's last new valse, a dreamy, haunting melody, with a touch of sadness in it, and Brian, lying lazily on the sofa, listened. Then she sang a gay little French song about Love and a Butterfly, with a mocking refrain, which made Brian laugh.

'A memory of Offenbach,' he said, rising and coming over to the piano. 'We certainly can't approach the French in writing these airy trifles.'

'They're unsatisfactory, I think,' said Madge, running her fingers over the keys; 'they mean nothing.'

'Of course not,' he replied, 'but don't you remember that De Quincy says there is no moral either big or little in the Iliad?'

'Well, I think there's more music in Barbara Allan than all those frothy things,' said Madge, with fine scorn. 'Come and sing it.'

'A five-act funeral, it is,' groaned Brian, as he rose to obey; 'let's have Garry Owen instead.'

Nothing else however would suit the capricious young person at the piano, so Brian, who had a pleasant voice, sang the quaint old ditty of cruel Barbara Allan, who treated her dying love with such disdain.

'Sir John Graham was an ass,' said Brian, when he had finished; 'or, instead of dying in such a silly manner, he'd have married her right off, without asking her permission.'

'I don't think she was worth marrying,' replied Madge, opening a book of Mendelssohn's duets; 'or she wouldn't have made such a fuss over her health not being drunk.'

'Depend upon it, she was a plain woman,' remarked Brian, gravely, 'and was angry because she wasn't toasted among the rest of the country belles. I think the young man had a narrow escape — she'd always have reminded him about that unfortunate oversight.'

'You seem to have analysed her nature pretty well,' said Madge, a little dryly; 'however, we'll leave the failings of Barbara Allan alone, and sing this.'

This was Mendelssohn's charming duet, 'Would That My Love,' which was a great favourite of Brian's. They were in the middle of it when suddenly Madge stopped, as she heard a loud cry, evidently proceeding from her father's study. Recollecting Dr. Chinston's warning, she ran out of the room, and upstairs, leaving Brian rather puzzled by her unceremonious departure, for though he had heard the cry, yet he did not attach much importance to it.

Madge knocked at the study door, and then she tried to open it, but it was locked.

'Who's there?' asked her father, sharply, from inside.

'Only me, papa,' she answered. 'I thought you were — '

'No! No — I'm all right,' replied her father, quickly. 'Go down stairs, I'll join you shortly.'

Madge went back to the drawing-room only half satisfied with the explanation. She found Brian waiting at the door, with rather an anxious face.

'What's the matter?' he asked, as she paused a moment at the foot of the stairs.

'Papa says nothing,' she replied, 'but I am sure he must have been startled, or he would not have cried out like that.'

She told him what Dr. Chinston had said about the state of her father's heart, a recital which shocked Brian greatly. They did not return to the drawing-room, but went out on the verandah, where, after wrapping a cloak around Madge, Fitzgerald lit a cigarette. They sat down at the far end of the verandah somewhat in the shadow, and could see the hall door wide open, and a warm flood of mellow light pouring therefrom, and beyond the cold, white moonshine. After about a quarter of an hour, Madge's alarm about her father having somewhat subsided, they were chatting on indifferent subjects, when a man came out of the hall door, and paused for a moment on the steps of the verandah. He was dressed in rather a fashionable suit of clothes, but, in spite of the heat of the night, he had a thick white silk scarf round his throat.

'That's rather a cool individual,' said Brian, removing his cigarette from between his lips. 'I wonder what — Good God!' he cried, rising to his feet as the stranger turned round to look at the house, and took off his hat for a moment — 'Roger Moreland.' The man started, and looked quickly round into the dark shadow of the verandah where they were seated, then, putting on his hat, he ran quickly down the path, and they heard the gate clang after him.

Madge felt a sudden fear at the expression on Brian's face, as revealed by a ray of moonlight streaming full on it.

'Who is Roger Moreland?' she asked, touching his arm — 'Ah! I remember,' with sudden horror, 'Oliver Whyte's friend.'

'Yes,' in a hoarse whisper, 'and one of the witnesses at the trial.'

29

Mr. Calton's Curiosity Is Satisfied.

There was not much sleep for Brian that night. He left Madge almost immediately, and went home, but he did not go to bed. He felt too anxious and ill at ease to sleep, and passed the greater part of the night walking up and down his room, occupied with his own sad thoughts. He was wondering in his own mind what could be the meaning of Roger Moreland's visit to Mark Frettlby. All the evidence that he had given at the trial was that he had met Whyte, and had been drinking with him during the evening. Whyte then went out, and that was the last Moreland had seen of him. Now, the question was, 'What did he go to see Mark Frettlby for?' He had no acquaintance with him, and yet he called by appointment. It is true he might have been in poverty, and the millionaire being well-known as an extremely generous man, Moreland might have called on him for money. But then the cry which Frettlby had given after the interview had lasted a short time proved that he had been startled. Madge had gone upstairs and found the door locked, her father refusing her admission. Now, why was he so anxious Moreland should not be seen by any one? That he had made some startling revelation was certain, and Fitzgerald felt sure that it was in connection with the hansom cab murder case. He wearied himself with conjectures about the matter, and towards daybreak threw himself, dressed as he was, on the bed, and slept heavily till twelve o'clock the next day. When he arose and looked at himself in the glass, he was startled at the haggard and worn appearance of his face. The moment he was awake his mind went back to Mark Frettlby and the visit of Roger Moreland.

'The net is closing round him,' he murmured to himself. 'I don't see how he can escape. Oh! Madge! Madge! if only I could spare you the bitterness of knowing what you must know, sooner or later, and that other unhappy girl — the sins of the fathers will be visited on the children — God help them.'

He took his bath, and, after dressing himself, went into his sitting-room, where he had a cup of tea, which refreshed him considerably. Mrs. Sampson came crackling merrily upstairs with a letter, and gave vent to an exclamation of surprise, on seeing his altered appearance.

'Lor, sir!' she exclaimed, 'what 'ave you bin a-doin' — me knowin' your 'abits know'd as you'd gone to bed, not to say as it's very temptin' in this 'ot weather, but with excuses, sir, you looks as if you 'adn't slept a blessed wink.'

'No more I have,' said Brian, listlessly holding out his hand for the letter. 'I was walking up and down my room all last night — I must have walked miles.'

'Ah! 'ow that puts me in mind of my pore 'usband,' chirped the cricket; 'bein' a printer, and accustomed like a howl to the darkness, when 'e was 'ome for the night 'e walked up and down till 'e wore out the carpet, bein' an expensive one, as I 'ad on my marriage, an' the only way I could stop 'im was by givin' 'im something soothin', which you, sir, ought to try — whisky 'ot, with lemon and sugar — but I've 'eard tell as chloroform — '

'No, d — it,' said Brian, hastily, startled out of his politeness, 'I've had enough of that.'

'Achin' teeth, no doubt,' said the landlady, going to the door, 'which I'm often taken that way myself, decayed teeth runnin' in the family, tho', to be sure, mine are stronger than former, a lodger of mine 'avin' bin a dentist, an' doin' them beautiful, instead of payin' rent, not avin' ready cash, his boxes bein' filled with bricks on 's departure from the 'ouse.'

As Brian did not appear particularly interested in these domestic reminiscences, and seemed as if he wanted to be left alone, Mrs. Sampson, with a final crackle, went downstairs and talked with a neighbour in the kitchen, as to the desirability of drawing her money out of the Savings Bank, in case the Russians should surprise and capture Melbourne. Brian, left alone, stared out of the window at the dusty road and the black shadows cast by the tall poplars in front of the house.

'I must leave this place,' he said to himself; 'every chance remark seems to bear on the murder, and I'm not anxious to have it constantly by my side like the skeleton at the feast.'

Suddenly he recollected the letter which he held in his hand, and which he now looked at for the first time. It proved to be from Madge, and tearing it open hastily, he read it.

'I cannot understand what is the matter with papa,' she wrote.

'Ever since that man Moreland left last night, he has shut himself up in his study, and is writing there hour after hour. I went up this morning, but he would not let me in. He did not come down to breakfast, and I am getting seriously alarmed. Come down tomorrow and see me, for I am anxious about his state of health, and I am sure that Moreland told him something which has upset him.'

'Writing,' said Brian, as he put the letter in his pocket, 'what about, I wonder? Perhaps he is thinking of committing suicide! if so, I for one will not stop him. It is a horrible thing to do, but it would be acting for the best under the circumstances.' In spite of his determination to see Calton and tell all, Fitzgerald did not go near him that day. He felt ill and weary, the want of sleep, and mental worry, telling on him terribly, and he looked ten years older than he did before the murder of Whyte. It is trouble which draws lines on the smooth forehead and furrows round the mouth. If a man has any mental worry, his life becomes a positive agony to him. Mental tortures are quite as bad as physical ones, if not worse. The last thing before dropping off to sleep is the thought of trouble, and with the first faint light of dawn, it returns and hammers all day at the weary brain. But while a man can sleep, life is rendered at least endurable; and of all the blessings which Providence has bestowed, there is none so precious as that same sleep, which, as wise Sancho Panza says, 'Wraps every man like a cloak.' Brian felt the need of rest, so sending a telegram to Calton to call on him in the morning, and another to Madge, that he would be down to luncheon next day, he stayed indoors all day, and amused himself with smoking and reading. He went to bed early, and succeeded in having a sound sleep, so when he awoke next morning, he felt considerably refreshed and invigorated.

He was having his breakfast at half-past eight, when he heard the sound of wheels, and immediately afterwards a ring at the bell. He went to the window, and saw Calton's trap was at the door. The owner was shortly afterwards shown into the room.

'Well, you are a nice fellow,' cried Calton, after greetings were over. 'Here I've been waiting for you with all the patience of Job, thinking you were still up country.'

'Will you have some breakfast?' asked Brian, laughing at his indignation.

'What have you got?' said Calton, looking over the table. 'Ham and eggs. Humph! Your landlady's culinary ideas are very limited.'

'Most landladies' ideas are,' retorted Fitzgerald, resuming his breakfast. 'Unless Heaven invents some new animal, lodgers will go on getting beef and mutton, alternated with hash, until the end of the world.'

'When one is in Rome, one musn't speak ill of the Pope,' answered Calton, with a grimace. 'Do you think your landlady could supply me with brandy and soda?'

'I think so,' answered Fitzgerald, rising, and ringing the bell; 'but isn't it rather early for that sort of thing?'

'There's a proverb about glass houses,' said Calton, severely, 'which applies to you in this particular instance.'

Whereupon Fitzgerald laughed, and Calton having been supplied with what he required, prepared to talk business.

'I need hardly tell you how anxious I am to hear what you've got to say,' he said, leaning back in his chair, 'but I may as well tell you that I am satisfied that I know half your secret already.'

'Indeed!' Fitzgerald looked astonished. 'In that case, I need not — '

'Yes, you need,' retorted Calton. 'I told you I only know half.'

'Which half?'

'Hum — rather difficult to answer — however, I'll tell you what I know, and you can supply all deficiencies. I am quite ready — go on — stop — ' he arose and closed the door carefully.

'Well,' resuming his seat, 'Mother Gutter-snipe died the other night.'

'Is she dead?'

'As a door nail,' answered Calton calmly.

'And a horrible death-bed it was — her screams ring in my ears yet — but before she died she sent for me, and said — '

'What?'

'That she was the mother of Rosanna Moore.'

'Yes!'

'And that Sal Rawlins was Rosanna's child.'

'And the father?' said Brian, in a low voice.

'Was Mark Frettlby.'

'Ah!'

'And now what have you to tell me?'

'Nothing!'

'Nothing,' echoed Calton, surprised, 'then this is what Rosanna Moore told you when she died?'

'Yes!'

'Then why have you made such a mystery about it?'

'You ask that?' said Fitzgerald, looking up, in surprise. 'If I had told it, don't you see what difference it would have made to Madge?'

'I'm sure I don't,' retorted the barrister, completely mystified. 'I suppose you mean Frettlby's connection with Rosanna Moore; well, of course, it was not a very creditable thing for her to have been Frettlby's mistress, but still — '

'His mistress?' said Fitzgerald, looking up

sharply 'then you don't know all.'

'What do you mean — was she not his mistress?'

'No — his wife!' Calton sprang to his feet, and gave a cry of surprise.

'His wife!'

Fitzgerald nodded.

'Why, Mother Guttersnipe did not know this — she thought Rosanna was his mistress.'

'He kept his marriage secret,' answered Brian, 'and as his wife ran away with someone else shortly afterwards, he never revealed it.'

'I understand now,' said the barrister, slowly. 'For if Mark Frettlby was lawfully married to Rosanna Moore — Madge is illegitimate.'

'Yes, and she now occupies the place which Sal Rawlins — or rather Sal Frettlby ought to.'

'Poor girl,' said Calton, a little sadly. 'But all this does not explain the mystery of Whyte's murder.'

'I will tell you that,' said Fitzgerald, quickly. 'When Rosanna left her husband, she ran away to England with some young fellow, and when he got tired of her she returned to the stage, and became famous as a burlesque actress, under the name of Musette. There she met Whyte, as your friend found out, and they came out here for the purpose of extorting money from Frettlby. When they arrived in Melbourne, Rosanna let Whyte do all the business, and kept herself quiet. She gave her marriage certificate to Whyte, and he had it on him the night he was murdered.'

'Then Gorby was right,' interposed Calton, eagerly. 'The man to whom those papers were valuable did murder Whyte!'

'Can you doubt it? And that man was — '

'Not Mark Frettlby?' burst out Calton. 'Surely not Mark Frettlby?'

Brian nodded. 'Yes, Mark Frettlby.'

There was a silence for a few moments, Calton being too much startled by the revelation to say anything.

'When did you discover this?' he asked, after a pause.

'At the time you first came to see me in prison,' said Brian. 'I had no suspicion till then; but when you said that Whyte was murdered for the sake of certain papers, I, knowing full well what they were and to whom they were of value — guessed immediately that Mark Frettlby had killed Whyte in order to obtain them and to keep his secret.'

'There can be no doubt of it,' said the barrister, with a sigh. 'So this is the reason Frettlby wanted Madge to marry Whyte — her hand was to be the price of his silence.

When he withdrew his consent, Whyte threatened him with exposure. I remember he left the house in a very excited state on the night he was murdered. Frettlby must have followed him up to town, got into the cab with him, and after killing him with chloroform, must have taken the marriage certificate from his secret pocket, and escaped.'

Brian rose to his feet, and walked rapidly up and down the room.

'Now you can understand what a hell my life has been for the last few months,' he said, 'knowing that he had committed the crime; and yet I had to sit with him, eat with him, and drink with him, with the knowledge that he was a murderer, and Madge — Madge, his daughter!'

Just then a knock came to his door, and Mrs. Sampson entered with a telegram, which she handed to Brian. He tore it open as she withdrew, and glancing over it, gave a cry of horror, and let it flutter to his feet.

Calton turned rapidly on hearing his cry, and seeing him fall into a chair with a white face, snatched up the telegram and read it. When he did so, his face grew as pale and startled as Fitzgerald's, and lifting his hand, he said solemnly —

'It is the judgment of God!'

30

Nemesis.

Men, according to the old Greek, 'are the sport of the gods,' who, enthroned on high Olympus, put evil desires into the hearts of mortals; and when evil actions were the outcome of evil thoughts, amused themselves by watching the ineffectual efforts made by their victims to escape a relentless deity called Nemesis, who exacted a penalty for their evil deeds. It was no doubt very amusing — to the gods — but it is questionable if the men found it so. They had their revenge, however, for weary of plaguing puny mortals, who whimpered and cried when they saw they could not escape, the inevitable Nemesis turned her attention from actors to spectators, and made a clean sweep of the whole Olympian hierarchy. She smashed their altars, pulled down their statues, and after she had completed her malicious work, found that she had, vulgarly speaking, been cutting off her nose to spite her face, for she, too, became an object of derision and of disbelief, and was forced to retire to the same obscurity to which she had relegated the other deities. But men found out that she had not been altogether useless as a scapegoat upon which to lay the blame of their own shortcomings, so they created a new deity called Fate, and laid any misfortune which happened to them to her charge. Her worship is still very popular, especially among lazy and unlucky people, who never bestir themselves: on the ground that whether they do so or not their lives are already settled by Fate. After all, the true religion of Fate has been preached by George Eliot, when she says that our lives are the outcome of our actions. Set up any idol you please upon which to lay the blame of unhappy lives and baffled ambitions, but the true cause is to be found in men themselves.

Every action, good or bad, which we do has its corresponding reward, and Mark Frettlby found it so, for the sins of his youth were now being punished in his old age. No doubt he had sinned gaily enough in that far-off time when life's cup was still brimming with wine, and no asp hid among the roses; but Nemesis had been an unseen spectator of all his thoughtless actions, and now she came to demand her just dues. He felt somewhat as Faust must have felt when Mephistopheles suggested a visit to Hades, in repayment of those years of magic youth and magic power.

So long ago it seemed since he had married Rosanna Moore, that he almost persuaded himself that it had been only a dream — a pleasant dream, with a disagreeable awakening. When she had left him he had tried to forget her, recognising how unworthy she was of a good man's love. He heard that she had died in a London hospital, and with a passionate sigh for a perished love, he had dismissed her from his thoughts for ever. His second marriage had turned out a happy one, and he regretted the death of his wife deeply. Afterwards, all his love centred in his daughter, and he thought he would be able to spend his declining years in peace. This, however, was not to be, and he was thunderstruck when Whyte arrived from England with the information that his first wife still lived, and that the daughter of his second was illegitimate. Sooner than risk exposure, Frettlby agreed to anything; but Whyte's demands became too exorbitant, and he refused to comply with them. On Whyte's death he again breathed freely, when suddenly a second possessor of his fatal secret started up in the person of Roger Moreland. As the murder of Duncan had to be followed by that of Banquo, in order to render Macbeth safe, so he foresaw that while Roger Moreland lived his life would be one long misery. He knew that the friend of the murdered man would be his master, and would never leave him during his life, while after his death he would probably publish the whole ghastly story, and defame the memory of the widely-respected Mark Frettlby. What is it that Shakespeare says? —

'Good name in man and woman . . .
Is the immediate jewel of their souls.'

And after all these years of spotless living and generous use of his wealth, was he to be dragged down to the depths of infamy and degradation by a man like Moreland? Already, in fancy, he heard the jeering cries of his fellow-men, and saw the finger of scorn point at him — he, the great Mark Frettlby, famous throughout Australia for his honesty, integrity, and generosity. No, it could not be, and yet this would surely happen unless he took means to prevent it.

The day after he had seen Moreland, and knew that his secret was no longer safe, since it was in the power of a man who might reveal it at any moment in a drunken fit, or out of sheer maliciousness, he sat at his desk writing. After a time he laid down his pen, and taking up a portrait of his dead wife which stood just in front of him, he stared at it long and earnestly. As he did so, his mind went back to the time when he had first met and loved her. Even as Faust had entered into the purity and serenity of Gretchen's chamber, out of the coarseness and profligacy of Auerbach's cellar, so he, leaving behind him the wild life of his youth, had entered into the peace and quiet of a domestic home. The old feverish life with Rosanna Moore, seemed to be as unsubstantial and chimerical, as, no doubt, his union with Lillith after he met Eve, seemed to Adam in the old Rabbinical legend. There seemed to be only one way open to him, by which he could escape the relentless fate which dogged his steps. He would write a confession of everything from the time he had first met Rosanna, and then — death. He would cut the Gordian knot of all his difficulties, and then his secret would be safe; safe? no, it could not be while Moreland lived. When he was dead Moreland would see Madge and embitter her life with the story of her father's sins — yes — he must live to protect her, and drag his weary chain of bitter remembrance through life, always with that terrible sword of Damocles hanging over him. But still, he would write out his confession, and after his death, whenever it may happen, it might help if not altogether to exculpate, at least to secure some pity for a man who had been hardly dealt with by Fate. His resolution taken, he put it into force at once, and sat all day at his desk filling page after page with the history of his past life, which was so bitter to him. He started at first languidly, and as in the performance of an unpleasant but necessary duty. Soon, however, he became interested in it, and took a peculiar pleasure in putting down every minute circumstance which made the case stronger against himself. He dealt with it, not as a criminal, but as a prosecutor, and painted his conduct as much blacker than it really had been. Towards the end of the day, however, after reading over the earlier sheets, he experienced a revulsion of feeling, seeing how severe he had been on himself, so he wrote a defence of his conduct, showing that fate had been too strong for him. It was a weak argument to bring forward, but still he felt it was the only one that he could make. It was quite dark when he had finished, and while sitting in the twilight, looking dreamily at the sheets scattered all over his desk, he heard a knock at the door, and his daughter's voice asking if he was coming to dinner. All day long he had closed his door against everyone, but now his task being ended, he collected all the closely-written sheets together, placed them in a drawer of his escritoire, which he locked, and then opened the door.

'Dear papa,' cried Madge, as she entered rapidly, and threw her arms around his neck, 'what have you been doing here all day by yourself?'

'Writing,' returned her father laconically, as he gently removed her arms.

'Why, I thought you were ill,' she answered, looking at him apprehensively.

'No, dear,' he replied, quietly. 'Not ill, but worried.'

'I knew that dreadful man who came last night had told you something to worry you. Who is he?'

'Oh! a friend of mine,' answered Frettlby, with hesitation.

'What — Roger Moreland?'

Her father started.

'How do you know it was Roger Moreland?'

'Oh! Brian recognised him as he went out.'

Mark Frettlby hesitated for a few moments, and then busied himself with the papers on his desk, as he replied in a low voice —

'You are right — it was Roger Moreland — he is very hard up, and as he was a friend of poor Whyte's, he asked me to assist him, which I did.'

He hated to hear himself telling such a

deliberate falsehood, but there was no help for it — Madge must never know the truth so long as he could conceal it.

'Just like you,' said Madge, kissing him lightly with filial pride. 'The best and kindest of men.'

He shivered slightly as he felt her caress, and thought how she would recoil from him did she know all. 'After all,' says some cynical writer, 'the illusions of youth are mostly due to the want of experience.' Madge, ignorant in a great measure of the world, cherished her pleasant illusions, though many of them had been destroyed by the trials of the past year, and her father longed to keep her in this frame of mind.

'Now go down to dinner, my dear,' he said, leading her to the door. 'I will follow soon.'

'Don't be long,' replied his daughter, 'or I shall come up again,' and she ran down the stairs, her heart feeling strangely light.

Her father looked after her until she vanished, then heaving a regretful sigh returned to his study, and taking out the scattered papers fastened them together, and endorsed them.

'My Confession.' He then placed them in an envelope, sealed it, and put it back in the desk. 'If all that is in that packet were known,' he said aloud, as he left the room, 'what would the world say?'

That night he was singularly brilliant at the dinner table. Generally a very reticent and grave man, on this night he laughed and talked so gaily that the very servants noticed the change. The fact was he felt a sense of relief at having unburdened his mind, and felt as though by writing out that confession he had laid the spectre which had haunted him for so long. His daughter was delighted at the change in his spirits, but the old Scotch nurse, who had been in the house since Madge was a baby, shook her head —

'He's fey,' she said gravely. 'He's no lang for the warld.'

Of course she was laughed at — people who believe in presentiments generally are — but, nevertheless, she held firmly to her opinion.

Mr. Frettlby went to bed early that night, the excitement of the last few days and the feverish gaiety in which he had lately indulged proving too strong for him. No sooner had he laid his head on his pillow than he dropped off to sleep at once, and forgot in placid slumber the troubles and worries of his waking hours.

It was only nine o'clock, so Madge stayed by herself in the great drawing-room, and read a new novel, which was then creating a sensation, called 'Sweet Violet Eyes.' It belied its reputation, however, for it was very soon thrown on the table with a look of disgust, and rising from her seat Madge walked up and down the room, and wished some good fairy would hint to Brian that he was wanted. If man is a gregarious animal, how much more, then, is a woman? This is not a conundrum, but a simple truth. 'A female Robinson Crusoe,' says a writer who prided himself upon being a keen observer of human nature — 'a female Robinson Crusoe would have gone mad for want of something to talk to.' This remark, though severe, nevertheless contains several grains of truth, for women, as a rule, talk more than men. They are more sociable, and a Miss Misanthrope, in spite of Justin McCarthy's, is unknown — at least in civilised communities. Miss Frettlby, being neither misanthropic nor dumb, began to long for some one to talk to, and, ringing the bell, ordered Sal to be sent in. The two girls had become great friends, and Madge, though by two years the younger, assumed the *role* of mentor, and under her guidance Sal was rapidly improving. It was a strange irony of fate which brought together these two children of the same father, each with such different histories — the one reared in luxury and affluence, never having known want; the other dragged up in the gutter, all unsexed and besmirched by the life she had led. 'The whirligig of time brings in its revenges,' and it was the last thing in the world Mark Frettlby would have thought of seeing: Rosanna Moore's child, whom he fancied dead, under the same roof as his daughter Madge.

On receiving Madge's message Sal came to the drawing room, and the two were soon chatting amicably together. The room was almost in darkness, only one lamp being lighted; Mr. Frettlby very sensibly detested gas, with its glaring light, and had nothing but lamps in his drawing-room. At the end of the apartment, where Sal and Madge were seated, there was a small table. On it stood a large lamp, with an opaque globe, which, having a shade over it, threw a soft and subdued circle of light round the table, leaving the rest of the room in a kind of semi-darkness. Near this sat Madge and Sal, talking gaily, and away on the left-hand side they could see the door open, and a warm flood of light pouring in from the hall.

They had been talking together for some time, when Sal's quick ear caught a footfall on the soft carpet, and, turning rapidly, she saw a tall figure advancing down the room. Madge saw it too, and started up in surprise on recognising her father. He was clothed in his dressing-gown, and carried some papers in his hand.

'Why, papa,' said Madge, in surprise. 'I — '

'Hush!' whispered Sal, grasping her arms. 'He's asleep.'

And so he was. In accordance with the dictates of the excited brain, the weary body had risen from the bed and wandered about the house. The two girls, drawing back into the shadow, watched him with bated breath as he came slowly down the room. In a few moments he was within the circle of light, and, moving noiselessly along, he laid the papers he carried on the table. They were in a large blue envelope much worn, with writing in red ink on it. Sal recognised it at once as the one she had seen in the possession of the dead woman, and with an instinctive feeling that there was something wrong, she tried to draw Madge back, as she watched her father's action with an intensity of feeling which held her spell-bound. Frettlby opened the envelope, and took therefrom a yellow, frayed piece of paper, which he spread out on the table. Madge bent forward to see it, but Sal, with a sudden terror drew her back.

'For God's sake no,' she cried.

But it was too late; Madge had caught sight of the names on the paper — 'Marriage

— Rosanna Moore — Mark Frettlby' — and the whole awful truth flashed upon her. These were the papers Rosanna Moore had handed to Whyte. Whyte had been murdered by the man to whom the papers were of value —

'Oh! My father!'

She staggered blindly forward, and then, with one piercing shriek, fell to the ground. In doing so, she struck against her father, who was still standing beside the table. Awakened suddenly, with that wild cry in his ears, he opened his eyes wide, put out feeble hands, as if to keep something back, and with a strangled cry fell dead on the floor beside his daughter. Sal, horror-struck, did not lose her presence of mind, but, snatching the papers off the table, she thrust them into her pocket, and then called aloud for the servants. But they, already attracted by Madge's wild cry, came hurrying in, to find Mark Frettlby, the millionaire, lying dead, and his daughter in a faint beside her father's corpse.

31

Hush-Money.

As soon as Brian received the telegram which announced the death of Mark Frettlby, he put on his hat, stepped into Calton's trap, and drove along to the St. Kilda station in Flinders Street with that gentleman. There Calton dismissed his trap, sending a note to his clerk with the groom, and went down to St. Kilda with Fitzgerald. On arrival they found the whole house perfectly quiet and orderly, owing to the excellent management of Sal Rawlins. She had taken the command in everything, and although the servants, knowing her antecedents, were disposed to resent her doing so, yet such were her administrative powers and strong will, that they obeyed her implicitly. Mark Frettlby's body had been taken up to his bedroom, Madge had been put to bed, and Dr. Chinston and Brian sent for. When they arrived they could not help expressing their admiration at the capital way in which Sal Rawlins had managed things.

'She's a clever girl that,' whispered Calton

to Fitzgerald. 'Curious thing she should have taken up her proper position in her father's house. Fate is a deal cleverer than we mortals think her.'

Brian was about to reply when Dr. Chinston entered the room. His face was very grave, and Fitzgerald looked at him in alarm.

'Madge — Miss Frettlby,' he faltered.

'Is very ill,' replied the doctor; 'has an attack of brain fever. I can't answer for the consequences yet.'

Brian sat down on the sofa, and stared at the doctor in a dazed sort of way. Madge dangerously ill — perhaps dying. What if she were to die, and he to lose the true-hearted woman who stood so nobly by him in his trouble?

'Cheer up,' said Chinston, patting him on the shoulder; 'while there's life there's hope, and whatever human aid can do to save her will be done.'

Brian grasped the doctor's hand in silence, his heart being too full to speak.

'How did Frettlby die?' asked Calton.

'Heart disease,' said Chinston. 'His heart was very much affected, as I discovered a week or so ago. It appears he was walking in his sleep, and entering the drawing-room, he alarmed Miss Frettlby, who screamed, and must have touched him. He awoke suddenly, and the natural consequences followed — he dropped down dead.'

'What alarmed Miss Frettlby?' asked Brian, in a low voice, covering his face with his hand.

'The sight of her father walking in his sleep, I suppose,' said Chinston, buttoning his glove; 'and the shock of his death which took place indirectly through her, accounts for the brain fever.'

'Madge Frettlby is not the woman to scream and waken a somnambulist,' said Calton, decidedly, 'knowing as she did the danger. There must be some other reason.'

'This young woman will tell you all about it,' said Chinston, nodding towards Sal, who entered the room at this moment. 'She was present, and since then has managed things admirably; and now I must go,' he said, shaking hands with Calton and Fitzgerald. 'Keep up your heart, my boy; I'll pull her through yet.' After the doctor had gone, Calton turned sharply to Sal Rawlins, who stood waiting to be addressed.

'Well,' he said briskly, 'can you tell us what startled Miss Frettlby?'

'I can, sir,' she answered quietly. 'I was in the drawing-room when Mr. Frettlby died — but — we had better go up to the study.'

'Why?' asked Calton, in surprise, as he and

Fitzgerald followed her up stairs.

'Because, sir,' she said, when they had entered the study and she had locked the door,

'I don't want any one but yourselves to know what I tell you.'

'More mystery,' muttered Calton, as he glanced at Brian, and took his seat at the escritoire.

'Mr. Frettlby went to bed early last night,' said Sal, calmly, 'and Miss Madge and I were talking together in the drawing-room, when he entered, walking in his sleep, and carrying some papers — '

Both Calton and Fitzgerald started, and the latter grew pale.

'He came down the room, and spread out a paper on the table where the lamp was.

'Miss Madge bent forward to see what it was. I tried to stop her, but it was too late.

'She gave a scream, and fell on the floor. In doing so she happened to touch her father.

'He awoke, and fell down dead.'

'And the papers?' asked Calton, uneasily.

Sal did not answer, but producing them from her pocket, laid them in his hands.

Brian bent forward, as Calton opened the envelope in silence, but both gave vent to an exclamation of horror at seeing the certificate of marriage which they knew Rosanna Moore had given to Whyte. Their worst suspicions were confirmed, and Brian turned away his head, afraid to meet the barrister's eye. The latter folded up the papers thoughtfully, and put them in his pocket.

'You know what these are?' he asked Sal, eyeing her keenly.

'I could hardly help knowing,' she answered; 'it proves that Rosanna Moore was Mr. Frettlby's wife, and — ' she hesitated.

'Go on,' said Brian, in a harsh tone, looking up.

'And they were the papers she gave Mr. Whyte.'

'Well!'

Sal was silent for a moment, and then looked up with a flush.

'You needn't think I'm going to split,' she said, indignantly, recurring to her Bourke Street slang in the excitement of the moment. 'I know what you know, but I'll be as silent as the grave.'

'Thank you,' said Brian, fervently, taking her hand; 'I know you love her too well to betray this terrible secret.'

'I would be a nice 'un, I would,' said Sal, with a scorn, 'after her lifting me out of the gutter, to round on her — a poor girl like me, without a friend or a relative, now Gran's dead.'

Calton looked up quickly. It was plain Sal was quite ignorant that Rosanna Moore was her mother. So much the better; they would keep her in ignorance, perhaps not altogether, but it would be folly to undeceive her at present.

'I'm goin' to Miss Madge now,' she said, going to the door, 'and I won't see you again; she's getting light-headed, and might let it out; but I'll not let any one in but myself,' and so saying, she left the room.

'Cast thy bread upon the waters,' said Calton, oracularly. 'The kindness of Miss Frettlby to that poor waif is already bearing fruit — gratitude is the rarest of qualities, rarer even than modesty.'

Fitzgerald made no answer, but stared out of the window, and thought of his darling lying sick unto death, and he able to do nothing to save her.

'Well,' said Calton, sharply.

'Oh, I beg your pardon,' said Fitzgerald, turning in confusion. 'I suppose the will must be read, and all that sort of thing.'

'Yes,' answered the barrister, 'I am one of the executors.'

'And the others?'

'Yourself and Chinston,' answered Calton; 'so I suppose,' turning to the desk, 'we can look at his papers, and see that all is straight.'

'Yes, I suppose so,' replied Brian, mechanically, his thoughts far away, and then he turned again to the window. Suddenly Calton gave vent to an exclamation of surprise, and, turning hastily, Brian saw him holding a thick roll of papers in his hand, which he had taken out of the drawer.

'Look here, Fitzgerald,' he said, greatly excited, 'here is Frettlby's confession — look!' and he held it up.

Brian sprang forward in astonishment. So at last the hansom cab mystery was to be cleared up. These sheets, no doubt, contained the whole narration of the crime, and how it was committed.

'We will read it, of course,' he said, hesitating, half hoping that Calton would propose to destroy it at once.

'Yes,' answered Calton; 'the three executors must read it, and then — we will burn it.'

'That will be the better way,' answered Brian, gloomily. 'Frettlby is dead, and the law can do nothing in the matter, so it would be best to avoid the scandal of publicity. But why tell Chinston?'

'We must,' said Calton, decidedly. 'He will be sure to gather the truth from Madge's ravings, and he may as well know all. He is quite safe, and will be silent as the grave. But I am more sorry to tell Kilsip.'

'The detective? Good God, Calton, surely you will not do so!'

'I must,' replied the barrister, quietly. 'Kilsip is firmly persuaded that Moreland committed the crime, and I have the same dread of his pertinacity as you had of mine. He may find out all.'

'What must be, must be,' said Fitzgerald, clenching his hands. 'But I hope no one else will find out this miserable story. There's Moreland, for instance.'

'Ah, true!' said Calton, thoughtfully. 'He called and saw Frettlby the other night, you say?'

'Yes. I wonder what for?'

'There is only one answer,' said the barrister, slowly. 'He must have seen Frettlby following Whyte when he left the hotel, and wanted hush-money.'

'I wonder if he got it?' observed Fitzgerald.

'Oh, I'll soon find that out,' answered Calton, opening the drawer again, and taking out the dead man's cheque-book. 'Let me see what cheques have been drawn lately.' Most of the blocks were filled up for small amounts, and one or two for a hundred or so. Calton could find no large sum such as Moreland would have demanded, when, at the very end of the book, he found a cheque torn off, leaving the block-slip quite blank.

'There you are,' he said, triumphantly holding out the book to Fitzgerald. 'He wasn't such a fool as to write in the amount on the block, but tore the cheque out, and wrote in the sum required.'

'And what's to be done about it?'

'Let him keep it, of course,' answered Calton, shrugging his shoulders. 'It's the only way to secure his silence.'

'I expect he cashed it yesterday, and is off by this time,' said Brian, after a moment's pause.

'So much the better for us,' said Calton, grimly. 'But I don't think he's off, or Kilsip would have let me know. We must tell him, or he'll get everything out of Moreland, and the consequences will be that all Melbourne will know the story; whereas, by showing him the confession, we get him to leave Moreland alone, and thus secure silence in both cases.'

'I suppose we must see Chinston?'

'Yes, of course. I will telegraph to him and Kilsip to come up to my office this afternoon at three o'clock, and then we will settle the whole matter.'

'And Sal Rawlins?'

'Oh! I quite forgot about her,' said Calton, in a perplexed voice. 'She knows nothing about her parents, and, of course, Mark Frettlby died in the belief that she was dead.'

'We must tell Madge,' said Brian, gloomily. 'There is no help for it. Sal is by rights the heiress to the money of her dead father.'

'That depends upon the will,' replied Calton, dryly. 'If it specifies that the money is left to 'my daughter, Margaret Frettlby,' Sal Rawlins can have no claim; and if such is the case, it will be no good telling her who she is.'

'And what's to be done?'

'Sal Rawlins,' went on the barrister, without noticing the interruption, 'has evidently never given a thought to her father or mother, as the old hag, no doubt, swore they were dead. So I think it will be best to keep silent — that is, if no money is left to her, and, as her father thought her dead, I don't think there will be any. In that case, it would be best to settle an income on her. You can easily find a pretext, and let the matter rest.'

'But suppose, in accordance with the wording of the will, she is entitled to all the money?'

'In that case,' said Calton, gravely, 'there is only one course open — she must be told everything, and the dividing of the money left to her generosity. But I don't think you need be alarmed, I'm pretty sure Madge is the heiress.'

'It's not the money I think about,' said

391

Brian, hastily. 'I'd take Madge without a penny.'

'My boy,' said the barrister, placing his hand kindly on Brian's shoulder, 'when you marry Madge Frettlby, you will get what is better than money — a heart of gold.'

32

De Mortuis Nil Nisi Bonum.

'Nothing is certain but the unforeseen;' so says a French proverb, and judging from the unexpected things which daily happen to us, it is without doubt a very true one. If anyone had told Madge Frettlby one day that she would be stretched on a bed of sickness the next, and would be quite oblivious of the world and its doings, she would have laughed the prophet to scorn. Yet it was so, and she was tossing and turning on a bed of pain to which the couch of Procustes was one of roses. Sal sat beside her, ever watchful of her wants, and listened through the bright hours of the day, or the still ones of the night, to the wild and incoherent words which issued from her lips. She incessantly called on her father to save himself, and then would talk about Brian, and sing snatches of song, or would sob broken sentences about her dead mother, until the heart of the listener ached to hear her. No one was allowed into the room except Sal, and when Dr. Chinston heard the things she was saying, although used to such cases, he recoiled.

'There is blood on your hands,' cried Madge, sitting up in bed, with her hair all tangled and falling over her shoulders; 'red blood, and you cannot wash it off. Oh, Cain! God save him! Brian, you are not guilty; my father killed him. God! God!' and she fell back on her disordered pillows weeping bitterly.

Dr. Chinston did not say anything, but shortly afterwards took his leave, after telling Sal on no account to let anyone see the patient.

''Tain't likely,' said Sal, in a disgusted tone, as she closed the door after him. 'I'm not a viper to sting the bosom as fed me,' from which it may be gathered she was advancing rapidly in her education.

Meanwhile Dr. Chinston had received Calton's telegram, and was considerably astonished thereat. He was still more so when, on arriving at the office at the time appointed, he found Calton and Fitzgerald were not alone, but a third man whom he had never seen was with them. The latter Calton introduced to him as Mr. Kilsip, of the detective office, a fact which made the worthy doctor uneasy, as he could in no wise divine the meaning of it. However, he made no remark, but took the seat handed to him by Mr. Calton and prepared to listen. Calton locked the door of the office, and then went back to his desk, having the other three seated before him in a kind of semi-circle.

'In the first place,' said Calton to the doctor, 'I have to inform you that you are one of the executors under the will of the late Mr. Frettlby, and that is why I asked you to come here to-day. The other executors are Mr. Fitzgerald and myself.'

'Oh, indeed,' murmured the doctor, politely.

'And now,' said Calton, looking at him, 'do you remember the hansom cab murder, which caused such a sensation some months ago?'

'Yes, I do,' replied the doctor, rather astonished; 'but what has that to do with the will?'

'Nothing to do with the will,' answered Calton, gravely; 'but the fact is, Mr. Frettlby was implicated in the affair.'

Dr. Chinston glanced enquiringly at Brian, but that gentleman shook his head.

'It has nothing to do with my arrest,' he said, sadly.

Madge's words, uttered in her delirium, flashed across the doctor's memory.

'What do you mean?' he gasped, pushing back his chair. 'How was he implicated?'

'That I cannot tell you,' answered Calton, 'until I read his confession.'

'Ah!' said Kilsip, becoming very attentive.

'Yes,' said Calton, turning to Kilsip, 'your hunt after Moreland is a wild-goose chase, for the murderer of Oliver Whyte is discovered.'

'Discovered!' cried Kilsip and the doctor in one breath.

'Yes, and his name is Mark Frettlby.'

Kilsip shot a glance of disdain out of his bright black eyes, and gave a low laugh of disbelief, but the doctor pushed back his chair furiously, and arose to his feet.

'This is monstrous,' he cried, in a rage. 'I won't sit still and hear this accusation against my dead friend.'

'Unfortunately, it is too true,' said Brian, sadly.

'How dare you say so?' said Chinston, turning angrily on him. 'And you going to marry his daughter!'

'There is only one way to settle the question,' said Calton, coldly. 'We must read his confession.'

'But why the detective?' asked the doctor, ungraciously, as he took his seat.

'Because I want him to hear for himself that Mr. Frettlby committed the crime, that he may keep silence.'

'Not till I've arrested him,' said Kilsip, determinedly.

'But he's dead,' said Brian.

'I'm speaking of Roger Moreland,' retorted Kilsip. 'For he and no other murdered Oliver Whyte.'

'That's a much more likely story,' Chinston said.

'I tell you no,' said Calton, vehemently. 'God knows I would like to preserve Mark Frettlby's good name, and it is with this object I have brought you all together. I will read the confession, and when you know the truth, I want you all to keep silent about it, as Mark Frettlby is dead, and the publication of his crime can do no good to anyone.'

'I know,' resumed Calton, addressing the detective, 'that you are fully convinced in your own mind that you are right and I am wrong, but what if I tell you that Mark Frettlby died holding those very papers for the sake of which the crime was committed?'

Kilsip's face lengthened considerably.

'What were the papers?'

'The marriage certificate of Mark Frettlby and Rosanna Moore, the woman who died in the back slum.'

Kilsip was not often astonished; but he was so now. And Dr. Chinston fell back in his chair, staring at the barrister in blank amazement.

'And what's more,' went on Calton, triumphantly, 'do you know that Moreland went to Frettlby two nights ago and obtained a certain sum for hush-money?'

'What!' cried Kilsip.

'Yes, Moreland, in coming out of the hotel, evidently saw Frettlby, and threatened to expose him unless he paid for his silence.'

'Very strange,' murmured Kilsip, to himself, with a disappointed look on his face.

'But why did Moreland keep still so long?'

'I cannot tell you,' replied Calton, 'but, no doubt, the confession will explain all.'

'Then for Heaven's sake read it,' broke in Dr. Chinston, impatiently. 'I'm quite in the dark, and all your talk is Greek to me.'

'One moment,' said Kilsip, dragging a bundle from under his chair, and untying it. 'If you are right, what about this?' and he held up a light coat, very much soiled and weather-worn.

'Whose is that?' asked Calton, startled. 'Not Whyte's?'

'Yes, Whyte's,' repeated Kilsip, with great satisfaction. 'I found it in the Fitzroy Gardens, near the gate that opens to George Street, East Melbourne. It was up in a fir-tree.'

'Then Mr. Frettlby must have got out at Powlett Street, and walked down George Street, and then through the Fitzroy Gardens into town,' said Calton.

Kilsip took no heed of the remark, but took a small bottle out of the pocket of the coat and held it up.

'I also found this,' he said.

'Chloroform,' cried everyone, guessing at once that it was the missing bottle.

'Exactly,' said Kilsip, replacing it. 'This was the bottle which contained the poison used by — by — well, call him the murderer. The name of the chemist being on the label, I went to him and found out who bought it. Now, who do you think?' with a look of triumph.

'Frettlby,' said Calton, decidedly.

'No, Moreland,' burst out Chinston, greatly excited.

'Neither,' retorted the detective, calmly. 'The man who purchased this was Oliver Whyte himself.'

'Himself?' echoed Brian, now thoroughly surprised, as, indeed were all the others.

'Yes. I had no trouble in finding out that, thanks to the 'Poisons Act.' As I knew no one would be so foolish as to carry chloroform about in his pocket for any length of time, I mentioned the day of the murder as the probable date it was bought. The chemist turned up in his book, and found that Whyte was the purchaser.'

'And what did he buy it for?' asked Chinston.

'That's more than I can tell you,' said Kilsip, with a shrug of his shoulders. 'It's down in the book as being bought for medicinal uses, which may mean anything.'

'The law requires a witness,' observed Calton, cautiously. 'Who was the witness?'

Again Kilsip smiled triumphantly.

'I think I can guess,' said Fitzgerald. 'Moreland?'

Kilsip nodded.

'And I suppose,' remarked Calton, in a slightly sarcastic tone, 'that is another of your proofs against Moreland. He knew that Whyte had chloroform on him, therefore he followed him that night and murdered him?'

'Well, I — '

'It's a lot of nonsense,' said the barrister, impatiently. 'There's nothing against Moreland to implicate him. If he killed Whyte, what made him go and see Frettlby?'

'But,' said Kilsip, sagely nodding his head, 'if, as Moreland says, he had Whyte's coat in his possession before the murder, how is it that I should discover it afterwards up a fir-tree in the Fitzroy Gardens, with an empty chloroform bottle in the pocket?'

'He may have been an accomplice,' suggested Calton.

'What's the good of all this conjecturing?' said Chinston, impatiently, now thoroughly tired of the discussion. 'Read the confession, and we will soon know the truth, without all this talk.'

Calton assented, and all having settled themselves to listen, he began to read what the dead man had written.

33

The Confession.

'What I am now about to write is set forth by me so that the true circumstances connected with the 'Hansom Cab Tragedy,' which took place in Melbourne in 18 — , may be known. I owe a confession, particularly to Brian Fitzgerald, seeing that he was accused of the crime. Although I know he was rightfully acquitted of the charge, yet I wish him to know all about the case, though I am convinced, from his altered demeanour towards me, that he is better acquainted with it than he chooses to confess. In order to account for the murder of Oliver Whyte, I must go back to the beginning of my life in this colony, and show how the series of events began which culminated in the committal of the crime.

'Should it be necessary to make this confession public, in the interests of justice, I can say nothing against such a course being taken; but I would be grateful if it could be suppressed, both on account of my good name and of my dear daughter Margaret, whose love and affection has so soothed and brightened my life.

'If, however, she should be informed of the contents of these pages, I ask her to deal leniently with the memory of one who was sorely tried and tempted.

'I came to the colony of Victoria, or, rather, as it was called then, New South Wales, in the year 18 — . I had been in a merchant's office in London, but not finding much opportunity for advancement, I looked about to see if I could better myself. I heard of this new land across the ocean, and though it was not then the El Dorado which it afterwards turned out, and, truth to tell, had rather a shady name, owing to the transportation of convicts, yet I longed to go there and start a new life. Unhappily, however, I had not the means, and saw nothing better before me than the dreary life of a London clerk, as it was impossible that I could save out of the small salary I got. Just at this time, an old maiden aunt of my mother's died and left a few hundred pounds to me. With this, I came out to Australia, determined to become a rich man. I stayed some time in Sydney, and then came over to Port Phillip, now so widely known as Marvellous Melbourne, where I intended to pitch my tent. I saw that it was a young and rising colony, though, of course, coming as I did, before the days of the gold diggings, I never dreamt it would spring up, as it has done since, into a nation. I was careful and saving in those days, and, indeed, I think it was the happiest time of my life.

'I bought land whenever I could scrape the money together, and, at the time of the gold rush, was considered well-to-do. When, however, the cry that gold had been discovered was raised, and the eyes of all the nations were turned to Australia, with her glittering treasures, men poured in from all parts of the world, and the 'Golden Age' commenced. I began to grow rich rapidly, and was soon pointed out as the wealthiest man in the Colonies. I bought a station, and, leaving the riotous, feverish Melbourne life, went to live on it. I enjoyed myself there, for the wild, open-air life had great charms for me, and there was a sense of freedom to which I had hitherto been a stranger. But man is a gregarious animal, and I, growing weary of solitude and communings with Mother Nature, came down on a visit to Melbourne, where, with companions as gay as myself, I spent my money freely, and, as the phrase goes, saw life. After confessing that I loved the pure life of the country, it sounds strange to say I enjoyed the wild life of the town, but I did. I was neither a Joseph nor a

St. Anthony, and I was delighted with Bohemia, with its good fellowship and charming suppers, which took place in the small hours of the morning, when wit and humour reigned supreme. It was at one of these suppers that I first met Rosanna Moore, the woman who was destined to curse my existence. She was a burlesque actress, and all the young fellows in those days were madly in love with her. She was not exactly what was called beautiful, but there was a brilliancy and fascination about her which few could resist. On first seeing her I did not admire her much, but laughed at my companions as they raved about her. On becoming personally acquainted with her, however, I found that her powers of fascination had not been over-rated, and I ended by falling desperately in love with her. I made enquiries about her private life, and found that it was irreproachable, as she was guarded by a veritable dragon of a mother, who would let no one approach her daughter. I need not tell about my courtship, as these phases of a man's life are generally the same, but it will be sufficient to prove the depth of my passion for her when I say that I determined to make her my wife. It was on condition, however, that the marriage should be kept secret until such time as I should choose to reveal it. My reason for such a course was this, my father was still alive, and he, being a rigid Presbyterian, would never have forgiven me for having married a woman of the stage; so, as he was old and feeble, I did not wish him to learn that I had done so, fearing that the shock would be too much for him in his then state of health. I told Rosanna I would marry her, but wanted her to leave her mother, who was a perfect fury, and not an agreeable person to live with. As I was rich, young, and not bad-looking, Rosanna consented, and, during an engagement she had in Sydney, I went over there and married her. She never told her mother she had married me, why, I do not know, as I laid no restriction on her doing so. The mother made a great noise over the matter, but I gave Rosanna a large sum of money for her, and this the old harridan accepted, and left for New Zealand. Rosanna went with me to my station, where we lived as man and wife, though, in Melbourne, she was supposed to be my mistress. At last, feeling degraded in my own eyes at the way in which I was supposed to be living, I wanted to reveal our secret, but this Rosanna would not consent to. I was astonished at this, and could never discover the reason, but in many ways Rosanna was an enigma to me. She then grew weary of the quiet country life, and longed to return to the glitter and glare of the footlights. This I refused to let her do, and from that moment she took a dislike to me. A child was born, and for a time she was engrossed with it, but soon wearied of the new plaything, and again pressed me to allow her to return to the stage. I again refused, and we became estranged from one another. I grew gloomy and irritable, and was accustomed to take long rides by myself, frequently being away for days. There was a great friend of mine who owned the next station, a fine, handsome young fellow, called Frank Kelly, with a gay, sunny disposition, and a wonderful flow of humour. When he found I was so much away, thinking Rosanna was only my mistress, he began to console her, and succeeded so well that one day, on my return from a ride, I found she had fled with him, and had taken the child with her. She left a letter saying that she had never really cared for me, but had married me for my money — she would keep our marriage secret, and was going to return to the stage. I followed my false friend and false wife down to Melbourne, but arrived too late, as they had just left for England. Disgusted with the manner in which I had been treated, I plunged into a whirl of dissipation, trying to drown the memory of my married life. My friends, of course, thought that my loss amounted to no more than that of a mistress, and I soon began myself to doubt that I had ever been married, so far away and visionary did my life of the previous year seem. I continued my fast life for about six months, when suddenly I was arrested upon the brink of destruction by — an angel. I say this advisedly, for if ever there was an angel upon earth, it was she who afterwards became my wife. She was the daughter of a doctor, and it was her influence which drew me back from the dreary path of profligacy and dissipation which I was then leading. I paid her great attention, and we were, in fact, looked upon as good as engaged; but I knew that I was still linked to that accursed woman, and could not ask her to be my wife. At this second crisis of my life Fate again intervened, for I received a letter from England, which informed me that Rosanna Moore had been run over in the streets of London, and had died in an hospital. The writer was a young doctor who had attended her, and I wrote home to him, begging him to send out a certificate of her death, so that I might be sure she was no more. He did so, and also enclosed an account of the accident, which had appeared in a newspaper. Then, indeed, I felt that I was free, and closing, as I thought, for ever the darkest page of my life's history, I began to look forward to the future. I married again, and my domestic life was a singularly happy one. As the colony grew greater, with every year I became even more wealthy than I had been, and was looked up to and respected by my fellow-citizens. When my dear daughter Margaret was born, I felt that my cup of happiness was full, but suddenly I received a disagreeable reminder of the past. Rosanna's mother made her appearance one day — a disreputable-looking creature, smelling of gin, in whom I could not recognise the respectably-dressed woman who used to accompany Rosanna to the theatre. She had spent long ago all the money I had given her, and had sank lower and lower, until she now lived in a slum off Little Bourke Street. I made enquiries after the child, and she told me it was dead. Rosanna had not taken it to England with her, but had left it in her mother's charge, and, no doubt, neglect and want of proper nourishment was the cause of its death. There now seemed to be no link to bind me to the past with the exception of the old hag, who knew nothing about the marriage. I did not attempt to undeceive her, but agreed to allow her enough to live on if she promised never to trouble me again, and to keep quiet about everything which had reference to my connection with her daughter. She promised readily enough, and went back to her squalid dwelling in the slums, where, for all I know, she still lives, as money has been paid to her regularly every month by my solicitors. I heard nothing more about the matter, and now felt quite satisfied that I had heard the last of Rosanna. As years rolled on, things prospered with me, and so fortunate was I in all speculations that my luck became proverbial. Then, alas! when all things seemed to smile upon me, my wife died, and the world has never seemed the same to me since. But I had my dear daughter to console me, and in her love and affection I became reconciled to the loss of my wife. A young Irish gentleman, called Brian Fitzgerald, came out to Australia, and I soon saw that my daughter was in love with him, and that he reciprocated that affection, whereat I was glad, as I have always esteemed him highly. I looked forward to their marriage, when suddenly a series of events occurred, which must be fresh in the memory of those who read these pages. Mr. Oliver Whyte, a gentleman from London, called on me and startled me with the news that my first wife, Rosanna Moore, was still living, and that the story of her death had been an ingenious fabrication in order to deceive me. She had met with an accident, as stated in the newspaper, and had been taken to an hospital, where she recovered. The young doctor, who had sent me the certificate of her death, had fallen in love with her, and wanted to marry her, and had told me that she was dead in order that her past life might be obliterated. The doctor, however, died before the marriage, and Rosanna did not trouble herself about undeceiving me. She was then acting on the burlesque stage under the name of 'Musette,' and seemed to have gained an unenviable notoriety by her extravagance and infamy. Whyte met her in London, and she became his mistress. He seemed to have had a wonderful influence over her, for she told him all her past life, and about her marriage with me. Her popularity being on the wane in London, as she was now growing old, and had to make way for younger actresses, Whyte proposed that they should proceed to the Colonies and extort money from me, and he had come to me for that purpose. The villain told me all this in the coolest manner, and I, knowing he held the secret of my life, was unable to resent it. I refused to see Rosanna, but told Whyte I would agree to his terms, which were, first, a large sum of money was to be paid to Rosanna, and, secondly, that he should marry my daughter. I, at first, absolutely declined to sanction the latter proposal, but as he threatened to publish the story, and that meant the proclamation to the world of my daughter's illegitimacy, I at last — agreed, and he began to pay his addresses to Madge. She, however, refused to marry him, and told me she was engaged to Fitzgerald, so, after a severe struggle with myself, I told Whyte that I would not allow him to marry Madge, but would give him whatever sum he liked to name. On the night he was murdered he came to see me, and showed me the certificate of marriage between myself and Rosanna Moore. He refused to take a sum of money, and said that unless I consented to his marriage with Madge he would publish the whole affair. I implored him to give me time to think, so he said he would give me two days, but no more, and left the house, taking the marriage certificate with him. I was in despair, and saw that the only way to save myself was to obtain possession of the marriage certificate and deny everything. With this idea in my mind I followed him up to town and saw him meet Moreland, and drink with him. They went into the hotel in Russell Street, and when Whyte came out, at half-past twelve, he was quite intoxicated. I saw him go along to the

Scotch Church, near the Bourke and Wills' monument, and cling to the lamp-post at the corner. I thought I would then be able to get the certificate from him, as he was so drunk, when I saw a gentleman in a light coat — I did not know it was Fitzgerald — come up to him and hail a cab for him. I saw there was nothing more to be done at that time, so, in despair, went home and waited for the next day, in fear lest he should carry out his determination. Nothing, however, turned up, and I was beginning to think that Whyte had abandoned his purpose, when I heard that he had been murdered in the hansom cab. I was in great fear lest the marriage certificate should be found on him, but nothing was said about it. This I could not understand at all. I knew he had it on him, and I could only conclude that the murderer, whoever he was, had taken it from the body, and would sooner or later come to me to extort money, knowing that I dare not denounce him. Fitzgerald was arrested, and afterwards acquitted, so I began to think that the certificate had been lost, and my troubles were at an end. However, I was always haunted by a dread that the sword was hanging over my head, and would fall sooner or later. I was right, for two nights ago Roger Moreland, who was an intimate friend of Whyte's, called on me, and produced the marriage certificate, which he offered to sell to me for five thousand pounds. In horror, I accused him of murdering Whyte, which he denied at first, but afterwards acknowledged, stating that I dare not betray him for my own sake. I was nearly mad with the horror I was placed in, either to denounce my daughter as illegitimate or let a murderer escape the penalty of his crime. At last I agreed to keep silent, and handed him a cheque for five thousand pounds, receiving in return the marriage certificate. I then made Moreland swear to leave the Colony, which he readily agreed to do, saying Melbourne was dangerous. When he left I reflected upon the awfulness of my position, and I had almost determined to commit suicide, but, thank God, I was saved from that crime. I write this confession in order that after my death the true story of the murder of Whyte may be known, and that any one who may hereafter be accused of the murder may not be wrongfully punished. I have no hopes of Moreland ever receiving the penalty of his crime, as when this is opened all trace of him will, no doubt, be lost. I will not destroy the marriage certificate, but place it with these papers, so that the truth of my story can be seen. In conclusion, I would ask forgiveness of my daughter Margaret for my sins, which have been visited on her, but she can see for herself that circumstances were too strong for me. May she forgive me, as I hope God in His infinite mercy will, and may she come sometimes and pray over my grave, nor think too hardly upon her dead father.'

34

The Hands of Justice.

Calton's voice faltered a little when he read those last sad words, and he laid the manuscript down on the table, amid a dead silence, which was first broken by Brian.

'Thank God,' he said, reverently, 'thank God that he was innocent of the crime!'

'No,' said Calton, a little cynically, 'the riddle which has perplexed us so long is read, and the Sphinx is silent for evermore.'

'I knew he was incapable of such a thing,' cried Chinston, whom emotion had hitherto kept silent.

Meanwhile Kilsip listened to these eulogistic remarks on the dead man, and purred to himself, in a satisfied sort of way, like a cat who has caught a mouse.

'You see, sir,' he said, addressing the barrister, 'I was right after all.'

'Yes,' answered Calton, frankly, 'I acknowledge my defeat, but now — '

'I'm going to arrest Moreland right off,' said Kilsip.

There was a silence for a few moments,

and then Calton spoke again.

'I suppose it must be so — poor girl — poor girl.'

'I'm very sorry for the young lady myself,' said the detective in his soft, low voice; 'but you see I cannot let a dangerous criminal escape for a mere matter of sentiment.'

'Of course not,' said Fitzgerald, sharply. 'Moreland must be arrested right off.'

'But he will confess everything,' said Calton, angrily, 'and then everyone will know about this first marriage.'

'Let them,' retorted Brian, bitterly. 'As soon as she is well enough we will marry at once, and leave Australia for ever.'

'But — '

'I know her better than you do,' said the young man, doggedly; 'and I know she would like an end made of this whole miserable business at once. Arrest the murderer, and let him suffer for his crime.'

'Well, I suppose it must be so,' said Chinston, with a sigh, 'but it seems very hard that this slur should be cast upon Miss Frettlby.'

Brian turned a little pale.

'The sins of the father are generally visited upon the children by the world,' he said bitterly. 'But after the first pain is over, in new lands among new faces, she will forget the bitter past.'

'Now that it is settled Moreland is to be arrested,' said Calton, 'how is it to be done? Is he still in Melbourne?'

'Rather,' said Kilsip in a satisfied tone; 'I've had my eye on him for the last two months, and someone is watching him for me now — trust me, he can't move two steps without my knowing it.'

'Ah, indeed!' said Calton, quickly. 'Then do you know if he has been to the bank and cashed that cheque for five thousand, which Frettlby gave him?'

'Well, now,' observed Kilsip, after a pause, 'do you know you rather startled me when you told me he had received a cheque for that amount.'

'Why?'

'It's such a large one,' replied the detective, 'and had I known what sum he had paid into his account I should have been suspicious.'

'Then he has been to the bank?'

'To his own bank, yes. He went there yesterday afternoon at two o'clock — that is the day after he got it — so it would be sent round to Mr. Frettlby's bank, and would not be returned till next day, and as he died in the meanwhile I expect it hasn't been honoured, so Mr. Moreland won't have his money yet.'

'I wonder what he'll do,' said Chinston.

'Go to the manager and kick up a row,' said

Kilsip, coolly, 'and the manager will no doubt tell him he'd better see the executors.'

'But, my good friend, the manager doesn't know who the executors are,' broke in Calton, impatiently. 'You forget the will has yet to be read.'

'Then he'll tell him to go to the late Mr. Frettlby's solicitors. I suppose he knows who they are,' retorted Kilsip.

'Thinton and Tarbit,' said Calton, musingly; 'but it's questionable if Moreland would go to them.'

'Why shouldn't he, sir?' said Kilsip, quickly. 'He does not know anything about this,' laying his hand on the confession, 'and as the cheque is genuine enough he won't let five thousand pounds go without a struggle.'

'I'll tell you what,' observed Calton, after a few moments of reflection, 'I'll go across the way and telephone to Thinton and Tarbit, and when he calls on them they can send him up to me.'

'A very good idea,' said Kilsip, rubbing his hands, 'and then I can arrest him.'

'But the warrant?' interposed Brian, as Calton rose and put on his hat.

'Is here,' said the detective, producing it.

'By jove, you must have been pretty certain of his guilt,' remarked Chinston, dryly.

'Of course I was,' retorted Kilsip, in a

satisfied tone of voice. 'When I told the magistrate where I found the coat, and reminded him of Moreland's acknowledgment at the trial, that he had it in his possession before the murder, I soon got him to see the necessity of having Moreland arrested.'

'Half-past four,' said Calton, pausing for a moment at the door and looking at his watch. 'I'm afraid it's rather late to catch Moreland to-day; however, I'll see what Thinton and Tarbit know,' and he went out.

The rest sat waiting his return, and chatted about the curious end of the hansom cab mystery, when, in about ten minutes, Calton rushed in hurriedly and closed the door after him quickly.

'Fate is playing into our hands,' he said, as soon as he recovered his breath.

'Moreland called on Thinton and Tarbit, as Kilsip surmised, and as neither of them was in, he said he would call again before five o'clock. I told the clerk to bring him up to me at once, so he may be here at any moment.'

'That is, if he's fool enough to come,' observed Chinston.

'Oh, he'll come,' said the detective, confidently, rattling a pair of handcuffs together.

'He is so satisfied that he has made things

safe that he'll walk right into the trap.' It was getting a little dusk, and the four men were greatly excited, though they concealed it under an assumed nonchalance.

'What a situation for a drama,' said Brian.

'Only,' said Chinston, quietly, 'it is as realistic as in the old days of the Coliseum, where the actor who played Orpheus was torn to pieces by bears at the end of the play.'

'His last appearance on any stage, I suppose,' said Calton, a little cruelly, it must be confessed.

Meanwhile, Kilsip remained seated in his chair, humming an operatic air and chinking the handcuffs together, by way of accompaniment. He felt intensely pleased with himself, the more so, as he saw that by this capture he would be ranked far above Gorby. 'And what would Gorby say? — Gorby, who had laughed at all my ideas as foolish, and who had been quite wrong from the first. If only — '

'Hush!' said Calton, holding up his finger, as steps were heard echoing on the flags outside. 'Here he is, I believe.'

Kilsip arose from his chair, and, stealing softly to the window, looked cautiously out. Then he turned round to those inside and, nodding his head, slipped the handcuffs into his pocket. Just as he did so, there was a knock at the door, and, in response to Calton's invitation to enter, Thinton and Tarbit's clerk came in with Roger Moreland. The latter faltered a little on the threshold, when he saw Calton was not alone, and seemed half inclined to retreat. But, evidently, thinking there was no danger of his secret being discovered, he pulled himself together, and advanced into the room in an easy and confident manner.

'This is the gentleman who wants to know about the cheque, sir,' said Thinton and Tarbit's clerk to Calton.

'Oh, indeed,' answered Calton, quietly. 'I am glad to see him; you can go.'

The clerk bowed and went out, closing the door after him. Moreland took his seat directly in front of Calton, and with his back to the door. Kilsip, seeing this, strolled across the room in a nonchalant manner, while Calton engaged Moreland in conversation, and quietly turned the key.

'You want to see me, sir?' said Calton, resuming his seat.

'Yes; that is alone,' replied Moreland, uneasily.

'Oh, these gentlemen are my friends,' said Calton, quietly; 'anything you may say is quite safe.'

'That they are your friends, and are quite

safe, is nothing to me,' said Moreland, insolently, 'I wish to speak to you in private.'

'Don't you think you would like to know my friends?' said Calton, coolly taking no notice of his remark.

'D — your friends, sir!' cried Moreland, furiously, rising from his seat.

Calton laughed, and introduced Mr. Moreland to the others.

'Dr. Chinston, Mr. Kilsip, and — Mr. Fitzgerald.'

'Fitzgerald,' gasped Moreland, growing pale. 'I — I — what's that?' he shrieked, as he saw Whyte's coat, all weather-stained, lying on a chair near him, and which he immediately recognised.

'That is the rope that's going to hang you,' said Kilsip, quietly, coming behind him, 'for the murder of Oliver Whyte.'

'Trapped by G — !' shouted the wretched man, wheeling round, so as to face Kilsip. He sprang at the detective's throat, and they both rolled together on the floor, but the latter was too strong for him, and, after a sharp struggle, he succeeded in getting the handcuffs on Moreland's wrists. The others stood around perfectly quiet, knowing that Kilsip required no assistance. Now that there was no possibility of escape, Moreland seemed to become resigned, and rose sullenly off the floor.

'I'll make you pay for this,' he hissed between his teeth, with a white despairing face.

'You can't prove anything.'

'Can't we?' said Calton, touching the confession. 'You are wrong. This is the confession of Mark Frettlby made before he died.'

'It's a lie.'

'A jury will decide that,' said the barrister, dryly. 'Meanwhile you will pass the night in the Melbourne Gaol.'

'Ah! perhaps they'll give me the same cell as you occupied,' said Moreland, with a hard laugh, turning to Fitzgerald. 'I should like it for its old associations.' Brian did not answer him, but picking up his hat and gloves, prepared to go.

'Stop!' cried Moreland, fiercely. 'I see that it's all up with me, so I'm not going to lie like a coward. I've played for a big stake and lost, but if I hadn't been such a fool I'd have cashed that cheque the next morning, and been far away by this time.'

'It certainly would have been wiser,' said Calton.

'After all,' said Moreland, nonchalantly, taking no notice of his remark, 'I don't know that I'm sorry about it. I've had a hell upon earth since I killed Whyte.'

'Then you acknowledge your guilt?' said Brian, quietly. Moreland shrugged his shoulders.

'I told you I wasn't a coward,' he answered, coolly. 'Yes, I did it; it was Whyte's own fault. When I met him that night he told me how Frettlby wouldn't let him marry his daughter, but said he'd make him, and showed me the marriage certificate. I thought if I could only get it I'd make a nice little pile out of Frettlby over it; so when Whyte went on drinking I did not. After he had gone out of the hotel, I put on his coat, which he left behind. I saw him standing near the lamp-post, and Fitzgerald come up and then leave him. When you came down the street,' he went on, turning to Fitzgerald, 'I shrank back into the shadow, and when you passed I ran up to Whyte as the cabman was putting him into the hansom. He took me for you, so I didn't undeceive him, but I swear I had no idea of murdering Whyte when I got into the cab. I tried to get the papers, but he wouldn't let me, and commenced to sing out. Then I thought of the chloroform in the pocket of his coat, which I was wearing. I pulled it out, and found that the cork was loose. Then I took out Whyte's handkerchief, which was also in the coat, and emptied the bottle on it, and put it back in my pocket. I again tried to get the papers, without using the chloroform, but couldn't, so I clapped the handkerchief over his mouth, and he went off after a few minutes, and I got the papers. I thought he was only insensible, and it was only when I saw the newspapers that I knew he was dead. I stopped the cab in St. Kilda Road, got out and caught another cab, which was going to town. Then I got out at Powlett Street, took off the coat, and carried it over my arm. I went down George Street, towards the Fitzroy Gardens, and having hid the coat up a tree, where I suppose you found it,' to Kilsip, 'I walked home — so I've done you all nicely, but — '

'You're caught at last,' finished Kilsip, quietly.

Moreland fell down in a chair, with an air of utter weariness and lassitude.

'No man can be stronger than Destiny,' he said, dreamily. 'I have lost and you have won; so life is a chess board, after all, and we are the puppets of Fate.'

He refused to utter another word; so leaving Calton and Kilsip with him, Brian and the doctor went out and hailed a cab. It drove up to the entrance of the court, where Calton's office was, and then Moreland, walking as if in a dream, left the room, and got into the cab, followed by Kilsip.

'Do you know,' said Chinston, thoughtfully, as they stood and watched the cab drive off, 'do you know what the end of that man will be?'

'It requires no prophet to foretell that,' said Calton, dryly. 'He will be hanged.'

'No, he won't,' retorted the doctor. 'He will commit suicide.'

35

'The Love That Lives.'

There are certain periods in the life of man
when Fate seems to have done her worst, and
any further misfortunes which may befall are
accepted with a philosophical resignation,
begotten by the very severity of previous
trials. Fitzgerald was in this state of mind
— he was calm, but it was the calmness of
despair — the misfortunes of the past year
seemed to have come to a climax, and he
looked forward to the publication of the
whole bitter story with an indifference that
surprised himself. His own name, and that of
Madge and her dead father, would be on
every tongue, yet he felt perfectly callous to
whatever might be said on the subject. So
long as Madge recovered, and they could go
away to another part of the world, leaving
Australia, with its bitter memories behind
— he did not care. Moreland would suffer the
bitter penalty of his crime, and then nothing
more would ever be heard of the matter. It
would be better for the whole story to be
told, and transitory pain endured, than to go

on striving to hide the infamy and shame which might be discovered at any moment. Already the news was all over Melbourne that the murderer of Oliver Whyte had been captured, and that his confession would bring to light certain startling facts concerning the late Mark Frettlby. Brian well knew that the world winked at secret vices so long as there was an attempt at concealment, though it was cruelly severe on those which were brought to light, and that many whose lives might be secretly far more culpable than poor Mark Frettlby's, would be the first to slander the dead man. The public curiosity, however, was destined never to be gratified, for the next day it was known that Roger Moreland had hanged himself in his cell during the night, and had left no confession behind him.

When Brian heard this, he breathed a heartfelt prayer of thanks for his deliverance, and went to see Calton, whom he found at his chambers, in deep conversation with Chinston and Kilsip. They all came to the conclusion that as Moreland was now dead, nothing could be gained by publishing the confession of Mark Frettlby, so agreed to burn it, and when Fitzgerald saw in the heap of blackened paper in the fireplace all that remained of the bitter story, he felt a weight lifted off his heart. The barrister, Chinston, and Kilsip, all promised to keep silent, and they kept the promise nobly, for nothing was ever known of the circumstances which led to the death of Oliver Whyte, and it was generally supposed that it must have been caused by some quarrel between the dead man and his friend Roger Moreland.

Fitzgerald, however, did not forget the good service that Kilsip had done him, and gave him a sum of money which made him independent for life, though he still followed his old profession of a detective from sheer love of excitement, and was always looked upon with admiration as the man who had solved the mystery of the famous hansom cab murder. Brian, after several consultations with Calton, at last came to the conclusion that it would be useless to reveal to Sal Rawlins the fact that she was Mark Frettlby's daughter, as by the will the money was clearly left to Madge, and such a revelation could bring her no pecuniary benefit, while her bringing up unfitted her for the position; so a yearly income, more than sufficient for her wants, was settled upon her, and she was allowed to remain in ignorance of her parentage. The influence of Sal Rawlins' old life, however, was very strong on her, and she devoted herself to the task of saving her fallen sisters. Knowing as she did, all the intricacies of the slums, she was enabled to do an immense amount of good, and many an unhappy woman was saved from the squalor and hardship of a gutter life by the kind hand of Sal Rawlins.

Felix Rolleston became a member of Parliament, where his speeches, if not very deep, were at least amusing; and while in the House he always behaved like a gentleman, which could not be said of all his Parliamentary colleagues.

Madge slowly recovered from her illness, and as she had been explicitly named in the will as heiress to Mark Frettlby's great wealth, she placed the management of her estates in the hands of Mr. Calton, who, with Thinton and Tarbit, acted as her agents in Australia. On her recovery she learned the story of her father's early marriage, but both Calton and Fitzgerald were silent about the fact of Sal Rawlins being her half-sister, as such a relation could do no good, and would only create a scandal, as no explanation could be given except the true one. Shortly afterwards Madge married Fitzgerald, and both of them only too gladly left Australia, with all its sorrows and bitter memories.

Standing with her husband on the deck of one of the P. and O. steamers, as it ploughed the blue waters of Hobson's Bay into foam, they both watched Melbourne gradually fade from their view, under the glow of the sunset. They could see the two great domes of the Exhibition, and the Law Courts, and also Government House, with its tall tower rising from the midst of the green trees. In the background was a bright crimson sky, barred with masses of black clouds, and over all the great city hung a cloud of smoke like a pall. The flaring red light of the sinking sun glared angrily on the heavy waters, and the steamer seemed to be making its way through a sea of blood. Madge, clinging to her husband's arm, felt her eyes fill with tears, as she saw the land of her birth receding slowly.

'Good-bye,' she murmured, softly. 'Good-bye for ever.'

'You do not regret?' he said, bending his head.

'Regret, no,' she answered, looking at him with loving eyes.

'With you by my side, I fear nothing. Surely our hearts have been tried in the furnace of affliction, and our love has been chastened and purified.'

'We are sure of nothing in this world,' replied Brian, with a sigh. 'But after all the sorrow and grief of the past, let us hope that the future will be peace.'

'Peace!'

A white-winged sea-gull rose suddenly from the crimson waters, and circled rapidly in the air above them.

'A happy omen,' she said, looking up fondly to the grave face of her husband, 'for your life and for mine.'

He bent down and kissed her.

The great steamer moved slowly out to sea, and as they stood on the deck, hand clasped in hand, with the fresh salt breeze blowing keenly in their faces, it bore them away into the placid beauty of the coming night, towards the old world and the new life.

We do hope that you have enjoyed reading this large print book.

Did you know that all of our titles are available for purchase?

We publish a wide range of high quality large print books including:
Romances, Mysteries, Classics
General Fiction
Non Fiction and Westerns

Special interest titles available in large print are:
The Little Oxford Dictionary
Music Book
Song Book
Hymn Book
Service Book

Also available from us courtesy of Oxford University Press:
Young Readers' Dictionary
(large print edition)
Young Readers' Thesaurus
(large print edition)

For further information or a free brochure, please contact us at:
Ulverscroft Large Print Books Ltd.,
The Green, Bradgate Road, Anstey,
Leicester, LE7 7FU, England.
Tel: (00 44) 0116 236 4325
Fax: (00 44) 0116 234 0205

Other titles published by Ulverscroft:

THE SEA-WOLF

Jack London

After embarking on a pleasure cruise, bookish young Humphrey van Weyden finds himself shipwrecked amidst a terrible storm. When he is picked up by a passing vessel, he initially believes he has been rescued by kind saviours. But Humphrey soon finds out that he has in fact boarded the *Ghost* — a seal-hunting ship captained by the incisive philosopher, brutal despot, and utterly terrifying Wolf Larsen. As Humphrey falls in love with Maud, a beautiful poet and fellow shipwreck survivor, he must contend not only with the dangers of being at sea, but also with competition from his cruel and scheming captain . . .

THE GARDEN PARTY

Katherine Mansfield

On a gorgeously sunny summer's morning, the Sheridan household prepares for an afternoon garden party: a marquee is pitched, exquisite sandwiches are created, and an abundance of canna lilies waits to be arranged. Young Laura flits pleasurably from task to task, all the while revelling in the sensory delights of nature and life. But her idyll is suddenly shattered by the baker's man, delivering both pastries and news — news that a man has just been killed in the nearby lane . . .

THE YELLOW WALL-PAPER

Charlotte Perkins Gilman

'The Yellow Wall-Paper' is Gilman's pioneering Gothic masterpiece, telling the story of a woman's descent into madness. Confined to a room, with only the intricate wallpaper for stimulation, the narrator slowly loses her grip on reality. She becomes increasingly suspicious of the people who care for her, convinced they are conspiring against her. As she becomes increasingly transfixed by the sprawling pattern on her walls, her horrifying fantasy becomes disturbingly real. Also contained in this collection are eighteen other stories, which exhibit Gilman's imaginative treatment of women removed from their traditional roles.

DR JEKYLL AND MR HYDE

Robert Louis Stevenson
& Various Authors

In seeking to discover his inner self, the brilliant Dr Henry Jekyll discovers a monster. Developing a serum with the intent of separating his good side from his darker impulses, he periodically transforms into Edward Hyde, a brutal creature, free of any conscience. The scientist's strange behaviour is investigated by his friend, the lawyer John Utterson. What follows is a classic thriller, and a terrifying study of the duality of human nature. Also included in this collection are five other classic tales of mystery and horror, from some of the greatest writers of the era.

KING SOLOMON'S MINES

H. Rider Haggard

Allan Quatermain, wild game hunter and explorer, narrates his adventures with Danish adventurer Sir Henry Curtis and Royal Navy Officer Captain Good. Hired by Curtis, Quatermain leads the quest to find Curtis's lost brother — who vanished while searching for the fabled diamond mines of King Solomon — and so becomes involved in a dangerous expedition through the unexplored African wilderness. Led by an ancient map passed down from a 16th-century Portuguese explorer, their journey takes them across deserts, over mountains, and into the hands of a sinister African tribe . . .

THE RED BADGE OF COURAGE

Stephen Crane

Henry Fleming is an ordinary farm boy turned soldier, with romantic notions about the glory of war. But, as the tedium of his regiment's encampment without action provides ample time for self-reflection, disquieting thoughts begin to prey upon his mind: doubts as to whether, in combat, he will stand his ground valiantly — or flee ignominiously. Then the regiment receives orders to march, and Henry finds himself flung into the maelstrom of battle. Amidst the blood, the acrid smoke, and the unworldly wails of the dying, his courage will be put to the ultimate test . . .